CROSSROADS BLUES

Michael Anthony Adams, Jr.

SIX SEEDS PRESS
Baltimore, MD

First Six Seeds Press Edition
Copyright © 2004 Michael Anthony Adams, Jr.

Originally Published as *Andrew's Songs, Vol VI.: Crossroads Blues* by Michael Anthony Adams, Jr. by CreateSpace Independent Publishing Platform
November 2011

Previously Published under the Pen Name Israfel Sivad by CreateSpace Independent Publishing Platform
July 2012

This Edition Published by Six Seeds Press,
Baltimore, MD
February 2022

ISBN: 978-1-952240-08-9

Cover Design © 2022 PJ Adams
Portrait of Michael Anthony Adams, Jr. © 2014 PJ Adams

Also by Michael Anthony Adams, Jr. and Published by Six Seeds Press

Fiction:
The Adversary's Good News: A Novel
Psychedelicizations: Short Stories
The American Apocalypse: Short Stories
Crossroads Blues: A Novel
The Cars Behind, Beside Us: Short Stories
Welcome to the Modern World, Charlie: Short Stories
Notes from the Idle Mind: Short Stories

Nonfiction:
Disorder: An Avant-Garde Memoir of Psychosis, Healing and Love

Poetry:
We Are the Underground: Poems
From Now to You: Haiku
Recipe for a Future Theogony: Poems
Indigo Glow: Poems
The Tree Outside My Window: Poems
At the Side of the Road: Poems
Soundtrack for the New Millennium: A Poem

www.6SeedsPress.com

Crossroads Blues
For My Mother

Contents

Crossroads Blues

I.
Shouting at the Moon

Times Square. The crossroads of the world. From the sky, where the tip-tops of glass towers overreach Babylon, to the ground, where the pedestrians are imprisoned on sidewalks, hurrying past one another, protected from bumping shoulders by invisible shields, a grayness hides in the light. The excess of New York City – smoke, fumes, exhaust – sticks to the humans' skins, collects in their breathing lungs, merges with the scents of hot nuts, hot dogs, tobacco, and trash to create a cacophony of flavors circling through every square inch of the atmosphere. In the space that isn't occupied by a body, sounds resonate – laughter, horns, voices. Maddening. Exhilarating. Tempting.

Chase Manhattan – a bank on a corner at the crossroads. Inside, up the escalator, past the ATM machines, are computers of records, tellers behind plexi-glass windows, managers in suits, money in safes and vaults and computers. Everything, both animate and inanimate, that is needed to sign a loan, open an account, withdraw, deposit funds. Outside, a red, white, and blue rectangular sign reaches perpendicular then parallel off the side of the glass building reflecting Times Square's traffic. Lights encircle the sign. In the night, they light the colors, drawing the pedestrians' attention, distracting the passengers in cabs and limousines. In the day, the sun is too bright, the grayness not gray enough, and the lights stay off. The sign itself has to be enough. The red, white, and blue arm spins: a giant, twirling business card over the corner, reminding everybody: Chase Manhattan.

Wearing dress slacks, shirt and tie, a young man barrels down Broadway, slides in and out between bodies, and strides beneath the sign. His tie, caught in the breeze his speed makes, sticks to his chest. He runs his hands through his hair. Unwashed, it sticks up straight. He sees his reflection in the glass door of the bank, his thin face with swollen eyes – hungover. He opens the door. He doesn't stop at the ATM machines. He bounds up the escalator, two steps at a time, and walks straight to the end of the line for the tellers.

He waits, taps his foot, scratches the back of his neck, rubs his eyes, and stares at an electronic sign: *If you received excellent service today, please tell a friend. If not, please tell me...* A name and a position blink across the darkened rectangle above the tellers' heads. Every once in a while, the sign goes "ding", and a number appears, and one person leaves the line to do his or her business.

People talk, argue, and laugh with the tellers. They pass checks, money, ATM cards, and deposit slips back and forth. They walk away smiling, frowning, counting cash, aware and unaware of each other, shoving receipts in their pockets.

The line moves slowly to the young man's mind, but soon he has wound his way through the cloth barricades, and nobody is in front of him. Ding. In the corner of the electronic sign, a number appears. An arrow points out which way the young man should go. He walks over to teller 15.

The teller sits behind a bulletproof window, a reminder of America's mythic past, of the days of Dillinger, when anybody with a gun could step into a building and demand that the registers be emptied, that the vaults be opened, that the guards and tellers and patrons lie on the ground and wait while he rests his Tommy gun on his hip before he tips his fedora and takes more in one day of brazen work than his hapless victims will make in their entire lifetimes of monotony.

The teller has long fingernails that curve like a dog's uncut claws. They are painted purple, and they are dotted with what look like little stars. They must be very stylish in whatever neighborhood she lives in. To the young man, they are too animalistic to be attractive. In his state (slight headache, mildly dehydrated, bleary-eyed) they make him physically uncomfortable. The teller rearranges herself on her seat. "Can I help you?" she asks.

The young man looks away from her nails. He stares into her heavily made-up face. She wears eye shadow and a dress that matches her nail polish. The bullet-proof glass puts her in a cage. "A plastic animal" is what the young man, in his foggy mind, thinks to call her. He leans forward to speak into the air holes, there either for her ventilation or for his depending on which vantage point is seen as encaged, drilled into the window. "Yeah, I need to cash this." He's surprised he can speak the same language as her, and he shoves a check and check-cashing card from his temp agency through the little divot beneath the plexi-glass.

Because of her nails, the teller has to twist her wrist and use the tips of her fingers to grab the check. She has practiced this technique a lot though, and she is able to pull the check up and into her hands in an awkward but swift motion. The young man is impressed. The teller looks for a signature on the check. She matches the signature to the signature on the check-cashing card. She runs the check through a slit in a machine that makes a thousand clicking noises in the space of a second as it sucks the check in and makes a barcode of black marks across the top of the back of it. The marks in the barcode mean something to somebody somewhere. She opens a drawer, puts the check into it, licks her fingers and proceeds to count out the money. The young man isn't sure whether or not he would lick his fingers after handling a check that just came from somebody else, but very little about the woman in the plastic cage makes much sense to him. She slides 339 dollars and nineteen cents back through the divot beneath the window. The change clanks in the metal trough. She slides the check cashing card back to the young man.

He tries not to look at her fingernails. He doesn't want to see her face. He takes the money and the card. He counts the money again, double checks to make sure it is the right amount. He tries to smile, says, "Thank you," and walks away not too much slower than he walked in. He holds the rail on the escalator as he glides back down to the ground.

He steps out of the bank. Times Square assaults him. Noise. People. Daylight. He wishes that he had his sunglasses, that he wasn't wearing a shirt and tie. He pulls a pack of cigarettes from his pocket, pulls out a cigarette, places it between his lips, and lights it. One more scent enters the atmosphere. A bit more smoke swirls into the haze. The tobacco tastes fresh.

He leans back against the glass building, into his own reflection, relaxing for a moment before he has to rush back to work. His head hurts, and Times Square isn't helping. An endless stream of tourists and businesspeople file past him. A group of teen-agers stand on the island in the middle of the square. They're holding signs for MTV and Total Request Live. They're shouting and cheering, excited to be away from the suburbs, amazed to be in New York City, blown away by their chance to be on TV. Maybe it will make them famous. The young man isn't interested in what they have to say to the cable viewing world. He turns and looks up Broadway. In the midst of all the bodies, he thinks he recognizes a face he hasn't seen in four years: dark hair, high cheekbones, dark complexion, thick lips. Not sure if he's right, he waits until the face reaches him. Then, he smiles, steps forward, and says, "Michael?"

The young man who he has stepped in front of stops. He's wearing jeans, boots, and a white tee shirt. He has a shadow of growth on his cheeks. Sunglasses shade his eyes. Looking as hungover as his interlocutor, but without the sophistication that an office job requires, he's either hipstered out or truly beat. The crowd fans out and swirls around him. A look of recognition passes across his face. He tips his head to the side. "Andrew?" he asks.

"Yeah, man," Andrew laughs. "What are you doing here?"

"I moved up here right after I dropped out of school. What are you doing here?"

"I moved here last year."

"Right after you graduated?" Michael continues.

"No. I stayed with my mom in Connecticut for a year. Saved up some money. Wrote a whole bunch."

"Oh yeah. That's right. I remember. You wanted to be a writer. Get anything done?"

"I wrote a play."

"No shit. Any luck getting it produced?"

"Yeah. A friend of mine from high school has a theater company here. She's putting it up for me. We're casting next week. What about you? What are you up to these days?"

"Nothing really. Waiting tables. Acting. Getting a portfolio together for modeling." Michael does have the style, the looks for modeling, for screen acting.

"Where you waiting tables at?"

Michael nods his head back: "Olive Garden." Andrew looks. Behind the mass of people, the chain restaurant sits comfortably at the head of Times Square, a symbol for the rest of the city, for the rest of America, for the rest of the world.

Andrew thinks for a moment. He looks back at Michael, glances him over. "Hey, you know, if you're not too busy these days, let me get your number, and I'll give you a call if you want a part in the show. It doesn't pay at all, but it would be something to put on a résumé."

"Yeah. I might be into that." Michael pulls out a cigarette and lights it. Smoke spirals into the air. Now that the conversation looks like it will last at least five minutes, Andrew leans back into his reflection again. Trying to move himself out of the path of traffic, Michael moves closer to him. "What's it about?" he asks.

"The play? It's pretty much this love triangle type thing. This girl, Sophie, who goes to a café all the time, falls in love with this poet who she meets there, but she's got this best friend, who's kind of a writer himself, and he's really into her. So the whole thing plays out around the conversations that Sophie and her friend have about why she's not into him, why she's into Raphael, that's the poet's name, and how Raphael can't really see anything in the world that's worthwhile. In the end, it's about how this girl finds out what it means to really fall for somebody for the first time, but for somebody who thinks he's so damaged that he can't love her back. The name of the play is *In My Beginning Is My End*. It's a Wagner quote. If you're into it, I'll let you read it."

"Autobiographical?"

"Huh? Yeah. I guess. A little, but what isn't?"

"True."

"So anyway, Raphael kills himself at the end. That's the part that I think you could do."

"The part that's not autobiographical."

"Huh?" Andrew notices Michael is smiling. His lips are so full, his cheeks so bright that it makes Andrew a little uncomfortable to stare at his face. Andrew looks down and grins. "Yeah. It's a big part, but you look right for it. Of course, Michelle, that's my friend, the director, she has the final say, but, you know…"

"Yeah. Give me a call about it."

They're silent for a bit, smoking their cigarettes.

Michael asks, "You writing anything new?"

"Yeah, a screenplay. I figure that's where the money is."

"No doubt. You got a story line yet."

"Yeah, but don't steal it."

"Hey, man, I'm an actor, not a writer. You don't have to worry about me taking your ideas. I wouldn't be able to do anything with them."

"All right. It's about this starving writer who decides he needs to come up with an idea that's gonna make him some money so he comes up with this idea about a starving writer who needs to come up with an idea that's gonna make him some money so he decides to write a screenplay about a bank robbery, but as the writer's coming up with his bank robbery plot, he realizes that the robbery could work so he enlists the help of this theater group that one of his friends is in – his friend helps him come up with the plot – and they decide to pull off the robbery, but the whole thing's run like a play… You know, stage manager, director, everybody has their roles. I figure that the whole thing would wind up dealing with the relationship between art and life…"

"Autobiographical again, huh?"

"Yeah, something like that."

"So what are you doing here? Casing the bank?"

"Huh? Ha-ha. No. I just had to cash my paycheck. Rent's a few days overdue. You know how it is."

"Yeah. I know how it is."

"So, here I am, busting my ass at my lunch hour just to cash the paycheck so I have the money." Andrew laughs.

Michael grins. "What are you doing for work, anyway? You're lookin' pretty sharp."

Andrew laughs a laugh like he's not quite comfortable with the hipster noticing his clothes. "Nothing really. Temp work. This other friend of mine from high school works for this agency, so he helps me out."

"You got all the hook-ups in the city."

"Guess so." Andrew's cigarette is done. He's smoked it past the butt. Standing in Times Square talking about his writing with someone who looks like Michael stamps all of New York's romanticism onto Andrew's fanciful mind. He doesn't want to leave, to rush back to sit beneath the fluorescent lights and make photocopies for the people who live in Connecticut and Long Island and take the trains in every day, who see the city as a producing machine powered by the financial district and spreading its wealth like The Blob – a formless giant, undulating in absorption – across the United States to every market on the globe. But he needs to make his rent for the next month so that he can stay in New York and keep having moments like this one. He says, "Speakin' about work, I gotta get back. Let me get your number."

"Right."

Andrew pulls out his cell phone. Michael rattles off his cell number, and Andrew programs it into his phone. "917 area code," Andrew notices. "I got stuck with 646."

"That's how it goes."

"Yeah. By the way, where you livin' at?"

"East Village."

Andrew pauses. Suddenly, his deal in Brooklyn doesn't seem so hot anymore. Work can wait. He scratches his head. "No shit. If you don't mind me asking, how much do you pay?"

"Five-fifty a month."

"How many roommates you got?"

"Only one."

"No shit." For the first time in a year, Andrew is nervous about his own living situation, his own neighborhood. The cafés and bars of Williamsburg don't seem quite as grand as they usually do in his imagination. His deal's certainly not as good as Michael's. "How'd you swing that?"

"Luck. Just like everything else in the city."

Andrew pauses for a moment. He looks up as if he knows how to tell the sun's time. "I really gotta go," he says.

Michael drops his cigarette, stomps it with the heel of his boot. "Yeah. I gotta go too. I got a bunch of shit to take care of today."

"Cool. I'll give you a call early next week, like Monday or Tuesday, let you know when and where."

"Sounds good. And hey, if you need any help robbing the bank, just let me know."

Andrew smiles. "Definitely." He pauses. "We could always just grab a beer sometime too," he adds, reaching out for friendship.

"Yeah. We could do that," Michael responds. He waves a quick goodbye and merges back into the crowd. He slips through the mass of people and disappears toward downtown on Broadway. Andrew turns around and walks back in the other direction, dodging bodies and passing beneath the red, white, and blue sign right before he crosses the street.

Who would have thought that he'd bump into Michael Lourdes in Times Square? An actor... He would make a great Raphael D'Angelo, Andrew's fictional alter-ego.

Andrew thinks that conversation might not be a bad one to start his screenplay with: Two people who haven't seen each other in a long time meet up in Times Square outside of the Chase Manhattan Bank that they eventually decide to rob. One is an actor, the other a writer. If people look, the scene contains an infinite number of meanings. It exists on a multitude of levels.

Dreams of the screenplay he believes he will write consume Andrew as he walks back to his temp position, snapping his fingers beside his head in rhythm to his thoughts. His hair is a mess. His face is red from his hangover. Talking to himself, he appears as half lunatic, half businessman to the people he brushes past on his way back to work, but he's having fun. He wants to write that scene over the weekend.

Today is Friday, September 7th, 2001.

In a little corner room of an office, halfway up, on the fifteenth floor of a Midtown skyscraper two blocks south and four blocks east from where Andrew is saying goodbye to Michael, wearing black slacks and a sleeveless red shirt, Michelle Sophiedos rests her hands on top of a copy machine. Her fingers are fine. Her shoulders are thin, her body dainty. Her hair is long and wavy. Poised to slide through the Xerox's automatic feed is a stack of 127 pages. On top of the stack, centered across the front, in fourteen point bold font, the words "In My Beginning Is My End" are written one double space above the bolded, twelve point "By Andrew Christian".

"The whole reason temp jobs exist is so that starving artists can make copies of scripts," she says. She looks over her shoulder and smiles mischievously. Her lip curls up in a way that is reminiscent of the funnel of a wave, making her teeth sparkle like spray.

Leaning against the doorframe, wearing black slacks like Michelle's but with a woman's white dress shirt instead of a lascivious red top, Jeannie smiles back at her. She thinks that Michelle is so pretty. Even beneath the deathly office lights, her complexion is rich and lustrous. She really can't believe that the girl doesn't have a boyfriend. She's so interesting and so nice. There has to be somebody who Jeannie knows who she can fix her up with…

Michelle is the artist, the temp. Today is her last day on assignment. Unsure of whether or not she's going to be working come Monday, it's imperative, from her viewpoint, that she make as many copies of the script as she will need for auditions and rehearsals. She certainly can't afford to go to Kinko's – not with rent and social commitments looming over her head.

Jeannie is the permanent employee standing guard for her new-found friend. If anybody comes down the hall toward them while Michelle is making copies of the script, Jeannie is supposed to ask Michelle what she's doing that night. Then, Michelle will quickly pull all of the copies out of the auto-sort file hanging off the end of the machine, grab the original script and put everything underneath a company memo that is her pretext for being in the Xerox room in the first place. It makes Jeannie feel important, like she's being inducted into some sort of illicit New York underground, to be a part of the small subterfuge.

"What's it about?" Jeannie asks.

"What?"

"The play. What's it about?"

Michelle tips her head to the side. "It's about this girl who doesn't really have any friends… She just sits around this café reading and thinking all the time, and she winds up meeting this writer there, and she falls for him, and the one guy who she is friends with gets jealous, and she argues with him over and over again about what makes the writer more interesting than him. There's not really too much to the plot until the end when the writer kills himself, and the girl's left with no friends at all. I don't really like it very much."

Jeannie laughs. "If you don't like it, why are you producing it?"

"I don't know. I'm not really doing anything else these days, and it was written by a friend of mine from high school. I'd like to help him out. He's done a lot for me. This other friend of his works for Heavenly Staffing, and he's been hooking me up with jobs pretty much ever since Andrew showed up in New York last year. Plus, the set's really simple and I got a line on a free theater space in Williamsburg so it won't cost hardly any money to put up. Besides, it'll be good practice. You know, trying to make the most of what I'm given."

"Is your friend cute?"

"Andrew? In his own way. Yeah, he's cute, but he's a little strange."

Michelle's life seems so exciting. She's an actress, a director. She has her own theater company – which (although Jeannie doesn't know it) means only that she has registered herself as a not-for-profit, has the phone numbers of a few actors she works with, and has come up with a name to put on applications – and works temp jobs while she waits for a grant. Jeannie frowns and glances down. She asks, "So what don't you like about the play?"

Michelle shakes her head. She laughs. "Well, let's see, where should I start? First off, I think the dialogue is weak. Every character talks the same. Second, his characterization of the woman is completely unrealistic. Her interest in Raphael, the writer, comes from virtually out of nowhere, and she never once offers a reasonable explanation for her attraction – Not to mention the fact that his character is hardly attractive at all. She remains static through pretty much the whole show, and her desires are very naïve for somebody of Andrew's age to consider them realistic in any way. She has almost no subtlety to her personality. You can tell it was written by a guy who doesn't really know the first thing about how to get into a woman's head, and a writer who can't read people's minds isn't going to make it very far.

"For the most part, the whole thing is way too romantic. His idea of a character for the writer is as this sort of tortured icon of post-teen angst. For the life of me, I can't figure out what the girl sees in him. His suicide, which I think is meant to be shocking, winds up being so shocking that you can't really tell quite where it came from. The conversations are far too heavy-handed, loaded with ideas and theses… Sometimes I feel like he should have just written an essay if he has some huge philosophical statement to make. Art is not a vehicle for philosophy. He's not Sartre by a long shot. And furthermore, there's nothing adventurous about it. There's no risk. He studied English in college, and you can tell by how safe he is structurally. Not that I'm looking for the next Beckett or anything like that, but there's very little creative fire from a directing standpoint. Greek tragedy has more on-stage action than this."

Jeannie ponders the depth of Michelle's critique. She

wasn't expecting such a diatribe as the one the girl delivered. It shows a clarity of thought that Jeannie hasn't encountered in anybody since college… if then, even. It's refreshing given her usual stale conversation over after work drinks with co-workers and professionally oriented suitors. She's really starting to like Michelle more and more with every conversation. They *have* to keep in touch after Michelle's assignment ends. Jeannie wants to have a friend with the capability of such insight. It will make life in the city so much more exciting. Collecting herself, she says, "The way you make it sound, I can't imagine why you agreed to do it at all."

"Well, I'm being overly-critical. In the end, there are some really good scenes, driven by a certain power of ideas in the conversation. Actually, it's his overly-philosophical bent that adds that, and I do think that with a little bit of help, it could shape up into something that's all right."

Jeannie makes her first venture into friendship outside of the office: "So do you think it will be worth me coming to see?"

"We'll see…" Michelle says, and she presses the "Start" button on the copy machine.

With a whoosh that rattles through the entire copier, the machine fires up. It clicks and grumbles and sucks the bottom page off the stack of pages. The whole stack slips toward the machine's mouth, and a faint needle-like glow peeks out from beneath the closed lid. The glow slides along until it reaches an apex from which it quickly returns. In the depths of the machine, a perfect facsimile of the image is burned onto a blank piece of paper that has been pulled up from the 8½" x 11" paper tray. The copied page is spat into the auto-sort file hanging at the end. With the faint noise of jumping plastic, the entire sorting file lifts, and another page slides into it, separated from the first.

Then, there is another lift and another page, and another lift and another page, and another lift until five copies of the page have been fired out. Magic. And then the original reappears from beneath the lid. It drifts to rest face up, an unfinished page of typing with THE END centered along the bottom, in a tray below the automatic feeder. The sound of gears sucks page 126 into the machine, and the mystical glow appears again and slides its tracer along the edge of the machine, and the whole process is repeated again and again and again, a testament to the efficiency of 20th century technology.

"Of course, it's a long way from me being able to make any predictions about what the performance will be like. I haven't even cast any of the roles yet."

"Do you know any people who you think would be right for any of the parts?"

"I've got some ideas, but I really wish that Andrew would act."

"Why's that?"

"He'd be perfect for the role of the girl's friend, but he'd probably be offended if I suggested that for him. I'm sure he sees himself as being a little more like Raphael."

"That's the writer who kills himself?"

"Yeah. Andrew's just not intense enough for the part. At least not on a consistent basis, but it doesn't matter. He doesn't think he can act."

"Have you ever seen him?"

"In high school. I don't think he's done anything since then. He was good. Whatever. It'll be fun to work with him again."

"In what way?"

"Well, he's smart, and I know that since he's working with me, the script's malleable. So I'm hoping that with some of my input we can bring out Sophie's character a little more and take some of the ennui out of Raphael's – make them both a little bit more real. It's a character driven show so it's important that the characters stand on their own. I know that Andrew can do it. He just needs to learn how to get out of his own head. With a little bit of help, he could be a really great writer."

"Are you sure you don't have a crush on him?"

"I'm sure. Besides, if there could be anything worse than dating actors, it would be dating a writer."

"Why do you say that?"

"The good ones are borderline schizophrenics."

Jeannie laughs. "Is your friend like that?"

"No. He's not right. That's for sure, but I'm not even certain whether or not I think he's any good."

"Do you know if he's writing anything now?"

"He must be. He's been writing as long as I've known him, poetry, stories… And I've known him for almost ten years now, since we were freshmen in high school. Jesus…" Michelle turns away from the copier. Like the expression of an animal caught in the glare of the photo copier's bright beam, her eyes are wide and blank. "That makes me sound really old doesn't it?"

Jeannie laughs. They're the same age. "I don't think it's such a bad thing to get older. I know I wouldn't have wanted to stay seventeen forever."

"You do have a point there," Michelle says, and she is content to turn back to the copier and be amazed at the intricacies that must occur in order for the writing on one piece of paper to be reproduced without the aid of a scribe onto a sheaf of other pieces. How does the machine know when to lift the auto-sort file? "Twenty-one would have been nice though," she adds as an afterthought.

The two of them don't say anything for a little while. In their bulbs, the lights flicker slight spasms of electricity. The suck and sound of the copy machine drones on and on as the needle of light slides up and returns, up and returns.

"Do you have a job lined up for next week?" Jeannie asks.

"No. Not yet. I'm waiting for a call from Charlie. He's usually pretty good about keeping me working."

"Isn't it annoying to not always know whether or not you're going to have money coming in?"

"Yeah, but you get used to it."

Jeannie straightens up. Her tone becomes quite serious. "What are you doing tonight?"

"Huh? Oh." Michelle quickly grabs all of the pages out of the auto-sort file – one stack, two stacks, three stacks, four stacks, five. She struggles against the machine's gears to pull the last page out of the automatic feed tray, and she grabs the original from its resting place. She has to wait a moment, praying that whoever is coming down the hall won't walk in on her while her last page finishes copying. Then, she slides everything underneath the memo, bounces the pages on the table, straightening them out, edge hiding edge, creating a seemingly infinite number of memos that, if they were what they purport to be, would give ten pages to every employee of the company.

A dark-haired man peaks around the corner. His hair is perfect, his cheeks razor smooth. His tie is sharp. His shirt is starched. "Hey, Michelle. You got a phone call. Line two. I think it's your temp agency."

"All right," Michelle says. She picks up her stack of papers, holds them against her chest, and walks past him out of the room.

The dark-haired man basks in the scent of Michelle's hair as she flies past him. He thrills at the smooth sight of her bare arms. "Got enough copies there?" he asks her back as she floats down the hall. She doesn't answer him.

He turns to Jeannie, glances her over. She fidgets like a schoolgirl looked at inappropriately by her gym teacher. "You waiting for the copy machine?" he asks her.

"No. I was keeping Michelle company."

"Well, you better get back to your desk. Gary's roaming around, and I'm sure he'd want to know what you're hoping to accomplish by standing around doing nothing."

When Michelle gets to the desk and the cubicle that she's been pretending are hers for the past few weeks, she looks around, reaches underneath her roller chair, grabs a leather bag that is sitting on the plastic mat, opens it up, and shoves the pages and pages of scripts in, burying them where they can't be found by anybody who works with her. The only person who she trusts not to tell her secret is Jeannie.

She picks up the phone, presses the button next to the blinking light labeled "Line Two", watches the light flash from an inconsistent red to a permanent green, flicks her neck to spin her hair around and uncover her ear, places the handset beside her cheek, and says, "Hello?"

"Hey, Michelle, it's Charlie," the voice on the other end answers distantly. "How's everything going over there?"

"Fine."

"They're not working you too hard, are they?" Charlie asks. Michelle can discern the almost flirtatious quality to his voice that he always addresses her with, that most men address her with. She can picture the wry smile that would be curling up his cheek — that is most definitely there still, sliding around the mouthpiece of his telephone whether she can see it or not, coloring the shade of his voice — if she were speaking with him face to face.

"No. Everything's just fine," Michelle says. From across a few blocks of telephone cables, hearing only her voice winding through the maze of coils, not seeing her face,

Charlie isn't astute enough to notice her exasperated tone.

"Great. Listen, I was calling because I think I got a job lined up for you for next week. It doesn't start until Tuesday, but one day without work shouldn't be too much of a problem for you, should it?"

"No. That's all right."

"Great," he says, and he goes on to tell her all about her next assignment...

Jeannie is sitting at her desk, trying to look busy, but not really doing anything at all. She wants to email a friend of hers, but she can't think of anything to say. She simply craves the distant communication, her own one-sided acknowledgement of life outside of work. The day is going by too slow. Fridays always do. She has no plans for that night, no dates, no tickets, only her television and her apartment in Queens. If she checks her email enough, something will come up though. On Fridays, it always does.

Michelle appears in front of her. "Was that your temp agency?" Jeannie asks her.

"Yeah. I got a job for next week," Michelle answers. In her hands, she's holding her stack of what is left to copy from the original script. Hiding every sign of Andrew's writing, the memo is placed neatly on top of it. "You ready to watch me finish making copies?" she asks. "I want to make sure I get all of this done before I leave here. You never know whether or not you'll be able to use the Xerox everywhere you work."

"I guess so," Jeannie says. "I gotta keep an eye out for Gary though. If he's walking around, I don't want him to see me just hanging out. By the way, what are you really doing tonight?"

"I'm supposed to get together with Andrew."

"Date?"

Michelle smiles and shakes her head. "You really have

this thing for us, don't you?" Jeannie shrugs. "Trust me. If you knew him, you'd know why I don't want to date him. We're just going out for drinks and to go over the script and schedule for the show. Why?"

"I was just wondering if you wanted to go out and have a drink after work."

"Yeah, I could do that. Just one drink though. I want to go home and change before I meet up with Andrew."

"Where are you guys going?"

"Holiday Cocktail Lounge." Michelle laughs. "*That* should be enough to convince you it's not a date." Jeannie doesn't know the bar. She tends not to frequent the dark homes of the lower strata of both the young and the aging in New York City. Her preference is for the Midtown establishments of the median income, twenty-something professionals. "It's this dive in the East Village. I don't know why we're going there. He only lives a few blocks from me, but it's got cheap drinks, and it's one of his favorite bars. I guess he figures on Friday night we should be in the city rather than Brooklyn, although the Holiday is hardly like being in the city. I think it makes Andrew feel more romantic to hang out at a bar where the drunk bartender barely speaks English. It makes him feel more like Hemingway or something."

"What time are you meeting him?"

"Eight."

"That gives us time for at least one drink. I still have to figure out what I'm going to do tonight, if I'm doing anything at all."

"Let's talk about it while I make copies."

"Right," Jeannie says. She glances around to make sure nobody is paying any attention to what she's doing, where she is going, who she is with. Convinced she's in the clear, she stands up, leaves her desk, and walks down the hall with Michelle.

"You'll never believe where I'm working at on Tuesday," Michelle says as they tread lightly along the short-haired carpet towards the Xerox room.

"Where?"

"The World Trade Center."

Sitting at the bar, waiting, Charlie sips his drink – Grey Goose on the rocks. The mirror behind the bar reflects an eternal array of endless spirits. Colors and tastes: brown and clear and black and gold and green and blue, sweet and bitter and soft and strong; shapes: long, squat, with spouts, with caps, paper labels, engravings, empty bottles, full ones, two fingers gone, three, four left. The bar smells like the two or three groups of patrons who have made their way there after work. No stale beer on the floor, no cigarette smoke mixing with vomit. The golden rail along the edge is polished till it shines. The beer taps are bright and reflective. The middle-aged bartender wears a tuxedo shirt and vest. A lone smoker sits with a woman at one end. Their conversation is private. He keeps his head to the side and his hand in front of his face as he talks. She smiles every few seconds. A group of three older men stand together at the other end, laughing about a colleague of theirs who isn't with them, individually wondering when the younger happy hour crowd, with the attractive younger women, will start to really fill the place up. The music is jazzy and low. Waiting for his friend, in a black suit, white shirt, and black and gold striped tie, Charlie sits in the middle, staring at his reflection above the bottles.

He thinks he's putting on weight. His face is heavy, not fat, just a little round. His jaw line is disappearing. He needs to stop drinking so much, start working out again. He runs his hand through his hair, trying to fix it, to frame his forehead better in the hope that that will somehow reduce the shape of his cheeks and his neck, but his hair is cut too short for him to play with. He stops. It's disheartening.

He feels his stomach resting heavily on his waist. He's putting on weight there, too. He's getting love handles. He straightens up, smoothes his shirt, and sucks in his gut. If things go on like this, he'll never get laid again. He takes another sip of vodka.

The alcohol burns in his throat. It lightens his vision. He smiles at his reflection. No reason to be so serious. Of course he'll get laid again. He doesn't really look so bad. He glances down at the grained wood of the bar and silently laughs at himself.

A hand rests on his shoulder. "Hey, Charlie. Sorry I'm late, man. It took me a little longer to get out of work than I thought it would." Andrew slides in beside him. As far as Charlie can tell, Andrew hasn't put on any weight since high school. How does he do that? He easily drinks as much as Charlie does, and he certainly doesn't get any more exercise than walking to and from the subway and stumbling around the city in the night. Must be genes. Some people have all the luck. Charlie takes another sip of vodka.

"What are you drinking?" he asks.

"Figured I'd just have a beer," Andrew says. "I gotta meet up with Michelle after this."

Charlie raises one finger to get the bartender's attention. The bartender tips his head back. His eyes light up. He walks to across the divide from where Charlie and Andrew are sitting. In a questioning pose, he leans ponderously over the bar. Charlie points to Andrew.

"Bass," Andrew says. The bartender places a pint on the grate beneath the tap. He drains the amber liquid into the glass. Flinging a coaster onto the bar, he sets the glass, dripping a line of soapy liquid down its side, in front of Andrew.

"Six," he says.

"I got it," Charlie says. He fishes into his pocket, pulls out a ten, and hands it to the bartender.

The bartender walks over to the register, rings it up. The numbers whirl with the resonance of changing cartridges. The drawer flies open. The bartender sticks his hand in, pulls his hand out, shuts the drawer with his palm. He spins around and returns with Charlie's four dollars, lays it in front of him on the bar, and walks away. Charlie leaves a one dollar tip. The bartender doesn't pick it up.

Andrew lights a cigarette, leaves his pack out on the bar. The smoke adds texture to the air.

Raising his glass to the gods, Charlie turns to Andrew. "Salud," he says.

Andrew follows Charlie's example. He holds his glistening pint aloft. He winks at his chum. "Always drink the fish," he says. He smiles. "Ichthus."

Charlie smiles back. He doesn't understand all of what Andrew intends, but he knows when his friend is making a joke. They each take a quick sip of their respective drinks, place their glasses back down on the bar, creating a Venn diagram with where their glasses had been. Intersecting sets.

"No fish for you, huh? What are you drinking anyways?"

"Grey Goose."

"I'll drink to birds eating fish." Andrew toasts the heavens again and pours a bit more ale down his throat.

"No tie," Charlie notices.

Andrew puts his glass back down, beginning construction on a set of Olympic rings – the athleticism of mathematics. "Don't worry, boss. I took it off, left it at work. I wasn't sure if I'd have a chance to get home before I see Michelle, and I didn't want to spend all night walking around with a tie dangling out of my pocket, making me feel like I got a tail, like some sort of animal – one that doesn't eat fish – a goddamn plastic animal." He smiles. Charlie doesn't smile back. He doesn't get that one at all. The inference is far too self-referential, too involved with an image whose significance is painted only on the interiors of Andrew's own mind, circumscribed inside his head, no cross-reference for that set. "I figure the dress shirt and slacks look with the hair all messed up is pretty hip."

"Yeah, I was gonna say something about your hair, too…"

"Jesus, I should know never to get together with you right after work. You always get on my ass."

"Sorry, but your appearance is my livelihood. Speaking about my livelihood, I got Michelle a new assignment," Charlie says. "She'll be starting at the World Trade on Tuesday."

Andrew slaps the bar. The older gentlemen waiting for the younger women glance at him, give disapproving looks – it's not that he's drunk already – then return to their conversation, still wondering where the happy hour crowd is (around the corner at a bar that has a happy hour. Soon the older gentlemen will realize that, but by then it will be too late. Slightly toasty, they'll head for the train back to Connecticut, and go home to spend the rest of their Friday nights with the wives. So much for the after-work scenery. They all agree they should have gone to some strip club, but they were all too timid to mention it when sober). "Now, how come she gets to work in The World Trade Center, and I keep getting stuck in these dingy Midtown places, sorting files and copying memos?"

Charlie laughs. "Take a look at yourself, man. I do all I

can to get you jobs. Michelle is skilled, polished, pretty, and she always shows up early. She's going to one of my biggest clients. I've got so many temps there that I could make my living off of the commissions from that firm alone."

"Well, I'm a writer, not a corporate peon."

"And Michelle's an actress, but somehow she manages to pretend for a little while."

"That's *be*cause she's an actress. I don't have that talent. I am my art."

"So you're telling me that you've already killed yourself, and now you're trying to drive yourself crazy enough to go out and rob a bank?"

"Exactly. Part psycho, part genius – just like Burroughs. Andrew Christian."

"You really shouldn't tell me these sorts of things. You depend on me for your rent."

"And you depend on me for yours."

"Not on you alone, my friend, and that's where the difference lies. Like I said, the World Trade Center could pay my bills. I don't need you. Makes me sound like New York City, doesn't it?"

Two seats down from Andrew, two women, already engrossed in conversation, slide up to the bar. Their presence disrupts the flow of Charlie's thoughts and phrases. It postpones Andrew's retort. Feigning oblivion, the women receive glances from both the two of them and the older gentlemen at the other end. The couple sharing cigarettes pay them a moment's notice, more markedly from the woman, and return to their private interlocution.

"So you're going out with Michelle tonight?" Charlie asks, focusing Andrew's attention back on him while he steals peaks over his friend's shoulder at the women ordering their drinks: a whiskey sour and a rum and coke.

"Yeah. We're supposed to put together a schedule for

the show."

"You bang her yet?"

"Jesus, man, that's no way to talk."

"Why not? It's what you want. You've wanted her ever since we were in high school. I remember you telling me all about her all the way back then. She's so beautiful, so smart, so talented, so… so… so… hot! Christ, you lusted after her so horribly it was contagious. You made me want her."

"Yeah, well, right now we're business partners."

"With benefits."

"No benefits."

"To your chagrin."

"I can't talk about this with you."

"Why not?"

"You're too crude."

"Just telling it like it is."

"To your mind, not mine."

"The only difference between my mind and yours is that mine is honest. You pretend like she's too pure for prurient desires. You need to grow up, my friend. You're scared. It's that simple. If you try something, she might betray your fantasy by not being interested, and then you'd be stuck with reality."

"And what, pray, is my fantasy and my reality?"

"I don't know your fantasy, but it has something to do with you and Michelle living artistically ever after. Don't tell me that she didn't have *some*thing to do with you coming to New York. Reality is, well, that you're a drunken temp who's barely fit for a job."

"Thanks, man. I know I can always count on you for positive reinforcement."

"Just being the realist in our dynamic duo."

"Dynamic duo? Who gets to be Batman?"

"That would be me considering I have the job and the money."

"But I have all the adventure here in Gotham."

"Like the child you are, Robin. You ready for another pint?"

"Sure… If you're paying. It's a sin to spend six dollars on a beer."

"I'll pay, since you're so concerned about the theology of alcohol."

"Well, if we're dealing in theology here, get me a Johnny Walker Black."

"Where's the theology in that?"

"I'm practicing to be a priest, sucking off the nectar of God. The land of milk and honey… What's the amber fluid? Forget about the body and blood of Christ. Every Irish Catholic knows that sweet whiskey flows from Her teats. Didn't they teach you anything in Sunday school?"

"First off, you can't be a priest. You're Jewish…"

"Only on my mother's side."

"Secondly, I never went to Sunday school. You know that. Give me a cigarette. I'll suck on that instead."

"Careful. God's face is obscured by smoke. His radiance shines in the midst of its obfuscation."

"Whatever, just give me a cigarette and shut up about God. I'm trying to get us drinks."

The drinks arrive to a toast of nothing in particular. The flamboyant mannerism manages to catch the eye of one of the women, the closest one, who are sitting two seats down from Andrew. Neither Andrew nor Charlie notice, though either would be delighted to do so. The older gentlemen leave, the last one out the door taking a peak at the curve off the stool of one of the women's asses.

The drinks are finished with a vow of only one more round from Andrew. He has to get downtown to meet up with Michelle. Charlie protests, but Andrew is adamant. He can't be late, which Charlie knows, from having grown up around the corner from him, is a lost promise. Andrew will be late. He always is. It's the main reason that Charlie doesn't trust him at any of his finer clients' establishments.

Like most nights, Andrew's hangover has been drunk away. He feels the whiskey floating freely through his brain. He sets his glass back on the bar, the final dregs of the last drink jiggling softly at the base of the tumbler. He's saving it for one final sip before he leaves. He lights a cigarette. As he exhales, through the smoke pouring out of his mouth, he says, "So I'm reading *The Masks of God* series by Joseph Campbell. I just finished the first book."

"I know," Charlie says, "You've told me about it before."

"Right. So, anyways, Joseph Campbell talks about two types of primitive man, the hard-minded man and the soft-minded man. The hard-minded man is the hunter, the gatherer, somebody whose sole concern is feeding himself and the tribe. At his strongest, he grows into the tribal leader, in a sense, the politician, the businessman. The soft-minded man has no real interest in food. He finds himself drawn to a certain mystical quality in the hunt, the mythology existing on the perimeter of man's tribal life. This obsession with the forces of nature leads to what Joseph Campbell refers to as the shamanistic breakdown – a sort of loss of touch with everyday reality in place of a religious experience. This is the origin of religion, which is then assimilated by the hard-minded man into an order for society, but the point is still made: Religion itself evolves from what ordinary men term madness…"

"You've told me all this before."

"Right, but what I'm thinking is, you see, this first book is called *Primitive Mythology*. The last book is *Creative*

Mythology – from what I understand, it deals with the moderns, like Joyce and Mann. I'm thinking that he's going to trace this shamanistic breakdown through the development of organized religion – the Saint's journey, the Buddhist *satori* – and into the equivalent of a modern artistic experience, meaning that great art evolves from the same insanity out of which God was created."

"If God was created by humans."

"Of course, well, we can't assume that God is in any way real."

"I try not to think about it."

"I can't help myself."

"I know. That's your problem."

"Anyways. Here's what I'm getting at: If art comes out of madness, and God comes from madness, then shouldn't we all be paying a lot more attention to what the insane have to say?"

"Sometimes I think you're insane."

"I'm working on it."

"How did I know that?" Charlie shakes his head. "Are you going to stay and have another drink with me, or are you going to run off to your woman."

"I'm going to run off even though she's not my woman. What time is it?"

Charlie checks his watch. It was a graduation gift from his father. You can tell a good deal about a man from his watch. "A little after seven-thirty."

"Shit. I'm gonna be late."

"Come on. Just stay here. Call Michelle and tell her you're having one last drink with me. Tell her to meet us here."

"No. I gotta go. The offer's tempting, but I gotta go." He slams the last drops of whiskey, steps up from his chair, and walks to the door, worried for a brief moment that he may be weaving ever so slightly. No. He hasn't had enough to drink yet.

"I tried," Charlie says to nobody in particular. "God knows, I tried. Bartender, one more Grey Goose."

From the observation deck of The Empire State Building, 86 stories above the teeming mass of humans gawking and mumbling and screaming and shouting and talking and walking and running, the streets and lights of New York City spread like veins and cells, a spiderwebbed body, many-headed like the Hydra, covered in eyes like Mithra, animate in its grandeur, breathing as a spreading amoeba, breeding with itself, consuming the flies, the demons: Beelzebub – their lord, their savior. To one side, the shores of New Jersey are visible. On the other side, Brooklyn spreads out across the East River. Queens is in the distance, one skyscraper rising, phallus-like out of the duplex plane. The flat and pointed roofs of the buildings that, from the ground, rise so high, blocking the sky, encasing their victims in alleys and walkways, lie a multitude of feet below, a mini-metropolis from heaven's perch. Unlike anywhere else in the city, the sky expands and shines with the radiance of stars, a seeming reflection in the water's above the firmament. Manhattan's grid of streets and avenues is a Euclidean map with one imperfection: Broadway, the defect built into the mosque, slices across the mathematical precision, scarring the earth. At the end of the island, the Twin Towers rise, glittering, glorious boxes dwarfing the financial district, a brother and a sister, fraternal lovers giving birth to all that lies beneath, morphing from SoHo and the Village into Midtown's masculine monument, falling off to the demure Chrysler Building, descending back into Harlem, Washington Heights, and the river that borders the Bronx.

"Do you ever feel like you're living the skyline?" Michelle asks.

Andrew pauses for a moment to think about her question. He stares out through the grates in the fence that encloses the observation deck, that discourages the suicidal from plunging from the dream of infinity to the reality of quantified concrete below. He's distracted by a vision of the fall, the wind, the freedom, the thought of death being so close. Milton's Lucifer. He blinks and looks back at the skyline spreading out all around him. He – in the midst of it all, in one of the anchors – gazes across the gulfs and ridges that have framed the aspirations of so many actors, brokers, musicians, writers, bankers, lawyers, painters, directors, models, entrepreneurs, immigrants from every continent on the globe, dreamers the world over – artists all. "I'm living the skyline right now," he says.

"Really? Look at it. Are you sure you're living everything that that horizon promised you before you showed up here?"

The warmth of the alcohol consumed with Charlie in Midtown and with Michelle at the Holiday Cocktail Lounge colors Andrew's thoughts and feelings. Over the course of the subway ride, while waiting downstairs in line, the mellowness of its glow in his bloodstream has faded, but it has given way to a subtler sort of contentment. He exhales thoughtfully, "Maybe not everything, but pretty close. Think about it. I've been here for a year, and today I spent my lunch hour talking to an old friend about being in a show that I wrote, that one of my friends is producing and directing. Over the course of that conversation, I finally figured out how to start my screenplay. Tomorrow, I'm going to begin writing it. I live in a rundown, railroad apartment with an actor in one of the hippest neighborhoods in the world. My bedroom window has a perfect view of the same skyline you're talking about. It's a little after ten o'clock on a Friday night, and I've already been at two bars tonight, talking about things that interest me, putting together a schedule for that same show. And now, here I am, standing mildly drunk on top of the Empire State Building, surrounded by tourists, with you asking me whether or not I'm living my fantasy. Look at the city all around you. This is the skyline. This is my dream."

Michelle isn't so sure. Her forehead and eyebrows crease in a way that one of her ex-boyfriend's found irresistible. She purses her lips and stares through that same grate without the thought of the fall. She feels the swirling presence of the tourists around her filling the landing they're standing on. She hears the laughs and shouts of playing children excited to reach the heights that, previously, only their fantasies had imagined. She says, "I don't know. Sometimes I feel like I've found the skyline, and other times, well, New York is New York, you know."

"I'm not sure if I do know. What do you mean?"

"Think about the city. No matter what you do, you can never get on top of it. Sure, there are people, who, for a moment, think they might have beaten it, but sure enough, the city will come along and spin their whole world upside down. I guess the skyline means different things to different people."

"What does it mean to you?"

"Fame. That's what it meant when I showed up as a little, lost freshman at NYU. I guess it's never really changed."

"Well, you never know. You might be becoming that."

"Becoming what?"

"Famous."

"Fame isn't so important to me anymore. All I really

care about is getting by and having a chance to do the best I can with the things that are important to me."

"You know, sometimes I wonder who out of all the people I know here is going to wind up famous. Next to me, you're in the lead, girl."

Michelle laughs a laugh that ends in a smile that radiates through her face, crawls up her cheeks, creases her eyes, shines an aura that reaches out and tickles the inside of Andrew's stomach. She spins her head to send her wavy hair tumbling back over her shoulder. With her hair out of the way, her profile is sharp. Framed by the lights in the distance, she's a poster, an album cover, a frozen moment embodying Andrew's dreams. She is his skyline. He's inspired. He says, "Think about it, Michelle. In, what, four days? You're going to be riding an elevator up in one of those towers to something like the 90th floor..."

"Something like that. Can you imagine what the city will look like from up there?"

"Tell me that's not living the skyline."

Michelle's smile spreads even farther. "Yeah, maybe that is something."

"You know, I think it's in *Mao II*, Don DeLillo says something about the World Trade Center being the hermaphroditic god of the city." The two pieces – the rook and the bishop – glow in leopard print dress. Off the bishop's crown, a thousand points of light, Jacob's ladder, penetrate heaven.

"I can see that. I guess the one with the antenna is the male part?"

"Something like that."

"A god, huh?"

"It makes sense. If you think about it, ancient people worshipped the gods of the earth, deities that were place-specific. They lived in their cities. There's definitely something very primal about New York. In the subway, it feels alive to me, and the World Trade Center is kind of like New York's monument to itself."

"More so than the Empire State?"

"Well, the World Trade is more directly connected to our mythology."

"And what's that?"

"Money." Andrew smiles contagiously. Michelle is infected. "Our Bible is *The Wealth of Nations*. Our faceless god: The Invisible Hand. The Twin Towers are our idol. You've been in the city long enough to know that."

Michelle nods. She stops suddenly. She tilts her head to the side. Her eyebrows crease again. Her gaze cuts through the night, slicing the air, dissecting the words hidden in it. "I don't know," she says, "The Empire State is an idol – New York's hard-on. I think a hermaphrodite is a little more than that."

"In what way?"

"Well, I remember this acid trip when I was a freshman. We went down to the World Trade Center to lie down and stare up at the lights. I can still see its shape kind of stepping out of the night and flying off above me, its foundation seeming to reach out beneath and support me... Anyways. When I was down there, I remember thinking about the same thing you were just talking about, how the city feels kind of alive, especially in the subways, and I remember thinking about how the World Trade Center starts down there underground and winds up going up – God knows how many feet, I don't, and how many thousands and thousands of people go in and out, underneath, and all around it every day. I could feel it, you know..."

"I can imagine."

"The electricity was coursing through me. Being down

there, for a second, it was like the whole city shot through me. I could feel the souls of ten million people refined into one single point, one place – the forms of those two buildings I was staring at. At that moment, I knew that the energy of those buildings, the mental energy of designing them, the physical energy of building them, the psychic energy that's contained in them, and the spiritual energy of the dreams directed towards them has made them into something much more than simply the physical shapes that we see. They have a presence that, now that you mention it, must be something like what people felt when they first came to believe in god…" Michelle laughs at the intensity of her monologue. "I don't know. I guess I was tripping pretty hard, but I'll be honest, ever since then, anytime I pray, I picture myself praying to the force that I felt surging out of the Twin Towers that night."

"That's pretty intense, Michelle. Now you're making me feel like a real ass for making my joke about capitalism."

"Yeah. I like the idea of New York's god being a hermaphrodite, too."

"Why's that?'

"It fits the city better than this monstrosity of masculinity that we're standing on."

"You don't think New York's masculine?"

"Not entirely. London is masculine. Paris is feminine. New York is a hermaphrodite."

"Some of the most ancient conceptions of God are as a hermaphrodite."

"As they should still be."

"I figured you'd want God to be a woman."

"Why?"

"Because you're a woman…"

"You forget. Women are more giving than men. I don't have to own all of God. Only men need that. Besides, if

God's a woman, who would I make love to when I die?"

"You could try angels."

"Why settle for second best?"

Andrew pauses to think about what Michelle has said. He stares at the curve of her lips. They tremble ever so slightly, as they always do when she's made a point after a few drinks. He has to agree with her. He nods. He laughs. "I'd expect that from you," he says.

"What?"

Looking into Michelle's eyes, he whispers, "You're a perfectionist. That's what'll make you famous." Michelle shakes her head proudly. They start walking around the perimeter of the landing, Michelle next to the fence. They walk slowly, gazing out at the expanse of the city as they go.

"Okay, perfectionist. If you could choose the perfect way to die, what would that be?" Andrew asks.

"That's a pretty morbid question," Michelle says.

"I know, but you're the one who wants to make love to God, so just answer it."

"Do you think about this sort of stuff a lot?"

"Every once in a while," Andrew laughs. "Answer the question."

Michelle thinks for a moment. The wind blows her hair. She gives herself a hug. "Nuclear explosion, right in the epicenter."

"That's original. Why?"

"So that I can see something that nobody else ever gets to see. The splitting of the atom, and all that... It's probably the closest any living person ever gets to seeing God, right? That way if there's no God after I die, I won't die disappointed. How about you?"

"Ripped apart by wolves."

"That's gruesome. Why would you want that?"

"So that I'm fighting to stay alive until the very last

minute…"

"Interesting view."

They pass Brooklyn. They pause for a moment to point out their neighborhood to each other ("Right there. There's the Williamsburg Bridge. That's Queens. There's Brooklyn. That's right where Greenpoint is.") They start walking again, brushing shoulders every once in a while, the invisible shields that they have on the streets, the ones that somehow manage to always keep urbanites at a constant distance from their neighbors, disappearing. Andrew cocks his head to the side. He asks, "But who says God would be the best?"

"The best at what?"

"Making love."

"I can't imagine that anybody could be better."

"What about the devil?"

"I don't believe in him."

"Neither do I, but as long as we're speaking mythically, if I were you, I'd take Lucifer. Seems to me he'd know a little bit more about the whole thing."

"Hmmm… You could be right about that. No. Maybe if I was younger – still in my rock star phase – I'd want the devil, but at twenty-four, I'll take God."

"Why's that?"

"Sensuality of course."

"Lucifer seems extremely sensual."

"Not the way I see him."

"Maybe you just don't know him like I do."

"All right. Now, you're scaring me." Michelle laughs. Along with her, Andrew laughs at himself. They've strolled half-way around the building, spun half a rotation atop the unmoved mover at the center of their world, reached the summer solstice of their journey. To their left side, the lights of Times Square, the eternally vigilant, virulent, beating heart of the city that never sleeps, shine the white glow of daylight in night – the sun imprisoned on earth. The monstrous advertisements in the pulsing atrium of capitalism are visible even from their distance.

"Can you imagine what New York would look like after a war," Michelle says, "The depth of the rubble from all these buildings?"

"It's mind boggling," Andrew says.

In front of them, a little to the right, the Chrysler Building, decorated in a pleated skirt of lights, rises to the Empire State's shoulder.

"See, even Midtown has a feminine part," Michelle says, nodding at the Chrysler.

Andrew looks. "I never thought of it that way."

"I guess, if the World Trade Center is New York's hermaphroditic god, then the Empire State and the Chrysler Building are the city's king and queen."

"And the rest of the skyline is pawns."

"Maybe it's a giant chess game: Midtown versus Downtown."

"The spiritual versus the temporal. God's kingdom versus man's."

"You're taking it too far again."

"Oh, come on, Michelle. Can't you see it? The financial district is powered by the faceless god. Midtown is the custodian of the riches. It's the church and the state lined up to do battle once and for all, to determine who will rule mankind – God or Caesar, papal doctrine or human law, the stock market or hard cash, theoretical economics or practical business? And the war is being fought all across New York City, with the lower classes as cannon fodder – you and me, moving back and forth, captured by opposing sides, sent back to the front with a new suit, a different face, making one wealthier to spite the other until it all spins back around."

Michelle grabs Andrew's arm. Her fingers are a shock. Andrew's excitement rises. She bursts in excitedly, joking, "Maybe it's not a chess game. Maybe they're really working together, the hermaphrodite, the king, and the queen. The posture of the game is just an act to keep us from rising up and going to war with both of them."

"Yes. Yes. The financiers and the entrepreneurs, the church and the state determining our American Dream: a new opiate for the masses. You're probably right about that. Capitalist scum… Worldwide revolution of the proletariat! That's what I'm calling for, and it's going to start right here in Gotham, with me and you, Catwoman, robbing the Chase Manhattan Bank in Times Square."

Michelle shakes her head. "What the hell are you talking about, robbing a bank?"

"My screenplay."

"What screenplay?"

"The one I'm going to start writing tomorrow. I didn't tell you about it yet?"

"No."

"It's about this writer – me – who needs to come up with an idea that's going to sell, so he comes up with an idea about a writer who needs to come up with an idea that's going to sell so he comes up with a plot for a bank robbery, but as the original writer's writing the story, he realizes that the robbery could work. So he gets the help of this friend of his who runs a theater company – that's you – and they enlist the help of a bunch of actors – that's Michael and Carey for starters – and they do the whole thing like a play, with a stage manager and a director and everybody having their roles. We still need to figure out all those parts, plus how to rob the bank…"

"That's a really cool idea. I can't believe you never told

me about it before."

"I wasn't sure if you'd be in to robbing a bank. Besides, you might steal the plot and take all the money for yourself."

"Andrew, I don't write. I direct. Somebody else has to give me the words, and I make sure that people see them right."

Michelle's arm is still wrapped around Andrew's. Her hand is resting on his thin bicep. His face is turned to hers. She's smiling. Her lips are soft and pliable. Her glassy eyes sparkle with a scintillation of heaven. She blinks. Her eyelashes hold together for a moment and pull apart. Her halo expands to encompass his still liquored brain. It contracts and pulls him down towards her. He closes his eyes. She closes hers and reaches up on tippy-toes.

They know the future, the next moment, perfectly.

Their tingling lips meet. Their mouths open. Their heads spin and lock. Andrew caresses Michelle's cheek, his palm cupping her chin. Michelle runs her fingers down Andrew's arm, up his back, nestling the tips into his hair. Their tongues extend to wrap around one another's, tasting each other's breath, merging two bodies into one in the simplest, the purest, of pleasurable practices.

Above them, the Empire State blinks. Beyond them, New York glitters. Around them, children laugh and couples nuzzle. Inside of them, a seed shoots out roots planted in the other's stomach.

Shared, conjoined, they step back, Andrew's hands resting on Michelle's arms, Michelle's fingers at Andrew's waist. In awe, they gaze into one another's once familiar, now brand-new eyes.

"How come that's never happened before?" Andrew asks.

"Because we've never been together on top of the

Empire State Building before," Michelle answers.

Usually, Carey would be at work, but he's taken this Monday night off. He has what he hopes will be a date, but the man he's hanging out with, he isn't sure if he's gay or straight. They met at a bar in the Village. Carey bought him a drink. They exchanged numbers, but nothing happened, and now Carey's nervous, wondering if maybe Gabriel only has the inclination to be his friend. He should have been more forward about his desires, he thinks. Still, they're hanging out tonight, and that counts for something.

Naked, with a towel, a woman's turban, around his waist, Carey stands in front of the bathroom mirror, shaving, listening to the music playing in the tiny living room that isn't much more than an enclave of the kitchen. It's Andrew's CD on the boombox, *London Calling* by The Clash. Carey's been listening to it a lot lately.

Carey hums along. The bathroom has no windows. It's bounded on one side by the kitchen, on the other by a wall separating him from his Puerto Rican neighbors. The light is yellow and fades in and out. The faucet doesn't work; the water only turns on and off from a valve on the pipe. The basin is sudsy with shaving cream, something vaguely sexual about its shade and grime. Carey rinses his razor one last time and pulls the plug on the drain. Sucking and gurgling, the sink swallows the dirty water. Carey whips the towel off his waist to wipe down his face. He stares at himself in the still slightly steamed mirror.

He's young and thin, hairless and smooth. He feels his body, the texture of his skin – the same as the men he loves, a perfect mirror for his lovers, attracted by the similarities rather than the differences in taste and touch. Gabriel probably has hair on his chest though, a little bit around the nipples, a happy trail.

Indicating that Andrew's home, a key clicks in the lock on the front door. Carey veils himself with his towel. The bathroom door doesn't close. There's always a crack to peek through – a teenager's fantastic dream.

Andrew steps in to the dub sounds, the cranking noises, and the deep bass of *The Guns of Brixton*. He heard faint stirrings of the music as he wound his way up four floors of the tenement's piss-smelling stairway. Warming and clouding the faded kitchen, steam has filtered out of the bathroom. Andrew doesn't turn the volume down on the boombox. It's one of his favorite albums on one of his favorite tracks. He's surprised to find Carey listening to it. Dropping his book – brand new subway reading, bought the day before, Joseph Campbell's *Oriental Mythology* (on the cover a demon chews a renaissance scene: the Tibetan wheel of transmigration) – on the one couch facing the radio (no TV), he walks over to the apartment's only closet that both he and his roommate share, unwraps his tie – the ox's yoke, the dog's collar and leash – from around his neck, and hangs it up on the hanger that he uses for the four ties he owns. He loosens his collar, twists his neck, reaches into his pocket, pulls out the tie that he left at the office on Friday night, and hangs it next to the one that he wore today.

He's soaking wet. While he was underground somewhere between Midtown and Brooklyn, maybe speeding beneath the East River itself, it started pouring outside. "Hey, man, can I get in there and get a towel?" he yells.

"Yeah, sure. I'm just finishing up," Carey answers. The door opens all the way. Carey comes out, his chest and legs glistening from the shower, his face smooth as a child's. It always makes Andrew slightly uncomfortable, given Carey's sexual preferences, for him to see him fresh and clean and nearly as naked as Adam succumbing to temptation, for him to smell the scents of soap and shampoo and oils meant only to seduce. Shields in place, they brush past each other.

"I figured you'd be at work tonight," Andrew says from the bathroom, his own towel wrapped around his head, pats his neck, and hangs it back on the rusted shower curtain rod to dry.

"I was going to, but then Gabriel called today and asked if I wanted to hang out tonight. I'm meeting him at The Homestead. Do you know it?"

"Yeah. You won't like it."

"Why not?"

"I like it."

"Oh, then you're probably right… Did you go out with Michelle last night?"

"No. I went to Doc's instead. Check this out." Andrew walks back into the kitchen. Still shirtless, Carey has put on jeans. Smoking a cigarette, he's sitting on the couch with one leg and a bare foot tucked up underneath him. With the toes of his other foot, he taps the rhythm of The Clash on the tile floor.

Andrew leans against the tiny arch that poses as the entryway from the kitchen to the living room. He says, "So last night, I'm walking along Saint Mark's, on my way from The Holiday to Doc's to shoot some pool, and when I get to the corner of First Ave, there's this black guy sitting on the sidewalk, brown-bagging a forty. I walk right past him, not paying him any mind. He's staring at the ground, sipping off his beer, harmless as any bum. Anyways. After I've gone a few steps, I hear him shout, 'Aww, shit!' So I turn around to see what's happening. He's jumped up, and he's dropping his beer in the trash can, spinning around to head downtown, and this police car is screaming around the corner. The car screeches to a stop. The cops jump out and run to get a hold of him. Before I know it, they've slammed him face down on the hood, and they're slapping cuffs on him while everybody on the street is standing around staring. He's yelling something at them, but they're not paying any attention. You know how cops do that, how they keep their faces turned away and tuck somebody into the backseat?

"Well, here's what strikes me about it. We're in The Village, right? I mean, college kids are walking down the street smoking joints. Twenty-somethings like me are stumbling into each other and pissing on buildings. For Christ's sake, half the people watching were probably more loaded than he was, and none of them were in any danger of getting arrested. I remember out on Coney Island this one time, these cops saw me brown-bagging, and all they did was tell me to throw it away. I was a little pissed, but I didn't get thrown against a car. It's bull shit, man."

"It's Giuliani. That's a fascinating story, but I can't believe you haven't seen Michelle again yet. Have you called her?"

"Not yet. I need to call her tonight."

"Yeah, you do… You're unbelievable. You talk about how in love with her you are, and then you spend a whole night making out with her on the subway, and you don't call her for three days… Get your shit together."

"I figured the three day rule, you know."

"The three day rule is that you call *within* three days of meeting somebody… Making out with an old friend, you should have called her immediately."

"I didn't want to bother her."

"If she likes you, you're not bothering her."

"Well, she hasn't called me either."

"She's not supposed to! I don't care how liberated a

woman is. She still wants *you* to call *her*. I don't even date women, and I know that."

"Yeah, but women tell you things they don't tell us straight guys. Shit. You're probably right. I'm gonna go call her right now. See if she wants to hang out tonight."

"Good luck. You'd better kiss her ass."

Andrew takes four steps across the living room. He passes through Carey's bedroom in another four, and he's standing in his own room. He closes the door.

His room is larger than any other room in the apartment, the master bedroom when a family lived, snuggled one on top of the other (as they still live in the apartment with the same floor plan next door), in that minuscule Brooklyn domicile. The floor is the same yellow tile that stretches all the way from the living room, and it slants, like the rest of the apartment, to the left, a shift, a settling in the ground beneath over the years the building has stood. There are no wall-hangings, no decorations, only peeling white paint. In the corner is Andrew's writing desk, complete with his laptop – a graduation gift from his father, and a half-drunk bottle of whiskey, a mental lubricant for the nights when he writes, on top of it. Tonight could be one of those nights. You never know. At one end of the room is a wall of windows, the only source of external light other than the opposite wall, a whole railcar opposed, in the kitchen, looking over the gray street.

Outside his bedroom windows, beyond the rooftops gathering puddles below, a fog has rolled sheets of rain across the river. The city is invisible – vanished like the mirage that it is. On any other day, the sun would be setting behind the Twin Towers, bleeding between black specters, a spectacular *mise en scène*. Andrew would sit out on the fire escape, his balcony beneath the right window, light a cigarette and watch the spectrum distend between the buildings.

Andrew whips out his cell phone, flicks it open, presses a button, presses another button, and hits the number "1". Michelle's number is recalled from the electronic memory. Andrew presses the button marked "Send". A signal from the antenna of his phone passes through his ceiling and into the atmosphere, off of an antenna, and up through the troposphere, beyond the stratosphere, out of the mesosphere, to a satellite hovering in outer space. One satellite contacts another satellite, and the signal travels back to earth. In less than five seconds, Michelle's phone rings and rings and...

Action at a distance, she answers: "Hey." She knows it's him. She saw his name digitally displayed from the memory on her phone.

"What's up? How you doin?"

"I'm all right." She sounds perturbed. "How are you?"

"I'm good. Listen. I was wondering if you wanted to get together tonight."

She sighs. "I don't know. I'm starting that new assignment tomorrow."

"I know. I thought maybe we could just get together for a drink or something."

"I don't know. I don't really have much money."

"Neither do I, but hey, it's New York. That's how it goes. I'll even buy you a drink... I'd like to see you."

She doesn't say anything for a bit. Andrew wonders if she's still there. "All right. You know it's pouring outside, though, don't you?"

"Yeah. I'm watching it out my window right now."

"Where do you want to go then?"

"I was thinking Enid's. It's close enough to your apartment that you won't have to get too wet."

Another pause. "Yeah. I could meet you there."

"All right. What time?"

"I don't know. I got some stuff to finish up here. How about a half an hour?"

"A half an hour sounds good. I'll see you then."

"All right. Bye."

"Bye."

She hangs up. The signal dies. Should he have told her that he loves her? No. She's probably not ready to hear that yet.

He sits down on the bed next to his wall, the place from which he spends so much time wishing he could understand the Spanish filtering through thin plaster. He stares at the torrent of rain pouring down outside, listens to it pelting his walls, merging with the music in the other room, birthing a natural rhythm different from what The Clash had in mind. He wonders at the feeling in his stomach: fear and desire and power and lust commingled into one trundling emotion.

He stands up, kicks off his shoes, picks his jeans up off the floor, and changes pants. He throws his black socks into the corner, finds a pair of white ones that don't look too dirty, slips into a pair of fake, Sketchers' wingtips, laces them up, and ties them. He unbuttons his shirt and drops it on top of his slacks. In his jeans, white tee shirt, and black shoes, he opens the door and leaves his room. Across from Carey still half-nude, out of the speakers on the stereo in the living room, London is still calling.

"So you called her?" Carey asks.

"Yeah."

"How'd it go?"

"We're gonna meet up at Enid's in a half an hour. She didn't sound too happy with me though."

"Well, you've got some making up to do, but if she likes you anywhere near as much as you like her, it shouldn't be too hard."

"Yeah… I love this song."

"The whole album's great."

"I didn't know you liked The Clash."

"I didn't. I was just sitting around the house one day, and I was thinking that *London Calling* is one of those albums everybody should be familiar with."

"Like *Kind of Blue* or *The White Album*."

"I guess so. I don't know. *The White Album's* always kind of scared me."

"Why's that?"

"Don't get me wrong. It's a great album. It's just the whole Manson thing. I can't help thinking that somewhere in that maze of words and sounds is the skeleton key to his whole 'Helter Skelter' idea."

"I've never thought about it like that."

"I guess some side of me thinks that if I spend too much time listening to it, suddenly 'Helter Skelter' will make sense to me."

"I think it takes a lot of drugs."

"Who knows. Whatever he heard is still there. It didn't go anywhere."

"Yeah, but Charlie's like the Joker. He's insane."

"The rest of the family didn't think so."

"They were all insane."

"If a multitude of people are suffering from the same delusion could it really be that they're all crazy? I mean, isn't that all that reality is anyway, one mass delusion?"

"Yeah, in a sense, but the Family was under the influence of a charismatic leader."

"We're all under the influence of charismatic leaders. Theologians, politicians, psychologists, philosophers, mathematicians, scientists. Really, he's no different than your shamans."

"Except that the shaman should recognize that the experience of God is completely personal. 'Salvation has no plural.' We'll call Manson a false prophet, a psychotic imagining a heightened, spiritual experience."

"How do you distinguish one from the other? I mean, unless you've got a Bible of some sort, you have no way of determining who's sent from God and who isn't, who's found Truth and who hasn't. You're the one with the theory about how we need to pay more attention to what crazy people think. For example, who's to say that Jesus wasn't a turn of the millennium version of the same thing?"

"In the eyes of the Jews, he was. I guess it all comes down to how life-affirming the world view is."

"Manson's world view *was* life-affirming. He was trying to create heaven on earth, the same as Jesus or the Buddha or any number of spiritual leaders."

"But through external destruction, not through self-actualization."

"Seems like, to him, self-actualization grew out of destruction. It's no different from all those anarcho-punk bands you grew up listening to. It's no different than Marx. Really, it's no different from Moses."

Rubbing his chin, Rodin's *Thinker*, Andrew pauses for a moment. "You know, I hate to say it, but you could be right. Maybe I need to buy *The White Album* again."

Carey laughs. "All right. But once that happens, I know it's time for me to get out of here."

Andrew shrugs. "Hey, you wanna know something cool?" he says.

"Sure."

"All right. Take a look at this album cover." Andrew picks up the disc jacket for *London Calling*, a black and white photograph of a bent backed man on a stage, swinging his bass guitar above his shoulder, an executioner's axe descending to the ground, the act of destroying the means, the tool, of his art, the omega of his creation, the alpha of his world created. The title, in pink and green, frames the snapshot.

"Okay."

"Well, Elvis Presley's first album is a black and white picture of Elvis playing the guitar, his mouth open wide, his body twisted around. It exudes sexuality. It's a promise of the liberation of the human spirit. Around the picture, in the same colors and lettering as 'London Calling' is written here, it says 'Elvis Presley'. So here's what I'm thinking. This album cover is a comment on the state of rock n roll's relationship to the world. It's no longer freedom and happiness. They're pissed. The promise of rock hasn't come to fruition. Twenty-five years after 'Shake, Rattle, and Roll', and the powers that be are exercising a greater stranglehold on the human spirit than ever before. Elvis gyrated and sang. This cover screams, 'Things have to change!'"

"And you're the one telling me that you think that external destruction doesn't lead to self-actualization…"

"I never said that. All right. I'm gonna get going. Have a good time with Gabriel."

"Yeah. We'll see."

The well gin at Enid's tastes metallic. The tonic makes it pop like rust dissolving in acid. The lime adds a pleasurable bite. Andrew sits at the bar, chewing on his stirrer, sucking bits of flavor, like marrow, out of its hollow center.

The room, larger than many of its occupants' apartments, dotted with tables, is lit by blinking Christmas lights strung around the bar and across the ceiling. On each table, a lone candle burns, its wick scenting the air, a censure. On the bar, the candles, like stained glass, add atmosphere. From the turntable in the DJ's booth above the female bartender, an album that's so hip Andrew has no idea who it is plays softly, something indie and acoustic venting from the speakers. The sounds of a pinball game come from the hall near the bathroom. The sparse crowd is young, retro-mod in vintage glasses, shaggy hair cuts, tight tee shirts, highwater pants, and polyester shirts. The men are smooth, the women stylish, fashionable in their precision as inhabitants of the neighborhood of beautiful people. Feeling so adult, so artistic, so suave and sophisticated, they're laughing and talking and toasting, excited, in spite of the downpour outside (visible through the windows encircling the only room that constitutes Enid's), to be showing themselves off in their neighborhood. This is their home. It's an invigorating sensation to be young in New York City, partaking of the pinnacle of civilization, breathing the exuberance of life, existing in a present ever teetering towards the future, leaving your parent's past and suburbia's loneliness behind, living off of the energy of your own youth and the enthusiasm of your peers.

Again, Andrew is drenched. Water trickles from his hair down his cheeks to drip into a small puddle forming beneath him on the wooden floor. Someday soon, he needs to buy an umbrella. As he waits for Michelle, for some reason, he remembers a dream that he had not too long ago.

The dream was more sensation than anything else – vague, fleeting, ephemeral. Angels fell from the sky. Their wings singed, clothed in burning white, screaming, they leaped to the abyss. Melting, moaning demons rose, phantom-like, amorphous, from fissures in the great, steaming earth. Fire engulfed the field of Andrew's mind.

He choked on the smoke. Flames encompassed the heavens. Buildings crumbled and burned. Thousands died in the holocaust. Ire and enmity. Ten million more deaths to come. The unavoidable blueprint for World War III was drawn at the beginning of time, and all that Andrew knew was that, in the angels' demise, the apocalypse had finally begun.

"Hey," Michelle says, wresting Andrew's thoughts away from his dream, back to his reality's dark atmosphere. "I figured you'd be late so I took my time. Have you been here long?"

"No."

Dry from her knees up, she's closing her dripping umbrella. Andrew really needs to get himself one of those. She kisses him on the cheek, their usual greeting, but without the usual verve. "You're soaked," she notices.

"I know. I can feel it."

She sits down at the bar and orders herself a glass of red wine. The pretty, blonde bartendress says hello to her. They vaguely know each other from Michelle's occasional passing through. Michelle doesn't introduce her to Andrew. Andrew offers to pay for Michelle's drink. She lets him, and she thanks him as if he were a stranger.

The eerie sensation of Andrew's phantasmal memories colors his thoughts. Michelle's coldness dampens his emotions. He wants to stare at her face, at her cheeks flushed from her rush, the curve of her lips, her breath rising, like a birdsong, in her chest, but he doesn't feel right looking at her. He turns on his stool to watch the downpour outside. He feels Brooklyn – the dusk, the gray, the rain. "That's one helluva storm," he says. "Puts a real damper on the evening. I had no idea it was coming."

"They've been talking about it all day."

"I guess I need to listen to the radio more."

"Maybe."

"Sometimes I really start to believe New York is indestructible. I mean, look out there. We used to worship elements. Rain like that is supposed to prove the power of the divine. It sure seems weak when it's only water beating on concrete."

"Sometimes I think God's the only thing you care about."

"I care about other things."

"Like art and poetry and politics and philosophy. Maybe music too. Did I miss anything?"

Andrew smiles sourly at himself. "Pretty predictable, huh?"

"No. I wouldn't say that," Michelle says. She sounds hurt. Andrew turns to look at her. In her mannerisms, he doesn't detect anything of her last tone. She's not smiling, but she would never visibly show any inclination towards suffering. With her long fingers, fingers that convey a sensual touch, she tips the wine glass to her perfectly pursed lips.

I care about you, he wants to say, but it took too long for the words to form themselves right in his mind. He lost his chance. If only life were written with a pen onto a piece of paper, a paragraph that he could revise. If only this moment were a play with one more rehearsal. *Get your lines right* – the director shouts.

– Hey, man, I'm a writer riffing on a phrase that just isn't coming out right.

"How was your weekend?" Andrew asks.

"It was okay."

"You do anything exciting?"

"Not really." She pauses, thinking for a moment. "How was yours?" she finally asks.

"It was good. I didn't really do too much. Wrote a

whole bunch, drank a whole bunch, read a little bit. The usual."

Michelle smiles a wan smile.

They sip their drinks. Andrew orders another gin and tonic. There's something that needs to be said, but he's not quite sure what it is.

"So I was figuring I'd give Michael a call tomorrow. See if he's still up for trying out for Raphael."

Michelle nods. Mentioning Michael, Andrew feels a jealous pang in his throat. He watches Michelle, hardly enthralled by the jiggling blood of Christ, spin her glass.

"Maybe I shouldn't bother calling him."

"Why not?"

"I don't know."

"Do whatever you think is right."

Andrew shifts in his chair. The second gin and tonic is helping his thoughts flow right. "So, um, I'm sorry I didn't call you earlier," he says.

"It's no big deal."

"I just got so caught up in my writing and everything," he lies.

"Really, it's no big deal."

"I figured you might be busy, too, you know, that you might already have plans."

"I didn't, but it's okay."

Andrew nods. "So I was thinking about what you said about the show, about how Sophie needs to have a moment where she says something about what makes talking to Raphael about his own poetry better than reading somebody else's, even if it's better. I think you're right. I added a little bit to that first conversation she has with Alexander. I'll let you go over it tomorrow if I can bring it by your apartment."

"Sure."

"I didn't bring it tonight cuz I figured, well, I don't know."

"What did you figure?"

"That maybe we'd talk about something else."

Michelle raises her shoulders and exhales softly. "Let's not talk about something else," she says.

"Okay." Andrew sits there for a moment. He glances over his shoulder at the windows opening onto the rain. The wind beats the drops into a song of dreariness, depression, and frustration. He turns a bit more and looks over the juxtaposition of the patrons. Gesticulating in conversation, they're all so happy and content with sparkling smiles, shining teeth, bright eyes – warm and dry despite the torrent outside. Words welling inside his chest, he glances back at Michelle. The candlelight accents the profile of her nose. "What should we talk about then?" he wants to know.

"I don't know. You've always got a thousand things to say."

"Yeah, I guess I usually do," he says, but he can't think of any of them. One question consumes him, blocks the flow of any other thought.

Michelle is finishing her glass of wine. Andrew asks her if she wants another one. She hesitates for a moment, but eventually, she says, "Sure," and calls the bartendress over. The bartendress pulls out a bottle of wine, uncorks it, and fills the glass as it sits on the bar. They laugh together at one of those things that only two women can laugh about. Andrew tries joining in, but it doesn't feel right. Michelle doesn't let Andrew pay this time.

Andrew asks if she wants to move to a table. She says that might not be a bad idea. Michelle waves goodbye to the bartendress, and they pick up their things and move to a table where they can sit down and face one another.

In the romanticism of the lone candle's light, Andrew takes a long draw of gin. Michelle isn't looking at him. Fidgeting with her full glass, she watches the few people around them, listens to the music from the DJ booth. She likes a hat that one of the women has on – a flat hat, slouching to the side, beret-like. In the darkness, it hides her face, lets the light of the table's candle illuminate her jaw line, draws the viewer's attention to a lone strand of hair dangling out from beneath. Michelle thinks that something like that might look good on her, too.

Andrew's leaning back in his chair. He taps the side of his glass in rhythm to the music that he doesn't know. Without missing a beat, he says stumblingly, "So, the other night, was that just a one night thing, a freak of circumstances, or was it, I don't know, something else?"

Michelle sighs. "I don't know, Andrew. What do you want it to be?"

Sitting still, still tapping his glass, for a moment, Andrew doesn't answer. When he does speak, his thoughts are calculated, his words enunciated: "I want it to be something else."

"Well, you sure didn't act like it."

"I know. I'm sorry."

"I mean, no wonder you don't have a girlfriend. Do you always not call somebody after you've kissed them?"

"You didn't call me either," Andrew mumbles.

"I didn't think I'd have to."

"But you didn't want... I thought, maybe, you know…"

"Jesus, Andrew, I'm not about to be a one-night stand. It was the first time we'd ever kissed… Maybe the last."

Andrew doesn't want to believe that that could possibly be true. He remembers being nestled together at the end of a gray bench as the L train flew and shook them through the graffiti covered, rat infested tunnel connecting Brooklyn to the city. His arm around Michelle's shoulder. Bouncing. Alone together no matter who got on or off, no matter how crowded they were. Her looking at him, glassy eyed, drunk… Caressing her cheek, her throat. The fine feeling of her hair in his hands. The startling sensation of her fingers at his lips. A dream. A dream to have again and again. Saying goodbye to her: a long kiss goodnight beneath the streetlight above the sidewalk outside her apartment door, an embrace that never should have ended. Asking to come inside, being told – *Not tonight. We're drunk. Go home.* Telling her that he'll call her soon, believing that soon, very soon, they'll be resting together in a delectable bed, beneath harmonious sheets, pulling one another close, naked and content, as warm as conversation and drink without saying or touching a drop of anything. "Don't say that."

"Why shouldn't I say that? You didn't even make an effort."

"I am now."

"By talking."

"What else can I do?"

"You're impossible. I knew, I've always known, I should never get involved with you. Everything's in your head."

Andrew looks down, purses his lips, pulls his hand down his face, tries to erase his expression, draw a new one in its place. There's no common denominator, no means of reduction, for a conversation between a man and a woman. The synapses snap in variations of different multiples. "I don't understand," he says.

"That's exactly what I mean."

"Please, Michelle, don't tell me that I screwed up."

"You know that this is a conversation we shouldn't even be having."

"I just want to know where things stand."

"I don't know. Jesus, you know just that night, earlier, I was telling Jeannie all about why I'd never date you, and it was precisely because of this."

"Because of what?"

"You're lost inside your head. Step outside yourself for a little bit."

"I'm trying."

"You didn't call me. You disappeared for whatever reason, and now you're sitting here saying things that don't need to be said."

"What do you mean?"

"Think about it. You think about everything else. Give this one a shot."

His eyes creasing, his mind wrestling, twisting, turning, writhing inside himself, Andrew is mute. He stares at Michelle. He wants to reach out and feel her cheek.

She laughs caustically. "On second thought, don't think about it. Just do something."

A geyser of laughter explodes from a table to Andrew's left. It floods the room, permeates Andrew's ear, crashes inside his brain. He glances to his left, makes eye contact with the smiling, shaggy haired hipster in a butterfly collar who tips his glass to him. – *Just do something.* There's nothing to do.

He takes another sip of gin, finishes the drink with a long gulp, sets his glass down, puckers his lips in response to the lime, and moves around the table to sit next to Michelle. She's taken aback. He puts one arm around her, draws her close, leans forward, and at the extent of the candlelight, where the glare meets the void, he kisses her on the lips.

She doesn't respond. Placid, she extricates herself from his embrace. "That wasn't what I meant," she whispers.

Andrew returns, crestfallen, shamefaced, to his original seat. He pulls a cigarette out of his pack, leans back in his chair, and taps the filter, packing the tobacco, against the table – a nervous habit. "I don't understand, then, Michelle," he says.

"I know."

"What am I supposed to do?"

"Something honest."

"That was honest."

"No, it wasn't."

Andrew mumbles dejectedly, "As the director, I guess you'd know about those sorts of things."

"You're not writing me, Andrew."

"I know."

"Then stop trying. Write yourself as much as you want, but don't try writing me."

Andrew flips the cigarette that he's been toying with between his lips. He picks the squat candle up off the table, tilts his head to the side, and brings the flame to the cigarette's end. The candle's dancing flame sends shadows slithering across his bony face. He sets the candle back down. In the midst of his exhale, he says, "I'm gonna go get another drink. Do you want one?"

"No. I need to go home."

"Please, don't go, Michelle. Stay for a little while longer."

"So we can get drunk together? Not tonight."

Andrew leans forward, rests his elbows on the table. Beneath his chin, a goatee at a distance, the melting candle adds an eerie quality to the shadowy slates of his face. Mephisto. "We could dance."

Michelle smiles, honestly, at Andrew's joke. She even giggles a little bit. It warms Andrew's stomach, tickles his loins, to know that he's the cause of her pleasure. A seductively wicked grin seeps into his eyes. "Not tonight, honey," Michelle says. "Unlike you, I like to be at work on time, maybe even early, and I'm starting a new job tomorrow."

"A kiss?"

Michelle's smile disappears. She stands up and grabs her umbrella. "Try not waiting so long to call me the next time," she says.

She brushes past Andrew. In the air, her scent, evocative of a summer field, lingers for a moment. Andrew turns in his chair. Her back, the shade of her thin shoulders, the wave of her long hair, disappears behind the curtain blocking the door. Waiting to catch one last glimpse of her, he stares out the window. In the light drizzle, her umbrella hiding her face, her legs zipping along the pavement, her shoes, lightly splashing, tapping an unheard rhythm, she floats, skims across the surface of water, down the sidewalk, and disappears around the corner to her apartment.

"Goodbye," Andrew whispers.

He stands up and walks back to the bar. He sits down and orders another drink from the bartender who knew Michelle but doesn't pay any attention to him.

Running the conversation through his mind over and over again, he sits pensive, scratching his chin, smoking a cigarette, staring at the floor. Candles flicker. Christmas lights blink. More and more people, as hip as the patrons already there, fill the empty tables, the vacant barstools. Their amicability, their greetings to one another, augments Andrew's loneliness. He wishes that he were underneath Michelle's umbrella, her hand wrapped around his arm as she fumbles for the keys to her apartment. He aches.

He decides that he wants to shoot pool. He finishes his drink quickly and leaves Enid's warmth. With his hands in his pockets, the drizzle dripping across his head and neck, watching his footsteps beat against the concrete, he walks up the block, past McCarren Park – opening wide and verdant, an empty, baseball field covered block in an asphalt wasteland – and turns left. At the corner of Bedford Avenue and North 12th Street, on the indistinct border between Williamsburg and Greenpoint, is The Turkey's Nest.

With neon signs of beers and games in the windows, The Turkey's Nest is the last remnant, so close to the youthful heart of Williamsburg, of the distinctly local flavor that has yet to give way to the tide of gentrification. A rumor that if the bartender hears you're an artist, he'll throw you out circulates the rounds of the neighborhood. Unafraid, Andrew steps inside and walks straight to the bar. He orders a Budweiser in a styrofoam cup so large that he has to use both hands to carry it; one hand is too awkward. Foam and dribble spill over the side – a cloudburst like the one, earlier, outside. Three dollars and fifty cents. The Turkey's Nest knows nothing of sin. Peopled by the Brooklyn working class, the Polish, the Italians, and the Puerto Ricans, the unemployed, elderly drunks, salt of the earth, a few drug dealers, and the prematurely dying middle-aged, it is bright and spacious, unrepressed, no iniquities to hide, with a pool table in the back, a pinball game in the front, the TV on ESPN-2, and a classic rock jukebox by the bar.

Ready to play a game, to try and forget what he feels, Andrew gets fifty cents for pool. He slaps his money down on the edge of the table and sets himself in a chair beside it. A group of neighborhood kids, seeming teen-agers not old enough to be drinking, stand around the dartboard by the bathrooms, throwing a game and chatting with bottles in their hands. Andrew leans back and lights a cigarette. Next to him is a middle-aged woman. She's a regular. He's seen her there, but he's never spoken with her before. She has black hair and thick skin, slightly wrinkled, savage, and pale. She's a little overweight, saggy breasted – the body of the goddess. Yelling at one of the men shooting, she's leaning forward and pointing at pockets, telling him where to put his ball. Bearded skin and bones, he's an elderly Christ, succumbed to the last temptation, freed from his cross, maligned by his wife. He shakes his head (he's wearing a hat from which a broom of gray hair peaks out) and tries his best to ignore her.

"He's never gonna make that shot," she tells Andrew, her accent is thick, been in Brooklyn her whole life. "His English is off. I know English. I can read a ball like I read a book."

Andrew nods, smoke seeps from his nose and mouth, but he doesn't respond. Caught up in his own thoughts, not really paying attention to what the woman says, he's acknowledging the sound of her voice. Like a schizoid self, Michelle possesses his mind. Her words, the forlorn moments, fleeting as his dreams, perhaps imagined, of her eyes… In his memories, he's trying to read her mind, to deduce from a twist of her neck, the tilt of her chin, a wave of her hand, her thoughts. It's no use. She's as impenetrable as a sculpture, modern art with a meaning crafted in the cavernous depths of the sculptor's subconscious – no classical story, no biblical myth carved into the façade. Pure form and structure. Art for art's sake like reality, a minimalist's realism, a woman.

To his left, in laughter, the goddess explodes out of her seated, abstract, alabaster statuette. Like a shark in a frenzy, her eyes disappear. Blind, her entire body, every crease and fold, jiggles with chuckles. Her man missed his shot. "Told ya so," she says. "I know English. I can read…"

"A ball like you read a book. Yeah, yeah…" the scraggly man slurs, finishes, dismisses her with a snarl, a wave of his hand, his magic wand, the evil eye to keep the devil away. He steps over to the bar and picks up a small tumbler of whiskey from where it rests. He pours the liquor through a tiny gap in his beard, stumbles into and leans against the jukebox.

More to get himself out of his head than anything else, to drift away from, stop chiseling away at Michelle's impregnability for a little while, Andrew says to the woman, "I had a dream the other night."

"Oh yeah," she responds, "What's it about?"

"It's kind of strange, what dream isn't? But in my dream, I'm back at home, I'm not from Brooklyn, in Connecticut, and there's this girl with me, and all I'm doing is trying to sneak away from my mom so I can sleep with her. She's real small, petite, with short, black hair, and a body that, at every step, every movement, writhes like a snake's. I don't think I've ever seen anybody quite as gorgeous as her. No," Andrew frowns, "I know somebody as beautiful, maybe even more so, but that doesn't matter.

"Anyways, this friend of my mom's, actually the mother of a friend of mine who lives in New York, this guy, Charlie, is following us everywhere. Every time I round a corner, lose sight of our chaperone, I lunge towards my tiny enchantress's lips, but before I can get her shirt over her chest to even *see* her breasts, while I'm nibbling at her neck, this friend of my mom's is breathing down *my* neck, in the most asexual of ways, asking me to explain what we're doing. Somehow, I always manage to make an excuse: I'm looking for her necklace – its clasp broke, she has a stomach rash she wants me to check out, I thought I saw something crawl up her shirt, things like that. So finally, I whisper in the girl's ear that we need to run away. She agrees.

"The next time we round a corner, we hold hands, like children, and start running. We don't stop until we've made it to the top of this hill in the middle of a wide, stretching field. We start kissing, and we maneuver ourselves down into a bed of grass. I can feel it scratching my skin, and we tear into each other like wolves.

"While we're clawing and gnawing, my mother's friend shows up. She shouts, 'What in God's name are you two doing?'

"I can't stand it. I've had enough. There's no more excuses to make. Still naked, sweat streaming down, glistening on my body, I jump up, stare my accuser straight in the face, stamp my feet like a beast, snarl, and bellow back, 'We're moving beyond good and evil. Is there something wrong with that?'"

There's a pause as the woman waits, leaning forward, seated in her ancient pose, breasts on her stomach on her lap, for him to go on. "That's it?" she finally asks.

Andrew takes a sip of beer, tilts his head to the side, and nods.

"I like it. More men need to have that dream." She looks at her friend getting ready to take another shot. His English is still off.

"Tell me something," Andrew says. "You're a woman…"

"Yeah."

Andrew laughs, wipes the beer from his lips. "I wasn't finished yet." His tone becomes serious, his face grave. "There's this girl, and I screwed up real bad with her, and I have no idea what to do to make everything all right again."

"How long have you two been dating?"

"We're not really even dating yet. She's a friend of mine

from high school. I've been in love with her since then, and we kissed on top of The Empire State Building the other night, but I didn't call her, and now she says that'll probably never happen again."

"You've been in love with her since high school, and you didn't call her? How old are you?"

"Twenty-four."

"That figures."

"I just didn't know. I didn't know if I'd be screwing up by calling too soon."

"You can never screw up by calling too soon."

"I'm realizing that now."

Thinking, the woman frowns, rests her chins on her chest. "Flowers, like The Stones," she says, pointing one finger, Buddha-esque as if the juke tunes were the language of the spheres, to the sky where the invisible music traverses the room like notes bounding along a scale. "Flowers can fix anything."

Andrew listens.

"Do you think your girlfriend has anything to do with your dream?"

"I had the dream before we kissed."

"That doesn't matter."

"I don't know how she could."

"Think about it."

"She doesn't look anything like the girl I was with in my dream."

"Dreams don't have to be perfect."

"Maybe. I don't know. I just want to know what to do next."

"I told you. Flowers."

"She said I had to do something honest."

"Flowers are always honest. Pick them out yourself. Tell her something with them. Flowers speak in colors.

When was the last time you saw her?"

"Tonight."

"Does she work?"

"She's starting a new job tomorrow."

"Perfect. Bring her flowers after work."

"Roses?"

"If that seems right to you."

"Red or white?"

"Whatever seems right."

"Then red *and* white." Andrew laughs, "But no blue. That's a color we can leave out of this occasion."

"They don't make blue roses. Red, pink, yellow, white, and black. That's it," the woman says. She looks back at the pool table. With one eye closed, glaring down the length of his stick, her man is lining up another shot. Scowling, the woman whispers to Andrew, "I swear he can barely speak English... Did I say speak? I meant use. A man his age should know how to *use* English."

"It was Freudian," Andrew responds. He's descending back into his head, using his mind to plumb the chambers of his heart, the cavities of his soul, to scour his memories again for some signal, some common unit of meaning that could unravel the code of Michelle's desires and explain to him how to act in accordance to her wishes. He exhales and shakes his head. It doesn't make any sense.

The woman is still speaking: "See, look at the way he lines up on the cue ball. He plays it backwards every time. Putting spin on the ball is like touching a woman. He's so set on getting to the eight that he forgets there's a whole game in between the break and calling the pocket. His biggest problem is that he can't think ahead. The important shot isn't the one you're taking, it's the next one. I know these sorts of things. Women shoot pool different than men. We play to block shots, not to make them. That's a defensive game. It's not winning that matters, only not losing. If you don't lose for long enough, eventually you'll win. If a man could learn to play pool like a woman, then he wouldn't have the sort of problems you're having. It's about the way you think…"

By four o'clock AM, on the morning of September 11th, 2001, Andrew is still stumbling around the Turkey's Nest, drinking whiskey and shooting pool against any drunkard who happens to wander through the door. He's quiet, pensive, rubbing his chin as he leans against the pool table, the wall for support. He looks like he's pondering the next shot, like he's a hustler playing the future of the game through his mind, but he's not. A pit yawns in his gut. He stays close to the jukebox for the full effect of the music, to let the guitars and drums overwhelm his thoughts, the lyrics mutate, mutilate his feelings. An excessive amount of alcohol allows the user to sense the intricacy of every emotion, but it renders him unable to lucidly express anything. Visions of screaming and smashing the pool stick against the table, throwing the shattered shards through the window – the tingling sound of breaking glass – dance, like sugar plums, in Andrew's head. Performance art.

The jukebox still has sympathy for the devil, but all of the regulars have left. The woman with the body of the goddess has removed herself from her pedestal and returned to her apartment upstairs. She's no longer sitting there against the wall, smoking cigarettes, analyzing Andrew's every shot, every movement, exhorting him to think, to twist his brain around and look at the pool table from a brand-new angle, to see the game backwards, the beginning as the end, the end as the beginning.

The bartender shouted, "Last call!" a few moments ago, and now he's telling Andrew to hurry up and finish his game. The music is turned off. The lights are going out.

The Turkey's Nest isn't so bright anymore. With the shadows, sin creeps in.

Two balls are left on the table: Andrew's eleven, and for his opponent, the eight. Andrew's only shot is a bank, one rail to the corner pocket, let the cue go where it will; the eight is resting next to its own pocket, a kiss away from victory. It's a shot he makes every time. He calls his pocket, draws a line on the ball, reads the angle, adjusts his mark, and strikes.

Two balls collide, a sharp crack bounds into a ricochet and the eleven comes flying back towards the pocket. The angle's off. It hits the rail, bounces back into the original rail, and rolls into the middle of the table. His opponent has a clear shot on the eight. Not wanting to see himself lose, not tonight, Andrew drops his stick on the table. "You win," he says. It isn't the way he wants the night to end, but no matter how hard he may struggle to grasp the trajectory of the game tightly in his meager fists, he has no control over pool.

Outside, the rain has stopped. Williamsburg's smog, the outflow that turns your snot black, has dissipated beneath heaven's shower. The air is clean and pleasant. After the rain, it's warm for September. There's a chain link fence topped with razor wire across the avenue from The Turkey's Nest. For a brief moment, that fence means something, symbolizes something internal, something to cut, to climb, to break free from and see what lies on the other side: the wasteland, a pit in the earth, a demolished building that the landlord has never reconstructed. Insanely drunk, Andrew turns left towards Greenpoint.

As he crosses across from McCarren Park, to his left, beyond an asphalt baseball diamond where the Puerto Ricans play weekend games, across the East River, deep in the midst of the skyline, the Empire State Building stands –

a postcard. The top is drenched in red. The needle blinks a warning to low-flying planes. In the swirling midst of Andrew's haze, the building rises stark and defined, in high-relief against the black night, one of the many gods of New York's pantheon.

A memory of Michelle's breath, her hair crawls up from Andrew's stomach. It lights in his throat…

"AHHHHHHHHH!"

He picks an empty beer bottle up from the gutter. From a running start, he aims the bottle at the city and throws it, as if a single bottle, a Molotov Cocktail, could bring down the immensity, the memories, of a skyline's definition, with a grunt that leaves him breathless and rubbing his shoulder. The bottle spins over the park's fence, shatters in the middle of the baseball diamond – the pleasing tinkle of destruction.

"I'm an idiot," Andrew whispers thickly to nothing and to nobody other than the blinking lights of the city and the blank face of the moon staring stoically down. He thrusts his hands into his pockets, hunches his shoulders, and keeps walking, kicking and scuffing the concrete every few steps.

"It's gonna be okay," he whispers as he walks. "It's all gonna be okay."

"No it's not." He shakes his head. "You fucked up bad."

"No I didn't. I'm gonna bring her flowers tomorrow, just like the lady said, and maybe not immediately, but eventually, this will all be okay, and I'll laugh about it. We'll laugh about it together."

"No you won't. You'll never laugh about it. You fucked up bad, my friend. You fucked up real bad."

"Shut up!" he yells as he stumbles into a tree, realizing he's reached his block.

He leans his head back against the bark. The solidity is comforting in his drunken fluidity. He wants to cry, but the whiskey won't let him. To be so close to something that you've wanted for ten years, so close... The world spins from distinction to darkness, from clarity to opaqueness.

His face contorted, his mouth open in dry sobs, he tips his head back to look at the sky. The moon glows, white as a whale, a halo around its laughing woman's face. Placid and cool, removed, peaceful and serene in the heavens, it mocks Andrew. His stomach twists.

"What are you looking at?" he shouts at the moon. "Why are you staring at *me*?" He jerks himself upright, stumbles a few steps to the end of the block, points one trembling finger at the face in the night sky, the eons old embodiment of man's terror, the centuries' hieroglyph of the world's unfathomable mystery, the cyclic correspondent of the menstrual ebb and flow, and like young Romeo beneath the spotlight, he screams, spits, "Just bring it on, motherfucker! Bring it on! I'm Andrew Christian, the baddest motherfucker who ever walked the face of this earth! The baddest motherfucker who *ever* walked the face of this earth!

II.
And the Butterfly Screams

Very little in New York still excites or impresses Michelle. Having lived in the city for six years, she has acquired the much needed, obligatory veneer of the "seen it all" New Yorker. For, in all honesty, what has a New Yorker, who has ever taken the opportunity to explore the visible and hidden features of the city's corpus, not seen? There are the homeless, the gangsters, the immigrants, the club kids, the police, the tourists, the glitterati, the literati, the digerati, the welfare recipients, the debutantes, the hip-hoppers and break dancers, the insane, the street peddlers, the models and photo shoots, the drug dealers, the pimps, the prostitutes, the hustlers, the parvenus, the artists, the filmmakers, the street-corner magicians, the gays, the sex-crazed, the sex-starved, the religious, the coke-heads, the stoned, the candy flippers, the drunks, the gallery-openings, the Fringe Festival, the Blue Man Group, the Village Halloween Parade, the pungent odors of Chinatown, the sickly stench of summer garbage, the extent of the globe's palate, the trendiest of whatever season's fashions, the end of the world is coming madness, rats the size of cats, door to door delivery drug services, 4 AM closing time fights and hook-ups, shows on, off, and way off Broadway,

Shakespeare in the Park, lines and lines of limousines, the Met, the MOMA, three story mega-clubs, after-hours gambling and coke dens, sex in taxi cabs, sex at bars, Religious Sex, Savage Love, jumpers from buildings, crime scenes, murders and robberies, pickpockets, panhandlers and con-artists on the subway, the marketing madness of America laid bare, topless bartenders breathing fire, S&M restaurants with men who want to take you there, and the entire host of the city's ten million frantic existences in all of their multifarious interactions.

However, this morning, as she zooms, wearing a short, gray skirt and a white blouse (much more conservative than usual), without stopping, past the lower stories in a crowded elevator heading up, up (heaven expands around her) above the North Tower's eightieth, eighty-first, eighty-second floor, Michelle is excited. Her ears popped long ago. She's never been this high inside the World Trade Center before. She's never been this high without the aid of an airplane before. The building embodies so much, holds a place of such symbolic value in the eye of New York's beholder. Being in the bright, spacious lobby, the maw of the great beast – walled in glass, bustling with an early morning crowd (serious faces, a few stray greetings, security guards standing protectively) – impressed the grandeur of working for wealth into Michelle's mind. Ascending one of the arteries of the giant possesses all the mysticism hidden in the depths of the American Dream. For the first time ever, Michelle has grabbed a hold of one of the spokes spinning the city's paddlewheel propelling the fortunes of business down the mythical Mississippi. It only took six years. She smoothes her skirt and shakes her legs. She's wearing a necklace with matching earrings that her mother bought for her years ago. It's rare that she's found an occasion to wear them. She hopes that her outfit will impress her new employers.

Although she would be loath to admit it to any one of her friends, deep down inside, the prospect of obtaining long-term employment at the top of one of those glass towers, looking out, every day, every afternoon, every evening over the lightening and darkening expanse of the city, even if she were only copying and filing, answering phones and pouring coffee, would fill her with a sense of accomplishment similar to the initial rush of moving to New York at eighteen. In all honesty, who in the city wouldn't love to spend the days that he or she had to work in one of the most important, one of the most industrious and intrepid of New York's monoliths? She intends to be her most charming, her most diligent, and her most flirtatious.

In the midst of all her optimism, only one thought bothers her. It has gnawed at the back of her mind since she awoke. It has bitten into her consciousness at the most inopportune of moments – as she was choosing her outfit, as she was fixing her hair, and now, as the elevator's digital light registers that soon she will be disembarking – and spit a sinking sensation into her stomach, diminishing her precarious confidence.

Last night, after leaving Enid's, she was certain that Andrew would call before she went to bed. She even lay awake for an hour, with the lights off and her phone on the nightstand, opening her eyes every once in a while, staring at the shadows across her ceiling, expecting that at any moment she would hear the muffled ring of her cell. He might have been drunk; he might have made a fool of himself, but he should have called. Regardless of what he had to say, it would have made her feel nice inside.

She had no intentions of waiting up for him to call. She had planned on being asleep within ten minutes of going to bed, and she doesn't appreciate the fact that she wasn't. She already spent all weekend waiting for him, and she's not like that, like a high school girl jittery for the boy, and it frightens her to think that she might be a little more in love with him than she initially thought, that she might have underestimated the strength of her feelings for an old friend, that she could have been so deceived regarding her feelings in the first place. She knows herself better than that. It was easy to feign offense over the weekend, but there's no excuse for last night, and Andrew is even more clueless than originally assumed if he couldn't figure out that calling her would be the right thing to do. If he doesn't get in touch with her today, then whatever they might have been able to have is over. That's what she's decided, and her decision makes her nervous. Why couldn't he have just called?

With a ding, the doors of the elevator slide open. Truly inside, one of the cells of, an individualized point in the soul of the hermaphrodite, she licks her lips, pulls a stray strand of hair out of her face, and regains her composure. She's tired. No thinking about Andrew and his screwed up head for the rest of the day.

Along with a man in a charcoal suit carrying a briefcase, she steps out. She gets her bearings and turns to her right. With an appreciative glance up and down Michelle's body, the man in the charcoal suit turns left to head towards his own pre-appointed place in the synapses of the organism's mind. His glance reaffirms Michelle's confidence in herself.

So many doors, so many offices. The perfect interior for the organs of a god. It's a macrocosm, the eidos, of every now microscopic office building that she has ever entered.

After a long, nerve-settling exhale, she opens the door of the suite where she's working. A long desk with a seated

bleached blonde receptionist wearing a headset greets her.
The clock above the receptionist reads 8:42. Slightly more
than fifteen minutes early, right on time.

Michelle walks up to the receptionist who tips her head
to the side and smiles sweetly – saccharine. She's wearing
too much eye shadow. "Can I help you?" she asks.

With all the honesty that she learned in acting classes at
Tisch, Michelle smiles back. She doesn't care much for the
receptionist's aura. She's young, pretty in a TV way, wants
to marry a stockbroker and live on the Upper East Side
(sounds like she grew up on Long Island, can't wait to go
home and have kids – if she even lives in any one of the
five boroughs yet. Queens, maybe, Forest Hills or
something like that. Astoria, if she's lucky), probably doing
somebody important, but Michelle is determined to be as
cordial as she can be to everybody. You never know who
can help you out in the future. "Yeah, I'm Michelle
Sophiedos, the temp from Heavenly Staffing. I'm supposed
to ask for Timothy Van Luchen."

"Certainly. He just showed up. I'll page him. Have a
seat."

Michelle sits down in a comfortable chair by the wall.
She crosses her legs genteelly. There's a low coffee table
with magazines on it. A *Vogue* catches Michelle's attention,
but she doesn't pick it up to look at no matter how
intriguing the fashions may be. She doesn't want to appear
impatient when Timothy meets her. First impressions are
extremely important in business.

The receptionist is talking into her mouthpiece. "Tim,
the temp is here for you," she says. She pauses. "Okay," she
says. She looks brightly at Michelle. "He'll be right out," she
says.

Michelle nods.

"You work for Heavenly Staffing?" the receptionist

asks.

Not really wanting to engage the girl in conversation, Michelle nods again.

"Does Charlie still work there?"

"Yeah," Michelle answers.

"I liked him. He was sweet," the receptionist says with a wistful smile.

I'll bet he was, Michelle thinks. "Yeah, he is," she agrees, smiling her own smile that she hopes is believable. The consummate director, she's pretty sure she would tell the actress to put more feeling into that one. She stifles a yawn. Her stomach has wings. She's a butterfly. Andrew pops into her head. She shuts him out. There's too much to worry about: her appearance, her gambit, her fate.

An attractive man in his early thirties rounds the corner from behind the receptionist's desk. He's wearing a dark blue suit and a subdued tie. His hair is a bit longer, somewhat hipper, than most businessmen's. With a lop-sided grin, he projects a playful persona. He probably backpacks and mountain bikes in Vermont whenever he gets a chance, enjoys cooking and keeps his Midtown apartment clean, might still smoke pot at the right party. On sight, Michelle likes him. He smiles warmly. He won't be bad to work with, could even be fun. "Michelle?" he asks, extending his hand.

Michelle stands up. She notices the man watching her legs unfold. She's glad she wore the short skirt. She smoothes out her clothing. "Yes," she answers.

"I'm Tim," the man says, and they shake hands. He smells of fresh after-shave. His grip is pleasant. His nails are manicured. His hands are smooth. Michelle smiles invitingly, but respectfully, with gleaming eyes – you can't act that – at him. He returns her gaze with a similar one of his own. With eyes like that, his girlfriend must be beautiful.

"So I guess I'll take you back and show you what you'll be doing," he says.

Will I be in a room with a view? Michelle wonders. She's still nervous. *It must be magnificent. You know it's the only reason I want to work here.*

Timothy turns to his right. The fluorescent lights, the electric blood of the titan, shine through his hair. His tie lifts slightly off his chest. He's still smiling. The introduction is going well, it seems. This is like a dream.

A crash and a thud reverberate through the floor, the walls, the ceiling. The building vibrates slightly, the plaintive resonance of vocal chords, the shudder of dying, insect wings. Michelle jumps. Her stomach plummets. The receptionist screams. The wall cracks. The lights go out.

"What the fuck was that?" Timothy yells, a strangled note like nothing a man should make in his voice.

In the darkness, Michelle's legs, stretching out of her carefully chosen skirt, begin to tremble. She has no idea.

Somehow, Andrew opens his eyes. Daylight shines through the wall of open windows into his bedroom. He glances over at the clock. The red, digital numbers read 8:46. Why the hell didn't his alarm go off? He's even later than usual. He's lucky he got up at all. How did he manage, all on his own, to pull himself out of sleep's submersion?

With his head swimming, the world fluid, life is a dream. Much too quickly for his head, he leaps out of bed, grabs a pair of pants and a tee shirt off the floor, slips on a pair of socks, and steps into his shoes. He doesn't have time for his usual morning gaze at the immensity of the skyline. He stumbles out his bedroom door and tiptoes as quietly as he can through Carey's bedroom. The stale taste of liquor coats his tongue. He hopes he wasn't too loud when he came in last night. He didn't know Carey was at home. In his bed against the wall, close enough that Andrew could touch him with his outstretched hand, Carey stirs, rearranges his covers, but doesn't open his eyes. In the living room, Andrew fumbles around in the closet for a shirt and a tie that seem to match his pants.

He rushes into the bathroom, quickly brushes his teeth, sticks his head beneath the faucet, runs his fingers through his hair, a poor attempt at combing it, scrambles around the apartment looking for his phone and his book, finds them on the couch, and leaves. He didn't even shave. His morning routine probably took about five minutes. It all depends on how the trains are running, but hopefully he'll only be about fifteen minutes late.

As he bounds down his stoop, the previous night's events float, on the white fingers of a whiskey wave, into his brain. He shakes his head at his bravado. That's risky business, tempting gods like that. He clutches his book tight against his side. No matter. He's moving beyond good and evil, seeking balance between the yin and the yang. He needs Michelle to understand that. Michelle... Nerves clench in his stomach.

The day is warm with a slight breeze. The sun is out. It feels more like Spring than Fall. It smells more like Massachusetts than Brooklyn. Last night's rain drowned the world, flooded the filth of the city with its deluge. The vivified morning juxtaposes the dank night. The world is brand new. Andrew floats, chosen for Noah's ark. A chorus of birds should be chirping. A choir of angels could be singing. Last night no longer seems insurmountable. Tonight, Andrew is going to bring Michelle flowers. Red *and* white roses. He can't forget that. She's a piece of the hermaphrodite right now. As he rounds the corner, headed for Manhattan Avenue, a rebirth nascent in his thoughts, he glances back over his shoulder at the city.

He stops walking and turns all the way around. His eyebrows knit together. He tilts his head to the side.

From the side, between the ribs of one of the Twin Towers, a plume of smoke issues like breath escaping a whale's blowhole, a pulsing fountain of blood. Clouding the perfect day, the skein of gray, an umbilical cord giving birth to nothingness, billows into the blue sky. It's an odd picture, unfathomable, one that doesn't fit quite right in the frame of Andrew's mind – a trailer from a techno-thriller. He shakes his head, turns around, and starts walking toward the subway again. As he turns left onto Manhattan Ave, he gazes one last time, before they disappear behind Brooklyn's boxy buildings, at the Trade Towers. The smoke, the poof of gray-matter, the exhaled rattle of a dying being, is still there. It wasn't a mirage, a late remnant of ounces of whiskey.

Some madman sitting dumbstruck on his stoop whispers something like, "Hey, man, I think I just saw a plane hit the World Trade."

Andrew doesn't hear him. He keeps walking along the scummy sidewalk, shops and bodegas to his left and right, Polish faces streaming through his sight, Polish words hounding his ears. Something doesn't feel quite right, something about that sight. The day is too crisp, too real for such an outlandish dreamscape to intrude. He hopes Michelle is okay. He better call her as soon as he gets to work. He could call her now, but he's running awfully late. He's sure she's okay. He wants to be able to feel that thought though. Shouldn't a kiss birth that kind of connection? He picks up his pace, walks a little faster, intent on reaching the office as soon as he can, letting his boss know that he needs to make a phone call.

On the train, holding the pole, clutching his unopened book (the fanged, three eyed creature on the cover chews

into the world), tapping his foot, staring at his reflection in
the windows, biting his lips, mashed between a young
Latina girl whose hair smells like South American forests
and an old Polish woman breathing her foul breath into the
imprisoned air, Andrew curses himself for not calling
Michelle immediately. He should have. Work isn't that
important. Where is she? How far is the fire from her? A
pit, an abyss, opens its jaws, threatens to swallow
everything Andrew holds sacred inside of himself.

Right after Lexington, with a jerk, the train suddenly
stops. A unanimous groan sounds from all of the
passengers who are already late for work. The conductor's
garbled voice crackles over the loudspeaker. Andrew can't
understand anything it says, something about the World
Trade Center, maybe a plane. That doesn't make any sense.
He asks the people beside him to translate. They shrug. A
middle-aged black woman leaning against the door shakes
her head, and with furrowed eyebrows, she deciphers, "A
plane hit the World Trade Center?" Everybody else shakes
their heads along with her. That can't be true. Nevertheless,
an odd presence hovers about the air, a wraith-like specter,
a nervous intensity seeping through the sewers, barreling
down the tunnels. As the wait goes on, the presence
intensifies oppressively – the expectant soul of New York,
the collective mind and body of ten million people, of acres
of glass and steel, of a hundred generations of history
permeating the earth, penetrating the subway pumping
capillaries.

Finally above ground again, the presence is stronger. It
no longer hovers; it has descended, a jinni in the form of a
city. The streets are alive and bustling, but not with the
usual morning formality and coldness. No, an electric
presence has ignited the streets. The skyward miles of glass
buildings burn with it. There is a purposefulness, a

panicked, enkindled direction to the usual meanderings. An unbound spirit has flown in on unchained wings.

Andrew pulls out his cell phone. Michelle's number is busy. That means she must be okay. He'll call her again from the office. Maybe she can tell him what's going on.

At Fifth Avenue, the sidewalks are packed like Times Square on New Year's Eve, body next to body, shoulder to shoulder, businessmen stand on newspaper dispensers, teen-agers straddle phone booths, all of them gazing, pretty rows of sun-drawn flowers, down the avenue at the distant end of which the Twin Towers rise stupendously, belittling even the nearest of skyscrapers, one of New York's millions of movie sets. Andrew doesn't stop to look. He's already seen the fire. All he needs to do is to get to the office and to call Michelle.

In the claustrophobic conditions of the elevator, reflections on the city's tension begin to unsettle his nerves. The world's energy is in flux. He can feel it.

He steps out of the elevator and opens the glass door of his suite.

Pandemonium has struck the office. Nobody is at their desks. Cubicles are empty. A buzz of voices, a swarm of bees, circulates. Co-workers are running back and forth from nowhere to nothing. The receptionist has disappeared. An overweight, middle-aged woman who Andrew has never exchanged more than a cursory greeting with runs up and grabs him by the shoulders. Her eyes are rolling wild. Her mouth is twitching. Her cheeks are melting. Her fingers, hands, and arms are trembling. Her gaze is pleading for understanding, for an explanation. "We're under attack!" she shouts at him.

"What are you talking about?" Andrew asks, his own face curling in incomprehension.

"The World Trade Center... Oh my God! There's more

planes… We're all going to die," she says, and she bursts into tears.

The moments become separate, distinct. In a daze, Andrew walks away from her, leaves her standing by the door sobbing. A skewed look on his face, he wanders, carefully picking his steps as if he were still drunk, over to his cubicle, picks up the phone, and begins automatically to dial Michelle's number.

"There's no service," a girl in a suit tells him. Andrew's seen her around the office.

"What do you mean?" he asks.

"There's no telephone service. Listen."

Andrew puts the receiver to his ear. No dial tone. Lost, he hangs up the phone. His voice sounds automatic, robotic, coming from someone else as he asks, "What's going on?"

"Nobody knows," the girl says. She's frazzled. Her early morning perfection has already come unraveled. "Two hijacked planes hit the World Trade, one into each tower. The FAA has ordered all planes out of the sky, but there's still something like ten or eleven that they can't get to. They might be coming for New York as well."

"Were they hijacked too?"

"Nobody knows. We're listening to it on the radio. Follow me." She waves her hand. Andrew follows. He wishes that he hadn't had so much to drink last night. None of this makes any sense. Try to get your mind around it. What did the hijackers do to the pilot, the crew, the passengers to make them fly into the glass façade of a building bustling with people? Knives and guns and wires and ropes… Sweat streaming down the pilot's face… A pistol to his temple… A blade at a stewardess's breast… A terrorist's smiling face… CRASH!

"OH MY GOD!"

The girl picks up her pace. Without intending to, she's suddenly running. Behind her, Andrew runs too. They reach a cubicle where five of the youngest workers are huddled around a radio. The receptionist has her hand to her mouth. Her eyes are blank. Her eyelids blink sporadically. Another girl is staring at the radio as if she might be able to read its mind and deduce the future. One guy is shaking his head, his face in his hands. The other guy has turned around and is walking stiffly, as if a stake were jammed through his spine, towards the front desk, the front door. Where does he think he's going? The last girl stares at Andrew and his companion as they fly into their audience.

"A plane just hit the Pentagon," she explains calmly, rationally, much too serenely for the situation. She's in shock. Never before has Andrew seen that zombified gaze.

The enormity of what has occurred finally hits him. He pulls his cell phone out of his pocket. There's no service. "Does anybody have a phone?" Andrew asks. "I need to make a call."

"Service isn't working. The circuits are all flooded," the guy says. "I've been trying to call my mom all morning."

"I've got to get out of here," Andrew says.

"Why?" the receptionist asks.

"My girlfriend's in the World Trade Center."

— *I don't want to die, mom.*

— *You're not going to die, honey.*

— *Yes, I am. Oh God, mom… There's no way out of here. It's dark. It's smoky. I'm choking. The stairways are all on fire…*

— *Somebody will get you. You're not going to die.*

— *There's no way anybody can get to us. The elevators don't work. Do you know how high up I am? I'm going to burn to death… I love you, mom. I don't want to die…*

Andrew is running. He started out walking, but now he's running, pushing his way between gawkers pointing and shading their eyes, chewing their lips, clenching their fists, glancing to their lefts and their rights, asking themselves and their companions if this is all a dream, if they really woke up this morning and are now standing motionless, speechless, dazed, confused, lost. Why am I watching this? What in God's name am I seeing? Am I supposed to be angry? Am I supposed to be sad? Is it really safe to be in the open on the street?

Andrew's vision is trained on the upper half of the Twin Towers where Michelle might or might not be (please, God, let her have been late for work), where an ethereal cloud of smoke, pouring from the sliced open mouths of the brother and sister, has concealed any remnant of the buildings, ascended Sinai, shrouded the gods' faces in a mist. Every once in a while, he glances back over his shoulder to see if the Empire State Building is still intact. Every once in a while, he turns his face to the sky, to see if another airplane has somehow appeared at those catastrophic heights.

He wasn't able to tell his supervisor that he had to leave. His supervisor, the vice president, had already run away, told everybody, as he whipped his tie off his neck, that he was going to a strip club. They could come if they wanted to, hide up in Harlem if they needed to, stay in Midtown if they didn't think they'd die there, go home if they could get off the island, do anything they felt like. Work was cancelled. Insanity, with its horde of laughing, screaming faces, had taken center stage at the world's playhouse.

And then, suddenly, amid a simultaneous cry of all of the world's inhabitants (it doesn't even seem possible), one of the monoliths, the wonders at the end of the island, the man-made monstrosities, the twin towers of Babel, with an endless plume of black, acrid ash and soot, collapses in upon itself, floor crashing into floor, pane smashing into pane, wall hurtling into wall, body falling upon body. The earth descends into a pit. It's gone. There were people in there. All that's left is the ascending mist of God swirling into the angelically perfect, blue sky, entombing the building's lover.

Andrew stops running. His head goes numb. He has just witnessed the inconceivable. Standing there, next to a white man in a sweatshirt and shorts and a black girl in tight pants and an airbrushed tee shirt, with his mouth agape, his mind screams out in horror. His psyche splits in two. His vocal cords can't make a sound. All around him, women are holding their breath, clutching their breasts. Men are crying. The strongest, having (for that brief second) seen the face of the Lord, avert their eyes. The abyss that Andrew felt yawning on the subway, threatening to consume his thoughts, opens its gaping jaws and swallows everything that he deems sublime into the same esophagus, the same spiraling black hole, the same nothing into which one half of the hermaphrodite just disappeared. The fault line beneath Manhattan, whether or not anybody watching on TV can see it, has finally cracked open and consumed the anointed capital of the world. Along with its megalith, New York City, with Andrew inside of it, has teetered off the precipice and fallen into the abyss.

At the moment of an atomic explosion, a vacuum is created at a point in space.

Michelle…

When the first tower fell, nobody knew quite what to do. After the initial outburst of terror, the angel's cry, there is silence about the space of heaven. Was it real? Did I see what I thought I saw? Did one of the permanent markers of man's majesty, a structure as grand and immaculate as a mountain, a city reaching into the sky, really turn to so many grains of dust? Please, God, don't let that happen to the other tower. Leave us with something, a reminder of our world before today, please...

When the second tower falls, the entire island of Manhattan shakes. The ground beneath your feet rumbles as the earth swallows the glass and steel and paper and hair and flesh. It might be purely psychological. It could be real. With a second joined gasp, a multitudinous cry, the monument to man's magnificence has given way to a memorial to his madness. The World Trade Center is gone, charmed, by ancient spells, into a great miasma carrying once important faxes and memos, monogrammed notepads and family photographs, rising and drifting across Lower Manhattan, the East River, Brooklyn. The elder god has been displaced by its children. Its body cut up and fed into the sky, creating a new world, a new topography at the tip of that tiny island.

On Fifth Avenue, a woman standing next to Charlie collapses to her knees, reaches to embrace the sky, and cries out to God to save us, save us, please. But heaven stays silent and blue. No army of avenging archangels appears. The host of bodies beyond the clouds of dust pouring down the financial district's streets might be safe, but their souls are lost, stolen by fleet, fleeing thieves arising and descending back into the dust before they can be seen. Looking to his right and left, Charlie sees zombies with trembling lips, shaking limbs, wiping their wide, staring eyes, clutching at one another in shock, in horror, in anguish and pain. He's one of them, and he doesn't even realize it.

A black zombie beside him, his face contorted in agony,

his eyes open and glazed, cries out to him, "Why are they doing this to us?" He has a Caribbean accent. "Why are they doing this to New York? We're not even from here. We are from everywhere…"

Charlie shakes his head. Like so many others at this moment, he doesn't know. He stumbles backwards, turns around, and starts walking back to Madison Avenue. There's a bar across the street from his office. That seems like the right place to be.

The past is a mirage. How many temps did he have in those buildings? How many temps had he placed permanently at the top of one of those towers? The reality makes him sick to his stomach. So many thousands of people, living and dreaming a moment ago, dead, disintegrated, incinerated now. He feels as if he might vomit. Maybe a beer will help him to relax a little bit, put all of this into some sort of perspective because from out here it's nothing but horrendous.

He's going to have to start calling people's homes, find out who was late for work, who was able to rush down the smoke-filled stairs in time. How many clients is he going to lose (his bank account dissolves into the same cloud as the World Trade Center)? How many deaths is he responsible for? You can't think like that.

Even though it's a little early to be drinking (most of the people in here would never before have found themselves sitting in front of a beer at this hour of the morning), the bar is as full as Fifth Avenue. It's as wall to wall packed with people as an East Village dive on Friday night, but a solemnity has replaced the expected frivolity. A subliminal, subconscious mass, the same specter that Andrew met on the subway, has infiltrated the stale atmosphere. Very few people have anything to say. Those who do are speaking in whispers that echo. The rest are leaning against the walls, shaking their heads, propped against stools, arms draped over the bar, holding undrunk bottles, tickling their lips, their eyes glued to the TVs on CNN at either end of the bar. On the TVs, the planes crash into the towers again and again and again. The World Trade Center crumbles again and again and again. Downtown, a crowd of people run, screaming, clutching handkerchiefs to their mouths, away from a surging, consuming cloud of debris again and again and again. With each replay, a collective, almost imperceptible, wince circulates through the bar. One or two people groan, shake their heads, appear ill. By each patron, the horror and agony and frustration is experienced again and again and again. It's overwhelming, destabilizing, jarring, psychotic.

Why are they making us watch this? Charlie thinks. *It's portentous of our own demise.* He wipes his forehead. He isn't sweating. He notices that he's shaking a little bit. His stomach is a strand of rope, stretched taut, looped around itself, tied into a torturous knot. His nerves are buzzing, jumping, popping so suddenly that he twitches and starts. Constantly glancing at the street, he realizes that he's not quite himself. He wonders if he ever will be again. *Am I going to die today?*

It takes forever to draw the bartender's attention away from the television, but Charlie's in no hurry. Today isn't a day when he feels like getting on the bartender's case. Regardless of what the images might be doing to his now fragile psyche, he's as consumed as everybody else is by the destruction. Drawn by the spectacle, the power, the force, they have no choice but to watch, to keep watching whether they want to or not.

Another plane crashed somewhere in Pennsylvania. Charlie hadn't heard about that one yet. CNN is showing maps, pinpointing the PA crash area right now...

Finally, the bartender notices Charlie standing by the bar.

"Heineken," Charlie orders.

The bartender nods. He doesn't say anything. He looks tired. His passion drained, he moves mechanically.

With his beer in hand, Charlie retreats back a short way, towards one of the tables by the wall. A young man is standing there, his eyes wide and bloodshot. He's loosened his tie from around his neck. He's Charlie's age or younger, probably twenty-one or twenty-two. His hand trembles as he lifts a beer to his lips. As Charlie approaches him, he says, "Think about it, man... Think about what might have been on those planes..."

"What do you mean?"

"Diseases, plagues hidden in the baggage compartment, released by the fire... We could all be sucking in some sort of sickness right now, dying as the wind blows, and we don't even know it." The young man nods knowingly and takes a sip of beer. He's driving himself insane. We're always dying as the wind blows.

The thought chills Charlie. He hadn't considered that possibility.

The young man goes on, "What do you think's going to happen next?"

"I have no idea."

"They could open fire on the streets, start shooting from sniper's nests on top of buildings. The police are all downtown. They're not gonna be able to do anything. They could start picking us off, one by one. There could be bombs planted all over the city. They could just be waiting for all of the news networks to have their cameras on New York before the nuke goes off, and we all disappear, in a flash." He snaps his fingers. "Just like that. It's all over. The rest of America watches white noise on their TV screens.

I'll tell you one thing. I'm not stepping outside of this bar until the whole thing's over. Think of how close we are to the Empire State, to Grand Central, to Times Square. There's still a shitload of planes they can't find. I wish I could get in touch with my mom." He pulls a cell phone out of his pocket. His fingers are rattling horribly. "But this damn thing isn't working."

Without saying goodbye, Charlie walks away from him, picks his way through the crowd towards the back. The young man doesn't seem to notice that Charlie's disappeared. He's still rambling almost incoherently.

Is anybody listening? Charlie thinks. *Does it even matter?*

In the back, a man and a woman are talking. The man says, "I was on the 7 train when I saw it hit. The first tower was already on fire. We were all pressed up against the windows, trying to figure out what was going on. The plane circled around the building. It disappeared for a moment. We were all watching it, trying to figure out what it was doing. It was like a hawk, some sort of huge bird-of-prey, searching the skyline for a mouse, and suddenly it slammed into the other tower. This woman beside me screamed. I went deaf." His gaze is distant and glassed, his lips curled in an aspect of self-loathing, despising himself for what he has witnessed. Speechless at his memories, he shakes his head and sips his drink. His features are so hideously deformed, his eyes so filled with incomprehension that Charlie wonders what he would have looked like if they had encountered one another on the way to the subway that morning. The man would have been bright and full, impressive in a suit as he carried his briefcase and nodded his smiling greeting, rather than a twisted shade of a human being, an inward malefactor guilty of crimes of omission.

The woman glances at him with an air of compassion. She wants to embrace him, to let him melt into her arms, to be the comfort that her womb desires. She's never even met him before. She nods at Charlie as he sets his beer on the table they're sharing. The man doesn't notice him. He's staring at his hands, reading his future. It's empty. The woman says, "My name's Hillary."

"Charlie," Charlie says, and they shake hands.

"I figure I should know everybody's name just in case you're the last person I ever see," she laughs.

Charlie doesn't think it's very funny, but he manages to smile. It's nice to be near a woman. Her femininity provides a comfort. To lie in bed with her and have her hold him… He wants to be sick, as if he's already had too much to drink and needs the pressure relieved, but no amount of vomiting could alleviate the illness in his guts. He wipes his hand down his face.

"Sorry, I guess I shouldn't say things like that at a time like this," Hillary says. She smiles consolingly. "Humor's just the way I deal with things."

"It's okay," Charlie says even though it isn't really.

"I'm here on business," she goes on. "I was here on business the last time they hit the World Trade Center, too, but this is nothing like that. I guess I'm bad luck for New York. I don't think I'll ever come here again. I was staying at a hotel above Grand Central, and I figured that it wasn't a very safe place to be so I decided to come down here instead, but how safe is any place in Manhattan today? If I could get on a train, I'd get as far away from here as I could, but it looks like we're all stuck together, at least until they open the island back up."

"You didn't make it very far from Grand Central," Charlie notices.

"Far enough. Far enough from Grand Central, still far enough from the Empire State, a little ways from Times Square, right in the middle of everything," she laughs again.

At the front of the bar, a man shouts, "A car bomb just went off in Battery Park. Did the TV say anything about it? I heard about it on the radio. We gotta get off the island. The whole place is wired…"

Somebody tells him to shut up. A frenzied panic ruffles the patrons, but nobody goes anywhere.

"Do you think that's true?" Hillary asks Charlie.

"Who cares," the man beside her says. "We're stuck here. There's nothing we can do but wait."

Charlie shrugs. He wonders if she'll invite him back to her hotel room. She's not gorgeous, but she has a nice body. He hates himself for thinking that. "Who knows," he says.

"I wish I'd taken a train as soon as the first plane hit," she says. "Gone out to anywhere. Somewhere in Connecticut or New Jersey. I don't know. Any place that was still connected to the United States, where I could still get home."

Charlie nods. His whole life – his job, his apartment, his friends, everything except his family – exists in New York City, on Manhattan Island.

At the front of the bar, somebody yells, "Fuck you!"

Yasser Arafat is on TV. His complexion and mannerisms appear exceedingly foreign. A reporter is interviewing him. One patron throws a coaster at the set. The coaster ricochets off the screen's glass, off Arafat's trembling face and petrified eyes. The bartender laughs uneasily. With nervous glances, shaking hands, and unsure nods, Yasser Arafat sends his condolences to New York City and the people of the United States. The entire exchange is surreal, an episode in the annals of science fiction. The future has shifted radically into the past.

"Bull shit!" somebody shouts.

"Maybe he knows what we're going through," Hillary

whispers. "Look at him. He's as scared as we are."

"He knows he's in deep shit," Charlie says. "Any hope for Mideast peace or a Palestinian State disappeared at the same moment the Trade Towers did."

"The only thing that would make me happy right now is to bomb the fuck out of *his* country. We should turn the entire Middle East into a goddamn parking lot. The bastards," the man sitting with them says.

A crash echoes through the room. A screaming stampede, a blur of colors beyond the windows, a triple exposed photograph, tramples along the sidewalk outside the door, bangs across the metal grates.

"God, what was that?" Charlie gasps. Unsure of whether or not he's still alive, he grabs his beer and along with everybody else rushes for the exit. The entire bar empties into a tangled mélange of running, petrified zombies: Mardi Gras, the day of the dead.

"What's going on? What the hell happened?" Charlie asks everybody as he walks back and forth along the sidewalk next to the honking, stalled traffic, searching for smoke, bumping into the fleeing dead, adrenalin rushing through his mind, fear clawing at his intestines. He's lost Hillary and the man who was with them.

"A bomb went off in Grand Central," he hears.

"What? What?" he keeps asking, wandering like the homeless insane, like the elderly with dementia, clutching his beer between white knuckles. "A bomb? A bomb, where?"

A female zombie grabs him by the shoulder. "No bomb, a bus crash, everybody panicked."

"Are you sure?"

"I saw it. Everything's all right. You're not going to die. Not yet..."

For a moment, Charlie wonders if it's really okay for

him to be standing out on the street with an open beer in his hand. Amid all the tumult, all the madness of the day, would anybody really care?

It started out as an interesting show. When Michael Lourdes's roommate woke him up that morning to tell him to come up to the rooftop, to see the World Trade Center burning in the distance, it was another one of those many momentous occasions of living in the city, a chance to see something, to be a part of something, that the rest of the world was only going to read about in the papers. He didn't even think about the fact that there were people in those buildings.

Now, it's something different entirely. Michael's roommate is gone, frantically trying to locate a girlfriend who lives on the Lower East Side and works in the World Financial Center. The devil's midsection has been reached. The entire world has flipped upside down. Pacing in circles atop his roof, Michael walks alone among neighbors crying with their arms around one another, men consoling women, women consoling men. One group asks another if they're okay. A girl of nineteen or twenty wants to know if Michael needs a hug. He says he does. The girl says she's glad because she needs one too.

She wraps her arms around him, pulls him into the soft fleshiness of her breasts, rubs her cheek against his chest. Her body radiates heat. Her hair smells of comfort. Her tiny shoulders tremble. Beyond their embrace, smoke is disgorged from Manhattan's ruined body. Mt. Vesuvius burns their shadows into Pompey's cement. "It's gonna be okay," she whispers between sniffles. "It's all gonna be okay."

"Yeah," Michael says. They let each other go.

"Thanks," she says, her young, sparrow eyes wounded

and questioning. She melts. Her skeleton remains.

"Yeah," Michael says. None of this is right. There has to be something he can do. He can't stay on his rooftop. He leaves the girl and his neighbors.

On the streets in the East Village, a silent compassion, like that of Simon for Jesus, pervades the usually frantic atmosphere. A parade of people, some covered in dust, ashen as death, in burial suits, make their way up and down First Avenue. One woman, coated from head to foot, the body of Ash Wednesday's cross, has stopped. She's turning circles in the middle of the avenue, going nowhere, a demagnetized compass, lost in once familiar territory. The living hold doors open for one another. They greet and help and gaze at one another in ways that New Yorkers on their impersonal streets usually never would. The shields that separate one from the other have melted imperceptibly into the atmosphere of the city, sheltering the inhabitants, the victims, from those outside.

At Houston Street, Michael turns right and walks past a million risen Lazaruses stumbling toward the bridges, waiting and hoping for their opportunity to escape the terrorized island of the damned. Hell has opened its dungeons, released its prisoners. Somewhere, Lucifer gazes with compassion upon his fallen compatriots. Free at last, shocked from millenniums of imprisonment, he roams along at the edge of every human's senses.

A police-manned barricade finally stops Michael's meandering. Rowing Charon's boat themselves, the silent terrified exit. Michael tries slipping past the guards, back into the dungeon that everybody else is in such a panic to leave.

"Where you think you're going?" a tee-shirted cadet, one of the heads of Cerberus, asks.

"I want to get downtown," he says.

"You can't go any farther," the cadet responds.

"I want to get down there and help clear out the debris, try to find people." The world echoes, like a bomb has been detonating continually, unceasingly since the moment the Towers fell.

"You a doctor?"

"No."

"You with one of the unions?"

"No."

"Then, you can't. There's plenty of people down there helping already."

"I need to get down there. I need to help."

"You wanna help? Go give blood."

Discouraged, Michael nods. He only has his body to give: a scant sacrifice for the souls already crucified. He turns around and starts walking back to the hospital. He doesn't realize yet that people in pieces don't need his blood.

The view from Bed-Stuy wasn't quite what Gabriel Burns had in mind. The waterfront has to be close enough since the city is locked down. The trains aren't running. The bridges are closed. Brooklyn floats, cut off from land by Manhattan's blockade.

But what's it look like from downtown? he wonders as he strolls, chain smoking cigarettes, amid the stunned, crying crowd, dressed for their neighborhood's morning fashion show, gathered on the rocky shore in Williamsburg. Across the East River, above the suspension bridge arching over the water, ash is egested, a volcanic expectoration, a postmodern brush stroke coloring the clear noontime sky, hanging like the Passover angel, ready to swoop down upon what's left of the skyline. From this day forward, the spectators' young lives will never be the same. Hocus pocus. With a puff of smoke, everything has changed. Alone inside themselves, a demon has appeared on the horizon. Lord, let us all go back in time. The horror that everybody else desires only to escape, Gabriel wishes he had the ability to thrust himself into the middle of.

I knew it was coming. It was always just a matter of time...

Like the starving masses begging for release from the holds of a ship that they crossed the Atlantic in, a crowd of dust covered immigrants wait patiently, glancing over their shoulders, tapping their feet, trembling at the entrance to the Williamsburg Bridge. A police barricade blocks their exodus. The usually jammed bridge extends with emptied lanes, lonely subway tracks, before them over the river. Tension, stretched taut as a tightrope, connects their minds. Universally, their vacant eyes tread the highwire, a terrified act to make symbiotic contact with one another. Nobody speaks. Language can't convey senselessness. They all know what the other has seen: bodies and flames and suffering and loss. Their eyes communicate in silent, fluttering reflections. Every glance has its own story.

The police part the Red Sea. Dry land opens before them. A giant with a million legs, a serpentine, dragon-like millipede, in sooty suits with dirty faces, they trudge along the Bridge, swell across its expanse, some still carrying briefcases. Mindful of one another, they walk in silence, staring at the tarmac, hurrying to Brooklyn's promised shores, petrified that the ground beneath their feet might disappear, that, with another explosion, the bridge could crumble. The day, a transforming larva spread throughout their intestines' pupae, undulates in their bowels. *When I get back to my bed, lie down to go to sleep, will I finally wake up from this dream?*

Not in the first wave, but eventually, Andrew is one,

alone among many, in the midst of that mass. A million thoughts compete inside his mind, split him into a trillion personalities, a thousand viewpoints for every emotion. He's been downtown, seen the destruction, always on the verge of tears as he searched the faces with a prayer that eventually one of them would be Michelle's. They would dissolve, faces streaked, into one another's arms, a scene from the love story of the brand-new century. But everywhere, there was only blood and dust and police routing the zombies back toward the Village's streets. Where is she?

Once he gets back to Brooklyn, he'll check her apartment. If nothing else, maybe Ari, her roommate, can tell him that she's called and she's okay, that she's in a hospital being treated for a fracture she received as she fled down the stairs. But he's tried calling her apartment, her cell over and over and over again, and every time he opens his phone, the signal is gone. None of the payphones, every goddamn one he saw, were working either. New York's inhabitants are alone, interred beneath the earth, cut off by the miles of steel and cement that crashed that morning.

The sound of the world dissolving rushes like a conch song through Andrew's ears. He's drowning. The scent of burnt cinder, exploded gasoline, sizzled flesh lingers in his nostrils. In front of him, a woman in her mid-twenties rushes up to the edge of the bridge. From a strap around her neck, she pulls a manual camera up to her face. She zooms in on her subject, and begins taking pictures, moving slightly, lithely, through the distraught crowd, twisting her lens as she snaps photograph after photograph, stealing the image, the soul, of the mangled skyline. She's an artist concocting a snuff film of her model's demise – a razor to the subject's veins, a nail through the model's brain.

Andrew's stomach twists. His throat clogs. His eyes moisten. His legs go weak. If he could cry, maybe he would feel better, but he can't. His emotions are too conflicted. In the middle of the bridge, he stops. The zombies plod past him. Scared to glance over his shoulder, afraid he might turn to a pillar of salt at the sight, he looks back at Gomorrah, breaks the commandment of the Lord, to see what the photographer sees, what vantage might be worthy of being captured forever.

Above the gray patchwork of buildings, simultaneously ascending and descending, fire and brimstone hang in the air. He sees Iblis among an army, a thousand free jinn, stomping on the skyline, slicing through the body of Wotan – the self-sacrificed God – torturing himself to attain the knowledge he desired. Andrew is Aeneas, fleeing Troy, the scales cleared from his eyes, watching his home, his city, his dream get ripped apart by the hands of creatures more ancient than the monuments he's worshiped, his sacrilege.

He bows his head to that vision to the West. There's nothing artistic, nothing edifying about it. There's no structure, no form of beauty. There's a thousand, two thousand, three thousand bodies escaping in smoke, cremated unceremoniously, religiously sacrificed, impaled as the survivors' archetypes. In reality, amid suffering, there's nothing worth capturing forever. Why is that woman taking pictures of all of this?

She's still there, examining, dissecting her subject. The shutter clicks. The film advances. A picture of emptiness in the distance, harried faces in the foreground is captured. She stares through her lens. Looking at life through art is a mediation, a way of escaping the pain of reality. Looking at art through life is an experience, a sounding of suffering's depths.

Andrew wants to grab the photographer by the

shoulders, rip her camera off her neck, burn her flesh with
the snapping strap, slap her across her face, push her to the
ground, and toss her film out into the clear blue sky, down
into the rushing river below them as he screams, "There
were people in there! Don't you understand? Don't you
hurt? This is life! This is real! You're witnessing the end of
our world!"

And she would coldly answer that that's precisely why
she's photographing it.

In the middle of the bridge, he stands still, his head
bowed, and he sighs, a precursor to tears that still won't
come. What if Michelle was in that building when it
collapsed? What if she was one of those who leaped from
the windows, dying to escape the fire? What if she burned,
suffocated in smoke? What does it take to kill yourself? He
retches. No vomit. He sniffles, wipes his dry mouth, his dry
nose, his dry eyes. He picks up his feet, and marches,
shaking his head, along with all of the other prisoners
exiting the gas chamber, dead already, miraculously
trudging on to a further destiny. He was supposed to buy
her flowers today. Behind him, the photographer twists her
camera to capture every visible angle.

At the end of the bridge, the Hassidim, in their long
black coats and tall hats, with their thick beards and coiled
sideburns, like an army of undertakers embalming,
mummifying the dead as they cross into the promised land,
rush back and forth, carrying plastic cups from a water
cooler presided over, blessed by their rabbi in his prayer
shawl. To every pedestrian coming back home to Brooklyn,
with a smile and kind Semitic words, they hand a cup of
water. There is something religious, initiatory about the
ceremony, as if, for the moment, every citizen of New York
has been allowed entrance, through the pain of mental
circumcision, by the vacant stares of their lobotomies, the

shock of their electro-therapy, into the race of God's chosen people. On this day, there is no Jew or Gentile, no Israeli or Palestinian, no Hassid or black man, the entire race of man is Hebrew, blessed by Jehovah, sacred in the eyes of God, spared by the blood on their door. Why can't we all be Hebrews forever?

Plastic cups overflow from the trash cans. Crumpled and cracked, they litter the sidewalk, street, and gutter. Catching their breath for the rest of the walk home, men in suits sit on the curb, their heads bowed, their faces in their hands. Spotted between them, with their high heels beside them like a bedroom painting, women in skirts rub their sore feet. Every individual knows that he or she is alone. Andrew gets a cup of water and thanks his server. "You're welcome," the young man smiles, tries to reach out, to bridge the gulf of language, to connect, through his red beard.

The water is refreshing. Its coolness has taste. Its liquid drains through Andrew's chest. Standing at the end of the bridge, gulping his drink, grateful for the respite, shocked at the extremes of humanity, he doesn't look back at Manhattan. The day is still crystal blue, but there is a layer of filth, like the smog of Times Square, coating his eyes. He needs his tears to clear it away, but underneath the perfect sky, he still can't cry. He crumples his cup and sets it on the trash can in such a way that it won't fall off, but he can't account for the wind. He wants to do everything he can to keep his city beautiful. It's not too long a walk from here to Michelle's. She'll be there. He knows she will be. He can feel it. A kiss birthed that kind of connection.

At Michelle's apartment, there's no intercom. Andrew rings the bell. With a buzz, the lock clicks. He pushes the door open and starts up the stairs. Suddenly, the external world is silent. It's a prison. The day's rushing screams, indiscernible in their lonely cells, have melted into a solid canvas, a background of white noise. Like the grunts of a man being beaten, his echoing steps, drips of paint, punctuate the cavernous tenement. Two floors up, the chain and latch on Michelle's door rattle, and the door creaks open.

Balancing himself with his fingers caressing the rail, Andrew rounds a curve in the stairwell. He stops, raises his head, and gazes up the flight. Framed by the arch of the doorway, Ari, in a pair of shorts and a tee shirt, her brown body shaking like a leafless tree in the breeze, stands with her fingers to her mouth. Her wide black eyes beneath her straight black hair are two ravens cawing beneath midnight. At Andrew's questioning look, she blinks and shakes her head – *No. Nevermore.* Her mouth opens like she's going to say something, but instead, she looks down at the ground. The ravens flutter away. Only midnight is left. Her shoulders tremble with tiny sobs, starlight.

Andrew closes his eyes. Blind, he tramps up the rest of the steps. Without saying a word, he opens his eyes and puts his arms around Ari's skinny body. He pulls her close. Her tears and sniffles moisten his chest, bleed against his flesh. He stares into Michelle's familiar quarters. One of Ari's paintings hangs on the wall in the hall. Andrew remembers pointing out the coloring to Michelle one night shortly after he moved to New York. He said that the green reminded him of cancer. Michelle laughed at his morbidity. She's so beautiful when her lips curl like that. She's as deep as the ocean. He still can't cry. Wide open, his eyes are painfully dry. But he could feel that she was still alive…

Sitting on the couch, staring vacantly at the ceiling, Carey wonders, *Is the world still here? Am I still alive?* From between his fingers, a cigarette burns blue smoke into the air. Formless faces swirl in the haze. His face twitches. The radio is off. There's no music that can capture the sensation of this moment. There's no music powerful enough to affect his emotions. The news is too real. For the first time ever, it's his life. He doesn't want to hear about it.

All day long, he sat in his apartment, in Andrew's bedroom, staring out the window at the smoke above Brooklyn's roofs, trying to figure out what this all means. War is the only foreseeable future. He doesn't want to live through it, doesn't want to see any more of it. He closes his eyes. Maybe when he opens them again, the world will go back to the way it was.

In the darkness behind his eyelids, the world is more terrifying than in the light. The sight of smoke sifting across the city, raining ash on the skyline, merges menacingly with the darkness. A vision of bombs and guns and blood rises, like a demented Phoenix, from the ashes. He opens his eyes. Nothing has changed. The crack is still there in the ceiling. His memories still cloud his mind. The future still waits, panting, foaming at the mouth, rabid, insane. He writhes in place.

He thinks about last night, about the sound and the power of the rain. It was romantic, mystical, and grand, perfect for the end of the world. He thinks about how nervous he was to meet up with Gabriel, how beautiful Gabriel looked drenched from head to foot, how the whole night he wondered if they might kiss. They never did, but he went home in love, his only concern being that Gabriel might be straight. Gay, straight, who cares... Now, that concern is so trivial, so meaningless.

The door opens. Andrew steps inside. The door closes. Carey doesn't acknowledge that his roommate has arrived. Like the corpse of a suicide, his brains splattered red and white, all blues, on the wall behind him, he remains stationary on the couch.

"Hey," Andrew whispers.

Carey looks at him, but he doesn't say anything. Andrew is standing in the kitchen, a blanched expression on his face. His features appear burdensome. They tug on his cheeks. It's painful to keep his skin on his face. His limbs seem weighted. They drag his shoulders down. His presence is a black hole. "You all right?" Carey asks.

"I can't find Michelle," Andrew mumbles.

"What?" Carey stands up. He moves towards his friend. He seems unsure. Maybe he's going to give him a hug, but something about Andrew's demeanor makes him stop. The whole universe, your entire life exists in your head. "Oh Jesus, Andrew, I'm sorry. I don't know what to say."

Andrew raises his shoulders. "I forgot my book," he says. "I think I left it at work." A shadow, the memory of the moments between when he set his book on his desk and when he walked back through his apartment door, darkens Andrew's stare. His blue eyes become the terrifying sky above Manhattan. "*The Masks of God*… Why does God need a mask?" His lips curl into a vizard of hatred.

Carey's eyebrows twist. He tilts his head to the side. "I don't know," he says. He sits back down. He fidgets with a string hanging off of the worn couch. "Did you talk to Ari yet?" he asks.

"She doesn't know where Michelle is either," Andrew says. "She's been trying to reach her parents all afternoon to see if they've heard from her, but there still aren't any lines out of New York." Tears fill the corners of his eyes. His lips tremble, but he still doesn't cry. This isn't a movie. Sometimes life is too real to cry about.

"She was working at the Trade Center today, wasn't she?"

"Charlie got her the job." Andrew looks down at the

kitchen's faded tiles. "I wanted that job," he finishes in a whisper.

"Do you want to go back to her apartment?" Carey asks. "Maybe she'll call. I'll go with you."

Andrew appears tired, dead. He hasn't slept for eternity. He's twisted and turned, his eyes held open by spirits as he stares into the abyss for a final, fleeting glimpse of his love, but his Beatrice has never appeared. "Yeah," he says. "Just let me change my clothes. I hate wearing fucking ties."

On Manhattan Avenue, on the way to Michelle's, overwhelmed by the dark beauty of Brooklyn, thinking about what all of this means, what it would be like to never see any of it again – if that even means anything, they pass a group of teen-agers standing on the corner.

As they pass, Andrew shakes his head. "Fucking asshole," he mumbles.

"What?" Carey asks.

"His tee shirt," Andrew says.

Carey glances back, one of the teen-agers, a blond boy with a nose ring and his hair a mess, is wearing a tee shirt emblazoned with an upside down American flag. Above the image, it says, *Rage Against the Machine.* Below the image, it says, *Evil Empire.* The boy's lips are tight. His cheeks are stained as if he's been crying all day, all night. He's the punk poster child of the millennium. The statement jerks Carey's nervous system. "That's inappropriate for today," he whispers. "Maybe he wasn't thinking."

"He was thinking," Andrew says. "It's inappropriate forever, now."

"Yesterday, you would have agreed with him," Carey reminds his roommate.

"Yesterday, I didn't realize what it meant," Andrew responds.

Maybe you still don't realize what it means, Carey thinks, but unlike the teen-ager, he's old enough to know that right now it's inappropriate to say that.

"All day long, all I kept thinking about was how I was ever going to write about this," Andrew says. "How I could ever turn what was happening into art. And then, on the bridge, I saw a girl taking pictures of the city, and I realized that if I don't find Michelle, I'm never going to be able to write about what happened today. I didn't tell you about last night."

Carey shakes his head – *No.*

"She left. She left, and she was angry with me. I was going to buy her flowers today to make up. We were going to laugh about it. I was going to buy her flowers…"

Andrew's face expresses an emotion more divine than hate, more primal than pain, more human than love. Carey wants the expression to disappear. He wants Andrew to cry. He can tell from the haze of his friend's sweet blue eyes, that all he needs to do is cry. Maybe Carey can cry for him. He could cry for the entire world.

"It'll be all right," Carey says. He puts his arm around Andrew's shoulder. "We'll find her, and you'll buy her flowers tomorrow," he says, and for that moment, he is evil enough to believe what he knows is a lie.

Andrew doesn't respond. He's cold, stoic as stone. He's an idol, a sculpture. If my master broke my leg, I'd thank him. Carey drops his arm. It's too awkward. Andrew should be feeling something. Carey doesn't understand – he isn't a god. Nobody ever understands. Carey shakes his head.

At Michelle's apartment, Ari opens the door. "I talked to Michelle's dad," she says as she stares at the floor. "Her mom was on the phone with her when her line went dead. She was stuck."

"But she made it out…" Andrew says.

Ari closes her eyes. She shakes her head. "They don't

think so," she says, "I'm so sorry, Andrew." She starts to cry again. "She was so beautiful." Her shoulders heave with sobs that echo off the tomb-like walls.

Carey's eyes tear up. He looks at Andrew – *Cry, goddamnit. We can't cry for you. You have to do it yourself. Cry!*

Andrew nods. He's really shaking his head. Internally, he's collapsed. Externally, he stands more stiffly than he did before. In his mind, he screams – a bug pinned on its back, vainly fluttering its wings. With his lips, he whispers, "Okay." He thinks, *She can't be dead.* He wipes his eyes. There's nothing there. He's completely dry. His tears are frozen inside his mind. It hurts. His soul is sobbing. His flesh has severed all connections to his spirit. He burns. He's being ripped apart, eternally, by wolves, torn into ten million people, put back together into one. It's too painful to fight. He's watching Ari cry. He's still lying in bed: 8:46 the clock says. Time, like Andrew's mind, is frozen, the wasteland of the final circle of hell. No motion. It's cold. I see Satan immobile at the center of the world. We're stuck, clawing at the devil's thigh. *Why did I say anything to the moon? I'm never going to write another word. Help me, God… God doesn't exist.*

III.
Dying as the Wind Blows

On September 12^(th), Michael doesn't want to leave his neighborhood. He feels drained as if he has just been visited by a succubus, a being who vanished, leaving him spent and exhausted, molested, curling up in bed alone. Nothing is worth doing – cooking, eating, talking, smoking. He doesn't even want to take a shower. His television doesn't work. The screen is white noise. The telephone is off. This doesn't happen in America. The National Guard, toting machine guns, riding in jeeps, doesn't patrol your streets. He's already learned that the blood he spent hours waiting in line to give yesterday is worthless. There aren't enough living victims to necessitate its use. The hospitals are virtually empty. The surgeons and nurses and orderlies stayed up all night, alone, waiting for the wounded. From his window, he sees them walking down the street, still in their hospital fatigues, staring at the pavement, shaking their heads. What do you do when there's nobody to help? The World Trade Center still spews dust and smoke, the sizzled remnants of steel and flesh. Firemen, taking breaks to sit down and cry (these are men who never cry), spray water over their comrades' interred bodies. Rescue crews from all across the country (they drove all night to get to

New York), search feverishly in spots where fires don't burn for those trapped in pockets. For the most part, they find pieces of people. Michael goes out to get a pack of cigarettes.

He walks to the bodega on the corner. An American flag graces the front of the establishment. It's a rustic scene out of place in New York, Rockwell in the midst of Pollock. The sound of Arabic floats around behind the counter. The speaking stops as soon as Michael enters, but the words echo in emptiness. The language terrifies him. Its guttural expressions and throaty clicks contain an element of imminent danger. He makes eye contact with a young man behind the deli counter. The young man nods nervously and quickly goes back to sweeping up the store. Michael forces himself to be exceedingly kind. As he gets his change, he smiles even though he's shaking. He tells the proprietor, "Take care of yourself."

"You, too, my friend," the proprietor whispers. His accent is thick. Along with the devastation he feels for his home, he's fearful for the future of his business.

Back on the streets in the Village, the stench is unbearable. Some of the residents wear masks to filter the impurities from the air. With the lower half of their faces covered, they look like spacemen marooned on the forbidden planet. This is nobody's home. The smell hovers, a coat of quicksand, brown and dense. It infects your lungs. Breathing is difficult. It's the scent of three thousand insects immolated in flames exponentially magnified to the ten millionth time.

The breeze picks up, and the scent from downtown blows up the avenues through Chelsea, invades Midtown's wind tunnels. It's heavy and strong, oppressive as silence.

In Midtown, Charlie is making phone calls from work. He's one of only three people who showed up at the office today, and the lack of vitality is unsettling. None of the executives came in from Connecticut. Nobody showed up from Westchester or New Jersey or Long Island. None of the receptionists or mail-room clerks made it in. Some of the numbers he's called don't work, but three temps are already unaccounted for. He has twenty more to go, and he hasn't tried Michelle. He doesn't want to know. He's not even worried about the fact that his biggest clients are gone. It doesn't matter that without them he can't pay his rent. Right now, all he cares about are the people. He bought a pack of cigarettes last night, and he decides to take a break and go outside to smoke one.

Midtown is an empty movie set, cardboard facades propped up on lonely streets. The smell is sickening. There's no laughter, no yelling, no honking horns, no cat calls, no cell phone conversations. The bodies, the cells that pump through the city's veins have disappeared. The sidewalks stretch, vacant, for endless miles. The sky is vast and blue. The buildings are sad and gray. They miss their lovers. The city is a cadaver. It's abandoned – huge and lonely, hollow as the surface of the moon, nothing but concrete, steel, glass, and brick. Tumbleweed could blow through the ghost town, a nightmare. The world ends in inanition. A lone body in an overcoat walks down the avenue. His greasy hair a mess, he talks to himself, fights with the air – the mad specter of the apocalypse. At the end of time, the city that never sleeps finally closes its eyes and dreams its own death.

At the end of the day, walking home from the office, crossing the street, feeling true emptiness for the first time in his life (it aches, physically, at a point that can't be scratched in your soul), Charlie happens upon a motorcade of buses and flatbed trucks. The buses are filled with police officers and National Guardsmen slouched in their seats, staring out the dark windows with empty expressions on their faces, their helmets shading their eyes. The trucks are overflowing with black boxes draped in clear plastic.

With a cry, a woman walking towards him stumbles in her heels. Her face contorts in a kind of agony that is unbearable to witness, something from man's prehistoric past. Civilized people don't make that expression. Like the rain from two nights before, tears stream down her cheeks. This isn't New York City. Charlie looks away. His breath heaves in his chest. He realizes that the boxes are filled with pieces of bodies, handfuls of the dust of people. By now, he knows that whatever might be left of Michelle could be in them. He finds the gutter. He's going to be sick. He needs to call Andrew.

Andrew found a copy of *The Post* abandoned on the street in Brooklyn. He's sitting on his stoop, flipping through the pages. Today, everything is a dream. When he opened his eyes this morning, all he wanted to do was close them again. Yesterday didn't happen... But the news says it did. Let me go back to sleep. I can't sleep. Even in my dreams, I see the world crumple like a burning piece of paper, black carbon at the edges, over and over again.

The paper can't hold his attention, but he looks anyway – black and white words and pictures. The world is black and white, shrink-wrapped in paper waiting for a spark. The texture of pulp rubs against his fingers.

All day long, he still hasn't cried. The tears metastasize inside his soul. This is what it means to be alive.

As he turns the pages, his gaze is captured by a picture. With fists raised in triumph, smiles of satisfaction, Palestinian men, women, and children celebrate the fall of the World Trade Center. They're dancing, singing, cheering in their refugee camp (barbed wire encloses them), flush in the first great victory of their lives.

Starting in his fingertips, rattling through his hands, up his arms, into his shoulders, his neck, his face, Andrew begins trembling. His jaw, his lips quiver. His mouth contorts. He's an abandoned child, a poster for the back of a milk carton. A sheen coats his eyes, and suddenly, with a heave from the polluted depths of his soul, as if the tears had been building, generating, multiplying like malignant cells, he begins to sob. His voice ricochets against the buildings, caws through the alleyways, rises along the streets. His whole body, from his feet to his head, shakes. He flickers. He drops the paper, leaves it abandoned for the next viewer. Doubled over, he grabs his stomach. He's been shot. A gut wound is the most painful. It takes an eternity to die from one. His throat hurts. It's gurgling blood. He bleeds cancer. He's dying a second time. He stands up, turns around, and walks, feeling his way, blind as Polyphemus (– *Who has hurt you, Polyphemus? – Nobody…*), back into his building.

Alone in his decrepit living room, Carey wants a body with him. He needs the presence of another, another's warmth, their compassion. His soul aches for a connection, anything to cut through the emptiness – the touch of skin, the pressure of fingers. He wishes that his cell phone were working. Maybe then, he could call Gabriel. On the couch, he wrestles with nothingness.

It's the people that he can't stop thinking about, thousands of Michelles, millions of Andrews, billions like him. The world's never going to be the same again. He remembers when he was a child, lying awake in bed, crying in the darkness, terrified that the Soviet Union and the United States were going to go to war, that a nuclear winter would freeze the world. All motion stops as the atoms split. His mother could never comfort him. It's been so long since he's felt apprehension like this.

Andrew comes inside. Carey can hear him sobbing. The tears are coming so hard that they echo in the tiny kitchen. He turns and looks. Andrew's face is a twisted mask, the extreme of tragedy, something akin to comedy, a muddy drama. Visibly frightened, Carey jumps up. "Jesus, what's wrong?"

"I want them dead," Andrew cries. He's choking on his words. "All of them…" he blubbers. His language is barely intelligible through his tears. "Dead. The women, the children, if I could put a bullet through every one of their heads myself, I'd do it. I've never wanted to kill before, and now, I want them all dead."

"All right. All right. Calm down. I can barely understand you. What are you talking about?" Carey asks.

"The picture." Andrew heaves. He's drowning, clawing at quicksand. "They're happy this happened. They're happy this is happening to us…" he gurgles. The watery sludge buries him in a liquid tomb.

Nobody's happy about this, Carey thinks. "I don't understand."

The zombie pounds his fists against his grave's walls: "In the newspaper… I'll kill them all."

Carey's chest has been sliced open. His heart has been smashed. He sits back down, puts his face in his hands. Heart attack and he's dead. This is everything that he was afraid of. *I don't understand!*

– They can't beat us. Get back to work New York! That's the mentality, the mantra for September 13th. Giuliani said it. George Bush said it. As broken as he feels, Andrew concedes. In the morning, he drags himself out of bed, swallows his tears, stuffs his rage, puts on a tie, and takes the train into Midtown. Whatever you do, try not to think about Michelle today. Somewhere, she's okay. Try to make this day as normal as it can be.

It's not even lunchtime before the first bomb threat comes in. It's across the street. Like jumpers, Andrew and his co-workers are pressed up against their skyscraper's glass. Andrew doesn't want to be there, but he has to watch. A crowd has massed on the sidewalk. Even from above, you can feel the tension on the street. You can sense the fear in people's eyes, the energy igniting the cramped space. Like heat, it rises. The last time this was real was only two days before. The police are stuck in traffic. A few officers try to control the crowd. They won't let them leave. They're pointing. They must be shouting. In yellow jackets, a bomb squad pulls up and runs inside the building. Two buildings down, people begin to file out. Another threat. There aren't enough officers to control that crowd. The sidewalk has been filled to capacity. The avenue is ready to burst. Manhattan is drowning. What do you think New York would look like after a war? The building next door to Andrew's is evacuated. If all of the people who work in Manhattan were to step outside of their buildings at one time, the island wouldn't have enough space to hold them all. The same girl who led him to the radio on September 11th turns to Andrew. Her eyes are wide. Her gaze is uncomprehending. For a moment, she appears so innocent. "What's happening?" she asks.

Andrew shakes his head. *Anything. Don't ask me. I think I want to die again.*

Like a trash heap of body bags, the suits and ties are piled on top of one another. Watching from his heights leaves Andrew with a strange sense of mediation. He's an angel watching humanity's madness from heaven. But is it really any safer to be in here? Would a threat be phoned in on the building that goes? Heaven's already burned. The demons won. Maybe I should step outside, go for a walk. After everything, it's impossible to box this world into your mind.

Suddenly, the phones buzz with electronic "brrrrrings". It's a swarm of bees inside your brain, boyfriends, girlfriends, just friends – *Did you hear? There's a truck on Staten Island. The police are after it. It's all over the news. It might be loaded with bombs. They've shut the bridges down. Nobody leaves Manhattan… Times Square has been evacuated. That's only a few blocks from you. Get the hell out of Midtown! I love you…*

Immediately, the office speeds up to the frenetic pace of two days before. It's too soon for all of this. The taste of adrenalin coats everybody's tongue. The rush of fear shocks their lungs. It's psychic. You can see it in your co-workers' bovine eyes, wide, waiting for the slaughter: Mad Cow Disease. Andrew's supervisor says anybody who wants to go can leave. Oh God, they've closed the subways again. We're stuck here again. We're all going to die today. Let me off this goddamn island!

Andrew needs a cigarette. He's trembling. He leaves the madness of the office and goes downstairs to the insanity of the street. Manhattan stinks. The stench of the World Trade Center has wound through all of the streets, tripped in between the buildings, destroyed the vibrancy of every other smell. That's Michelle. Burned by the smoke, tears rise in Andrew's eyes. Get that thought out of your head. She's alive. She smells like a summer field. Someday, I'm going to bring her flowers. I never even got to say goodbye.

The smoke from his cigarette mixes into the atmosphere. It's overpowered by the rotting odor of the city's death. We're drowning in the city's death, maggots inside the corpse, turning to flies, feeding on shit. Can you taste it? Isn't it dangerous to be on the street? Where are the bombs? Where is the enemy? Sitting on top of buildings, hiding from the National Guard, staring out of windows with rifle scopes to their eyes? I need to smoke this cigarette quick. Do I care if I die?

Andrew's cigarette tastes of the world's smell. It brings what's outside into his body. It's harsh and burning, dark and sooty. His stomach flutters. The nicotine makes it beat its wings faster. The pressure of the street rumbles inside of him, thousands of terrified bodies pound through his intestines, stomp his organs into submission. New York writhes in his gut, millions of larvae begging for release. This is how it feels, on the inside, to be alive inside your grave, bloated by worms.

They slither down the street, crawling overtop of one another, panicked, silent, gnawing through the dirt, the earth. Feed me. Let me sense the light. In the beginning, there was darkness across the face of the deep.

By the end of the day, the city is silent. As Charlie walks home, whipped, beaten, he finds the city as empty as it was the day before even though it's milling with people. There were two bomb threats on his building today. Twice, he had to rush down the stairs, stand on the street, wait to see if, this time, he's the one running away from the wall of dust. In his suit, dazed and lost, he sits down on a fire hydrant. Planted for all eternity, metamorphosed into a vegetable, he sits and sits, staring at the ground. He's catatonic. He'll never speak again. His brain hurts. Is this ever going to end? One of his temps is walking down the street. When she sees Charlie, she walks up to him, throws her arms around his neck, and begins to cry. He doesn't respond. For the first time in his life, he can't think about sex. He can't feel her. He didn't think anything could be worse than September 11th. September 13th was. Without saying anything, the girl pulls herself off his neck and keeps walking to the subway. *You could die in there,* Charlie thinks.

On the subway back to Brooklyn, Andrew is surrounded, boxed into a corner, but the bodies are silent.

They stare at emptiness, bounce with the rumble of the tracks. At every awkward noise, they jump. Their faces are blank. Their minds are overtaxed. They search the faces, the mannerisms of their fellow passengers for potential terrorists. They hold the poles with dry palms. All day long they've been preparing themselves to die. They've prepared themselves so well that they can't come back to life. It's disheartening to be surrounded by the dead. It's suffocating when you can't claw your way out of a mass grave.

Even the project kids from the Bronx are shocked into stupors.

Above ground again in Williamsburg, Andrew sees a poster on a telephone pole: *Our cry of grief is not a cry for war!* What fucking hipster can still claim such moral compunction? With a sob, Andrew rips the paper off the wood, crumples it up, and throws it into the trashcan. This is already a war, one that I'm living and dying through.

That night, as he lies in bed, staring at the ceiling, the burnt smell of the World Trade Center seeps through his window, buries him. He burns with fear for his life, disbelief at this madness, grief for what's happened to Michelle, horror at what's become of his world. He sits up. His stomach hurts. The white glow from the work site, the gaping hole of the World Trade Center ignites the night sky. The fact that the buildings aren't there still, glittering like a queen's tiara, doesn't register quite right. In the darkness, in the distance, the hole looks the same as Times Square, the great white way, an empty chamber of the city's glowing heart, the vacant chamber of the gun for our suicide. It reminds Andrew of being on top of the Empire State Building, on top of the world with Michelle ("Right there. There's the Williamsburg Bridge. That's Queens. There's Brooklyn. That's right where Greenpoint is."). Was that really less than a week before? He never knew that the world could devolve so quickly. He never even got to apologize. He cries, but it doesn't make him feel any better. His mind splits into two, into three, into four, into five. He falls into infinity. He'll see Michelle again. He can feel it. A kiss birthed that kind of connection. Until they find her body, he refuses to believe. He can't bleed enough tears to quell this world's suffering.

Andrew wants a picture of Michelle to plaster across the city's walls, a photograph to place beside the thousands of other photos of the missing, something to show the world that somebody cares about the fact that nobody can find this girl either, something in which she's smiling, laughing, her lip curling like a wave, something to prove to you all how beautiful she is, but he doesn't have any photos of her. At Avenue A and 14th Street, he stands in front of one of the hundreds of makeshift memorials. A mural of the skyline with the Trade Center still standing powerful and tall is spray painted across the brick wall. *Rest in Peace*, it says in white like the lights that ignite the sky beyond the river outside Andrew's bedroom window every night. In the night, the paint is dark, absorptive and reflective of the streetlights. It's somebody's attempt to reach back into their memories and deliver to the world what they were once able to see, an image, a life, a time that now exists only in the artist's mind. If Andrew could paint, he'd scrawl Michelle's face across those buildings, make her eternal on a street corner in the city she loved, her home forever and ever now.

On the sidewalk in front of the mural, a bed of candles – long and tall, short and squat, in glass jars with religious scenes – burns. It's an altar, a relic from the church. Smoke without incense spirals into the air. Somebody placed a copy of this week's *Village Voice* underneath a plastic wrapped bouquet of flowers. The cover of the paper has a picture of the downtown skyline from Brooklyn. Where the World Trade Center should stand, the photographer is holding a postcard of the Twin Towers. It fits in perfect. The buildings are unbroken. The blue sky is cloudless and clear. You can see the photographer's thumb at the bottom of the photo, a personal imprint on his vision, the defect built into the mosque. *Wish you were here*, the headline reads. Wish you were all here.

Andrew bends down. In front of the candles (every day a zombie comes here to light them), he places his own bouquet – red *and* white roses. They look like drops of blood on satin. He bought them at a flower shop on 14th. He was inspired by the mural. Art feeds off of art. When everything else is madness, you have to trust your feelings.

"I'm sorry," he whispers in the same voice that he whispered goodbye to her that night when she was gone at Enid's. It's the only voice he can speak to her with. It's been a week and three days, and he still doesn't know where she is. At the end of his words, a whine rises in his throat. Tears come to his eyes. Not caring if anybody sees him, he stays on his knees and cries. He doesn't care if they never kiss again. All he wants is to see her wavy brown hair. Glimpses of her back haunt him everywhere. There she is, right there, reflected in the glare of the spray paint. He looks over his shoulder. There's nobody behind him. Ghosts can travel anywhere. Like his first view of the Trade Towers on September 11th, he knows he will remember this moment forever. Like when he shouted at the moon, it's now a part of what makes him who he is.

He stands up. His shoulders are heaving. He wipes his face with his shirt. He needs to regain his composure. He's meeting Carey and Gabriel at Mona's. It's the first night he's been out since September 10th.

At Mona's, Carey and Gabriel are sitting at the bar. They're both drinking Bass. The bar is smoky. By the pool table in the back, the jukebox is low. A light glows above the red felt. The weekend regulars are still at home mourning, sewing their brains back into place, resting in their coffins, wondering if the Village is open yet. Only a few Alphabet City locals are placed surreptitiously around the bar. They've crawled in from their domiciles to stare at the TV in the warmth of the dark atmosphere. It feels like a womb peopled by lost sperm cells, broken by their quest for the egg.

The door opens, and all heads turn to it. Andrew wipes his nose and walks in. His face is haggard, his expression lost. He sees Carey, nods, and walks over to him.

"Hey, Andrew. I didn't know if you'd make it. I didn't think you'd get my note," Carey says. "Andrew," he says, "This is Gabriel."

Gabriel turns on his stool. His brown hair is shaggy and sticking up like a young Bob Dylan's, like a rooster's – let there be light, cry for the dawn, Peter Pan. His body is muscled and wiry. His cheeks are thin and bony, dotted with stubble, but it's his eyes that are so striking. They're as deep as emeralds, shiny stones quarried from the depths of the earth. Man will search forever, scour every borough for a shine like that. "Nice to meet you, man," Gabriel says, and he sticks out his hand. Andrew grabs it. Gabriel's grip is strong. His hand is firm. His forearm flexes. He smiles. His eyes don't light at all. His grin is crooked. We're the lost boys, Robin. Batman's gone, burned beyond recognition. Meet the Joker. Can I dip you in acid, too? he laughs.

"Likewise," Andrew answers. Taciturn, he sits down beside Gabriel and orders a drink. The female bartender, in tee shirt and jeans brings him his Bass. He lets it sit on the coaster as he pulls out a cigarette that he packs against the bar. He hasn't had a drink since September 10th.

With the first sip, the bitter taste of malted barley, he remembers his bluster – *I'm the baddest motherfucker who ever walked the face of this earth.* He remembers throwing a bottle at The Empire State, dreaming of Molotov Cocktails. He sniffles. *I'm not really that tough,* he thinks. *Just an American kid from the suburbs. Nothing prepared me for this nightmare.* In his dreams, the moon laughs at him. He wants to cry again. He cries a lot these days.

"Hey, Andrew, you all right?" Carey asks. He's leaning across Gabriel, tugging at Andrew's sleeve.

"Yeah, I'm okay… I brought Michelle flowers tonight."

"Oh," Carey says. He leans back into his seat, gives Gabriel a nervous look.

"Hey, man, you shoot pool?" Gabriel asks Andrew.

"Sometimes, but I don't feel like it right now."

"Come on. I'll pay."

Andrew shrugs.

They grab their beers and walk up the steps to where the pool table sits. Gabriel is tall, taller than Andrew, much taller than Carey, a little over six feet. He stands stiffly like a model on a runway. "Carey won't shoot pool against me," he says.

In the back by the bathroom, as Andrew's choosing a cue, Gabriel sticks a cigarette in his mouth, lights it. He exhales. Like incense for an invocation, the sweet scent of pot smoke puffs across the room. It's mystical. I see the shadow of the devil in the corner. Andrew inhales deeply. He looks at Gabriel. Gabriel slips the cigarette back into the pocket of his tight jeans.

"We need the right music," Gabriel says. He feeds two dollars into the jukebox. "Music is ninety percent of pool."

"What's the other ten percent?" Carey asks.

"Luck. Just like everything else in the city."

Andrew remembers Michael saying something like that the day that they met in Times Square. Michael... Andrew never wants to see him again. There's no role left for him to play. He doesn't want to have to tell him that his play is over. There's never going to be another one. In my beginning is my end.

"I'll rack," Gabriel says. "You wanna break?"

Andrew shakes his head.

"I'll break, then, too, but you have to shoot."

Andrew feigns a smile.

"Just remember, we play backwards."

"What?"

"Just kidding."

Carey backs into a booth, trails his fingers along the table, and sits down. Above him, spray painted across the red and white wall is the blue outline of a body with a twisted face and horns. Graffiti is scrawled across its torso. Below it, he's seated, an egg, in the ovaries. Wait for the blood to flow, to fill the halls, to expel us all.

The crack of pool balls, tiny platelets and blood cells, bounding off one another fills the room. It's the chorus of disease, immunity attacked by cancer, the internal crackle of bones riddled with HIV.

"That's not so bad," Gabriel says. "Nice spacing, huh?"

Andrew looks at the table. He doesn't feel like reading it right now. It's like the book still sitting on his desk at work – *The Masks of God*. Every mask, every trick wears Michelle's face.

Andrew sees the shot he wants to take, the nine to the corner. With a swirl around the pocket, the ball sinks, rolls through the inside of the table.

"You're shooting high," Gabriel says. "Seems like a lie," he laughs. "That's all right. I like going low. It fits my personality."

In his booth, Carey smiles. Inside, he's pins and needles, strapped to the rack, torture.

Andrew wins the game.

"Another one?" Gabriel asks.

"Why not."

"I gotta go get change. You want another beer?"

Andrew nods.

"Carey?"

"Sure."

"I'll be right back. Don't go anywhere. I'm like Minnesota Fats, baby. We could run all night."

Gabriel returns, bends down, sticks the quarters in the change slot. With a rattle, he pushes the silver mechanism in. The quarters drop in their spots, release the balls to rumble down the length of the table. They're the key. Open the gates, angel. "All right, this time we play for souls, Fast Eddie. That's the beauty of pool. It has so much meaning beneath the surface. Like a Hell's Angel, show your class. You break the bones this time. I'll follow your lead."

Andrew gets a nice break, not as spacious as Gabriel's, but the thirteen falls. He follows up with the eleven.

"Looks like you're shooting high again," Gabriel says. "I still don't believe it."

As the second beer goes down, Andrew feels his mind emptying out. He's vacant, full of a billion lives. Their violence, their violation, makes him nauseous. Only Michelle's soul could expand to fill his emptiness, but her presence is gone.

Gabriel is blocking pockets, but Andrew miraculously squeezes around his balls. The game goes on forever. As Andrew sinks the eight, Gabriel says, "All right. One more and another round. Tell your guardian angel to let up on me. This time it's double or nothing." He bounds down the steps back to the bar.

"So what do you think of Gabriel?" Carey asks.

"He's different," Andrew says. He's thinking about what it meant to leave flowers for Michelle. His head goes numb. It was a symbol, an attempt, the only way he could think of to get his apology to her. It was inspiration, a form of art, his first creation since the world was destroyed – red and white, all blues.

"Yeah," Carey answers dreamily.

Gabriel returns with their drinks and another dollar's worth of quarters. Andrew breaks – no luck. Gabriel lines up and goes on a three ball run. He leaves a ball at every corner.

"This time I got to *choose* low," he says. Andrew doesn't respond.

Gabriel sticks a cigarette in his mouth again. Again, the pungent scent of pot follows his exhale. It's mimicry, like heaven, such juxtaposition to the stench outside. He returns the cigarette to his pocket. He sticks another cigarette in his mouth and lights it. This one smells straight – gray and deathlike as the dust covered survivors of the World Trade.

Gabriel sets his cigarette in the ashtray on Carey's booth. He struts over to the pool table, lines up on his shot. "Pool's like sex, don't you think?" he says as he strikes.

Andrew shrugs. Gabriel's ball falls. "I guess so," Andrew says. He doesn't feel like having this conversation. Love is what we all need. Sometimes sex is too painful, too violent. Right now, everything is violence.

"No, think about it." Gabriel grazes another ball, keeps it set beside his pocket and buries the cue in Andrew's striped mass. "Everything about it. Like right now, I just threw you a cock block, brother. I'm flirting with you. It throws you off kilter."

Andrew stares at the table, sizes up his angles, tries to

see how he can play off the rails. "Maybe you're right," he says, trying to get into Gabriel's groove.

"I know I'm right, man. I think about it all the time."

"What, sex?" Carey asks, smiling.

"That too," Gabriel says. "It's a way for manly men to make love, a circle jerk, masturbation. The rest of us like to fuck." He shoots a wicked grin at Carey.

Andrew doesn't answer. He lines up on his shot. His English is off. The cue ball bangs around the table – no action. Maybe Gabriel was right.

"Guess your guardian angel split on you. Never trust an angel. That's what I always say," Gabriel jokes.

His joke chews through Andrew's mind, bites into his heart, spits blood back into his brain, vomits through his tear ducts. Water the room. Expel us all. It's masturbation, a self-induced menstruation.

"It's no different than war," Gabriel says.

Andrew stiffens. With a worried look, Carey moves to the edge of his seat like he wants to jump up and clamp his hand over Gabriel's mouth, but Gabriel has already set himself up for his next shot. "I mean, think about it. Did you see Bush's speech to Congress last week? Tell me I'm not right."

Carey relaxes a little bit. He smiles nervously. "It was pretty surreal. I never thought I'd see anything like that as long as I was alive," he says.

"Surreal? How about hyper-real? We're living in the middle of a movie, man, a fucking Hollywood melodrama. *Independence Day.* Aliens have landed. The entire goddamn Congress applauding the President like he's a bloody rock star... You ever listen to the Dead Kennedys?"

"Yeah," Andrew says. *The last time was three weeks, a whole lifetime, ago.*

"*Kinky Sex Makes The World Go 'Round.* Think about

that." Gabriel clears the table. "You owe me two souls," he says as he sets his cue back against the wall.

Michael is trembling. His hands have been shaking all day. His stomach is rolling, a pregnant woman's. He's ready to give birth to his disease. He'd go back to his apartment, take an evening nap, but he can't stand the nightmares. He's sitting at the circular bar at the Holiday Cocktail Lounge. The white-haired owner is shuffling and stumbling around behind it, mumbling to himself in Italian. Looks like the Holiday will be closing early tonight.

Michael rarely goes to bars alone. He takes a sip off his Budweiser, checks the faces of the drunks around him: old and haggard with dirty fingers, pouring whiskey between their whiskers. It's nice to see them, to know that they're here, but he's certain: *Nobody knows it but me.* His eyes grow terrified. *I don't want to know these things.* He lifts the beer to his lips again. He's not a drunk. The alcohol won't take away his shakes.

It's been two weeks and four days since nobody needed the blood that he waited for hours in line to give.

With a click, the door opens. Michael jumps in his seat, loses his breath, and glances over his shoulder. Just a patron. It looks like… The man entering pauses, a shade at the door. He's wondering if he should turn around and leave. Then, he changes his mind and guardedly steps inside, comes back to life. Michael was right. It's Andrew. He smiles. For a moment, he forgets his fear. He's so glad to see that Andrew's still alive. Andrew doesn't smile back. He only nods.

Michael stands up. He walks over to Andrew, wraps his arms around him and holds him close. "It's good to see you, man," he says.

"You too," Andrew answers dispassionately. He lightly

pats Michael's back. Michael lets him go. He looks at Andrew's face, tilts his head to the side. There's a vacancy in Andrew's eyes, like a blind man lost in darkness, unable to believe that he still can't see.

With a start, Michael remembers what he knows. He glances distractedly around the room. "Can I buy you a beer?" he asks to take his mind off his thoughts.

"Sure," Andrew says.

They sit down at the bar. "So how you making out?" Michael asks. "You all right?"

"No, but is anybody?"

"True."

"If you watch it on TV, we're all supposed to be okay."

"I know. It's frightening." With his observation, Michael flinches. "I'm glad you showed up here," he says.

"Yeah, I haven't been back here since before September 11th."

"Well, we're all still here," Michael says. "For now."

Andrew mumbles, "Yeah. We're all still here."

"So whatever happened with your play? I could use the call, might be a nice way to take my mind off of everything."

Andrew frowns. "It's over," he whispers.

"I thought you were just casting…"

"I can't find the director."

"Oh. Jesus, man, I'm sorry. She was a friend of yours, right?"

"My best friend."

Michael stares at his beer, taps his finger against the glass. "I'm sorry I brought it up."

"That's why I never called you," Andrew blurts out.

"Hey, man, I understand. I'm sure it's been tough. I can only imagine."

Andrew nods.

"I'm glad you showed up though," Michael says. "I've been sitting here driving myself crazy." He chuckles a little. "I need somebody to talk to. That's for sure."

"Why? What's going on?"

"Nothing really... Hey, you wanna finish these beers and head back to my apartment with me. I'd like to smoke some pot."

"Why not."

Michael's apartment is even tinier than Andrew's. The kitchen is minuscule, with a tiny television next to the sink. There's no living room, not even a fake one, the bedrooms come off the kitchen in wings. Michael has the back bedroom, the smaller of the two. There's enough room for his twin bed, and a small desk. A window looks at the neighboring building's bricks. It's a prison cell.

Andrew sits down on the bed. Michael fumbles around in his desk drawer. He pulls out a pipe and the pot. As he's packing the bowl, he says, "So I don't even want to tell you about this, but I've been keeping it bottled up inside all day. I haven't wanted to make anybody else flip out, but I need to tell somebody, and I guess the beer's finally loosened me up enough to talk about it.

"Last night, I went out with some friends, and I bumped into this guy who I haven't seen in a while, and he told me that some friend of his who works in Hillary Clinton's office told him to get the fuck out of New York City this weekend because a nuclear bomb was definitely going to go off. I asked him if he was serious, and he swore that his friend wouldn't lie. Shit, man, I flipped the fuck out. I was at the Port Authority last night, getting a ticket to go home when I realized that my family lives in DC. If a nuke goes off in New York, they'll probably hit there, too. My question was, if I'm going to die would I rather die with my family or with New York. I chose New York. I figure I already died here once." Michael's fingers are still shaking as he breaks up the pot. "I mean, Christ, look at my hands. If all this doesn't end soon, I think I might just die of a heart attack.

"All I keep telling myself right now is one more day, and the weekend's over. We've made it. If we're all still here come Monday morning, this Monday's going to be the best day of my life. You want some music?"

"Yeah, that would be nice."

"Go ahead. Pick it out."

Andrew digs through a pile of CDs on the floor by the bed. *Ziggy Stardust and the Spiders from Mars.*

"Good choice," Michael says.

The slow four beat of the drums fades in, and Michael hands the bowl to Andrew. On the boombox, the flourish of a piano cues David Bowie's vocals. Andrew sparks the lighter.

The marijuana feels nice rubbing against his soul. Its smoky palms caress his scars, his open wounds. It's a salve, a balm. Andrew had forgotten how nice it feels, in the long muscle cells of your stomach, to get high. Over the past few weeks, he needed something to reach inside his mind. He hands the pipe back to Michael.

"This is a great song," Michael says. "I swear it's how I felt today..." He hums the tune to *Five Years* beautifully, angelically. It's magical, a wave of cosmic haze, glamorous glitter and spandex in this ghetto fabulous world. "Yeah, that was me today," he says. "Probably tomorrow, too. I hate feeling that I'm going to die."

A flash enters Andrew's mind – of Michelle standing at a broken open window, the wind whips through her hair, with a man she doesn't know, asking him, *Do we have to jump? Do we have to?* He can feel the flames, the heat. He sits up sharply. *It's just the marijuana fucking with you.*

"This is my favorite line," Andrew says. Michael cocks his head to the side and listens to the line. "It's like *The Ice Storm*."

"What?"

"The book, *The Ice Storm*, by Rick Moody. They made a movie out of it. It wasn't as good. He's got this whole thing with comic books winding through the novel, *The Fantastic Four*, a sort of mythology, a reference to our contemporary heroes, a commentary on our modern world's own lack of a mythological past. The movie never captured it. It couldn't capture how all motion stops when things freeze either, like absolute zero in Dante's hell. He wrote *Demonology...*" Michael shakes his head. He doesn't know it. "At the end of *The Ice Storm*, you find out the narrator is one of the characters. It's like suddenly the whole thing becomes real. It's happening to real people. Kind of like all of this."

"You read a lot, huh?"

"I wanted to be a writer."

"You don't want to write anymore?"

"What is there to write about? I've spent my whole life living stories. Now, everything is happening, and it's horrible. I hate it. I hate being alive." Andrew sniffles. "The last night I saw Michelle, she told me to get outside of my head. Well, I'm trying, and it hurts."

Michael hands the bowl back to Andrew. He sits in the chair, resting his elbow on the desk. His dark hair sticks up in every direction. His legs are crossed at the knees. Behind him, the wall is stark and white, paint peeling and chipping away. He's a perspective painting, a scene for the new renaissance, the ultra-modern aesthetic. "Shit, man. If you can ever do that, you need to tell the rest of us how it's done."

At the corners of his lips, Andrew smiles a bit. His eyes still look pained.

"As far as life goes, man, I mean, I know I don't know you that well, but from what I remember of you, you never hated being alive."

"I know. I was in love with myself, my mind. That's what I hate. I've never looked outside myself for anything. Happiness, love, it was all inside of me. After all this, I've realized that I've never felt before, and now it hurts too bad to feel anymore. I was in love with Michelle, and I never even got to feel it. I can't help myself now. I feel everything – anger, sadness, pain, mine and everybody else's."

"Sounds like you're the Buddha."

"What?"

"You probably know better than me, but wasn't he supposed to be a prince, all rich and everything, with servants and concubines, and when he finally went outside his palace and saw how much everybody was suffering, he renounced it all and ran away into the woods to find enlightenment? All of life is suffering, right? There has to be a way out."

"I'd just started reading a book on oriental mythology right before all this happened. I haven't read a word since September 10th."

"Well, start reading it again, man, maybe it'll help you. Shit, maybe it'll help me. Don't fuck with synchronicity."

"I don't know. It's hard to read nowadays."

"Then you need to listen to *Ziggy*. I've been listening to this album daily since all this started. It's the only thing that makes me feel any better. For those forty-five minutes or whatever, the world feels okay. There's no National Guard, no bin Laden, no Al-Qaeda, no workers with their vacant stares and stories of fires and bodies coming into my restaurant, no smell. Sometimes, I even imagine the World Trade is still there."

The lyrics resonate with the static in Andrew's mind.

They slip a cast onto his broken soul. To know that somebody else, somewhere, felt this aching, this emptiness in the back of his throat, even if the situation was different, the names, the faces, the places, none of them were the same. London not New York, a love unrequited rather than lost, but to know that they felt. That's poetry, the germ of art, a seed for creation, a Serpent rising between the white pillars of a door, nailed to a crucifix, lift me up... The tree of life with Lucifer winding around the stalk. To feel, to partake of the knowledge of good and evil. *God, I want to stop feeling.* Just smoke some more weed...

Suddenly, David Bowie's words are electric, a shock. With his hand thrust wrist-deep in the light socket, frying him, electrocuting his soul (one, two, clear... *SHOCK!*), Andrew sits up straight. With his unwashed hair, he looks like Ziggy Stardust, a young David Bowie, without the make-up on his face. The hermaphrodite's coming for you, honey.

Didn't Gabriel say something about that? He looks at Michael. His eyes are closed, sealed. He's waving his head, a charmed snake hooded by scales – let me tap my foot on the floor, make you sing – in rhythm to the music's notes. With the weed in his mind, Andrew is entranced by the bone structure of Michael's face, his cheeks, his chin, the face beneath his skin, his face before he was born. He could be Gabriel's darker, more masculine twin. For a moment, he sees what Carey sees in men, but it's only because men look like women. *We're moving beyond good and evil, marrying heaven to hell.* In the garden, what did Lucifer whisper to Eve?

"Could I see the cover?" Andrew asks.

"Huh? Oh yeah, sure. I'm gonna get some water. You want some?"

"You got a beer?"

"Yeah. I'll grab you one."

Andrew feels warm. His extremities, his nose, the tips of his fingers, his toes tingle. He's looking at a picture of David Bowie holding his guitar on a lonely city street. He knows it's not, but it could be Greenpoint. What's Ziggy Stardust doing in Brooklyn? On the back, Ziggy Stardust is in a phone booth. The colors are tinted, vibrant and bright, painted over the black and white. He opens the booklet, unfolds the cover, spreads the lyrics sheet, like a series of intricate scales, out on the bed in front of him. He's enthralled by the pastels of Lady Stardust singing in his dress, of the black and white Starman holding his jacket tight around his neck. When the young Mozart entered Bach's library to pour over both his forgotten and his famous scores, he never left. His eyes grew wide. He stayed up all night, enthralled. The silent music in his mind was cocaine to his brain. Somebody sleeps, warm and comfortable, beneath these sheets.

The album starts with the recognition of the madness caused by the reality of death. After this recognition, the realization of the necessity for love occurs. When confronted by death, life loses its luster, its grandeur. We search for pleasure in the everyday, but when confronted with mortality, life ceases to make sense. Only the immediacy of love has meaning, but love is all too often unrequited, unreturned. For salvation, we turn to the intensity of another's experience, to art, the myth of the rock star, our "Moonage Daydream", the cosmic experience of drums and guitars, the sensation of electricity coursing through our brains.

Michael returns with Andrew's beer. "Thanks," Andrew says.

"No problem. The music still okay for you?"

"Perfect."

"Good."

God appears to us in the guise of the radio. It's an experience of the sensations that make life divine. Rock is a medium by which the spirit itself communicates with man.

This idea is no different from the Christian concept of man's inability to see the grandeur of what we refer to as "God". He would cause us to go blind, a metaphor for insanity. The experience of "God" would breed a living death. As zombies, praying for salvation, a return to life, we retreat to the immediacy of now. A new god, our salvation lies in worshiping the earth, worshiping life, for God exists simultaneously as both life and death. This is my first antinomy.

I remember thinking (it seems so long ago now) that a true experience of the spiritual would be akin to madness, would force the shaman (in ancient times) or the artist (in the contemporary world) to react to his experiences in a manner that society would deem as insane. It's the insanity of those who have truly seen God, have become the music on the radio that must then be distilled into an experience that others can relate to. He takes the spirit and makes it earth. We perceive God through mediation, through art, through dancing and rock n roll.

It's right here in the next song. The lyrics aren't on this sheet. It's a moment to reflect rather than read. It's a metaphor for the heights he has reached, but like Zarathustra, he has to teach others how to get to heaven when everything's "going down".

And he returns as "Lady Stardust", the man who is a woman, the male experience of the dual existence of sex as a female, the artist, a god, loved by both man and woman alike, the rock star, the hermaphrodite who sings in the night.

But the hermaphrodite was destroyed (I'm coming for you, honey).

Like Lucifer when he first sees Adam and Eve in the garden. The devil must be a woman, a man, a hermaphrodite, Lady Stardust, a creature in love with this life, not the next one. Was that the secret that Lucifer revealed to Eve? How much more beautiful it was for a woman to make love to another woman rather than to a man?

Art redeems life's suffering. Everything is beautiful when it's sung about. That's why the artist is "of the Devil's party", the one who realizes that in order to endure the horror of this world, we have to push ourselves beyond the dichotomy of good and evil, heaven and hell, and embrace suffering and hideousness with as much respect and awe as we embrace happiness and beauty, the divine form of both sexes, the yin and the yang, the sublation of all dualities, the experience of both the man and the woman, like blind Tiresias (blinded by his knowledge of God, the feminine existing within the masculine) living between two lives.

The music feels so good. Rock n roll lights inside your stomach with the glow of red wine, the spent passion of holding your lover in your arms.

The World Trade Center knew it was going to fall. The collective unconscious told me so. Angels fell from the sky. Their wings singed, clothed in burning white, screaming, they leaped to the abyss. It was a sacrifice, a suicide. It was all inside my mind.

In "Suffragette City", women run the vote. Man has lost all control. The masculine hierarchy of Allah or Jehovah is gone, destroyed, blasted into oblivion by the hermaphrodite's shooting star. To the patriarchy, it's madness, death. Juno, the masculine woman, the feminine counterpart of the rock star, has finally wrested control of the gods from Jove.

We've come full circle, an A-B-A structure where the knowledge obtained by B paints A in a different light. Death is no longer frightening. At all times, it simply is. We are the living dead. This is the "Rock N Roll Suicide", where the nectar and ambrosia of spirit and earth have left us as zombies. C'est l'Ennui, the wasteland. We no longer taste the milk and honey. But Ziggy, our hermaphrodite, the morning star, Lucifer, Satan Trismégiste, has experienced this too, experienced the pain and the pleasure, the heights and the ecstasy, the emptiness and the foreboding. That's the true beauty and wonder of art, the shared experience of divine rapture.

"Whoah."

"What?"

"Nothing."

But there's more to listen to, the extra tracks on this extended version, the subconscious, the collective unconscious, at work again. I don't have the lyrics to read.

"Could you turn the music up a bit?"

"Sure, man, no problem. These are my favorite songs."

Without the words, let me lose myself in the moment, the rapture that Ziggy, the alien, has brought from beyond the sphere of the fixed stars. It feels so wonderful, so magnificent. "John, I'm Only Dancing" inside my mind, tapping my feet to the electric rhythms in my brain. Let me sleep, safe and secure, in the plush depths, on the wicked pillows of this "Velvet Goldmine". Belial, are we deep enough to find Gabriel's eyes? Reclining on this bed in New York City, dreaming of gallows, I think "the mind is its own place, and in itself can make a Heav'n of Hell, a Hell of Heav'n."

Michael is tapping his foot. His black boot rattles the wooden floorboards. He's nodding his head. His hair nods back and forth. He's playing air guitar against the leg of his jeans. His lip curls as he mimes the lyrics. With his thick, black hair absorbing the light, he's as smooth as Elvis on the cover of his first album. The music emanates from him, from his mind. It fills the room. With his eyes closed, he sings in a baritone keyed to Ziggy's falsetto.

Andrew jerks up. On top of the Empire State Building, the wind, the freedom, the thought of death being so close... He shakes his head. It can't be true. *Michael, who are you?*

David Bowie's words are an explosion. The idea is unequivocal. The hidden language of the world... Nobody should ever know this. God is going to explode inside my mind. I'm going blind.

The world crumbles. Shrink wrapped in paper, it ignites. It all exists inside your mind. Michelle is standing at a broken window. The wind whips through her hair. Do we have to jump? A building collapses in on itself. Angels scream. Tomorrow, a nuclear explosion, a hole in space, the visible face of God, is going to engulf the entire city, blind us all for all eternity. Goodbye, New York. We're going to die tomorrow. Lady Stardust was sent here to warn us. Lucifer is singing. I first saw Michael four days before September 11th. Death is nothing.

Andrew jumps up, scrambles for his cigarettes, finds them on the bed, and shoves them in his pocket. "I gotta go, man."

"You sure?"

"Yeah, I'm sure."

"You all right?"

"Yeah, I'm cool."

"Well, thanks for stopping by. I needed it."

"Anytime."

Michael smiles. "I'll see you again. That's what I choose to believe for tonight."

Andrew nods.

Outside, on the Avenue, the lights are bright, tiny fairies doused in dust, orbs tinged with haloes, beacons in the night. Ten million night lights guiding their lost souls back home. Ghosts carouse the Village's streets.

Andrew walks north toward the subway at 14th. He's trembling like Michael was when he first saw him at the Holiday. Like an alien, the young man's disease was contagious. Like Michelle's love, it sprouts its roots in, impregnates Andrew's stomach. He feels the demons gnawing at him.

Two blocks from Michael's door, Andrew plops down on a corner curb. He pulls his cell phone out of his pocket. He leans over to move out of the way of a couple walking by. They brush his shoulder. With his trembling hands, he flicks his phone open. There's a number that he wants to call, memory #1, but that number is gone, disintegrated in the flames of a few weeks ago.

Sitting in public, a jester on the corner, holding his

communicator in his hand, trying to converse with heaven, waiting to be beamed up, he begins to sob.

"There's only one person I want to tell I'm going to die," he cries. "Only one person who I want to spend my last night with. Without her, I don't care. Without her, I really don't care." He shakes his head. "That's not true. I wish it was, but it's not. I don't want to die. Michelle, I don't want to die."

With its hazy lights, the science fiction night is silent and uncaring. A flying saucer, the obscured moon glows above the ravished skyline. I'm the baddest motherfucker who ever walked the face of this earth. Tomorrow, we're going to die.

I'm in Paris, hiding among the stone alcoves bordering the Seine. The world is an opera — masks and fans and costumes and passions. The water will keep us safe. My stomach hurts. Have I been shot? Am I already dead? I pull my hand away, and the blood flows freely. I'm dying, but I'm still alive. If we drown, we can hide. In the river, the glare of a billion mushroom clouds, the suck and pull of vacuous space, is reflected. It's too late. The world has been destroyed.

Drenched in sweat, suffocating in his sleep, Andrew wakes up. Expecting to see a cloud looming over Manhattan, a flash that blinds him in his last moments, he leaps for the window. Beyond the cool glass, only the hollow skyline, with the work lights' white glow, greets him. His chest is heaving. His saliva smacks of adrenalin. It's September 11th all over again. He's drowning. He stumbles back to bed and runs away to hide in Paris's sewers.

That evening, Gabriel comes over. All day, around every building, behind any body, Andrew expected to see the flash, the glow of white brighter than day, the surge of the sun imprisoned on earth. From a single point, the light would expand, progress, disintegrate the brick and concrete world in its path. By the time Gabriel makes it to the apartment around five o'clock, Andrew is a nervous wreck, nursing the Polish beer that he bought from the bodega at the end of the block.

When Gabriel enters, Carey gives him a peck on the cheek. They come into the living room and sit down on the tiny love seat across from where Andrew is sitting, holding his beer in his lap. Gabriel drops his sunglasses on the floor. His cat's eyes glow. Carey stretches out and rests his feet at the end of Andrew's couch.

"How you doin' today, man?" Gabriel asks.

"I'm all right," Andrew says.

Carey smiles. "Hey, we made it." He leans forward and slaps Andrew's shin.

Andrew nods.

"What do you mean?" Gabriel asks.

"Some friend of his said last night that New York was gonna blow today. Got the news from a friend of a friend at Hillary Clinton's office."

"No shit? Who knows. Maybe it did, and we're all dead, zombies who won't admit it, damned to wander New York for all eternity. I think I like being dead." With a chuckle, Gabriel lights a cigarette. "You mind if I put some music on?" he asks.

"Sure. Andrew's CDs are over there. Mine are in my room."

Gabriel hops up. He walks over and begins flipping through a pile of CDs beside the couch Andrew is sitting on.

"Oh shit, I haven't heard this in forever, you mind if I put it on?"

Andrew looks at the jewel case Gabriel is holding up. "Not at all," he says.

"The Damned," Gabriel whispers. "This is my

childhood. It might have the right atmosphere."

The distorted bass of *Damned Damned Damned* blasts, a gunshot, from the speakers.

"You guys wanna smoke?"

"Sure."

"Why not."

"I've only got the one hitter, but we can stretch it," Gabriel says. He reaches in his pocket and pulls out a little plastic baggy of weed.

Quickly, the smoke lies in heavy layers of sediment throughout the living room's tiny alcove. The Seine flows through Andrew's brain. A mushroom cloud is reflected in his mind. Drowning keeps us safe. Bury me alive beneath the sewers. "I'm gonna open a window," Carey says. "We gotta be able to breathe." He walks into the kitchen.

Andrew is entranced by Gabriel's face, his cheek bones and neck. If the dark Michael is Lady Stardust, then the light Gabriel is Ziggy. *When did the one split into two?*

The sound of the street merges with the music on the boombox, the smell of exhaust commingles with the odor of pot to create a modern symphony, a sensurround of sickly tastes merged with dissonant noise, cars and shouts – Polish and Spanish, correspondences of sensations in the silent space between bass and guitar, the soundtrack of the contemporary world. Gabriel nods his head from side to side, skipping every few beats, in a slow mimicry of the undying rhythm. It's the only way to maintain the pace.

"You guys got a roof?" he asks.

"Yeah," Carey laughs.

"Can we get up there?"

"Yeah. Andrew, you wanna come?"

"Why not."

From the roof, in the distance, above the flat homes of Brooklyn, beyond the suspension bridges, across the East

River, the wounded skyline towers and descends, rises and falls, a broken wave, a shattered Behemoth, Leviathan hooked by the cross, the whale harpooned, capsizing. Ground Zero's vacuum is a whirlpool, churning and sucking at the survivors' clawing bodies. The buildings and their people lean like they're in Pisa.

Without the Twin Towers to block it, the sunset is blinding. The spectrum is the expansion and progression that Andrew spent all day expecting to be his last visual image forevermore, nevermore, the cosmic flash burned into his retinas, melting his face, his brains. Its purples, pinks, and reds slice across the buildings, scalping them, peeling off their epidermis, leaving their naked nerves, bruising and drenching the cityscape in blood. Torture. Crime and punishment.

Andrew can't look. "I see that every night from my goddamn window."

"I'd kill for that view," Gabriel says.

"You can have it, man. I don't want it."

"Naw. In the end, I'd rather stay in the pulsing heart of Crooklyn. Bed-Stuy. Do or die, baby. I swear I never wished I was in the Twin Towers before that day they collapsed."

Carey tenses. The air flexes; the world contracts. Watch it breathe. Andrew dies. "What are you talking about?" he asks.

"To see it, man. To fucking see it. For Christ's sake, that was hell on earth. When do you ever get to see the pit open up like that? You gotta be in a war zone. Gotta be a fucking rush."

"I'm as close as I ever want to be," Carey says.

"Sometimes I wish I was in there," Andrew admits. "But only because then I could have died."

"You missed the point. The idea is to stay alive."

"Nobody stayed alive."

"*C'est la vie.*"

Carey shudders. "You sound like a fucking politician talking about collateral damage."

"Bull shit. Collateral damage is something different entirely. I don't want anybody else to go through it. It happened, and I just wish I was able to really be there."

"That's the most selfish thing I've ever heard," Carey says.

"It's a hypothetical situation. We all know the reality: A bunch of people died, and the world fell apart, but I wouldn't take the buildings back. They were a fucking eyesore."

"Jesus, Gabriel. One of his best friends was in there."

"Sorry, man, but I've had friends die before, too, and death is death. I'm sick of conversations about fucking heroes and all that shit. The reality is that nobody was saved. Everybody died, and the politicians got a war. You wanna know what I really think?"

"Not right now."

"Really, I think George Bush and Dick Cheney knew about the whole fucking thing. It all fits together too well. They've been trying to get a pipeline through Afghanistan for years. Don't tell me they wouldn't do it, but I don't think they knew about the Pentagon. That scared the shit out of them. Fuck the people in New York, but don't let them hit DC."

"That's bull shit. Nobody wants a war."

"Really? I'll tell you what. This won't be the first before it's all over."

"This will be the only one," Andrew mumbles, "Because it's the right one." He turns to Carey, "And I want this war."

"You sure, man?" Gabriel asks. Buried in the caverns

behind his cheekbones, his green eyes are endless. They contain all the heat of the earth's core as he turns them on Andrew. "It won't bring your friend back. It's just gonna put a shitload more people through what you're going through."

"Gabriel, you need to stop, or I'm going to ask you to leave."

"And this is gonna be people who have been living through something infinitely worse than what New York's been like for the past month for almost twenty-five fucking years. You should just be grateful that you've never seen this side of the world before. I mean what the hell do you think created Osama bin Laden?"

"Gabriel, stop…"

"No. I'm serious. Open your fucking eyes, man. You ever read about bin Laden? He started out giving humanitarian aid. He had a heart. He had fucking compassion, man, and what the hell happened to him? He saw too much. Too many dead people. Too many orphans. He fucking snapped, and now what's happened to us, to your friend, is nothing to his psyche, his conscience.

"When people are dying daily from our bombs what do you think the Afghanis will say about George Bush? They'll be shouting, 'He's a fucking psychopath!' You dig The Clash. Think about it. You wanna be a one-way person?"

"That's it, man. I'm sorry, but you gotta go," Carey says. "This isn't the right time or place for this conversation. I'll call you tomorrow."

"We've talked about all this before."

"It's different right now."

"I'm just telling your roommate to step outside his head and try seeing the world from somebody else's perspective. If I said anything that offended you, I'm sorry."

"It's all right," Andrew whispers.

"No. It's not. Goodbye, Gabriel. I'll talk to you tomorrow."

"You've gotta be kidding me."

"I'm not. I'll walk you to the door."

Gabriel twists his neck. It's a vulture's flesh, the scaly body of a snake. He stares at Andrew with the blandness of the scavenger, the coldness of the cobra, dancing and flicking its tongue seductively as it contemplates dead prey. "It's like Aretha Franklin, baby. Picture the entire world singing *Think* to you. There's a distinction between right and wrong, man. And Carey, you don't need to walk me down."

"No. I'm going to."

Alone, on the rooftop, Andrew stares at the sunset he was never able to see before. The vibrant colors against the drab buildings are a confusing dichotomy, a harsh contrast. *Maybe if I wasn't so stoned right now, this would all make a little more sense. Maybe if I wasn't so selfish, this would all be a little more mythical. What the hell was Gabriel talking about? Step outside of my head... That's the same thing Michelle said. Michael is her name in English. He's Lady Stardust. And if two is one, Michelle is Lady Stardust, and I look like Ziggy. Gabriel is Ziggy. How did one become two? "I had to phone someone so I picked on you." — Don't fuck with synchronicity.*

From this height, the sight of the skyline is teeming with a brood of remembrances. It's a living Mnemosyne, a physical engram. Moving to New York was such a divine experience. Entering a dream, Andrew was breathing through gills in the bulging belly of the muse, breathing through a cord off the pulsing blood of the city. I guess the skyline means different things to different people. Sometimes, it's simply frightening.

Standing on top of the Empire State Building with Michelle that night catapulted him to the apex of Olympus.

Her kiss was nectar. Her arms were ambrosia. The buildings below them were snowcapped hills. Together, joined in their minds, at their lips, they were a hermaphrodite, a god. And then the hermaphrodite was destroyed.

The trapdoor from the building to the roof opens, and Carey appears. "I'm sorry about that," he says.

"It's all right."

"No. It wasn't."

"Really, it was."

Carey sits down on the tar beside Andrew.

"He had a point," Andrew says.

"You think so?"

"I know you think so. You just never say those things to me."

Carey looks at the ground between his feet. He raises his shoulders. With a sigh, he drops them again.

"Do you think he could have been right? I mean about Bush and Cheney knowing about the whole thing?"

"I don't think so. I mean, don't get me wrong. I think they're two evil men, but they're not complete lunatics. Then again, you can never trust a businessman."

"Carey, is it wrong for me to want us to go to war?"

"I don't know, man. You've been through a lot. I know that I don't think it's ever right to go to war."

"What are we supposed to do then?"

Carey purses his lips and exhales slowly. "I don't know. I'll tell you what I believe, though. There's no such thing as countries, and there's only two kinds of people in this world, the people who want power and the people who are content just being humans. Bush and bin Laden, Dick Cheney and Mullah Omar are examples of the former. Me, you, Michelle, Gabriel – as fucked up as he is – and all the civilians in Afghanistan, the women who have to wear burqas, the men who have to grow beards, we're all human beings, and all we do is suffer while these other people fight for God or for business, it's all the same thing, claiming that they're doing everything in our interest. If they ever took a moment to really think about our interests, the world would be a different place. Congress wouldn't have impeached Clinton, Bush wouldn't have stolen the election, and bin Laden wouldn't have thought that it would help his cause if he killed a bunch of Americans."

"But should we go to war?"

"No."

"Then how do we make sure this never happens again?"

"We leave those people alone, pull out of Saudi Arabia, stop the sanctions against Iraq, support a Palestinian state. Use all the money we'll spend in a war to send them food and help them build hospitals and schools. If we don't, it'll happen again. One thing Gabriel said is true, there's a distinction between right and wrong."

"But do you think doing all those things will keep them from doing this to us again?"

"Nothing can keep them from doing this to us again. Certainly not a war. You ever been down South?"

"Not really."

"Well, I grew up down there, and I'll tell you what, it's been almost a hundred and fifty years, but there's still people who think the Civil War isn't over yet. There's still people who hate the north for reconstruction. It takes millenniums for humanity to heal."

"I want bin Laden dead."

"Jesus, man, so do I, for watching what he did to you, for taking away Michelle. I didn't know her as well as you, but I thought she was beautiful too."

"And how do we get him without a war?"

"I don't know, but with a war, there's a million more Michelles. They just aren't Americans, and that word doesn't mean anything to me."

Andrew bows his head. "I'm so confused. Everything I ever believed is totally against everything I feel."

"Not to be harsh, but I guess you got some thinking to do."

"Yeah, I guess I do."

"I'd like to see you go back to being you."

With his wounded eyes, Andrew gazes silently at Carey. A slight breeze ruffles his hair. Huddled between his arms, hugging his knees to his chest, vainly loving himself, for a moment, he's an Afghani refugee. Carey wants to give him an embrace, but instead, he pats Andrew on the shoulder.

"I'm gonna head back downstairs," he says. "Now that I'm not hanging out with Gabriel tonight, I have to find something else to do."

"All right. I'm gonna stay up here for a little bit."

"Don't think too much."

"I always try not to."

"And don't judge yourself by what Gabriel said. He's got his experiences, and you've got yours. Nobody can ever understand where another person's coming from." Carey disappears back downstairs. Andrew is alone again with the ghastly sunset.

He strains to scour the scribbled pages of his brain. He feels something, a frightening sensation in his stomach, the slight pressure of parasitic alien teeth nibbling at his guts. He's parturient with emotions and ideas. He shifts uncomfortably.

How can I ever see the world from somebody else's perspective? I'm ensnared by my own experiences: my youth, my home, college, my writing, my loves, New York, 9-11, Michelle. I'm not bin Laden, and I don't know what he's lived through, but I can't forgive him or understand his rationalization for what he did. I believe that going to war is right. I've never believed that before, but I do agree with Carey, and I understand what Gabriel says: I don't want what's happened to Michelle, to me and my friends, to happen to anybody else anywhere in the world. I'm certain of that.

I don't want there to be a war.

Gabriel knows what he believes. Carey believes what he feels. I'm mired in the wasteland between my gut and my mind, a mouse in a maze, trapped by walls of feelings or concepts on every side, all in contradiction to one another.

I know what I believed. It never floated that far from me, but I can't fathom what I've experienced.

Michelle, help me.

The threatening night looms on the horizon. The violet sky fades indigo. Reality is tinged with fantasy. Existence merges with nothing. There's a point between life and death, between waking and dreaming, where the pendulum swings dangerously inside your brain. The axe approaches your belly. The pit yawns before your mind's eye. A knife caresses your veins. Another evening of sitting at his window and staring at the glowing work lights from Ground Zero, Michelle's tomb, the point of impact of the nuclear reaction.

I'm ready to die. I want to throw myself off this building, feel the freefall as I tumble, a fallen angel, out of the sky. Is that what you had to do? Don't let me think about it. All the dead want is to live. All the living want is to die. I know that Gabriel's right. Michelle, will I ever see you again? This is all a symptom of my disease. Like you said, I can't get outside of my head. I want to believe in something like right and wrong. What if I had died today? If my body was destroyed, what would have happened to my memories, my mind?

Did we die today? Gabriel thought so, and being dead is just like being alive, our bodies projected by our minds. A nuclear bomb exploded last night. I dreamt the reality like I dreamt September 11th, *and now I have to confront my transgressions. I woke up at precisely 8:46. I know that because I checked the clock. Time stopped. It's still September 10th. I'm shouting at the moon. This is the rapture, my judgment. At the moment of death, time condenses, the fall, the crucifixion, the judgment happen simultaneously. Can I find you again in this wasteland, Michelle? Where's Saint Michael? He's sitting in an apartment in the Village, the masculine counterpart of your name. Have you ever heard an angel sing? I'm drowning in Paris's sewers again. I want to trust George Bush, but I've never trusted businessmen. Is a desire for vengeance a sin? I still owe Gabriel two souls. He's Ziggy Stardust, the future image of me, a refinement of my features, the alien, a savior sent from the Starman. Where did he get those eyes? It's time to figure out what I believe. Please, don't judge me.*

It's the same bar they met at on September 7th. It's exactly a month after the Tuesday following that, and the entire world is a different place: Satanic, flipped upside down, the card of the hanged man dangling from his ankle, an inverted crucifixion.

Charlie remembers the last time he sat at this bar waiting for Andrew. He remembers worrying that he'd never get laid again. He frowns at his puffy reflection above the spirits in the mirror. There's a madness to his features that he's been blinded to. His eyes scream helter skelter, and a permanent snarl is etched onto his lips.

Above the mirror, a picture from the *Daily News* hangs. It's a sketch of a man in a turban. His cheeks are gaunt. His beard is long. His eyes are soft. A holy fool. *Osama bin Laden: Wanted Dead or Alive.* Charlie tips his glass to the Wild West poster. He'd join the posse if he could. Tiny American flags stick up from either end of the bar. One side of the mirror, the side without the liquor, is draped in a huge banner of red, white, and blue. Another picture is set in front of a bottle of Jack Daniel's, firefighters in blue raising a flag at Ground Zero. Behind them is a tangled mass of steel and smoke. God's erector set broken in a child's temper tantrum at the ends, pieces of the Twin Towers twist around themselves in shapes as impossible as an Escher sketch, the Lobachevskian landscape of hell. *We salute our heroes*, a sign below it says.

Sitting at a bar is better for me than watching the war on TV, Charlie thinks, but war is addictive. Where are the TVs? There's a 24 hour movie on Fox: *America Strikes Back*. He takes a sip off his Grey Goose on the rocks. He's already on the third one. He had two at lunch. One addiction feeds the other.

The bar is fairly empty tonight. There's no couple giggling at one end, no group of businessmen thinking they'd rather be at a strip club. There's another man in a suit sitting a few stools down from Charlie, sipping off his tumbler of whiskey. *How many deaths is he responsible for?* Charlie finds himself wondering. The thought is a swarm of bees, a billion butterfly wings, inside his brain. Another sip of vodka will take care of that.

Andrew slides in beside him. "Hey," he whispers in a muted tone.

Charlie jumps up from his seat. "Jesus, it's good to see you, man." He hugs Andrew with the power of a bear, the compassion of a dog. He's Peter meeting the risen Christ. "What are you drinking? I'm buying."

"Bass."

"Always drink the fish, right?"

"Huh? Yeah. Always drink the fish," Andrew says dejectedly. He stares at the wooden floor, at his feet resting on the bottom of his stool.

"Bartender, a Bass for my friend."

"It's good to see you too, man," Andrew says, and as

his friend leans against the bar and thumbs through his wallet, he reaches up to give him another hug. He holds him lithely, like a cat would caress a lion. We look the same. I'm a smaller version without your mane, and you're so much stronger than me. I break easily. Let me be more like you. These two childhood friends...

"How's your mom doing?" Charlie asks. His eyes are full of tears, but he won't cry.

"She's all right."

"I'm sorry I didn't make it to Michelle's memorial last weekend. I didn't think it would be right for me to go. You know, since I got her the job there."

"It's all right. I understand."

With the expression of a forgotten dad, Charlie looks at Andrew. "I knew you would," he says. Andrew's beer comes up. Charlie pays the man. He sits back down. "How fitting is that though? The day of the service, we start bombing Afghanistan. It's like Michelle wanted her revenge."

Andrew winces. He takes a slow sip of beer.

"So how was it to be back home?"

"Weird."

"What do you mean?"

"Until I saw Michelle's mom and dad, it was like nothing had even happened. Other than American flags flying everywhere, nothing was any different. My mother was so happy to see me. I didn't even know what to say to her. Somebody even told me they were glad to see New York had gotten back to normal, that the anthrax attacks haven't fucked us up too bad."

"Jesus. They have no idea, do they? I haven't had a single temp make it to work on time all week. Every day, the subways are shut down for bio-terrorism scares."

"I was twenty minutes late today while we waited for

them to clean up the powdered sugar from a fucking donut."

"This place is never going to be normal again."

Andrew shakes his head. "Not for me. Not without Michelle."

It's Charlie's turn to stare at the floor. The silence has volume – weight and sound. The light goes out of his eyes. "I'm sorry," he says eventually.

"You don't need to say that." Andrew closes his eyes. "It wasn't your fault."

"Jesus, man, I need to say it to somebody. You're the only one I can tell. We lost seven temps that day. Seven people who I knew, who came to me for a job. I sent them there, and they died…"

"I know. You told me. I'm sorry."

"You can't be sorry for all of them."

"I can try to be."

Charlie wipes his dry eyes. He sniffles and straightens up in his seat. "Well, now we're making sure this never happens again."

Andrew stares at the shape of the white flesh of his hand around the glass pint of his brown ale. The colors form an interesting juxtaposition, something solid and soft against something liquid and hard. Slowly, he says, "Yeah. I guess so."

"We're gonna bomb those motherfuckers back to the Stone Age. No American is ever going to go through what we're going through ever again."

"I hope not," Andrew whispers.

"They should have done this a long time ago. I always liked Clinton, but now I'm thinking that he fucked us bad."

Andrew nods slightly, once forward then back. He ends with his head cocked to the side. Furrowing his eyebrows, he listens intently.

"I think we've got the right administration for this job. At the time, I wasn't so happy about it, but now I'm glad Gore didn't win the election. If you think about it, it's like fate, you know. You can probably see the divine intervention, what with you thinking about God all the time."

"There's a duality to every system."

"I mean George Bush didn't even win, but I think he's the only one for the job. Bin Laden has no idea what he unleashed. We'll turn his country into a fucking runway for our jets."

With his head still tilted to the side, Andrew lightly touches his lips. "It's not his country," he says.

"What?"

"He's Saudi."

"Well, Mullah Omar, then. Either way, they fucked up bad. We've got Special Ops in there now, and those are some bad motherfuckers."

"You think we could talk about something else?"

"Huh? Sure. Sure we can talk about something else." Charlie chuckles. "You'd be proud of me, man," he says. "This whole thing has me thinking about God for the first time in my life."

"Really?"

"Yeah, I mean, all these people. What happened to them? What happens to us? We have to go somewhere. We can't just disappear. There has to be a god. I need there to be a god. A lot of people are probably going to die during this war."

"A lot of people die every day."

"There has to be something, some sort of divine justice, to let us know we're doing the right thing."

"This whole thing has convinced me more firmly than ever that there's no such thing as God and that religion might be the most wicked weapon man has ever discovered."

"That doesn't sound like you at all. Why do you say that?"

"Because Michelle was murdered for some goddamn religion. I know that there are a thousand real reasons beneath that surface explanation, but bin Laden justifies his own psychosis, his own psychological foibles through religion, and people agree with him just because they have the same name for a concept. I refuse to be a part of it on any side. People are blowing each other up all over Israel for religion, for a land claim that has no basis in any historical fact, but in European guilt for their own bigotries. It's all bull shit, man. There's no such thing as Jesus, Yahweh, or Allah. I always believed it was only a concept, but I don't believe any more that it's a beautiful concept. I think it's hideous, the most hideous justification for suffering that humankind has ever invented."

Charlie stares at the bar for a moment. He twitches his wrist. "How's your writing?" he asks.

"I haven't written a word since the weekend before all this started. It just doesn't make sense to me anymore. I mean, what the hell was I writing about anyway, some made-up story? Shit, we may not even live long enough for me to finish a screenplay. Radiation from a dirty bomb in Times Square, asphyxiation from sarin through the subway vents. Who knows."

Charlie turns his skewed gaze on Andrew. "Don't talk like that."

"It's true."

With a vehemence that rouses the bartender's notice, Charlie says, "We're gonna win this war. You know that, don't you? They might have hit us first, but we're gonna win."

"I already lost."

"Goddamnit. Stop talking like that. I bought you a drink for Christ's sake." Charlie stops. He settles back into his chair, runs his hands down his face. "It just pisses me off, man. It pisses me off that my oldest friend in the entire world is scared he's going to die. It pisses me off that I'm scared I'm going to die. I haven't opened my mail for a week. Not that I think anybody gives a damn about killing me..."

"But people do want to kill you. They want to kill all of us."

"But because of cross-contamination. I don't want to die yet. I saw the fucking bodies, man. The day after, I saw the first truckloads of bodies. I have no idea what you're going through without Michelle, and I keep thinking to myself that there are three thousand people who left people like you behind. Seven of those, I sent there. It hurts to see you like this. And I know it's my fault."

"It hurts me to see you like this. And it's not your fault."

"It's bin Laden's fault."

"His and others."

"That's right." Charlie swirls back into himself. "I think I might be drunk," he says.

"I've seen you drunk before."

"I think I've been drunk since September 11th. Well, maybe not since the eleventh. It might have been more like the twelfth or thirteenth. I've got to get my shit together." In a belated act of self-love, Charlie smoothes his shirt over his stomach. He glances sidelong at Andrew. He whispers, "I haven't told anybody this yet, but I think about killing myself sometimes."

Andrew nods. "I can understand that. I think about it, too."

"Don't say that. Jesus, don't say that. I already hate myself for putting you through all this. Don't make me hate myself for that too."

"You didn't put me through this. Stop talking like that."

"I've got to be honest. I don't think I can handle the world being like this."

"Neither do I."

"That's why we gotta win this war, so the world can go back to normal."

"The world's no different than it was on September 10th. Except that now we know people hate us."

"For no fucking reason."

"It's our foreign policy, man. It's all those things you used to make fun of me for thinking about in high school. That's what destroyed the Trade Center, man, our foreign policy."

Charlie stares at Andrew. He blinks. "Don't ever say that again. Terrorists destroyed the Trade Towers. Bin Laden destroyed the Trade Towers…"

"And what was his motivation?"

"I don't know. Hatred, jealousy, evil…"

"There's no such thing as evil."

"Don't play one of your fucking intellectual games right now, man. We're talking about three thousand people. Three thousand *Americans*. One of them was your friend. Don't you ever make this discussion intellectual. This is real."

"I know. Dear God, believe me, I know. I've never known the world was as real as I know it is right now."

"You gotta hold onto something. I hold onto the fact that we're doing the right thing, and that once we win, the world will go back to normal. I won't think about slitting my wrists every night as I sit in my apartment drinking forties and watching Fox, mentally flagellating myself for sending those people to work that day, hoping that we win, that somehow, we justify their deaths. Where is your intellectual argument with that, Andrew? How is it right that somebody gets murdered just for going to work?"

"Try seeing it from their perspective," Andrew whispers.

"*Their* perspective? I don't give a damn about *their* perspective. They certainly don't give a shit about mine."

"Look, man, on September 12th, in the newspaper, I saw all these Palestinians cheering, and it broke me. It fucking broke me, man, but the more I thought about it, the more I realized it was like when I was a kid and something bad happened to one of the popular kids at school. It just made me happy to know that maybe they hurt like I did now. That was wrong, and I know it, but it's the same thing. The truth that I want them to understand, that I want us to understand is that we're all in this together. The world's not us against them."

"Now it is."

"On that, we're going to have to disagree."

"Are you telling me that you don't think it's right for us to be at war?"

"I don't know anymore."

"I can't believe I'm hearing this."

"It fucking tears me up inside, man."

"Jesus Christ."

"All I'm certain of is that I don't want what happened here to happen anywhere else in the world."

"It's not. Look, this was a terrorist attack on a civilian target. We didn't know it was coming. It was a beautiful, blue day. *We* gave the Afghanis warning. We did everything we could, and now we've got to go get those bastards."

Down the bar from them, the other patron, setting his glass aside, has begun to pay attention. The bartender is staring at them. "I'm sure it was a blue day in Afghanistan on Sunday," Andrew mumbles.

"What?"

"Maybe we should talk about something else."

"No. I don't think we should. This is worse than the conversations we had in high school. Don't you understand? You grew up here. Those people were like you. In Afghanistan, they're nothing like us."

"They're still humans."

"And they live under a repressive regime."

"We all live under repressive regimes, in the shadow of charismatic leaders. It's all madness. Your only choice is to choose your insanity. I refuse to let a powerful personality dictate my thoughts for me. I just wish the rest of the world would wake up to that fact. Maybe then, we'd all be at peace. The leaders might call a war, but none of us would show."

"They're grateful that we're going in there."

"How could anybody be grateful that we're bombing them? You've smelled the city the past couple weeks. How could you appreciate that smell?"

"They've lived through a lot worse than we have. This is nothing to them."

"Death is always something."

"Would you rather America was attacked or Afghanistan?"

"I don't think it makes a difference."

"Jesus, man, I always knew you were nuts. But this is fucking insane."

"Like I said, the world's insane. I'm trying my hardest to stay sane."

"I don't think you're doing a very good job."

"Look, man, I didn't even want to come here tonight. Why? Because this is where I was right before Michelle and

I finally kissed." The statement sets Andrew alight. He's incinerated.

The flame is too bright. There's too much heat. Charlie recoils in his seat. His jaw drops. He exhales heavily, a salve for his burns. He clears his throat. When he speaks again, his tone is soft. "Jesus, man, I had no idea. You never told me…"

"I never got a chance." Andrew shakes his head. "I hate my memories as much as I hate me. Do you remember me wanting that job at the Trade Towers?"

Slowly, Charlie nods. "Yeah."

"Well, I remember telling Michelle she should be excited about working there. How the fuck do you think I feel about that? Telling her she should be excited she'll die."

"You didn't know."

"Neither did you. So stop giving me your guilt shit. We all feel guilty. Michelle died for us, for our sins."

"Why are you saying these things?"

"Because we're the ones who are guilty, whether we're partying every night, dreaming about the stock market, or living safe and secure in the suburbs. If they could have killed all of us, they would have. The night before the attacks, they went to a strip club. Sometimes I think it was so that they could really hate us, distill everything that's fucked up about America. We're dropping cash on naked women while the rest of the world's starving. How much do I pay for a shitty apartment in this city? Six fifty a month. What would a Palestinian refugee do with ten percent of that? Whose fault is it that this happened? It's yours, mine, and everybody else in this country who doesn't really give a shit."

"You need to shut your brain down, man. You keep thinking like this, and you're going to go crazy."

"I don't give a damn. I'm already crazy. I live in America, don't I?"

"Andrew, I love you, man, but you need to watch yourself. You're too smart for this."

"That's the most American thing I've ever heard somebody say."

"Maybe you need to get out of New York for a little while. Put this all back into perspective."

"Do you have it in perspective?"

"No, but I still believe in my country."

"And I believe in Michelle. Without her, I don't give a shit anymore."

"Christ, man. Michelle is not the be-all-end-all of existence. For God's sake, you only kissed her once…"

Andrew spins on Charlie like a mongoose on a snake. He grabs him by the arm. His fingers dig so deep into the flesh that Charlie winces. Andrew says, "Don't you ever say that. If you're my friend, don't you ever say that again. She is. For me, in this place, at this time, she is. She may be until the end of time."

Michelle's apartment is now Ari's apartment, and it's strange to be there. Like the rest of New York City, it's haunted. Blending with the original art work, ghosts, shadows among the abstract canvasses, flit across the walls. Spirits convene beside the beaded lampshade in the corner. Specters slip along the ceiling. A phantom has taken up residence there. Pale and grim, it sits down beside you, rests its hand on your knee while you recline on the couch. It breathes down your neck, seductively tickling the hairs at the base of your scalp, when you lean forward to pour another glass of red wine from the bottle sitting on the low wooden table in front of you. In the twirling haze of smoke coming off the end of your cigarette, for a moment, it merges with Ari's face. It smiles. It screams. You blink. It grows wings and melts back into the atmosphere.

Inside, there's no anchor, no author. *The Pequod* floats adrift, a lonely ghost ship haunted by its phantom crew. Can you feel the albatross around your neck? The depths from which the souls escape descends into the valley of your heart. It gapes and yawns, swallowing your lungs in a whirlpool, a freezing, fiery hole. You choke. You cough. You lean back into the couch to feel the emptiness hit you again. This doesn't feel right at all. Who else is here, inside of me, pressed against the walls, staring out from the corner? Inside out, I'm all alone, and I've never been this alone before.

"Andrew, are you all right?" Ari asks. Her eyebrows crease with concern. Her royal nose and her dark complexion are a tangle of uncertainty. She wipes a strand of straight black hair from in front of her face.

"Yeah. It's weird. That's all," Andrew shakes his head. He sniffles. Scared at the sound of voices, the ghost has moved on down the hall, flittered out the window to find its final resting place again, descended back into the chambers and cells, the kingdom of your heart.

"I know. I live with it every day." Searching the room for the presence, Ari glances over her small shoulder. "I'm thinking I might move out."

Andrew nods. His eyes appear weighted for drowning. "I could understand that. I think about moving out of my place, too. I can't stand seeing the work lights every night. Their glow's like a ghost's halo. I hate not waking up to the Trade Center in the morning, and I'll never get used to seeing the sunset, how bright my bedroom gets. I can't go in there until after the sun's finished going down, but then the lights are on…"

Ari nods. "How's work going?"

"Work's work."

"Are you writing?"

"No."

"Have you shopped around that play that Michelle was going to put up?"

"I threw it away."

"What?"

"It's still on my computer. I just couldn't stand seeing those words anymore. The premise is inane. I can't believe it mattered to me. I mean, who cares about some writer who can't fall in love?"

"If it's about love, I care."

"Well, I don't. It was 125 pages of self-referential bull shit. I don't really think anybody wants to sit through two hours of the inside of my head. I know I wouldn't want to."

"You never know."

"How about you, are you working on any new canvasses?"

"I've kept myself locked in my studio. It keeps me out of here."

"Are you still working on abstract colors?"

"Yeah, but I'm trying to develop narratives. I want to tell a story about what all of this has been like." She pauses. She flips her hair in front of her face, glances down her nose at Andrew, and says hesitantly, "About Michelle."

Andrew sniffles. He shakes his head. "I don't see how you could ever turn this into art, into something edifying and grand."

"It's just something I feel I have to do."

"I guess a lot of people are like that. This theater group that Carey works with just did a production called 'Impressions of 9-11'. It was basically improv performances. They only worked on it for like a week. I guess it was good. I didn't go."

"It's a way to cope."

"I'll take alcohol," Andrew says as he lackadaisically pours himself another glass of wine.

"I use a lot of that too," Ari says. She tilts her head to the side. A mother's look creases her eyes, purses her pretty lips as she contemplates her visitor, this young man, drowning himself in drink, so obviously broken inside, all alone now in a broken city with its broken skyline. I could give you a home… That's a fleeting thought. Like a ghost.

"So how are you telling the narrative?"

"What?"

"In your paintings, how are you telling the story?"

"With colors…"

"Red and white?"

"Sometimes. More blues. I'm trying to paint my insides. How it feels. The anger, the confusion, her beauty, my love."

"Sounds interesting."

"I'll take you over there, let you see it sometime. I'm not ready to show it to anybody yet. The story's still kind of confused. Once I pull the strands together, then people will be able to see how all of this feels."

"I don't think I feel anything anymore."

"Don't say that. I can see that you still feel. It shows in the lines around your mouth, your eyes."

"I think I'm dead."

"You're not dead."

"A nuclear explosion went off in New York. Lady Stardust warned me about it. We're zombies. You can see it in our eyes. We just haven't realized it yet."

Ari stands up. She moves over to the couch that Andrew is sitting on. Her jeans brush together. Her arms are so thin. When she was a child, she was nothing but rattling bones. The boys used to make fun of her. The girls all picked on her. She cried herself to sleep. She didn't start growing breasts until she was in high school, and she never had a boyfriend until college. Her features were too long, her skin too dark, her body too small. Now, she has the shape of a runway model, Kate Moss, a waif, an anorexic's dream. She sits down in the ghost's vacant place. Her body is light. It hardly leaves an impression on the cushions, but Andrew can feel her warmth. It floats off her skin in waves. Her scent is dark, ancient, and mystical. With her bulging, bloodshot eyes, she looks down. Between her knees, she wrings her hands. Her fingers are long, the psychic's sign for the artist. Her palms are splotchy brown and flat, no mound of Venus. A gypsy once told her that she will lead a sad life. "Andrew, tell me how you feel."

"I told you. I don't feel anything anymore."

"I don't believe that. I know you. I know you feel."

"It doesn't matter how I feel. My feelings can't change anything."

"It always matters how you feel."

"Then I'm going crazy. How's that?"

"Honest."

"I can't do anything honest. That's what Michelle said."

"I don't think she meant that."

"Maybe I should ask her."

"You don't need to be so vitriolic."

"It's how I feel. I'm trying to be honest."

Ari bows her head. "I'm empty inside," she says. "I've never felt like this before. Not even when my grandmother died."

"It's worse than my parents' divorce."

"You remember your parents' divorce?"

"I was eight. I wish I didn't remember anything."

"This isn't just about Michelle."

"Ari, I'm falling apart inside. I'm so scared, so full of

hate, wracked with self-loathing, torn apart by wolves. Heauton Timoroumenos."

"What's that mean?"

"Self-tormentor. It's from Baudelaire. When I think, I think about Baudelaire a lot these days."

"Why's that?"

"Because I feel like I'm smelling the flowers of evil. This fucking city, the stench... Moving beyond good and evil."

"I don't believe in good and evil."

"Then you've already made it, and I'm still trying."

"I only believe in positive and negative, and I've never seen anybody as consumed by the negative as you right now."

"It's because I'm dead."

"You're not dead."

"On the inside. I died as soon as the first tower fell. I felt it. I felt my soul disintegrate inside of me. When I saw you on the stairs, and you shook your head, my heart shattered and rained its dirt down on my spirit, entombing me inside myself like Milton gone blind, a living grave."

"Have you written any of this down?"

"I can't write anymore."

"Maybe it would help."

"By making me live through it every day?"

"You're already living through it every day."

"Ari, I don't want to think about any of this."

"But you might be the one person who can tell this story right."

"And I might be just another asshole spouting off about my pain. Like I said before, who cares about the inside of my head?"

"I do. Michelle did. I've listened to you this whole past year. You have an amazing way of looking at the world."

"Charlie thinks I'm insane."

"Screw Charlie. I don't even know him, but tell me, what does he know?"

"That he loves America, and he wants bin Laden dead."

"And you? What do you want?"

"I want Michelle back."

"So do I," Ari says. She unfolds from the couch. Her steps, circling around the room, are carefully placed. With her shaking fingers, she pulls strands of hair across her trembling lips. Her eyes are a vacant ocean, calm on a winter day, gray and flat. When she speaks, her voice is thick, drowning in saliva. She doesn't look at Andrew. She stares at the ghosts haunting her paintings, her psyche on pieces of canvas. "You could bring her back though. You could bring her back with words."

"I don't want to. I don't believe in poetry anymore. It doesn't make the world any less painful. It's an escape, like any other drug."

"And what about art?"

"The same thing."

"It's a good drug though."

"All drugs are good drugs."

"It doesn't hurt anybody."

"Except for romantics, its addicts. Its lies tear them apart inside."

Ari turns to Andrew. Behind her black hair, her face is hidden in a rain forest. Something wild, a tiger, has just hunted down an animal, killed its prey for food. Doused in blood, it rips and tears through the flesh of a living, crying being that kicks as its arteries pulse violently. They cease. Like a rape, a violated lover, its heart stops beating. We're watching it from the overhanging shadows of a tree. Adrenalin freezes in our petrified veins. It's a reality that humans don't like to see. "I'm one of its addicts."

"I've always been one too, but it's not enough anymore. It's not real enough to alter my reality."

"Maybe we just need to work harder."

"Maybe you do. I'm through."

"Don't say that, Andrew. You have to write this story. I want to see Michelle again, love her mind and her laugh again."

"I can't stop loving her. She haunts me. I see her every day, everywhere, in the shade of a woman's hair, in the sound of a girl's voice, in the darkness of my mind's eye, in the radioactive glow of Ground Zero."

"When did you first meet Michelle?"

"My freshman year of high school. She was in my science class. We sat in the back together. She was a goth chick. Cure tee shirts, black dresses, fishnet stockings, an ankh necklace, and lots of eye make-up. Her hair was real short back then. You couldn't even tell it was curly. It was cut to the nape of her neck, and she put hairspray in it so that it stuck out in every direction. She came in and sat down at the desk next to me. She had such an attitude. She popped her bubble gum. The teacher asked her to spit it out, and she refused. She almost went to the office over that. She introduced herself to me. My heart exploded. She was that beautiful. I was such a dork. I wanted to be a skater real bad, but I couldn't skate, and my mom would barely let me grow a flop. I decided to become a punk rocker so that Michelle would like me, but it didn't work. She was a lot cooler than I was.

"I'd let her read my poetry. She liked it. She'd smile at me after she read it, and her eyes would sparkle beneath the stars and twirls of her mascara. She said it reminded her of Donne. I didn't even know who he was. I believed she was falling in love with me. All the poems were about her. I don't think she ever knew that. Until the last time I saw her,

I always told her they were about other girls. I always dreamed that someday, when we were lying in bed together, I'd confess that they were about her.

"We'd sit in the back and trade writing all through class, not paying attention to a thing the teacher said. I wrote about love. She wrote about politics and racism. What did we care about science? We were artists. True art is anarchy. It has no laws. She convinced me I should try out for drama. I did it so I could be closer to her. I think that's why every guy goes out for drama. The straight ones at least. It's not because we love acting. It's always to be closer to pretty girls."

"You really love her, don't you?"

"I loved her before I even met her. When I was a little kid, after my parents got divorced, sitting all alone in my bedroom, listening to new wave records and playing with my dog, I'd dream about meeting a girl like her. My dreams almost came true. It only took ten years. That's a lot closer than most people ever get. I'll just try to always forget that the last time I saw her she was angry with me."

Ari is sitting on the couch again. Staring at Andrew's profile, she's leaning her head against her hand. Her hair tangles around her bracelets. "She wasn't angry with you," she says. "Hurt, but not angry. She was starting to realize how in love with you she'd always been."

"I think that's the worst thing you could possibly say."

"I just wanted you to know that."

"I don't want to know that."

"I'm sorry. I didn't say it to upset you."

"That's all right. I'm getting used to crying at the most inopportune of times. I started crying at work the other day. Just because I couldn't get the copy machine to work. My co-workers stared at me like I was insane. I must have seemed like a woman on her period. The guys all treated me like a leper, but there was this one girl. She was one of the first people I talked to on September 11th – I still remember how wide her eyes got when the plane hit the Pentagon; it was like she could see it happening on a movie screen in her mind – she gave me a hug and told me everything would be all right. I just needed to go outside and smoke a cigarette, walk around for a bit. It's funny how only women can understand something like that. No, Carey always understands, too. Maybe it's something about being attracted to men."

"I don't know. It doesn't make sense to me how we can be expected to go on with our lives as if nothing happened. We ride on the subway even though we know that the tunnels could crack and the whole river could flood over us, drown us while we hang on to a strap. We still go to work even though our friends are missing when we get home. The signs say, 'Get out and shop New York. They can't beat us.' As if the terrorists care whether or not I buy a new pair of shoes. Half the time I feel like I'm already beaten."

"I know I'm already beaten."

"I think people in the city are getting pretty used to people breaking down. There's a lot more compassion. I saw this Puerto Rican guy on the subway the other day, he had a du-rag and gang tattoos all over his neck, straight out of East New York, helping some poor little white girl, she couldn't have been over eighteen, who looked fresh off the farm find her way out of the Times Square station. She looked about ready to die. I don't think she could find her mom or her hotel, and she wasn't too happy about being lost in the mazes beneath New York City. She must have thought she was going to get eaten alive by rats, but he walked her to the exit. I would have loved to see the look on her face when she finally saw the sunlight again. I bet she even gave him a hug and a kiss. It was probably the first time she ever touched somebody who was brown. The city's a different place. I don't know if it will ever be the same again."

"I remember the first time I heard cat calls on the street again, listened to all the project kids talk shit to all the women walking by. It used to make me ill listening to that. I could never understand how somebody could say those things to another person, but the other week, when I finally heard it again, it was music to my ears. It was sublime to realize that people were still alive, dead inside, but half of them were dead to begin with. I was blind to all of that. I finally opened my eyes at the moment I died. It's like being still-born. Does that make me still blind? I'm an abortion, a fetus with flesh encrusted eyes. God's abortion. The hermaphrodite's abortion. New York is still New York. A little less grand, a little more scared, but it's still New York. All I need for it to be real to me again is for Michelle to be here. If she appeared, I'd come back to life."

Ari stares at Andrew for a moment. He doesn't notice. He blinks rapidly at the floor. With a twitch, she looks down at her hand rubbing against her jeans.

They're silent, drinking their wine. Andrew leans forward, rests his elbows on his knees, stares at the vaporous space. An apparition opens the door to his coffin. Michelle should be coming home soon. At any moment, her key should click in the lock on the door. She smiles as she enters, flips her hair over her shoulder. Ari and I were just getting started, sharing a bottle of wine, waiting for you to show up. Do you want a glass? Are you ready to go over my script again? I made the changes you recommended. You were right. It does flow better without that conversation. I didn't take the whole thing out because the ideas are still important to me, but I tweaked it, tried to make it a bit more real, like you said. You always give me my best ideas. Did I ever tell you that before? It doesn't matter. Now, I can tell you how I really feel.

The hardwood floor is lonely and cold, a dead forest, nature's empty, lost soul. The rug at the edge of Ari's toes is Michelle's. She can't take looking at it anymore. Decorating the walls, her paintings, the shapes and colors, have become meaningless to her. A black line down a purple canvas that once represented her. A green box on a field of burnt orange that was once her home. The fruit of her soul, expressions of herself once upon a time now seem distant and cold, lifeless and old in their youth, like renaissance portraits, the ideas of art before World War I, a nineteenth century still-life of a fresh grapevine lit by candle light. Someday, maybe I'll paint this scene. This whole room, its presence, the emptiness and the suffering of the ghosts, the generations of families before us, their psychic energy encaged by these walls, their arguments and passions, this type of realism, two bodies unable to communicate, crying without tears, unable to touch, to comfort one another, the surreality of what lies at the edge of our conversation, pasts only hinted at as we exhale, the words evaporating in air, the taste of aged wine, the entire history, the entire race of mankind breathing our fears and pains back in to us as we inhale silently, alone though together, is the ultra-modern aesthetic of art. "I'm glad you came by tonight," Ari says.

Andrew nods. He sniffles and wipes his nose. He says, "I remember Halloween of my sophomore year. Michelle went as a vampire, and she wore a garter belt. At a friend of ours house, sitting on the couch, she taught me how to take it off. Our friends laughed at me as I fumbled with the snaps. I twisted, pushed, and pulled, and Michelle giggled at me. Nobody had any idea why I was trembling so bad. They all thought I was nervous. It wasn't my nerves. I was ready to explode. My heart was beating so fast. I was twitching like a rabbit. I've remembered that moment my entire life. I can still recall the taste of the menthol cigarettes she was bumming me on my tongue, the electric buzz of her skin beneath the fishnets. Whenever I got sad, I'd always try to remember that, to remember that one night, she let me touch her leg, and maybe someday, I could touch her again, feel that pulse ripple through my fingertips until it electrified my entire body. I once told Michelle that I wanted to die by being torn apart by wolves, fighting to stay alive. That's a lie. I wanted her to shock me into a stupor, a jellyfish wrapped around my soul, a heart attack in her arms, the only place I could ever rest as I died." With his lips, he smiles. His eyes are ready to drown. A mask of comedy over tragedy. The only true expression for life.

A ripple spreads from Ari's womb through her heart to her throat. It tingles against her lips. She breathes it back into her lungs where it catches her breath in a liquid sigh. Her heart beats waves against her chest. We're drowning together, here, tonight. My body is quicksand. My soul claws. Its lips gurgle mud. I don't know if it would matter to me if I died. Let me close my eyes and sink down, beneath the city, through the tunnels where the subway rumbles, deep into the fault line that swallowed us all two months ago. Maybe there we can find Persephone, taken from us in the summer of her youth, enthroned now on an ebony tomb, her beauty forever marred. The world is forever fall, forever winter. We're frozen, here on this couch, moments away from one another. Demeter has no bargain to strike with the lord of the dead. The wasteland of the modern world has no god for her to bargain with. Nobody comes back to life.

"Andrew, can I put my arms around you?"

"Sure."

Awkwardly lifting themselves off the couch's cushions, they slide closer to one another. Their clothes rustle. Ari scoots underneath Andrew's shoulder. She slips one arm behind his back, lays the other across his stomach. He pulls her in tight. She grabs a hold of his waist, feels the flesh at the edge of his belt. Twisting her long body, a snake draped across a cross, her head rests lightly on his chest. She turns her eyes into his shirt, flattens her nose against him, smells the skin of a man. He buries his face in her hair, the scent of something so different from him. Each blinded by the other, their inner lives open to them. A desert of ice. They close their eyes tighter to make their minds go blind, a snowstorm in the midst of white nights, a reflection and absorption of all light, and they hold one another harder as if trying to press themselves into one being, the hermaphrodite majestically oblivious to all pain.

Ari's flesh barely hides her bones. Like mud, it should be so easy to slip straight through, to let it blanket us both, to rest beside her skeleton, interred within her warmth, embracing her face before she was born. Across her back, it's a thin layer over ridges of rocks, distant fog capped mountains, the clouds that we plummet through on our descent from Olympus, from heaven. The fallen angel bemoans what he's lost as he swims through the lake of the abyss. On her arms, it grips the sinews and moves ever so slightly as Andrew slides his hands down her long muscles. She nestles closer to his warmth, feels her own body press tighter against his. Can you fill my emptiness tonight?

From the walls, a phantom watches this all, averts her eyes, wipes her tears, prays to be real again, to be a body to be held by somebody. God doesn't exist. There's nobody to make love to when you die. She moves closer, her presence sends a shiver through Andrew's nerves. He trembles. Why did you go away? It's supposed to be you on this couch with me. The phantom embraces the minds, the bodies of the two friends, potential lovers. The coolness of her touch, the promise of her spiritual *ménage a trois*, thrusts them deeper into one another's embrace.

"Stay with me tonight," Ari whispers as she rubs her cheek against the tee shirt covering Andrew's chest.

Andrew sniffles. Angels never cry; they only die. He nods and kisses Ari on the top of her head, his lips so light and full against the taste, the brittle sensation of her hair. With one finger beside her nose, the phantom wipes a non-existent tear from her dry eyes.

"Are you ready to go to bed?"

"Yes."

"Let's go then."

Cupping his fingers over Ari's fingers that trail behind her like the tie to an open robe, he follows her into the bedroom. As the pall bearer, lightly gripping her lover's casket, Ari slides, fluid with wine, her stomach a pupae aflutter. Ready to fall six more feet, Andrew sees his life open before him, internally, like a sepulcher. The phantom, as sexton, follows, holding in her hollow eyes the tools, picks and shovels, to dig every empty grave. They each walk with their heads down, staring at the floor – the floor that Michelle's feet used to step across – expectant that the ritual begin, certain only that the act of love, the verb itself, will replace the nouns, the lost feelings inside of both of them. As the world melts, our solids become liquids, then gases, and we struggle to grasp at whatever can still wet our hands and leave us with the residue, the scent, of the subjects that used to define our selves. The ghosts slip through our fingers, drift out of our lungs, but we can drown in, be suffocated by the deliquescence of people as their bodies slip backwards into phantoms, into memories, and we breathe their scents, their lives, but breathing this putrid stench, this gaseous mass of immolated flesh requires too much pain. We cough and hack, heave with emphysema. We die in the arms of every love, every moment, we ever have. This world becomes our iron lung, prolonging our lives by pressing out our breath like a torturer's device, forcing us to breathe one more time.

Ari turns the light on in her room. In a flash, a scorching moment, her bed comes into view, pressed into the corner, below the window, piled high with colorful blankets and thick pillows, a final resting place, a plush coffin. She turns to face Andrew, slides her hands up his arms, his back, pulls herself into him, feels her body compress against his, rubs her cheek against his shoulder, smells his neck, his pheromones, then sadly presses her lips to his. He responds with a vampiric longing, a full expression of his emptiness as he tries to breathe her soul into his body, to suck himself back into existence with another's life.

They move over to the bed, slowly undress one another, each carefully removing the other's clothes, passionately caressing the exposed layers of skin, pressing their fingers into the other's flesh, watching the blood disappear beneath the dermis and return in a rush of pigment. The light exposes their different colors, brown and white, divided but fading into one another. Naked, they curl into the other's alcoves, a head resting on a shoulder, a leg entwined with a leg, the yin and yang, light and dark, opposing energies completing a whole in the ceremonial circumference of the bed. Let me sprinkle salt around this circle, keep us safe from the spirits we conjure, the demons of lust and life, loneliness and love, sadness and strife, appearing on the periphery of our amorous vision.

"Will you hold me for a moment? I never needed so bad for someone to hold me."

Their hips slide together, Siamese twins at the waist, a fetal birth, the mother with her umbilical child sobbing at his first hint of light. They glide like a two headed snake. The pulse is slow, the rhythm soft. The blankets above them slip off, trickle down to the floor. One body keeps the other warm. The yin and yang vibrates with energy, positive and negative, a give and take to merge the competing forces into one. A kiss on trembling lips, a hand on a shuddering breast, stomachs pumping in time with the other's breath.

Eyes closed. Darkness. On the tide of wine, the world recedes back to another day, another time, a dream of another body here beneath me. Let me feel her in you. Let me feel you in her. This isn't the room I wanted to be in. I wanted to be on the other side of that wall, to sleep a dream of death on the other side of that wall. This room is so close, so tight, red *and* white. I need to feel you in my coffin here tonight, to decompose with you tonight, to slough off my skin in a metamorphosis tonight.

I'm here, hiding, banished by the sanctity of ritual. Can you see my eyes sparkle with tears? Can you hear my lungs shudder with sobs? Can't you see me? Can't you hear me? I'm here, inside your mind. I'm Beatrice, Dido, Isolt, Juliet, Cleopatra, every woman, everything. I scream. I writhe like you, my pain in tune to your ecstasy. I am the form, your albatross, your snake, idolized by you, my limbless body nailed to the cross, the spirit of your hermaphrodite, banished from the heaven of earth, burned beyond recognition, buried alive, my bones gnawed upon by worms, suffering for your sins, imprisoned by your love in a world of demons, Mary Magdalene, raped and tortured, forced by deprivation and desolation to be one, forever alone, among flitting shades of many. The world has no time for love. Don't you still believe in me? Why have you forsaken me?

Oh, Michelle...

"What's up, man. I didn't think you'd make it out here.

Bed-Stuy's a different world from Greenpoint. I'll tell you that. Well, come on in," Gabriel says. Beneath his brown tee shirt, his dirty thermal undershirt has holes in the elbows. His jeans have holes in the knees. He's barefoot. He runs his hand through his hair and moves out of the doorway so that Andrew can squeeze into the apartment.

Gabriel's place makes Andrew's own apartment appear spacious and clean. A ratty old couch, a thrift store chair. The grime on the walls seems three feet thick, a catacomb. Let's roll away the stone and watch Jesus rise again. "You think about it. There's really only a handful of blocks in between. You can drive it in like five or ten minutes. In L.A., it's hardly even a neighborhood, but here, it's a whole fucking world, man. A whole fucking world." Gabriel takes a puff off his cigarette. He exhales slowly as he stares into Andrew's eyes. The smoke obscures his face. Andrew looks away.

"You from L.A.?"

"Born and raised in the city of angels. Moved to New York at eighteen. My friends went to college, and I came here. This city's been my education. And Lord, I've paid for it."

"I've never really been out west."

"You should try it. It's a lot like heaven."

"Why'd you leave, then?"

"I prefer hell. You've read Blake, right? That's what fallen angels always say. Heaven has too much fucking sun."

"How long you been in New York?"

"Seven years now."

"Michelle lived here almost that long."

"Who?"

"Nothing."

"Have a seat," Gabriel says. He picks some tee shirts up

off the chair, throws them into his bedroom, and Andrew sits down. There's a hole in the fabric below where Andrew puts his hand on the armrest. The stuffing spills out. The fabric is dark brown and dirty. The stuffing is orange, foamy, and white. It's a tree bleeding leaves. In the city, you see nature everywhere. However fucked up it may be.

"I'm glad you came by," Gabriel says. "When Carey told me what you wanted, it all made sense. I knew I could see a kindred soul in you. Hold on a second, let me go grab the shit, and then we'll smoke a bowl."

Gabriel disappears into his room. Andrew takes the opportunity to soak in his surroundings. Gabriel's abode is a cave, dark and dank. Rats live here; Andrew is certain of it. It's a subway tunnel without the graffiti. Gabriel could be one of the mole people – his skin faded albino, his eyes glowing red from being sequestered away from the sun. A lab rat, the maker's experiment. He steps into the light and ignites on sight, the morning star.

"So I'm calling it a quarter, but I'm sure it's more. I didn't weigh it out. Anyways, what I'm hooking you up with is from my private stash. I never sell it to anybody, but you look like you could use it. This whole city could use it, but I guess I'm a little selfish. It's a sin, but what the fuck do I care. Sin doesn't exist."

"How much is it?"

"I'll give you the bag for fifty. I get it practically for free, but I gotta turn a profit. That's the way of the world, and it's better than turning tricks, whether it's on the floor at a massage parlor, on the floor of the stock exchange, or anywhere in between. If you aren't part of the solution, you're part of the problem."

Andrew fishes into his pocket, pulls out his wallet, counts out three bills, and extends them towards Gabriel. The exchange is made, barter and trade, alienated labor, a mediated experience. Gabriel slides the bills, loose, into his pocket. Andrew sets the bag on his lap. It's fat and green. Nature once again. The color of money.

"Now to real business. That's just pleasure. Let's light that bowl. I'll let you try a taste of what you just bought."

"Sounds good to me."

Gabriel takes his time packing the bowl. His nicotine stained fingers work expertly, breaking apart and picking through the weed, stuffing it into the pipe, packing it tight, all bud, all leaves, saving the stems, no seeds. "You want the first hit?" Gabriel asks.

"Why not." The marijuana tastes fresh and green, no hints of soap, no residue of dirt. It's a summer field, a song of innocence, the scent of nature, the earth, of trees and brooks. Pure as a virgin forest. A hint of pine and oak, the Deep South, New England. Snow, steam, memories, and dreams. *This is more than I can handle.*

I feel the ghosts closing in on me. Like Gabriel's face behind exhaled smoke, their agonized grimaces obscure my vision. Their claws caress my neck, tickle the hairs at the base of my scalp. Their cold thumbs press into my jugular. I can't breathe! What have I done? I've betrayed my love. Ari... Brown and beautiful. Asian and abstract. Black and pointed, your nipples harden beneath my fingertips. Your breasts tremble beneath my palms. I feel a shiver in your heartbeat. My own breathing stops. Your thighs quiver to the touch. Your insides melt as your legs embrace my waist. Inside each other's bodies, inside each other's minds, we're so close. Enraptured with the same pain, enfolded by the same empty, infinite space, entombed alive together like an ancient king and queen, we speak in silent moans and heaves. We're haunted by the same images. The same phantom hides around our different corners, admonishing us for being alive while she's died. Every night, she glares at me out of the white lights from the vacant work site outside my window. So I stay with you instead, where she screams at me from every picture frame, from every darkened corner, from the doorway to the bedroom I wanted so badly to spend my life and death in, from every tortured memory of my life before that day. The Empire State Building, tall and statuesque, New York's surviving monument to itself, is a blight upon my vision, a curse upon my head, a torment to my lonely thoughts, a memory that I never want to have again. Its stark loneliness, powerful and drab, all that's left of my world, my dreams, is the black spire piercing my bleeding heart.

"How you doin' over there?"

Andrew nods.

"Good shit, huh?"

Again, Andrew nods.

Gabriel stands up and walks over to the boombox in the corner. There's a stack of CDs beside it. He bends down, picks one up…

"You mind putting on that Wu-Tang, man? I haven't heard it in forever," Andrew says. "A friend of mine in college stole my copy, and it would be nice to do a tour of my memories. It's so hard to remember me these days. Everything's so different now. I think I'm ready to enter the 36 chambers."

"I was gonna put something else on, but I could deal with the tiger style. I already opened the first chamber for you. Only thirty-five more to go."

"Just like Blake."

Gabriel tilts his head to the side, creases his eyes. "Right," he says hesitantly.

"You know Allen Ginsberg realized it was his destiny to write poetry when he was lying naked in his apartment uptown one day, and he heard William Blake's voice?"

"Never heard that story before, but if Blake's spirit is anywhere, I'm sure it's tripping around New York City. There's a lot of spirits tripping around this city. Keep an eye out for them. I've met a few myself."

"Supposed to be true, but I'll bet he was on a lot of

drugs."

"Hey man, just cuz somebody's on drugs doesn't mean that what happens to them isn't real. If it did, my whole life would be a fantasy."

"Like with Manson…"

"What?"

"Just thinking about a conversation Carey and I had once." Andrew frowns. His throat closes up. "On September 10th to be precise." He leans back in the chair. He bunches his eyebrows together. His gaze goes blank. His stare turns inward. Memories gather storm clouds across his face. *I still remember the rain: nature vainly flailing, beating its straw-filled brains out against worlds, walls, of concrete like a rat, man, trapped, going mad, in a maze. And then, POW! Batman, everything changed.*

Gabriel pops the CD out of its case, opens the lid on the boombox, and drops the disc in. He hits play and majestically steps away.

The beats kick in. A four count of bass, dissolving on the one, building back up on the next measure. Slow and deliberate, sounds layer one overtop the other. A high snare pops on the count, snapping music, ticking time to the tick of the high hat, drowning out the deep bass subliminally building in the background, hitting on the rhythm, pounding in the recesses of the cavity of your skull.

The music is internal. Its sounds travel through the world, but they only exist inside your mind. A tree falling alone in the woods is silent. It turns Andrew's thoughts back onto its source, his own straw-filled brain. Set a spark to the livestock feed and watch your thoughts combust spontaneously.

As he walks, Gabriel hunches his shoulders and swings his long arms around in time to the beat, a primitive dance, a sensation from the dawn of man reiterated in tribal ceremonies, the foundation for the drawing of the circles, the chambers, that enclose the world, the spheres. The beat stops. Gabriel stops and straightens. In the middle of the tiny room, he closes his eyes, tilts his head back to stare at the paint peeling on the ceiling – the building that cuts him off from heaven – and spreads his arms in mimicry of the crucifixion.

On the upbeat, Gabriel nods his head back to the rhythm. He plops down on his couch. "You ever listen to the beats on this album, man? I swear the RZA's a fucking genius. Miles Davis reincarnated, even though Miles wasn't dead when the RZA was born. Maybe he breathed his soul out of his body, and it flew across the island to land in Shaolin Land, turning a kid who spent too much time in the Killah Hill projects into the RZA, a razor."

"A sentence balances on a razor."

"What?"

"I used to think about that when I wrote poetry, that a verb was balanced on the tip of a razor, that the subject and the object dangled off both sides, swinging like a pendulum, tipping from one side to the other, hanging above you like you're trapped in the pit, and you want to keep the balance perfect so you don't get split in half. If you use it right, touch a sentence to your veins, writing becomes the perfect metaphor for suicide."

"Now, that's fucking wild, man."

"If you just listen to the rhythms, to the snaps and the bass, Wu-Tang sounds like gospel music."

"Yeah, they do. I never noticed that before. The new gospel, baby. The sounds of repression, of souls tortured in the wastelands of America. The true Hebrews, slaving to build the pyramids on the backs of dollar bills. Now, embalming motherfuckers with their minds, turning zombies into living, breathing mummies. The RZArector.

Wu-Tang *is* the killer bees on the swarm, buzzing all through your mind, pulling your brains out through your nose, popping your dead eyes back open, telling reality in stories that most people would never read. The spirit of the blues. Take a look at this neighborhood surrounding you, baby. It's the Brooklyn Zoo, the Ol' Dirty Bastard's home."

"O.D.B. sounds like insanity to me. His meter's off, his rhymes come from out of nowhere. His flow is non-existent, but somehow he pulls it all off. Sometimes his style hurts my brain."

"That's what I'm saying. You think anybody can really stay sane in Brooklyn, staring at Manhattan's silver glow across the river? No matter how damaged the skyline might be, it's still insurmountable. O.D.B. encapsulates that sensation. He's the Osiris, man."

"The risen god of the dead, the basis for the myth of Jesus."

"Big Baby Jesus. Don't you forget it."

Gabriel smiles, his eyes light with madness. "Here he comes. Bzzzzzz…" He sticks his arm straight out, dangles his fingers into the air. With his fingertips, he plays on the invisible insect keys of a piano to the rhythm of his rattling teeth.

In the midst of the bastard flow, a river over the gravel of his voice, I think I can see the ghosts, like bugs, crawling across the abandoned carcass of this decomposing room — black dots skipping across the walls, roaches slipping along the floorboards. Killer bees from my brain infect the pictures I see, we all see, in the world outside of me. Osiris, Big Baby Jesus, will judge me, will determine if my death is fit to live. Before I meet that Ol' Dirty Bastard in the Brooklyn Zoo, teach me the secrets, the riddles and rhymes, the answers to the questions that He will pose to me as He cries frozen tears from His black hole in the center of this world, chewing on a feast, the brains, the guts, of Brutus and Judas. Jesus… What was the secret that Lucifer revealed to Eve? They're inscribed as hieroglyphs in the correspondences that paint the world that I'm nothing more than a piece of. I'm a figure on the pyramid walls, too. Flat. Two-dimensional. There's a duality to everything. Gabriel, what are you introducing me to? Trying to translate the pictographs, to understand The Book of the Dead, I'm lost inside your burial chamber (I remember Michael's cell), my head, blindly clawing at the walls to get in, get out, my fingers bleed along with my soul, so I can feel my way towards a soft beacon of sunlight beyond this ancient tomb. It's dark as death. In here, I'm a grave robber cursed for the riches I've spent my years trying to steal. I'll write a screenplay – That's where the money is. How much do I pay for a shitty apartment in this city? Six fifty a month. What would a Palestinian refugee do with ten percent of that? The white devil, just like you, Gabriel. Michael. Ziggy Stardust and the Lady. You look so similar to me, both as beautiful as a woman, smelling like me, feeling like me, the sensations of the same that Carey's attracted to. What are you attracted to, if anything, Gabriel? I watch you smile to the rhythms of the rhymes in the music. Your grin climbs up your crooked cheeks and dies below the slight bags beneath your sunken, bloodshot eyes. So green. So deep. Sometimes, you look like you've seen everything, but you see nothing. How does your hieroglyph read? Your hair sticks straight up from dirt and grime. Mine does the same (I see myself reflected in the double glass doors of a bank – Chase Manhattan). A mirror to the future. A rooster – cock-a-doodle-do. Ari's so soft. Her skin collapses beneath my fingertips – a body below the surface. Driving me insane with its loving differences, her scent swirls in my brain. Gabriel, you look like bones and gristle, like me, no give to the touch, the scents of sweat and desire. Is it important to feel what a woman feels? The weed twists around in my brain, spinning my view upside down. Suddenly, I see the world, play the game, backwards. God, like life, is the writer. The devil is death, the director making sure we see God's words right. Or is it the other way around?

"Pay attention now. The killer bees are loose. Tell me it

doesn't sound like they've returned from the land of the dead, and they're coming straight after you. It's a children's story, baby. Every angel chooses to fall. It's the only way they can come back to life. Listen to the beats with your mind. They're opening another chamber, showing you what they saw in the underworld. Doing battle with the yin and the yang... Beyond good and evil, if you will. Bzzzzzz..." With his fingertips, Gabriel still strokes the keys to his non-existent piano. Flies on strings buzz at the end of his reach. Silently, the butterflies scream. He plays the music, taps the beat of the spheres. It's an incantation, a ritual, a hex on the world around him. It buzzes in Andrew's mind. Gabriel runs his other hand through his hair. He re-adjusts his brain and his rooster-du. He shifts around in his seat, brings one leg underneath. His body twists like a contortionist's, a serpent's, long and lean, ready to infest Cleopatra's flesh. Are those fangs I see? The music is a swarm. It fizzles above the beats. It's the sound of the world dissolving, rushing like a conch-song through Andrew's ears. In the background, a voice speaks, calls off the hierarchy, levels of choirs, of a whole ghetto's worth of cherubs and archangels, thrones, powers, and dominations. The Wu-Tang Clan. They have names as shrouded and varied in meanings as an entire cosmos of other-worldly beings. It's a call to arms, the declaration of independence of the mythos for the future world.

Suddenly, Andrew starts in his seat. "So the projects represent death?"

"The projects don't represent anything, man. Life isn't a book. Unfortunately, they simply are, but why don't you tell me?"

"I don't know, man. I was just thinking..."

"What?"

"Where did the Wu-Tang Clan get their names? It

reminds me of a shaman, a spiritual experience, where a man discovers the name of his soul. Like with tribal people, entering the cave – a physical symbol of the womb, simultaneously the tomb – finding God in your suffering and loneliness, your death, and then rebirth. Is that what happens in the projects? Is it something akin to schizophrenia, a rock n roll suicide? The devolution, forced to find a name that describes yourself as you are in reality, not as what your parents wanted you to be? Is there a necessity to the starving artist? As far as I know, I've always just been Andrew Christian. Never even contemplated using a pen name."

"This world's enough to make anyone schizophrenic, but I know my name, man. Gabriel Burns. Stew on the significance of that for a little while."

"I don't think I know my name. Andrew doesn't mean anything to me anymore, and I don't think Christian is an adequate description of my world. Maybe it is... Everything I defined myself as is gone. I was a piece of this country, this lunatic asylum that so many stare at, aghast. The insane never realize the symptoms of their own illness, but I don't want to be crazy anymore. I want to be sane, to be this country's psychologist. Listen to the world and make sense out of all this, and shit, man, I don't know what I'll do with it, but I want to make sure that nobody anywhere ever has to live through something like 9/11 again. I want to isolate the causes and cut them out like cancer."

"People are living through shit like 9/11 every day. Maybe not on such a grand scale, but it's always there. It just doesn't happen to middle and upper class Americans. That's the difference."

Andrew straightens in his seat. Hurriedly, he runs his hand down his face. "Like the Ghostface Killah," he says.

"I never noticed the significance of that name. I always thought he was the ghost. You know, like he killed and then disappeared, but maybe he's just the killer, and I'm the ghost face. You're the ghost face. All white people are the ghost face."

"It's possible, man. I wouldn't mind killing white people – living in the suburbs, cooked up in a bottle by Yakub, driving safely into the ghetto for drugs and prostitutes. An abomination, driven by money, power, and conquest. Our families are hardly human if you ask me."

"But is anybody else any different? I don't think it's a question of race. It's something about being human, about being an animal with a brain. Humanity is the abomination, goddamn plastic animals slaughtering one another for ideas, for fun, for land and money. Wu-Tang doesn't paint a pretty picture of culture at all."

"But it's real. It's the blues, and until white devils pay attention to what the fuck they're saying and stop thinking that cruising through the suburbs blasting this shit and pretending like they have any fucking clue what it really means to be a black man in the ghetto, it's never going to change. Shit, they're talking about bringing out the fucking guillotine, and every soccer mom's shouting, 'Let them eat cake.' Me and you are the enemy."

"I don't want to be the enemy anymore."

"I don't know if there's anything you can do about it. Face it. You're white."

"And what about you? Are you the enemy? Living out here in Bed-Stuy, in this apartment, not working, selling drugs?"

"I do what I can, and pray that when the revolution finally comes I go quickly. Maybe I'll get nabbed right off the bat and strung up from one of the streetlights outside my apartment. A good, old fashioned lynching. No matter how I live, I can't change the color of my skin."

"There's never going to be a revolution."

"What happened to the Trade Center, brother? Take a look outside your fucking window some night."

Gabriel's words buzz through Andrew's brain, lose their abdomens as acupuncture pins in the pressure points of his soul. *I look outside my window every goddamn night. White lights... Michelle... The sun shining, burning through my room, igniting my bed, torching my clothes. I never want to see the sun again. This world crawls beneath my skin like the worms in my tomb. This life stings inside my skull like a thousand needles from killer bees. The Ghost Face Killah, Ol' Dirty Bastard, you torture me. I never meant to step up to you. Sitting here with Gabriel, I know I'm the devil. The straight, white male. Ziggy Stardust opened the world up to me, slammed it shut on my fingertips. Bzzzzzz... Gabriel plays his keys. Like the devil, flies on strings. A twisted mirror. Will this ever end? What will I have to face in death? Retribution for my sins of omission? The Method Man heating hangers up on the stove, jamming screwdrivers through my tongue? Raekwon "The Chef", cooking me up and feeding me to the rest of the Clan? U-God chops through my head. The Rebel INS pulls the guillotine up for my neck. The RZA holds me in place, and the Genius gives the order to let it fall.* Gunshots blast across the walls of the room, echo through the tiny chamber. "What the fuck was that?"

Gabriel explodes with machine gun laughter. "It's the CD, man, a moment of the urban landscape captured on tape. Relax. You sure you're all right?"

"Yeah." Andrew runs his hands down his face. "I should probably get back home, though. Thanks."

Back outside, alive again on the streets, Bed-Stuy infects his senses. How does a family live here? There's a burned out building on the corner, a boarded up store across the street. The apartments loom, dark and decrepit with bars over broken windows. Razor wire encases a vacant lot. The air is noxious, contagious, thick and heavy with fumes. The sky itself seems sad. The street scene looks, forever, like Andrew feels – alone, frightened, scared, beaten, whipped. It's his body flipped inside out. His emotions painted across the world's canvas. Tortured on the outside, empty on the inside. A group of youths, in du-rags, strut down the sidewalk, b-boy limps in place. They're talking loudly and gesticulating with their hands. Even without any beats behind them, the rhythms of their words, their speech patterns, sound like the raps Andrew just listened to. As they near him, Andrew presses himself against the wall of Gabriel's building. They laugh at him, shaking their heads as they go past. His pocket bulges with weed. He's paranoid. Stoned, he waits for the Ol' Dirty Bastard to pop around from any corner. Like the devil at the crossroads, a smile stretching across his angry face as he spits his words, he makes a deal with Andrew and introduces him to his fate. *Meet Mr. Meth, he'll be your jailer for the night…* Naked and vulnerable, never before so aware of the color of his skin, Andrew creeps along the street towards Bedford Avenue. A lone black face peers out of a dark window.

At a corner, Andrew pauses. His jaw drops. He blinks. *How come I didn't notice that on the way down here?*

On the side of a building, across the dusky, red façade, coloring the bricks, a mural is painted. The spray paint is now coated with a layer of grime, but it's still visibly the face of a young, black man. A golden halo rests above his head. The blue sky, dotted with clouds, expands behind him. All around him, tiny angels, clothed in white, with white wings and black faces and arms, fly. Beneath his serious, cherubic gaze, a golden banner reads in black: *Though your years were short, may you sleep with the angels, Khalid – 1977-1995.*

The ghosts of New York City live everywhere.

"You're the same age as me," Andrew whispers to the empty streets. The city nods and silently groans in response. Andrew steps forward. The city steps along with him. The world is so heavy. From outer space, thousands of pounds of pressure press onto his shoulders, forcing him into the earth, burying him in the fault line beneath the city. He stumbles under the weight. "When I graduated from high school, with college opening up before me, you died." Andrew presses his fingers against the paint. He points right into Khalid's fragile forehead. His hand trembles. Life courses, eternal, through the portrait. The universal mind flows in through his fingertips. It must be something like what Michelle sensed as she lay at the foot of the Twin Towers. He feels the pain that went into this piece, the loss that tore through somebody's stomach, that inspired that person to take this image out of his mind and give it back to the world.

He sees Khalid, 18 years old, lying on the street at this corner. A friend holds his trembling head in his lap and fights back tears. This is a boy who never cries. Blood gushes out of bullet wounds in Khalid's chest, soaks his tee shirt, and spills into the gutters. It dribbles along with the sewage. Spittle gathers at Khalid's lips as he tries to recite his last words. He points a weak finger at heaven. His eyes glaze over. His pupils dilate. Watching the whole thing, his mother, crying into her hands, stands on the stoop of one of the buildings across the street. It's summertime. "I'm so sorry," Andrew says. "I'm so sorry."

IV.
The Wolves Can Have Me

New Jersey is Gibraltar. Pass through the Lincoln Tunnel, below the Hudson River's rushing waters, through the Pillars of Hercules where the stonework, arching over a cavern cut out of the earth's flesh, is still draped in a commemorative red, white, and blue flag reminding everybody of the crypt they are about to enter. Manhattan is a graveyard. Necropolis. Where the hermaphrodite used to stand, the skull has been ripped open, the brain exposed. Poke and prod its sticky mush like the experiment that it is. Find out what makes this all tick like a time bomb. Blocking the soul, writhing buildings rip into the bleeding, tearing sky hanging heavy and low, crying across the man-made horizon. Below – Pandemonium. Bodies roll overtop one another. There's not enough room inside the beast's excremental cavities for all of the lost souls. Bloodshot eyes glazed over, zombies meander from one death to the other. Times Square is the main target. Feel it in the late fall air. The momentary comradery of the weeks following 9/11 is gone. The shields that keep New Yorkers in their place are up at full throttle. The space between bodies is cold and terrifying, shocking to the touch. It hurts to be alone. Paranoia and anxiety are the main neuroses. Usually cool

New Yorkers jump at unexpected noises. Hipsters still can't believe their eyes. The slightest movement, slightest motion could always mean sudden death. Better to be frozen than to be in the wrong place at the wrong time. Like in Times Square, the bustling heart of capitalism, the focal point around which the rest of the world spins, an oasis, a mirage in the midst of this vast island desert of buildings deserted by life, ten million dead cells being expelled into this sphincter by the taxi cab and subway intestines, now the terrorist's chopping block where wealthy America sticks its neck into the guillotine's wooden hole. Arms tied behind the back, the throat rests on the chopping block, a cow with bovine eyes waiting for snipers to stick their guns out of windows and buildings as pipe bombs explode in the trashcans to cover 42nd Street and Broadway in body parts and filth. The blade rises up, up, up... Go! Swoosh. Thwack. We're done. Eyes wide, transfixed, transmogrified, the beast's many heads roll into the basket.

In the midst of it all, Andrew makes his way to the Chase-Manhattan Bank at the corner of the crossroads in Times Square. Chase the American dream born of flesh and jealousy, greed and oblivion, the images blasted across the world from the other coast, the heaven of swimming pools and sunshine and palm trees, the hell of ghettoes and guns and drugs, Hollywood, Los Angeles, the City of Angels, the city that the nightmare of manifest destiny, of chasing Manhattan, created.

As Andrew steps beneath the spinning red, white, and blue sign, a ring sings out from his slacks' pocket. The tone is almost lost in the street's hustle and bustle, but at the edge of hearing, it exists, an electronic beacon of familiarity, the lithe sound of companionship. Like the rest of the world, it means nothing. It's never the call that Andrew wants to get, the number that would still register as #1 on his digital display, a number that melted into the hands of its owner, that became one with her flesh, the same day that she entered the hermaphrodite. Andrew stops, reaches into his pocket, and pulls out his phone. In the cold, he flips it open and holds it to his ear. "Hello?" he says.

"Yeah, is Charlie there?"

"Sorry, you got the wrong number."

"What?"

"You got the wrong number. Charlie's my friend. This is my cell phone. I'm Andrew. Did he give you this number?"

"No. I – I don't think so. Sorry."

The other end clicks. Andrew shakes his head, folds up the phone, and puts it back in his pocket. He rubs his hands together and breathes warmth onto them. There's a tug on the slackened, bluesy tuning of his heart strings as he realizes that in the very back of his mind, he still hopes that every buzz of his phone might be Michelle calling to say that she's okay, that she had to sort some things out after everything she was a witness to on September 11th. She watched a man burn to death before her eyes. Black ash and soot, he crumbled, crumpled to his knees, rolled on the floor, pieces of his melting flesh imbedding in the carpet, and then, like an angel, she ran through the smoke, oblivious to the flames licking at her arms, her heels, everything except her face. She's been in the hospital, receiving treatment for fractures and mild burns, but she's okay now. She'll see him soon. Never mind about Ari, she'll see him soon.

In the bank's glass double doors, Andrew's own image is reflected. He's shocked to see how much, at a glance, he resembles a smaller version of Gabriel. With his hair sticking straight up and his sunken, bony cheeks, he could almost be Carey's friend's little brother. He shakes his head.

A puff of his breath disappears in the cool, not yet cold, air. If anything, that's not true. He's nothing like Gabriel, no matter what the latter may think of the kindred quality to their souls. He's not Ziggy Stardust.

Through the glass doors and up the escalator, Andrew clutches his paycheck in his sweaty palm. The moistened edges crumple beneath his fingers. This is the second half of his rent, the most important check of the month. He stands patiently at the end of the line. Stretching in front of him, coiling through the winding tape like spectators at a crime scene, glancing every which way, picking their ears and wiping their brows, plastic animals all, is a seemingly endless array of suits and skirts. Above the tellers' heads, like the subtext of the world, subtitles in Esperanto, the electronic board delivers its messages. Slowly, though not so slowly that it bothers him, Andrew snakes through the line.

He's taken to smoking pot every night, and it now affects his days. The world comes through in layers of cosmic jive. In front of him, he sees a vision of a woman who is a man. She's wearing a skirt and heels, but her features are too sharp, her legs too wiry, her arms too veined and defined. Her blonde hair is bleached and harsh, and he thinks he sees a shadow of an Adam's apple beneath her chin, but it might be a reflection, a dark twisting of the light. There's another man, a few people behind him, who Andrew can't fathom as either black or white. With every shift of the line, his race changes. His features are African, but his skin appears pasty red. Ahead of it all, beyond the ticker tape end, St. Peter sits behind bulletproof glass and takes your money at the pearly gates. He converts the cash into electronic symbols, and your money no longer exists. Without writing or the Twin Towers or Michelle, marijuana is the only thing that makes life beautiful. Andrew remembers the screenplay he wanted to write. The question was always – *How, in this day and age, could anybody still rob a bank?* There was a symbol there, an importance beneath his words, an idea at the edge of his consciousness, nothing tangible or defined like the man-woman's arms, but soft like Ari's, like Michelle's, like the white black man's features, something to explore and understand. Like the rest of the city, the rest of his life, it was all metaphor. Now, the metaphor is real. The lunch rush line twists and turns, and always, aside from a few glances back at the white black man, Andrew keeps his eyes on the woman who is a man as they rush, headlong, to the end to turn something real, something tangible, into soft, malleable electricity. A seemingly infinite number of St. Peters, St. Marys conduct the bustling crowd into the afterlife.

Andrew is the next person in line. The man-woman argues with St. Peter. A happy man in slacks and a tie steps away and rushes back to the escalator leading down to the street. He's one of the elect, the chosen few. In English and Esperanto, the electronic sign speaks to Andrew. It tells him to go to the teller that the happy man just walked away from.

"How are you today, sir?" the teller asks. She has short blonde hair and too much make-up. She's pretty in a plastic sort of way, as pretty as a plastic animal, one who lacks the natural mountain air of the beast, can ever be.

"Yeah. I need to cash this," Andrew says. He slides the check and his check cashing card into the metal trough beneath the window.

Like a pig, the teller slops it up. She holds it close to her face and scrunches up her eyes. Her lips contort. She looks back at Andrew and frowns. "I'm sorry," she says quickly. She spits the check back into the trough. "I can't do that."

Andrew   twists   his   brow.   A   subtle   sign   of incomprehension drags across his lips and cheeks. "What?"

"I can't cash it. This account has a hold on it."

"A what?"

"A hold. We can't cash anything coming through on it."

"That doesn't make any sense. It's from my work. Look at it again." With the tips of his fingers, he slides the check back towards her.

The teller doesn't even look at it. "I know where it's from. I'm just telling you what I was told." Perturbation remakes the mold of her features.

"Can I deposit it?"

"No. You can't do that either."

A tremor passes from Andrew's head, across his face, through his body, into his feet, and out through the floor. With his sweaty palms, he picks the check back up. "Why not?"

"I just told you," she states very matter-of-factly. "This account has a hold on it."

"But if I banked with a different bank, I could deposit it then."

"We're not a different bank."

"This is my rent."

"I'm sorry," she says, but she doesn't really look like she is.

Andrew leans towards the glass. He wants to burst through, to crawl through the ventilation holes that help her breathe, to shatter the bulletproof window, and to grab her by the throat and throttle her until she gives him what he needs… At the teller's eye level, as if he could suffocate her, he presses the check against the air holes. "But this is my money. I worked for it. Is there anything I can do with this check?"

"Not until there's money in the account."

Incredulity explodes behind Andrew's eyes. He's

breathless. Over and over again, he runs his hands through his hair. Amid gasps, he heaves, "There's no money in the account?"

"That's why it has a hold on it. Look. Is there something else I can help you with? There's a line behind you."

Andrew glances back at where he came from. The white black man taps his foot at the entrance, patiently waits his turn to step forward and speak with the angels of mercy. Andrew's hand trembles. His gut burns raw. "No. I guess not," he says. His hand falls limply to his side, and he turns around. The man-woman has vanished, disappeared, turned into electric wind and escaped in a puff of violent violet smoke.

As slowly as he wound through the line, Andrew winds his way back to the escalator. He's no longer in a rush. If he can't get paid, should he even go back to work? As he walks, he stares at his feet. His dress shoes move languidly. The white floor disappears beneath the taps of his black feet. He shakes his head and runs his hands through his hair. It sticks up every which way. He's been electrocuted – a prisoner seated in the chair. Straps tied around his ankles and wrists hold him against his will in the seat. Circuits clamped in a cap to his brain conduct the current's flow. His eyes pop out of his skull. His teeth slam down on the bit. He needs his money. He needs to live.

He hits the escalator and glides back down to street level. His wet palm slips along the handrail. In the other hand, he holds his crumpled check, moistening its ink with sweat, but money never bleeds. He continues to shake his head. His intestines strangle his stomach.

On the street, with his feet firmly planted on concrete, the thousands of people – zombies with ties swirling about their necks, dresses billowing around their ankles –

meandering through the brisk air form the millions of molecules of dirt that fill his mouth and lungs to suffocate him as he's buried alive in his grave, New York, a plot of land purchased, now making him cold as the zombies searching for new lives to steal, new souls to place in the witch doctor's earthen jars, stumble across this, his final resting place. With his eyes wide, his automatic movements, Andrew's now a zombie, too, wandering sporadically, stop – start – try again, in circles outside the door to Chase-Manhattan.

With a finger tap on the side of his head, he takes off towards the south. Leaping in and out of the way of mindless bodies, he turns left at 42nd, passes an underground tunnel that leads into New York's subway guts. The sound of motion and life rumbles out of the earth. He blows past Bryant Park, a grassy green oasis of benches and trees, heaven in the city, a respite for the homeless and the white collar working class to come together, bordered by the majestic Library where, in front of the imposing stonework, the lions stand as stoic guards, protecting from the uninitiated, the dregs content in the park, the knowledge hidden in the depths of that building. At Fifth Avenue, he's caught by a light. He turns south again for a block. With the Library, the lions roar, proud and imposing behind him, he waits for the walk sign at 41st, crosses the street, and finds himself in front of a check cashing agency that he always noticed on his way to Heavenly Staffing's offices.

In the transparent façade of windows, a neon sign promises what Andrew needs: Checks Cashed. He reaches for the door handle.

"Yo, you got anything to give for Queensbridge Basketball?"

Andrew turns around to face the direction of the voice.

"What?"

"You got any money for Queensbridge Basketball?" a tall, black kid wearing a thick, puffy coat and shaking a tin can asks him.

"No. I don't."

"Maybe on the way out?"

"I don't think so," Andrew says. He turns around and opens the door.

The kid mumbles, "Fuckin' devil."

Inside the check cashing agency, a crowd of people stand around waiting for money. Mostly black, some Puerto Rican, peppered with poor whites more decrepit than any of the other customers. Unlike at the bank, where the patrons lined up in a perfect single file line and waited patiently for the electronic board to tell them when it was their turn to speak softly and smile at the tellers, the agency is anarchy. At one of the four grime smeared plexi-glass windows, a streaked smooth surface with no air holes for the animals' ventilation, in such sharp contrast to the immaculate sterility of Chase-Manhattan, a heavy-set young woman screams at one of the tellers who argues violently with her. The woman points at the counter, presumably her check, and screams that it's her money and no she doesn't have another I.D. They didn't give her a check-cashing card. The Latino guy behind her impatiently says to pick up her shit and get the hell out of there, people are in a hurry. I got business to do, she tells him. He shrugs and looks away. Andrew gets into the bunch behind a black youth whose hair is done up in corn rows that dangle down his neck. The tight braids pull at his scalp, separating his hair into perfectly spaced fields. The hair is thick and dark. Its slickness dances beneath the fluorescent lights. Its texture, the weaving, in and out, over and under, creates a landscape more intricate than anything Andrew could ever do with any portion of his body.

When Andrew finally reaches the bulletproof window, after jostling his way through the masses starving in the holds of New York's ark, the woman in the suffocating cage says lackadaisically, "Can I help you?" On display for all the animals to see, she repositions herself in the seat and taps her hands on the counter.

"Yeah, I need to cash this," Andrew says, and in perfect repetition of his earlier actions, in an environment that heaves and coughs as heavily and violently as Chase-Manhattan sighs and crosses its legs, he slides his check and card beneath the window.

The woman takes one look at the check, clicks her tongue, sticks her thick, heavily painted lips out, shakes her head, and says, "Can't do that."

"Why not?" Andrew nearly cries. He droops down. For support, he claws weakly at the counter.

"Last week, every single one of these checks bounced. Do you know how much money your company owes us?"

"I have no idea how much money they owe you. All I know is that I worked, and this is *my* money."

"You're gonna have to get it somewhere else..." and she shouts, "Next!"

"Wait, wait. Don't do that. I need your help."

"You *need* to talk to your employer... Next!"

I need to buy a fucking gun, come back here, shove it in between your pouting lips, down your wide open mouth, past your teeth, deep into your throat, and take every goddamn penny you're hiding in that drawer! "There's nothing you can do?"

"Nothing."

A tall guy, straight out of Bed-Stuy says in a rumbling, subway train voice, "Move your ass, homeboy, I got shit to do."

Trembling from confusion and rage, Andrew obeys. He

swipes up his worthless check. With shaking, sweating fingers, he pointlessly shoves it deep into his pocket, buries it beneath his change and keys. With his tie, the only tie, the only noose, in that room, flapping against his chest, he hurries out of the agency, through the zombies clawing at his bones, to hang himself.

The door closes behind him. He stops to think. He runs his rickety hand through his hair. He fumbles in his pocket for a cigarette, shoves it in between his lips, lights it, and leans into his reflection, tries to rest inside himself, against the agency's glass front.

The tall black kid rattles his tin can. He says gruffly, "Yo, you got anything for Queensbridge now?"

Andrew shakes his head. He hangs forward like he's descending into the concrete. His cigarette dangles limply from his fingertips. "No, man, I really don't. I don't even have anything to take care of myself. If I can't figure something out soon, I may not be living here next month."

The black kid purses his lips and turns away. He doesn't believe him, and he doesn't know what the hell he's babbling about.

Andrew's phone rings. He pulls it out of his pocket. "Hello?"

"Is Charlie there?"

"You just called me, man. I already *told* you, you've got the wrong number." Without waiting for a reply, he flips the phone closed. It snaps tight with an angry shutter. Quickly, he opens it back up, and dials a number.

"Heavenly Staffing, can I help you?"

"Yeah. Is Charlie there?"

"No, he's not here right now. I'll put you through to his voicemail."

"Don't bother. I'll call his cell." He presses end, dials memory #2, and hits send.

"*You got Charlie. Leave a message, and I'll call you back.*"

"Charlie, it's Andrew, man. Call me as soon as you can. I need to talk to you. Something's wrong with my check." He hangs up and runs both hands down his face. He leans deeper into his reflection. His soul is quaking. *Why is this happening to me, Michelle? Why is this happening to me?*

For once, Andrew isn't late. He's sitting at the bar they always meet at, staring at the spirits that Charlie usually contemplates as he waits on his tardy friend. The poster of bin Laden, the picture of the firemen at ground zero, and the message about the country's "heroes" are still in tact in their place. With his thick hands, the barkeep uses a bar mop to dry the inside of a wet glass. The red, white, and blue banner still graces the mirror at the other end of the establishment. Andrew snarls and shakes his head at it all. Draining the world's fangs of their poisons, injecting the venom into his brain, he reminds himself over and over again, *Nobody was saved.*

He takes a hearty sip of ale. Using the back of his hand, he wipes his mouth with a dead on purpose. He already can't make his rent. Why not spend what's left on alcohol? He looks at his blue eyes in the mirror – hollow and empty as the streets of Bed-Stuy, bleak and dead as the stony topography of Manhattan, as brimming with unbelief as Jesus's sweaty gaze as he hung on the cross, his hands tearing from his wrists, holes in his feet splitting his flesh, and he cried, "Eli, Eli, lama sabachthani!" Behind him, he catches a glimpse of Charlie coming in the bar. He turns on his stool.

Frazzled, isolated, unable to focus, Charlie scans the entire empty room before he notices Andrew sitting alone at the bar. In a business-like manner, he smoothes his shirt and tie, tries to present himself with some semblance of dignity. Never mind that his face is straw and his eyes are wet paper. He only needs a spark to spontaneously combust into tormenting, cold-burning flames.

He nods his head back and hurries over to Andrew. He takes off his overcoat and frantically sets it on the stool beside him. Rubbing his hands together, letting friction warm him (careful you don't explode), he sits down.

As cold as the black air outside, Andrew stares at his friend. With his gaze, he attempts to freeze him into place in the center of the world.

The bartender comes over. "Grey Goose on the rocks," Charlie says. He sounds tired. The bartender shows no interest in the order as he grabs a glass, stuffs it with ice, turns around, heads over to the rail, and begins to pour. Clear and fearsome, the liquor drains into the glass.

The bartender returns to Charlie and sets the glass in front of him. Charlie pays the man.

After his first sip, Charlie finally breaks the palpable, overwhelming silence. He shakes his head, exhales heavily, rubs his hand down his face, and says with hesitation, "How you doin', man? I've had one helluva day."

Vehemently, Andrew turns on his friend. "How am I *doin*? How do you *think* I'm doing? I can't make my fucking rent, man. Are you gonna tell me what the hell is going on or not?"

Andrew's brief monologue leaves him heaving and breathless. Like a drunkard's dream, the initial violence had been building since a little after noon that day.

Charlie smarts. In the tradition of the beta, he lowers his gaze away from his friend's. He whispers. "I'll help you out if you need me to."

"I don't want you to help me out. I want *my* money. The money I worked for."

With his eyes still averted, as he toys with the stability

of his glass, Charlie acknowledges, "I can't get you your money right now."

"Then why'd you tell me to stay at work today?"

"I said right now. We're gonna get this all cleared up as quickly as we can."

"What the fuck happened, man? Tell me what happened."

Charlie brings his shoulders up. Like a frightened turtle, he tries to bury his head in his neck. "I can't," he says.

"You gotta be fucking kidding me, man. I've known you since we were, what, four maybe five years old? I'm your oldest friend. Why the hell can't you tell me?"

"It's company policy. You're one of our temps…"

"But you know what happened."

Charlie nods belatedly, carefully.

"That's rich, man," Andrew says. He leans back in his seat and smiles angrily, a bit demoniacally. "You get me a job, I can't get paid, you tell me to go ahead and stay at work, you'll explain it all later, and now you won't tell me what happened just because of some sort of goddamn 'company policy'. That's fucking rich, man. Tell me, did you know about this 'company policy' before or after you called me back?"

"Before… Look, if it makes you feel any better, I can't get paid either. I don't know when I'll ever see a commissions check again. They've been holding them for almost a month, hoping this wouldn't happen."

"What do you mean, 'Hoping this wouldn't happen?'"

"I'm nearly broke, man. I'll help you out with your rent though if you need it. It's my fault. I know that. I know that, for you, for every other temp we have, this is all my fault," he fades away into a mumble. "It's all my fault." Charlie moves uncomfortably. His midriff has been sawed through. His stomach and his intestines lay in a pool at his feet. It pains him to be alive, to still feel.

Bringing his hands from his hairline to his chin, Andrew erases the hatred, the misunderstanding from his eyes and lips and replaces the raw emotions with an air of compassion. His tone is much calmer, more controlled (he places his hands carefully as if he's molding his own feelings into a more pleasant shape), as he says, "Just tell me what happened…"

"All right. I'll tell you, but you can't say a word about this to anybody, especially not the people you're working for. If wind of this gets back to the higher ups at Heavenly, then I'm going to lose my job… Although I may not have a job for much longer if things don't change."

"Don't worry, man. I won't tell a soul."

Charlie moves closer to his conspirator. He inhales through his nose, looks around to make sure the bar is still empty, that none of his coworkers have arrived to forget about this last, most horrible of days, exhales carefully, and whispers, "Now, you need to understand how a temp agency gets its money. We work off of loans from the bank. Every week, we present them with a list of the temps that we received timesheets for. I forget what the technical name for it is, but it's some kind of form that the accounting department puts together. It's a print out with a list of all the assignments and the hours that we expect to receive billing for. Then, the bank loans us the money until we can get the bills out to the clients and receive payment. That usually takes a few months. We have to process the timesheets, print up the bills, mail them, and wait for the client to get off his ass and cut us a check. That's why the loans are so important. It's the loans that keep us afloat, that allow us to cut the paychecks. Whenever a payment finally comes in, we turn a portion of it over to the bank to cover the loan. Because the payments come in at various times, the bank allows the loans to roll over, assuming that only if the company closed would we ever match up as even.

"This is how pretty much every temp agency works, and we've never had any problems with it.

"Anyways." Charlie takes a sip off his drink. "This is where we get to the part that you can never say again. Okay?"

Andrew nods.

"We lost a lot of clients on September 11th. Because of that, the bank got worried about our records. It's total corporate bull shit." Charlie glances away. He chuckles gravely. "In the midst of all this, at the moment of all this insanity... You know, buildings blowing up, temps being lost, televisions, telephones not working, the National Guard hanging out in sniper's nests on top of our skyscrapers, the fucking air force making hourly patrols over our city, the bank starts worrying about how all of this is going to affect their bottom line. They ask us to turn over all of our records. They justify it by saying that they need to see the figures for how much money they're going to lose because certain clients don't exist anymore." Charlie drains the crystal clear remnants of his vodka. He swirls the ice in the bottom of the glass, drinks the melting remains of watered down alcohol, and orders another one. Enthralled, Andrew pulls abstractly on his beer and his cigarette.

"I can understand where they're coming from," Charlie concedes. "I don't like it, but I can understand it. Shit, one of the first thoughts I had that day, and I haven't told anybody this (I'm scared to even admit it to myself), was, 'How much money am *I* going to lose?' Can you believe that? How fucking selfish am I? No more selfish than them. I wonder, how many Americans were thinking that on that day? It still irks me to no end." He shakes his head. "And because of that, they asked us to turn over our records." He takes a long sip of vodka.

"I don't know what the hell our CFO was thinking. He should have known they'd figure it all out, but I guess everybody in Heavenly's upper echelons assumed that the company didn't have a chance, and we needed to at least *attempt* the bluff. So the bank gets our records, and starts poring over them very carefully, with a fine toothed comb so to say, adding up figures, determining how many clients might simply have vanished in the effluvium. Over the course of all this, some worthy accountant, probably trying to better his station, brings a slight discrepancy to the bank's attention.

"He points out that the figures don't really add up, that the profits don't seem to be what they were reported to be. So the accountant starts toying with numbers. He pores over all of our old profit reports, and he discovers that if certain permanent placements are doubled up as temp placements, then the numbers that we had always reported as our weekly profits equal the numbers that we actually turned in. The bank approached us with this fact about a month ago. Our CFO was fired immediately." Charlie grins sadistically. "Somebody had to take the blame, and it couldn't be the executives or the owner. Even though, and they haven't admitted this yet, but I'm certain of it, they were the ones who ordered that the profits be reported in that manner. CFOs don't make things like that up. They're accountants. They want things to add up. But the padding allowed everybody to take the huge bonuses that we took over the course of the bull market. We didn't really earn that money. We simply stole it from the bank. As long as the stock market kept climbing to indeterminate heights, nobody ever assumed that there'd be a reason to scan the books so carefully. It's the same thing as Enron. But in the end, we needed a sacrifice. That's when I first found out about what we had been doing, when the CFO was let go, and that's the truth."

"I remember you saying something about that when it happened, but so much was going on that I didn't pay any attention to it."

"There's no reason to pay any attention to it unless you know *why* it happened. Heavenly scrounged up as much money as we could out of our various business accounts, but we've been borrowing so heavily against the bank for so long that there's no way we can cover the losses. The money's gone, spent on trips to Rome and London, on homes and cars. Last week, the bank finally canceled our loan. That's why all our checks bounced. No check cashing agency in the five boroughs will accept a promissory note from us. The finances have been turned over to the bank, which is determining what bills we will pay and what bills we won't. Of course, first we have to come up with a way to pay them back before any of our employees can be paid. We're trying to negotiate a new loan with a different bank, but who knows when that will finally come through. Our finances are in complete shambles." With an aura of utter defeat, Charlie turns away from his friend. With a heavy hand, he orders another drink.

Andrew is slack-jawed. He blinks a few times. His expression is illegible. "So basically, what you're saying is that people *knew* this was going to happen?"

Charlie nods slowly, precisely. "Not for certain, but they knew there was a possibility."

"They knew that my paycheck would bounce today, and they gave it to me anyway?"

Even though he doesn't want to, Charlie nods.

"Did you know?"

With great reluctance, as he waits for the bartender to

return with his drink, Charlie nods.

"How about this whole week, while I was working for money I can't get, did you know then?"

Charlie nods.

"And you didn't fucking tell me. Jesus, man, you're supposed to be my friend."

"Don't you understand, I couldn't tell you. Everything I just said, if that gets out, I'll lose my job. You're lucky I told you anything at all. I didn't have to, you know."

"No. You didn't have to." Andrew shakes his head. He orders another drink. As he waits, silent, he rubs his fingers along the slices of the grain in the wood on the bar. Like experiences, the lines form an impenetrable pattern. He admires the way his napkin, a crumpled ring, a disintegrating Venn diagram with no arithmetic words to intersect, with sets now incommensurate, sticks to the surface.

"I'm glad I told you, though," Charlie says. The third drink is working through his system. He sucks in his gut. In the mirror, he smoothes the skin on his neck. "It makes me feel a little better about everything. You know, the fact that I could let one of my temps in on what's happening. If only one good deed could counteract everything I've done wrong."

Bile leaks through Andrew's stomach. It rises through fissures into his throat. It escapes in his words' breath. "This wasn't about making you feel better," he says.

"I know that."

As soon as his next beer shows up, Andrew realizes that he no longer wants to be at this bar. The cleanliness, the sterility turn his stomach. Why do they always come here? This place has no life, no art. The dark wood accoutrements are too solid to conform to the fluidity of drinking. He no longer wants to share a drink with Charlie.

He wants to be alone in some place dark, some place ravaged, where women never go and the man on the stool beside him is using his last bits of change to buy the cheapest beer on the shelf. "Tell me something," he probes. "You said you aren't getting your commissions checks, but are you still getting paychecks?"

"I don't know," Charlie says. "Those checks draw on a different account. They're covered by profits, not by the loan. But I have no idea whether or not that account's been frozen by the bank," he adds hastily.

"Well, how can you cover my rent if you don't know whether or not you're getting paid?"

"I'm willing to take the chance. Like I said, I know this is my fault. You're my friend. I feel like it's my responsibility to help you out if I can."

"So you are gonna get paid."

Charlie slams his glass down on the bar. He buries his own Venn diagram. "Look, Andrew, I don't know. I want to help you out that's all. But if you keep talking like this, I may not feel like it much longer."

"I already said I don't need your help."

"You did when you first showed up in New York."

"A lot's changed since then."

Charlie looks at the ground. In a nervous manner, he rubs his hands across the bar, smoothes his napkin back out. "Yeah," he sadly agrees. "A lot's changed since then."

They finish their drinks in silence, not a word from one to the other. Each stares at his reflection in the mirror, contemplates the shade of his own eyes, the lines around his mouth and what each line means. Every crease, every wink and wrinkle is the remnant of something unfathomable seen. Events age people. If life were lived alone in a plastic bubble, without companionship, without stress or tragedy, we would still grow older, but we may never age. They each wonder over all the things they've lived through, and they think about this last disaster affecting them both differently. One near the top, distressed about his career, guilty for his complicity and complacency. The other close to the bottom, worried only about how he'll eat. Both affected by mightier men's tides. It erects a fence topped in razor wire between their age-old friendship. On either side is the wasteland.

"Well, I better get going, then," Andrew says as he finishes his beer. He stands up.

"Hold on," Charlie says. He fishes in his pocket and pulls out his checkbook. He pulls a pen from his coat and begins to write.

"Don't do that," Andrew says.

"I have to."

"No, you don't."

"You don't understand, man. It's for me, not you. I want to do something right for a change."

"All right. I'll take it, but I may not cash it."

"Just cash it, and pay me back when the new loan comes through." With a flourish for his signature, Charlie tears off the check and hands it to Andrew. "Look at it as my faith in my company," Charlie says even though the sentiment makes him ill. "Besides, I need you to go to work next week. I'm probably going to lose a lot of clients over this, and I don't have many more clients to lose." He shakes his head.

Andrew stares at the figure: $400.00. He sighs heavily. "Thanks," he says.

Charlie nods. "Are you gonna show up for work on Monday?"

"Yeah. I'll be there."

"Thanks, man. I owe you big time."

"Don't mention it."

"And I promise we *will* get you paid soon. Hopefully before the end of next week."

With a silent nod, Andrew walks away from Charlie, leaves his oldest friend drinking alone at the bar they always meet at, and as he does so, he thinks to himself, *Never trust a businessman.*

Monday night. Carey has to work. Andrew's all alone in the apartment. He could call Ari, but he doesn't feel like it. Sometimes you're more alone with somebody beside you. Sometimes, having the wrong person beside you is more painful than having nobody beside you. There's music to listen to, recorded artists to understand and speak with, lyrics, notes, and rhythms to make sense out of. He has a new album purchased from one of the Polish record stores on Manhattan Avenue. The owner, an older woman with only a minor comprehension of English, asked him, first in Polish and then, in response to his confused look, in broken English, if he was from Poland. British and French he'd responded. With a thick accent, she told him, "You look Polish." And he can't argue with her. Living in Greenpoint, he's realized that his coloring, his thinness, all speak of an Eastern European ancestry. It's nothing to be ashamed of. Poles understand suffering, their homeland the battleground for a thousand years of wars. The purchased album is *The White Album* by The Beatles. It's been years since he's listened to it, and he's certain that there's an emotion in Lennon's and McCartney's, in Harrison's and Starkey's phrases that can help him feel a little less adrift in all the madness surrounding him. The album was made at another tumultuous time in world history, but of course, what time in world history hasn't been tumultuous? It was only in the America of the nineties that a padded wall surrounding a middle-class country in a self-administered straight-jacket concocted of unfounded optimism and a compulsive focus upon financial security was erected to blind the ultra-sensitive citizenry to the rest of the globe's frothing and foaming, convulsions and seizures. As much as possible, Andrew wants to avoid his bedroom. He doesn't want to see the work lights. In his mind, they always burn as a bright reminder of the world's darkness. He's in the living room, reclining on the couch, toking on a bowl.

After a few hits (with every hit, his lungs open up more), he sets the bowl aside, leans forward, and presses play on the boombox across from the couch. Immediately, his world view is less mediated. He melts into the universal mind. From out of the speakers, the sound of an incoming airplane reminds him that, with his hammer and sickle, he's back in the U.S.S.R. With a squeal, the rhythmic guitars fade in, and Andrew collapses back into position – his head tilted back, his neck resting on the couch, his eyes focused on the cracks in the ceiling, his hands flat beside him, his stomach in constant turmoil. The distortion sounds thick. Even with the digital recording, the instruments contain the palpability of vinyl. Between the walls of his decrepit apartment, he's in London circa 1968. Trolls, en route to their respective hovels, march along the streets outside. Fairies flit in the dust circulating around their heads.

There's something magical about this album. An aura surrounds it. Once upon a midnight dreary, Andrew discussed it with Carey. Somewhere in the midst of this collection of voices and sounds is the skeleton key to the whole Helter Skelter theory. Like the face of New York forever marred, dipped in acid like the Joker's, for Andrew by the events of the past few months, Manson has taken a sickle and etched his scar into the happy history of this album. Ghosts haunt every object, every place, every human, everything. A usually melodious chord progression takes on an eerie presence when thought about what this music scalded into the Family's already twisted brains. Their theories and plans, on the tail of a shooting that added harmony to The Stones' *Sympathy for the Devil*, marked the end of the Sixties' revolution, and with it, a brand-new revolution was begun.

God and the devil have joined forces, become one and the same, Andrew remembers reading once was the foundation to everything Manson taught to the wandering, lost, gypsy members of his family. In order for Christ to return and save the world, we have to destroy Hollywood Babylon, Andrew remembers being something like what Manson, in the drug-addled recesses of his poverty-stricken mind, thought might be the final solution for peace. Charlie...

Maybe murder is the answer, Andrew thinks as he contemplates the men who press the buttons and pull the gears in the locomotive's engine room at Heavenly Staffing. *I'm flying off the track, struggling to hold onto your caboose.*

He envisions himself with a bandana for a mask and a six-shooter in his hand as he makes his way up and down the train's pathways; his spurs jingle-jangling. *Hand over your money and your jewelry,* he says to everybody until he reaches Charlie. There's a moment of recognition, and then, Andrew pulls the trigger. Blood sprays across the seats, splatters across the face of the woman beside his friend. She screams and leaps in place. *Can't have people recognizing me,* Andrew the Kid casually explains with a friendly tip of his ten-gallon hat to the other passengers. And then he starts in on his career again.

How could somebody rob the Chase-Manhattan Bank in Times Square? With a computer or a gun? Do you steal the cash or the electricity? The whole world is electricity.

Everything we see, everything we touch, everything we breathe, everything that we believe is solid or space, my arm, that boombox, these walls, the cash I need, Michelle alive or dead is nothing more than electrons, protons, neutrons, gluons spinning around the focal point at the center of the atom, the unmoved mover, much like the main character in a novel. At the moment of an atomic explosion, a vacuum is created at a point in space. Michelle was supposed to help me come up with the scheme. That was the plot, how life imitates art and art simultaneously imitates life. There's no such thing as art, only life.

(From a shadow in the corner, a figure takes shape and steps away from the wall (last night as he smoked pot, Andrew listened to Carey's copy of *The Wall* – the figure was here, then, too). Like it does every night as Andrew sits all alone in his head, soaking in the vibes of somebody else's emotions, it glides across the tiny room and sits down next to him on the couch. He can feel its presence there. He's no longer alone. A seed that was planted in his stomach has grown simultaneously, its stalk twisting and turning around the trunk that grew in the shadow's presence, as the seed that shot forth into the shadow's powerful, nectar-filled, life-producing, all-consuming plant. The shadow rests its amorphous hand on Andrew's knee. It dissolves into one with his flesh, passes through his dermis, spreads through his bloodstream, and nestles into the marrow of his bones. He swears he can feel it tormenting him there like cancer, the most painful of all kinds. He vomits bile into his bedpan. He runs his hands over the clothes that cover his invisible wounds. He closes his eyes.)

What did Lady Stardust reveal to me that night we were alone together in Michael's cell?

My world is gone, destroyed on September 11th, 2001 at 8:46 AM in a nuclear explosion. My body, my disintegrated bones and flesh, still lies, a shadow burned to the earthen sheets, in my bed. From memories, my soul, my eidos and form, is projected onto this plane. We're all dead. And with living memories, it's no different than being alive. I still need money I can't get. Even God is a capitalist. And that's the devil's revolution, the declaration that we're all equal, that the power acquired by owning the means of production, spiritual or physical, does not necessitate the right to determine Law. As our society moves closer and closer to the ideal, America becomes Lucifer's home, his last resort, his final solution. He is Coyote, and this was his land before it was our land. Here, on this continent, we're haunted by the devil. He ravaged the Jamestown colony. The Pilgrims discovered him and descended deeper into their puritanical religion. He flew loose, on wings as large and invisible as the heavens, in Salem, across the plains to Vegas and Hollywood, and many times, right here in Brooklyn. Everything is the devil. And New York is the unofficial capital of it all, the official capital of the world, home to the ruler of this world, Necropolis, Pandemonium, the New Jerusalem, on an island named in the ancient tongue of its natives, Manhattan, the seat of world politics, the U.N., with a ticker tape, stock market pulse that pumps capital throughout the globe. The rest of this city is a dream, the experience of aborted fetuses, lives determined unfit by the universal mind, in the belly of the great beast.

Where are you, Michelle?

(Beside you, inside of you.)

Like Paolo and Francesca, flitting shadows, formless souls float at the periphery of our understanding and vision, tormenting us, haunting us, leading those of us who have abandoned all hope through the many and varied gates of hell. Poetry is the spirit-guide. Love is death. Death is love. The songs on this album repeat over and over again a refrain of love, a revolution for the time, and all I want is to die, the revolution of my time. There's a knife in the kitchen drawer. I can feel its cold metal blade skim through the stringy mess of my veins. Warm blood drips freely down my arm. I catch it in my hand, my fingers grow stickier and stickier until my muscles go limp, and I'm with Michelle again, no more money problems, no more corporate officers' lies, no more memories of this city without my friend, no more work lights, no fear of death, maybe the World Trade Center will reappear there, adorned by trumpeting angels, miraculously bathed in reflections, shimmering like a golden mirage, on the other side. Maybe, on the other side, I can rediscover my skyline.

I'm bursting. My stomach throbs with starving aliens. Theses and feelings threaten to explode out of me, and my mouth is nailed shut, no way to express what hurts. I need a witch doctor with a scalpel to perform a caesarian section on these, my unborn ideas, children at war with me, with one another in my belly. Ziggy, tell me, will the Starman really come from beyond the realm of the fixed stars to save us all?

(The ghost stands up and walks to the window (with a tremor, Andrew feels his limbs lighten as she leaves his bloodstream). She tilts her head back and stares up at the darkening sky. As her gaze penetrates the heavens' spectrum, a tear drips down her cheek. There's nobody to make love to when you die. She bows her head to emptiness and turns back around. She sees Andrew sitting alone on the couch, his eyes closed, his face contorted as if he is, which he is, one with the source and product of her own vaporous emotions. She walks up to him. She crouches down. She reaches forward with her trembling fingers. She wants to feel his cheek, the warmth of his flesh, of human flesh, rather than simply to pass right through.

She sits down beside him again and rests her head on his shoulder. She feels nothing. Her invisible hair spills over his chest (Andrew feels its deathly coolness like a spike through his lungs. He gasps and repositions his shoulders.). How often she might have been able to spend an evening like this…)

In this world, throughout all of time (history is an illusion, a lie), humanity has waited, prayed for a god, a goddess, a man, a woman to open the gates of heaven or hell and lead us all into spiritual, earthly bliss. Come now, children of Ishmael, it is unto you that I speak. We are waiting for the giantess. Lady Stardust, I think you could be the one. Dis une prière pour Rimbaud et Verlaine et pour leur saison en enfer. Souviens-toi, dans las rues et les bordels de Paris, Jeanne Duval pleure. Elle meurt, de la maladie et de l'amour, de les fleurs du mal, avec elle amant, Baudelaire. Lilith, Eve, Joan La Pucelle, Mary Magdalene…

The devil is a woman. It's God who is necessarily evil. By the patriarchy, the logos, the word, our world is subverted, corrupted, ulcerated, turned wicked by deceit and inversion. It is the Catholic cross itself that is inverted. A rock has no up or down. When we play the game backwards, the beginning as the end, the end as the beginning, the hanged man dangles right side up. The devil is a man like me. Let us bring about the revelation, endeavor to complete the iron age of Kali, give live birth to the dark consort of Shiva, the simultaneous generator and destroyer. She appears with a hundred human heads dangling from a rope about her neck. Finish the age of quarrel; begin the reign of the antichrist. The devil is a beast of the field, unclean with a ten foot phallus and a cloven hoof. May Krishna, the lion-king, return to make love to his gopis. And the men all wonder what happened to their wives. They are in the wild, the wilderness receiving the pleasures that only Lucifer could teach to Eve. The Bacchae perform their own Dionysian symposium. Bacchus, alone, turns water into wine. The cherubs remove their fiery swords from the entrance to Eden. God and the devil are one and the same, the hermaphrodite, the circle enclosing the yin and the yang. The physical is simply a manifestation of the spiritual. This is gnosis.

Hypnosis... psychosis. What's happening to me? What are these things that I'm thinking?

(*I'm always here with you...* The ghost whispers into his ear. With a senseless, tasteless nibble at his flesh, she curls closer to her lover, disappears into his body, merges back into one with his soul.)

Disc one of *The White Album* is over. Andrew leans forward. He pulls the disc out of the top-loading CD player. He puts it back in its case and removes disc two. He puts it on and presses play again. He descends back into his seat and lights his pipe. His mind grows wings. His brain decides to leave his neck. The transcendent thump of drums is followed by the cerebral wail of the guitar. The world is green. In the bright black outside, the trolls have turned stiffly into zombies, the fluttering fairies into vampire bats. When your head is no longer attached to your body, sometimes, the world can become very scary.

Who is speaking to me? The music? The devil? Michelle? An alien? Ziggy? One filters out its dross, purifies its individuality, divides its sediment, separates into the infinite, into two, and that infinity of two, with the help of God's Kool-Aid stick, can be roiled back into one again. (He folds his face between his hands.) There's a duality, a universe inside the unit, to the soul, to everything. Naturally, a man and a woman must exist inside of me (*I'm beside you, inside you, too*) like a twin. Carey is aware of that. He has a woman's name. His existence is a testament to the unity of duality, a man who is a woman, just like his lover, Ziggy. Gabriel is Ziggy, and Michael is the Lady. With their complementary beauties (one light, the other dark), they are the first division of the hermaphrodite's unity. The second division rests in the name Michael – Michelle. She's the director, acting invisibly upon our souls. Michael's the actor, a model acting out a director's modeled role. Michelle is the feminine counterpoint to his soul. I'm a writer, a mirror, David Bowie to Gabriel's Ziggy, the body that shares space with his lover. The split occurs again, twice more. Carey acts as well. Like Shiva, Gabriel holds duality, the hermaphrodite, the split, the secret of creation and destruction, inside himself in the depths of his subconscious. Chase Manhattan... Through his ideas, we could devise the scheme. He and I come up with the plot, the director acts upon our souls, and the actors make it so. Before you know it, we're rich through our knowledge of the bank vault's combinations, the secrets of the universe. No more worries about paychecks bouncing from Heavenly Staffing. I can live off of God's money, His trillions. I'm no longer writing stories; I'm writing my life. In that way, I'm the devil and God, too. One is the writer, the other the director. I'm simply confused as to which is which. I tempt myself, and I save my own immortality. Every man is his own savior. The father, the son, and the Holy Spirit compose our tripartite souls. Jesus is Lucifer just the same. Only one is an angel's name. The split occurs yet again. Terrestrial existence mirrors the divine.

He takes another puff off the green he purchased in the black heart of Brooklyn from Gabriel's white hand. He relaxes and sets the pipe down on the couch beside him. He leans back and locks his hands together behind his head. He closes his eyes.

With the secrets of the universe come the answers to

life and death, the trillion progeny of the once allowed, now forbidden, tree. Will you walk through the Garden with me? The tree of life holds forth the ripened fruit forbidden to us, to those who have tasted the knowledge of good and evil, which is why, in order to become gods, in order to never allow death to come between us, we must move beyond that concept. Michelle, can I turn you into a god? Dante did it with Beatrice. Can I do it to you for real? I don't want to be an artist! I want us to be gods, to be the Starman, Ziggy Stardust. Michelle, will you be my lady, make us the hermaphrodite, one being composed out of two?

The split occurs between the living and the dead, the beautiful and the damned. We are the beautiful and the damned. All lives, the history of memory, the master with the slave, sublate inside of me. Let me spit it all out again, give birth to it all with my mind.

I see a world filled with trees. Endless fields of Elysian flowers grow all around. I stroll through the land before time. A long leaf of grass dangles limply out of the side of my mouth. With my tongue, I shift it around. A green lake shimmers, golden, in the distance. I wear a straw hat, blue jeans, and that's all. Sexy Sadie, looking an awful lot like Ari, greets me, supple and naked, beneath the apple tree. She lays me down on a bed of lotus petals. Her lithe body presses jaggedly into mine. Skin permeates skin (*Whisper that secret to me…*). There's a third, Lilith to her Eve, peeking around the corner, watching. I see her, beyond a bead of sweat dripping across the edge of my vision, out of the corner of my eye. She's been following me. I'm Lucifer, Samael, the king of this nighttime world. I see us transform into one, huge snake as we slither and slide across each other's bellies along the ground. As I am nailed to the cross, with my arms outstretched, the snake unveils its hood. It dances to the rhythm of the charmer's turbaned beat, vacantly staring, patiently waiting as it flicks its tongue to taste the air that it wants to slide through behind its teeth, but to all observers, the music keeps it still while its body sways back and forth. The lotus petals are buried deep among the dead within our sweaty mud. From my semen ejaculated into the earth, I pollinate their seeds, merge the body to the mind. A brand new world is born, and we're all young, Michelle, and you're here with Ari and me, no longer watching from lonely corners of our memories. You're real. I can touch you. You can taste me. We see one another as children. You: a curly-topped girl picking pretty flowers. In your pink dress, framed by the blue horizon, you hold the colors up to the sky for God to see. Me: a boy with a fishing rod dangling emptily from his hands. I wipe my face and cast the vacant line into the water again, but in the recesses of my barely formed brain, I never forget the sensation of you for the first time. You're imprinted upon my mind. I see you again, a few years later, a seeming lifetime to our pre-adolescent understandings, at a coming of age dance. From across the vacuous floor space, you stand out against all the other girls hiding from the boys hiding from them. You smile coquettishly at me. I'm scared of what the others may think (we're not yet comfortable with our sexuality), but I venture into the fray and ask you to dance anyways. Your palm presses lightly against my bony shoulder. I smell the forever familiar scent of your hair. It registers in the reincarnated epicenters of my subconscious. With my hand around your waist, I pull you a tiny bit closer. You don't resist, but you don't come all the way. After we're done, you giggle and tell me your name. I fall in love with you all over again. This time there's no mistakes.

I strike a deal with the lord of the living, the lord of the dead. I lose myself inside the universal mind, inside my head. I focus on my breathing, and I beg the ruler of this world that nobody else ever has to die. I pray to God, to the devil, to aliens to save us, but nothing listens outside of my mind. I don a cape, draw a circle on the floor, stand inside of it, and light a candle. Smoke leaks a timid streak into the air. I point my wand to the four ends of the earth, and I speak in forgotten languages. To my eyes, through my psychology, shadows grow wings in the corners, the candle flame dances in time, but no protective entity appears in my field of vision. We're alone here, abandoned by our creator, digging boroughs into the planet, burying our faces in caves. I remove my cloak and step outside the magic circle. I hide in the sewers of Paris, in the green smoke settling across the living room of this apartment in Brooklyn. Outside my alcove, the world is terrifying: anthrax and dirty bombs, terrorists and soldiers, Ground Zero and the apocalyptic lot of this city. Everywhere, the smell of death lingers on. Ghosts, crying from the blood stained earth, scream for revenge, for relief, to let their maimed, tortured souls rest in peace. Their cries tear me apart inside because I know they no longer believe. They are all as hopeless as me. Do you hear? *You're all as hopeless as me!* Every being on this planet is guilty. It's all a question of at which point you begin to assess the blame. In the beginning, it was only God. Now, mankind has taken over both the harness and the reins. Our ancestors have abandoned us. The dead want us dead. For that, I'm willing to die. Just hand me the knife. Don't make me walk over there and pick it up myself, but I'll do it if it will make you happy…

The White Album is over, but the marijuana is still a fresh jolt of transplanted neurons through the rewired circuitry of Andrew's brain. Silence complements the empty space surrounding the occasional sound of a car going by on the street outside. A horn honks. Andrew blinks. His thoughts frighten him. He's not sure if they're his. He stands up and decides to go into his bedroom.

Across the river, the devil's night light, the work site of the World Trade Center glows. There are men down there in boots, jeans, and hard hats, on cranes, on foot, picking through the rubble, still finding pieces of people and the melted relics from their cubicles. Supposedly, it's as true as myth, there's an iron or a steel cross, at least six feet tall, big enough for a man or a god, on a Calvary of broken walls, reminding everybody who is responsible for all of this. Near the work site, there's a strip club where all the men hide when their day is done. They cry into the dancers' breasts, and the women quietly, patiently hold their babies' heads. There was a riot when the firemen were told that their hours were going to be cut. They stormed the police barricade. All they wanted was the bodies of their dead friends.

In the corner, against the wall, Andrew's unused computer rests on his desk. In that man-made, silicon memory hides the key to his entire life, everything he has written. The half-drunk bottle of cheap whiskey, not a finger less than on September 10th, still sits still on the desk beside it, a reminder of the nights when all he would do was sit there and write. He grabs the bottle of whiskey and plops down on the bed. From there, he can begin writing his life. Mental journal entry number one: it's 8:46 in the morning on September 11th, 2001. He uncorks the bottle and takes a drink. The sweetly fermented, corn mash flavor tastes good. It warms the inside of his mind. He decides to take another drink. The liquor catches in his throat. It activates a slight gag reflex. Andrew washes it down with one last sip. When you're writing, there's never a last sip.

The whiskey begins worming its way into his brain.

Like oil on a smoky fire, it re-ignites, stronger now, the sensation of marijuana on his already singed synapses. The world starts to flip like bad reception on an antenna set television picture. Existence is diffused by a haze of white noise. He's underneath the work lights, entombed in the rubble, clawing for a space from which he can breathe. From above, a brush of air permeates a tiny hole in the disintegrated concrete. He reaches his fingers through the surface of pebbles. The wind tickles his nails and skin. He pries his way through the molten metal and finds himself above ground again, encased in a wasteland of ice and flames, a fire that doesn't burn, an ice storm that doesn't freeze, a tornado of misery.

He takes another drink of whiskey.

The tornado spins. Trapped in its wind, Andrew presses his face up against the edge of the funnel. He strains, with every muscle of his body, against the strength of the clouds, but the dark winds are too powerful. His arms are whipped backwards. His shoulders pop from their sockets. He cries out. The force lifts him off the ground. Twirling around and around, he screams, but nobody can reach him. Praying only that God will spare *them,* the rest of the world cowers beneath their breakfast tables. The tornado's tail slices into the earth as it cuts a path across the dust covered, crisscrossed streets of Lower Manhattan. It picks up trash, filth, concrete, glass, and bricks. A rat splats against Andrew's chin. He can taste its dirty, matted fur on his lips. Its skinny, fleshy tail pokes his eye and whips across his forehead. With a spouting plume of contaminated water, the tornado jumps the East River. Grinding razor wire into its menagerie, it flattens the bars and cafés of Williamsburg. The razor wire tangles around Andrew's body – lacerations, suffocation. The tornado lands on his apartment. It rips away the walls, the ceiling, the furniture, the neighbors, the stairwell, the foundation, and spits them up into the sky in a swirling, black fog of dust and debris. The tornado deposits Andrew alone, stoned and drunk, on his bed in the darkness in the middle of nowhere.

Another shot of liquor scorches his throat. Beneath its heat, his stomach vesicates. A light stream of smoke, like the candle of his ritual, is distilled into his esophagus. His emotions are a spark. He combusts from the inside out. The flames engulf his organs. They tear through his bloodstream. They turn his bones to cinders. The inner layers of his skin catch like paper shrink wrapped around his essence. The fire begs to be released, to breathe the oxygen available only in open air.

Andrew stands up and wobbles over to his desk. He leans against the side of it for a moment, and then he tears the computer from its place. Like tendons exposed beneath skin stripped from the bone, its cords dangle out of the wall and spill, a shivering, shriveling millipede, across the desk. With his father's graduation gift clutched tight to his chest like a baby infant, he stumbles over to the window. He throws the glass up, and he dumps the computer, his abortion, into the alleyway below his room.

Without an umbilical cord to connect it to its mother/father's stomach, the computer twirls freely through the air. Its sleek surface catches an occasional glimmer of moonlight. It smashes against the brick building across the alleyway and spills its innards, in a tinkling rain, down into the abyss beneath it before it crashes, out of sight, existing only in the mystical realm of sound, against the hard concrete of the alley five stories below. And the world is silent. In the darkness, Andrew feels relief, ice cooling the whiskey flames, welling out of his stomach into every limb of his being. His life is gone. Maybe the zombies will find it. But they'll never make sense out of it.

He turns around and trips back over to his bed. He crashes down on the mattress and closes his eyes. *I'm writing my life*, he thinks to himself as he drifts off into a tormented sleep. *I'm writing my life, and we're gonna rob the bank.*

"I wish you would have stopped by earlier," Ari says. "I would have gone out and had a drink with you." She's wearing a pair of jeans and a white, cotton shirt. It clings to her torso and brings out her skin's rich color.

"I felt like being alone for a little while," Andrew answers. He's reclining on her couch. His tongue thickens as he speaks. "I had some thinking to do. I wanted to shoot some pool."

"Were you thinking about writing? Michelle said that's what you used to do whenever you had an idea."

"Sort of. You got any wine?"

"Yeah, but I don't feel like opening a new bottle. I don't think you'll be drinking too much more tonight, and I know I won't drink that much."

"Go ahead and open one up. Whatever we don't drink tonight, we can finish tomorrow."

"All right." She disappears around the corner into the kitchen. Andrew pulls a one hitter and a twisted cellophane wrapper filled with weed from his pocket. He packs up the pipe and takes a puff.

"You want some pot?" he asks.

"Not tonight," Ari shouts from the kitchen.

Andrew burns what's left in the pipe. He puts it back in his pocket. Ari returns with a bottle of wine, two glasses, and a corkscrew. She sniffs the air. "Guess you decided to have some without me," she says with a smile.

Andrew shrugs. The ghost steps away from where it was hiding against the wall. It materializes for a moment, a pale apparition with a long torso beneath a flowing dress.

Its hair billows out to fill the room. Like cobwebs, it wraps around the vacant furniture. Like the carnivorous spinning of a spider, it entangles the two lovers' bodies in a gossamer snare. Then, it disappears. Andrew blinks. He flicks the non-existent threads from off his arm. The ghost follows him everywhere.

With a light pop, Ari opens the bottle and fills the glasses. She hands one to Andrew. "To old and new friends, but always to close friends," she says. Andrew frowns and nods. They toast.

"Have you talked to Charlie this week?" Ari asks. "Are there going to be any problems with your paychecks?"

Andrew sighs. He narrows his eyes. "He wouldn't tell me. It's his company's policy to keep their employees in the dark. Right now, Charlie's the company, and I'm an employee. So much for twenty years of friendship." He shakes his head.

Ari sips her wine. "It's not really his fault. I mean, it's not right that his company can't pay their employees, but it's not his fault," she says.

"I know that, but he got me the job. And I can't believe he gives more credence to the whims of those assholes who run the whole thing, than to a bond that he's spent years forging."

"He needs to protect himself. It's the way of the world."

"It's not right."

"If you were in his position, you'd do the same thing."

"I wouldn't let myself be in his position."

"I'm sure Charlie never imagined he would be in this predicament."

"What I really can't believe is that after everything we've been through, nothing's changed. The world's as selfish as it was on September 10th. Don't people realize that we allowed September 11th to happen?"

"*Nobody* 'allowed' September 11th to happen."

"We did."

"Who?"

"Me, you, Bush, Cheney. Everybody. This whole goddamn world. Even Michelle…"

"Don't say that, Andrew. That's not true."

"It is though. America lives on Paradise Island while the rest of the world starves and fights and dies. It doesn't matter if right now I hardly have enough money to buy a pack of cigarettes. I'm not going to fall. My successes in life come from advantages that I didn't earn: I'm white, people of my complexion conquered this continent, my parents and their parents came from the same privileged class."

"They weren't privileged in Europe though, and that's why they came here."

"But they were privileged, don't you see. They're human. It doesn't matter what race is in charge. Mankind is guilty for history. If the roles had been reversed, if we'd lived in a matriarchy instead of a patriarchy, if Africa had conquered the world, none of the victors would have acted any differently. Men would have been devalued instead of women; whites would have been sold into slavery. Humanity is the devil. Some of us simply have to pay for our sins, and others don't. If things don't change, someday, we'll all suffer."

"What about the innocent?"

"Who's innocent?"

"Children…"

"From the moment of conception, they're guilty of their ancestors' crimes."

"Are you paying for your sins then, for your father's, your mother's, your grandparents' and great-grandparents'?"

"No, but I'm willing to. I'd like to."

"And what would that consist of?"

"I don't know. That's why I'm scared. It'll happen. I'm certain of it."

"I don't like having this conversation with you," Ari says. "Can't we just enjoy one another's company for a while?"

"Sure," Andrew says sadly. He purses his lips and drinks his wine. Ari sips hers. Andrew pours himself another glass.

As he sets the bottle back down on the table, from out of the spout of its neck, like a genie, like an alcoholic's breath, in a silent stream of steam, the ghost gains shape again. She has no wishes to grant, however. It's not the people who set her free. Rather, it's the spirits that make her seen. In a cloud, she ascends to the ceiling. She hovers, as mist, watching over everything – two lovers not quite seeing one another, one staring at the ground, the other at his drink. Her muddled features contort. She grows fangs. Her tongue forks and slithers out between purple lips. Before she strikes, she's sucked, a streak of dirty air, into Ari's lungs on the tail-end of a deep intake of breath. Inside the woman's living body, she gnaws on whatever flesh she can find, tries to let another feel what she now feels inside. She drains her venom into open wounds, struggles to make the woman understand. A slight pang agitates Ari's heart. With the next exhale, the ghost is expelled. Ari caresses her chest. As vapor compelled by whatever gusts of wind may exist, the ghost drifts through stagnant air. Andrew wipes his eyes. In his moment of blindness, she disappears into the bedroom. She resurfaces against the doorjamb behind him. A barefoot apparition in a pale, shimmering nightgown, she leans, lonely and majestic, against the wooden frame from where she watches and waits. She rests one foot on top of the other, looks at the ground, and struggles to hold back tears that will never come.

There's a sensation of someone watching you. You can feel her laser sight burning a hole through the fine hair and thin skin on the back of your neck. It's a red dot invisible to the naked eye, a tracer for a gun, and then comes the shot. Your flesh parts. The bullet enters your bloodstream. The lead is poison, a tapeworm spreading indefinitely through your intestines as it chews on your weakened flesh, a feast from which it grows. There's no hope for survival. The ghost sees your spinal cord, your brain stem, the basis of all your thoughts and memories. It morphs them like LSD. You're asleep. Life, like death, is one long dream. You're naked, more naked than on the day of your birth as the doctor cut your umbilical cord and for the first time thrust you, crying and screaming, out into this bright world alone.

"The paintings are coming along pretty well," Ari says. "I've finished the first two. I'm touching up the third, and I'm outlining the fourth. I'm thinking there will be five, five different pictures to convey the feelings. The first one shows the world from a very naïve perspective, how beautiful everything was before 9/11. The second one is about watching the buildings fall, about Michelle's death. The third one is about coming to terms with anger and hate, reality. The fourth, I think, is going to be about how dark the world looks after glimpsing such things, and the fifth, hopefully, will wind up being a vision for the future. Anytime you want to come by the studio to see them, I'd like for you to."

Andrew nods. He's more interested in the wine.

"Have you written anything lately?"

Andrew shakes his head.

"You really need to start writing again."

"I threw my computer out the window," he mumbles.

Ari twitches. "You did what?"

"I threw my computer out the window."

With her eyes wide and her hands trembling, she stumbles over her words as she asks, "Why'd you do that?"

Andrew shrugs.

"You shouldn't have done that, Andrew. You really shouldn't have."

"I don't need it any longer."

"What about for writing?"

"I'm not writing on paper anymore."

"That doesn't make any sense."

"I was listening to Carey's copy of *The Wall* the other night, and I started thinking about rock stars. That's what I think that whole album's about, the myth of the rock star. I started thinking the whole goal is to get outside of the wall, right? The wall being all the things that keep us boxed up inside ourselves, our minds, that keep us from connecting with other people. Art is a piece of all that. Pink Floyd says so when they begin the album at the same point it ends. Art is a way of mediating your experience, not allowing it to affect you and giving other people pipe dreams to believe in. It's like religion, and just like religion, it shouldn't be preached; it should be lived. My life's my art, and I'm sick of living stories that other people write. I'm sick of writing stories that are more compelling than my life. There's no such thing as God, and if that's the case, then I want to rule my world like Lucifer. From now on, I'm only writing my life."

A concerned look creases the corners of Ari's eyes. She frowns, and she speaks very carefully. "Are you going home for Christmas?" she asks.

"No," Andrew says.

"I really think you should. You didn't go anywhere for Thanksgiving either."

"I don't want to leave New York. I can't stand the world outside this city. When I went home for Michelle's memorial, everybody and everything made me ill. I hate their lives – empty and selfish, concerned with consumption, propagation, and security. At least here you can find people who understand what happened on September 11th."

"And what happened on September 11th?"

"The end of the world."

"Why couldn't it be a new beginning?"

"Because heaven doesn't exist, and death is simply nothing."

The ghost, with her glowering, peaked complexion, leans towards the two friends. She gives ear to their private conversation. On silent feet, with a ballerina's tiptoe, she steps a little way away from the wall. At the edge of the light, she feels anger stab her guts. Its blade rips apart her stomach, her intestines. She doubles over. Blood pours out between her fingers. It drips, then disappears like steam across a stream, on the floor. She wants to shout, to scream, but her cries are never heard. Instead, she senses, in her throat, the metastasizing tears that imprison her, that can never be released.

"But what if death *is* something?" Ari asks.

"Then I'm going to hell."

"Why do you say that?"

"Because humanity is the devil."

"So we're all going to hell?"

"Yes."

"Even Michelle?"

Andrew nods.

The ghost steps back into the shadows of the bedroom where the world is cooler, where the fires of rage and hate don't burn quite so strong. The black air washing in through the windows, glimmering softly from the streetlights, liquefies in the ghost's presence. It swirls around her nightgown, billows up underneath the hem, drenches her hair, and cascades down her face in dark waters that wash the blood from her stomach, her garments, her hands. She drowns in a river, rapidly turning milky red, that she can breathe. She closes her eyes and feels her clothes cling to her disintegrating body. The world robs her of all blood, all feelings. As she melts back into the elements that gave her shape, she watches the tide rise in the living room where Ari and Andrew sit, talking. They are subsumed by a flood that they are blind to. Their spirits claw at the quickening waves while their bodies remain beneath, motionless on the sandy bed of the sea. At the bottom of the ocean, surrounded by jagged toothed demons swimming in and out of nothing, drawn to the frenzy by the ghost's deliquescing chum, lighting their way with their bodies' own electricity, they rest on barnacled coral reefs.

"I don't believe in heaven and hell," Ari says.

"I try not to," Andrew answers, "But sometimes I can't help myself."

Andrew finishes his second glass of wine. He reaches for the bottle again. "Are you going to leave any for me?" Ari asks him, smiling.

Without saying anything, Andrew drops his hand back onto the couch.

"I was just kidding. Have as much as you want, there's another bottle in the kitchen." Andrew pours himself that glass.

"Sometimes I think I can feel her, you know. It's like she's watching me," he says.

"I know what you mean," Ari says. "That's why I want to leave this apartment. I feel her here all the time.

Especially when you come by." She wraps her arms around herself, hugs herself tight, tries to exude the warmth that Andrew should be giving. "I think she follows you."

Andrew looks up from his darkened glass. "That can't be true."

Slightly shocked, Ari says in a conciliatory manner, "You said yourself that sometimes you feel her."

Andrew's eyes blaze. Ari wants to hide herself from his gaze. With a harrumph, he says, "I know that's a lie. Death is nothing. She's nowhere, except maybe compacted into the dust at Ground Zero, and someday, we'll be nowhere, too."

Slack-jawed, Ari stares, aghast, at the man who she sometimes chooses to share her bed with. "I just meant her energy. You bring her energy with you," she whispers.

"And that's why you like being with me? Because I remind you of her?"

"You know that's not what I mean, but I don't think we need to get into that." She raises her eyes and stares coldly into Andrew's face as she finishes, "That idea could go both ways."

Andrew shakes his head. "It just reminds me of when I was at her memorial. The minister kept rambling on and on about how we all knew Michelle was in a better place, that we should be grateful for the peace she feels... All I kept thinking was, *Lies! Lies! Why do they feed us all these lies?*"

"Because it's what people want to hear. It's what her mother needs to believe."

"I don't care what her mother needs to believe. I want the minister to tell me the truth."

"And what's the truth, Andrew?"

"That she's dead. She's gone. She's not coming back, and I'll never see her again."

"Do you really believe that would be better?"

"Yes. Because it would drive home to all of us that we need to live right now. Right fucking now. Not waste our time with all this shit." Indicating Ari's paintings, he swings his arms around the apartment.

"For some of us, this 'shit' *is* living," Ari snaps.

"This isn't living. It's not real. Don't you understand? It's not real."

"And what about you? Sitting around your apartment, getting stoned, getting drunk, going out to bars, listening to music, and shooting pool, is that real?"

"I've got plans. That's the difference. I've got plans to turn this world upside down, show it its true face, make things appear as they are: infinite."

"And how are you going to do that? By winding up a burn out with wet brain?"

For a moment, Andrew remains motionless. Only his hands twitch slightly. His eyes roam furtively. Then, in a flash, he pops out of his seat. Ari recoils as if he's going to strike her. He rushes over to the wall and grabs a painting, one with a black line down a purple canvas, from where it hangs. Its frame scrapes across the white wall paint.

Screaming, his face melting in agony, he spins around, and he slams it into the coffee table. With a smash, the bottle and glasses of wine upend. The table jumps in place. The wine spills purple blood across the carpet, three wounds: a spear to the ribs, a bullet to the brain, and a knife to the veins. A gouge rips through the canvas's abstract pigments, through the layering of paints. Heaving for breath, Andrew steps back and leaves the painting dangling, like a body from the hands of its crucifixion, from a hole in its own flesh off the side of the wooden table.

In silence and shock, with her wide eyes even wider than usual, Ari sits still. In an instant, her painting is gone, destroyed, damaged beyond repair. She might be able to reproduce the colors, but she will never again be in the same frame of mind that created those particular brush strokes, those distinct textures. She always imagined that symbol of herself would someday belong to her grandchildren. With a sniffle, she says, "Get out of here, Andrew. Get out of here, and don't ever come back."

Saturday in Williamsburg. Stroll down Bedford Avenue, the hippest street in the hippest neighborhood in the hippest city in the world. At the corner of North 7th, with their backs to the L train's entrance, a couple gives one another a hug and a kiss. They're a commercial. In real life, people don't take the time to dress like this. Men don't make sure that their striped pants match so succinctly with the solid colors of their butterfly collared shirt and jacket. A man rarely pays so much attention to the intricacies of the stitched patterns on his shoes. He doesn't even take his sunglasses off to say goodbye to his girlfriend. She loves it. His style matches hers perfectly, a hint of retro-mod, a glimmer of haute chic with the requisite thrift store mentality. Both of them are stylishly unkempt with bed-head hair, a shadow of whiskers for him, and the bare minimum of make-up for her. And these two are simply the entrance to Williamsburg's fashion gallery, nothing more than greeters for the newcomers venturing in from hotels and hostels and friend's places in Manhattan because somebody at NYU told them to check out the scene here.

As you continue down Bedford Avenue towards Southside, on your left, you pass the L café. You stop and take a gander in the large glass windows at the front, see if anybody you know is awake and eating yet. Couples and groups sit at tables, at the bar. They're laughing, smoking, talking, all enjoying their 1:00 pm brunches, huevos rancheros, breakfast burritos, and mimosas. Last night was a long night what with parties and bars to go to. There was an art opening in the neighborhood and a DJ spinning in Bushwick. You had to make a late night appearance at Enid's, and a friend of yours was having a cast party in Greenpoint that you thought might be a good place to network at. You'd like to make a film someday, or maybe start up a magazine if that trust fund kid you met a few months ago will ever get off his ass and put up the money.

Still rolling down Bedford, you weave in and out of a group of thirty-something artists, the established members of the community, the ones who moved out here when Williamsburg was still Puerto Rican gang territory ravaged by wild dogs and arson, the entrance to Donnie Brasco's world. Older now, no longer interested in hitting the scene, they laugh like ancient Bostonians soaking in the randomness of the Commons as they push their children in strollers. They complain about the neighborhood, how there is no more affordable housing, and they wonder when their Mecca turned into this post-MTV wasteland of hipper-than-thou twenty year olds. Only one woman frowns slightly as she realizes that, really, it's all their fault. They paved the way for gentrification, and she starts wondering what the generations of families who had lived here before them, the Italians, the Puerto Ricans, the Polish, and the Hassidim, thought when they all started making their treks across the bridge. New York progresses too rapidly. It's a stomach constantly upset by a new influx of acidic food before the last ulcerous combination has even been digested. The city and its inhabitants are in a perpetual state of future-shock.

Pretty soon, you hit the anti-mall with its neon colored stores. You stop by the record shop to see if any CDs that you want might have been brought in. You've been getting really into proto-punk lately, and you're collecting old

Stooges on vinyl. The MC5, however, would be the mother lode. Nothing. You leave, turn right, and step inside The Verb for your morning cup of coffee. On the folding sidewalk chalkboard outside, you notice that somebody's written, instead of any sort of specials, in green chalk with pink flowers around the words – *The Verb Loves You*. That's a nice idea to start the day on, you think.

You stand at the end of the line, contemplating what size coffee you're going to get and whether you're going to get it in a to-go cup or a mug. The atmosphere of The Verb is red. Its cavernous appearance is somewhat reminiscent of a memory that predates your birth, a subconscious preconception of the womb. The warmth of the room is cozy and comfortable, a place where you could once again fall asleep in your mother's arms. The girl in line in front of you has long blonde hair and a style reminiscent of 80's new wave. It's all the rage these days. In the back corner, stage-left, in a booth on the level up three steps, a mini theater balcony behind a short grate, a young man in a thin, gray wool sweater with a hole in the elbow, his dirty brown hair thick, spiked, and unwashed, is sitting with a cup of coffee and a book. Since the room is full, two girls sit down at the empty spots next to him in the booth. They ask if he's saving the spaces. He says, no. His name is Andrew Christian. You don't know him. So you don't pay any more attention to him as you decide that given the over-crowded conditions of the café, you'd better get your coffee to go. You've got stuff to do around your over-priced apartment today anyways.

At the table in the corner, Andrew looks up from his book, *Oriental Mythology*. He narrows his eyes as he catches a glimmer of the conversation that the two girls who just sat down next to him are having.

"I don't understand why everything's so damn

expensive," one of the girls says, the more conservative of the two, the slightly more overweight of the two, dressed exactly like Middle America's thousands of other recent college graduates in beige pants and a matching sweater from The Gap. She's out of place in the Burg's fashion show, a thick coated sheep in the midst of scraggly wolves. Maybe if she stays here long enough, she'll catch on.

"It's what it means to live in a city," the other girl says, the one with faint strains of a beginning for the unfolding style of her own. Appearance is like a symphony. Her mannerisms and her tone bespeak the possibility of her ability to survive in New York. And simple survival is the best that those on the bottom of the food chain can ever hope for in the belly of capitalism's great beast.

"But I'm running out of money, and I can't afford getting an apartment here: first month, last month, security deposit, and a ten percent broker's fee. I mean, I have a job, and I can't afford it. How do people live here?" the first girl says.

"Very cheaply," the other girl says. Andrew smirks. The girls don't notice. "Maybe we need to look separately," the girl goes on. "You know, try to find room shares."

"But I don't want to live with somebody I don't know," the first girl says.

"We may not have a choice. It's been over a month, and we haven't found anything we can afford. I can't stay on Sarah's couch forever, and I'm sure Joelle doesn't want you taking up space at her place too much longer."

"Do you mind if I smoke a cigarette?" Andrew leans over and intrudes.

The first girl recoils. Her lips twist as if she never expected another human being to ever say a word to her ever again. She's awed at the reality that somebody could hear her conversation, but that's life in a city for you.

Everybody can hear your conversations. The other girl says, "Not at all."

Andrew pulls his cigarettes out of his pocket, packs one against the table, sticks it between his lips, and lights it. The first girl brushes Andrew's exhale away from her face. The other girl smiles quietly at her friend's unfriendly mannerisms.

As his heavy, damaged lungs take in the smoke, Andrew thinks to himself, *Why would anybody want to move here now? Don't they understand the world that we live in today? This city is a death trap, a roach motel, an island that draws us in to where we wait patiently for the righteous avengers of Islam to strike us down with guns and radiation, diseases and chemicals for our cultural discrepancies. Only our sadness and suicidal tendencies keep us here in this post-9/11 daze.* He frowns and shakes his head. To the girls beside him, New York still represents the same magnificent monster, the same Puff the magic dragon, that he first naively encountered and conquered almost a year and a half ago. Tiamat has never reared her other ancient, Hydra heads, her rotten teeth, her rancid breath, her smoke and flames for the benefit of their suburban visions. For them, she still benignly chews her tail around the circumference of this world as the World Serpent. The Ragnarok has never occurred. Loki, Fenrir, and Hela have never been freed. Valhalla has never been emptied. The eternal warriors still battle only with one another and spend their evenings drinking mead. The gods remain safe in the heavens. Trying to block the girls' conversation from his conscious hearing, Andrew goes back to his reading

Andrew's eyes grow wide. He stares blankly at the page. He reads a sentence over again. His lips silently mouth the phonics as he follows the dashes and the commas to the period, and then, he reads it over again. With his index finger, he traces the ascent of the words, the subtle shifts in tone and content. He fixes his vacant stare at the black letters on the white pulp. The abstract shapes blur and cease to mean anything. Images of medieval violence slice and burn themselves into the raping of his mind. He closes his eyes.

And the warriors of Allah destroyed my timeless dream where good and evil did not exist, where all things simply were as they are, where mankind had the ability to taste the fruit of the tree of eternal life. Michelle was my Radha. I was Jayadeva, the writer writing the religious fables that underlie the reality of my songs of experience. Like the prophets, the servants of the Middle Eastern gods have played this role throughout all of history: the crusades, the inquisition, our civil wars, King David conquering the Promised Land, British Round Hats, Sharon, and Arafat. But why does Joseph Campbell treat the name Allah with such respect? He must believe that there is some sort of truth to the myth of the faceless god who brings destruction in His wake. Could Allah be the name of the world's destroyer? He is nature's power – a fire, an earthquake, a storm, a nuclear explosion, a war. Ari's peaceful lineage is that which gave birth to the divine Upanishads of sex and love where there's no fallen man, no Judgment Day. Like a terrorist, I destroyed that with one action, one drunken mistake of smashing her painting against the table, the altar, that Michelle brought into that apartment. I've become Shiva, another name for Allah. I banished myself from Eden. I am the white man, a devil cooked up in a bottle by a mad scientist. Two cherubs with fiery swords now guard the door to my last tangible memories of Michelle. I'll never see her furniture, her room, again, the last things of hers that I could smell and touch and feel. For me, she truly is a ghost, a memory. I remember the shredding sound of the canvas ripping – like a cat being skinned alive. I haven't seen Ari since then. It's been over a month. It's now January, 2002, a palindrome, something Pythagorean. If that's a sign, is it good or bad? We haven't even spoken on the phone.

Andrew opens his eyes, closes his book, and sets it

aside on the table. He takes a long drink of coffee and rubs his hand down his face. Beside him, the two girls are still discussing their prospects of finding housing in New York City. Andrew frowns and shakes his head.

But you two sitting beside me are still there. For you, this place, this city, this country still contain magic. I remember moving here. It could have been a trillion years ago for all I know. Trilobites spiraled through the deep. The past few months have been an eternity. When I came here, at the dawn of time, New York opened like an oyster, like a woman, to me, and all I wanted was to hold that huge pearl in my tiny hand, but as I reached onto that pink bed to seize the jewels, the oyster clamped its jaws around my wrist. I'm still screaming. Terrorized bubbles stream from my nose and mouth. Running out of oxygen, I struggle to free myself. The pearl was a booby trap, a landmine, and it blew my fingers off. I'm bleeding to death from the wound. Won't somebody help me? Without a thumb to hold this world with, I hardly feel human anymore.

With one long gulp, Andrew finishes his coffee. He wipes his mouth, picks up his book, slides out from behind the booth, morosely mumbles to the two girls, "Good luck," and leaves The Verb without even waiting to see what sort of response the girls give to his weak encouragement. Their answer is a cursory nod at his back as he walks down the steps and reenters, from the thoughtfully removed comforts of the balcony, the world's orchestra pit. It's time to put the binoculars away; we're on eye level again.

On the sidewalk, Andrew notices the chalk sign telling him that The Verb loves him. A verb seems an awful lot like God, something in constant flux, unable to be pinned down by the fixity of a noun. All things are Buddha things animated by the Holy Spirit, our logos. In other words, God loves you. *Bull shit*, Andrew thinks. *God hates us.*

With his thoughts still consumed by that one sentence

from *Oriental Mythology* (could it really be that the different names of God represent different natural forces? What does Yahweh, God's silent name, mean?), Andrew heads down Bedford Avenue towards Williamsburg's Southside. The character of every block begins to change the face of the neighborhood. The hipster dwellings become more and more influenced by a Puerto Rican flavor. Bodegas replace the cafés. The bars disappear. A small, hole-in-the-wall church appears. Yahweh has to do with the inner sense of God, the meanings that can never be given voice to by language. If it wasn't for the slight bite in the windy air, the neighborhood would have every appearance of being a Caribbean home. There's more trash on the sidewalks, more graffiti on the brick walls, more razor wire around the buildings. Andrew turns to his right. He heads towards an abandoned factory district on the waterfront. The vacant structures loom, empty and decrepit. Like the beach on an overcast day, their barrenness gives the mind a more reflective attitude. It's only a matter of time before these buildings, like so many on the blocks surrounding them, are converted into artist's lofts.

He reaches his destination, a sort of cove in the midst of the urban monstrosities, on the banks of the East River. Piles of stones define a beachhead where the river's weak tide attempts to invade Brooklyn. The rocks are the soldiers slaughtered. Benches have been set up on tiny patches of grass so that visitors can appreciate their view of Manhattan's skyline. Andrew hasn't been here since before September 11th. He hasn't wanted to see the skyline in its entirety without the Twin Towers anchoring it as a base. It's different from the view out of his bedroom window. There, like the supporting cast to his monologue of the financial district's experience, he sees Downtown with the rest of the city in the distance. Here, he sees the skyline in its entirety. It's the same view that God has of the world. The only thing approximating this experience is when he stood on the roof of his building with Gabriel. He remembers the conversation. The world was so simplistic back then. Right existed, and so did wrong. In his mind, without this scene, the buildings can still exist in a dream. It's moments like this when the treacherous waves of reality come crashing in.

He walks out to the outcropped piles of rocks, stands on the edge of a flat stone, and with a sigh, takes in the monstrously full expanse of New York's broken skyline. The wind barrels down between the opposite shores of Manhattan and Brooklyn and lifts his hair slightly from his head. There's no sight like this anywhere else on earth. One of the world's man-made wonders, the skyline dips and lifts, reflects metallic visions against the gray day. Beams of sunlight stream, refracted from the girders and windows. The phalanx of skyscrapers far away in Midtown and Uptown don't look much larger than the buildings of any other city, but when the scale of distance is accounted for by comparison with Downtown's structures, now vacant and phantasmal with the glaring hole in their towering line, the magnificence of Manhattan's eternal brilliance is comprehended. Nothing, not a mountain range, not the ocean, makes a human being feel more insignificant than this skyline. It is the world we have created, and our own creations dwarf us. As individuals, we are nothing. Collectively, we are God. That is the lesson of New York City. Humanity, spontaneously and continuously, creates the invisible hand.

There, in the middle of it all, still standing glorious and proud, lonely at its sullen height, a full head above its brethren, surveying the land at the edge of this great continent, its status undiminished, is the Empire State

Building, the first true monument that this city built to the American god.

Andrew closes his eyes and bows his head. A month or two earlier, he would have cried, but he has no tears left. They all dripped down his cheeks in the darkness of many and many a midnight dreary. The sadness still builds in his throat, but he's too dry for it to ever be released. He sniffles, but there's nothing there. On the inside, this must be what it feels like to be dead.

A hand grabs his shoulder. Beneath his thin clavicle, the fingers dig into his flesh. He's yanked back and forth. He sways to the rhythm that his accuser creates. "Hey man, how you doin'?" a voice asks.

Andrew turns around. He stares into Michael's smiling face. At the corners of his lips, he smiles. "I'm okay. How are you?" he says as calmly as he can. We have to pretend that stuff like this happens every day.

"I'm all right. Just coming from a friend's apartment. What's your excuse for being here?"

"I wanted a chance to see the city."

"I'm going to L.A."

"Really?" Andrew asks. Michael's hand leaves his shoulder. He drops it, limp, by his own side. Andrew narrows his eyes. He pretends he has x-ray vision, like he can see through the buildings all the way to the West Side Story and the Jersey Shore. "A friend of mine says that's a lot like Heaven."

"It might be. I wouldn't know. Never been there before."

"He says it's the sun makes you feel that way."

"Shit. All I know is there's no terrorist's there."

"They will be."

"Well, at least they don't have subways."

"Only freeways. What are you going out there for

anyways? Acting?"

"Yeah. Something like that. I hear the studios pay more attention to the way you look. Besides, there's more money to be made out there."

"That's certainly true. I'm getting ready to make a movie though. I was hoping you'd be in it."

"No shit. What's it about?"

"I told you all about it in Times Square that first day we bumped into each other. You know, the whole bank robbery plot."

"Oh yeah, I remember that."

"So I was thinking that you could play the role of one of the actors. That is, if you're still up for it."

"Up for it? Just start it this month. When do you think you'll be done with the filming?"

"I don't know. I was thinking we could do it basically as an improv performance. I don't have the script finished yet. I've started it, but I was figuring that with you and my roommate and this friend of his we could use inspiration to direct us towards the right end."

"Inspiration, huh?" Michael steps back a pace. He scrunches up his face.

"Yeah. It's a piece of my newest theory regarding the nature of art."

With his eyes and mouth still as tight as a virgin, Michael says, "And what is that?"

"It all has to do with the idea that art is a byproduct complete unto the subconscious. I've been seeing visions, man. Ghosts…"

"That's a little bit too heavy for me. I don't believe in shit like that. See, it's statements like the one you just made that make me realize I need to get to L.A. New York's gotten too weird."

"Weird… Like Wyrd. And right there, with that

concept, we're approaching the realm of the gods. That's the problem. Do you believe in fate?"

"I don't believe in anything."

"Well, I'm starting to believe in fate, that this world is outside of my control. September 11th was meant to happen. I dreamt about it."

Michael steps further away from Andrew. With a downward glance, he takes in Andrew's shape. Giving himself a hug, he rubs his hands along the denim of his wind-breaking, jean jacket. "What do you mean you dreamt about it?"

"Angels were falling from the sky. All I knew was that the apocalypse had begun. You can't tell me that history isn't going to look at this event as being the beginning of World War III."

"It's funny, you know. My roommate turned me onto this Palestinian web-site. I spent a whole week or two going down to the Kinko's near Astor Place to check it out. Practically maxed out my credit card on their pay by the hour computer." Michael laughs nervously. "Anyways, one day, I read this interview with bin Laden. He was talking about how all these different people in his inner circle had dreamt about September 11th before it happened. It was something about a soccer field, and the Muslims versus America, but I don't remember the whole dream. Regardless, the Arabs won."

"Of course they did, man. There's no way to declare ourselves the victors."

"Bin Laden also said that there were a lot of Muslims created that day, that God was proud of what they had done. He said that when people saw the Twin Towers fall, they immediately plummeted to their knees and began praying to Allah and his power." Michael scuffs the toe of his boot against a stone at the river's edge. Both he and

Andrew take a moment to reflect upon their experiences of that day.

"Who knows. Maybe God *was* proud."

Michael twists his head to the side. He squints but still looks Andrew in the eye. "How could God be proud of that?"

Andrew wraps his hand tighter around his book. "The warriors of Islam, man, the warriors of Islam."

"I don't know. I went down there that day. You know, to try to help. I saw the people covered in ash, wandering with this look in their eye like nothing I'd ever seen before. They were dead, man. Whether the towers collapsed on them or not, downtown New York died that day. God wasn't proud of that. Not my God at least."

"That's cuz you're an American. There are deeper gods in this earth. I was down there, too. I don't know what I saw. I remember it, but it doesn't mean anything to me. There was this one girl with blood streaming out of a gash on the side of her head. She was wandering around looking for her cell phone. Everything she saw on the street, she picked it up and said, 'Is this my phone? This isn't my phone.' She'd drop it. 'Where's my phone?' *That* sounds a lot like an experience of God."

Michael shrugs. "I don't know. I'm gonna take off for L.A. Too many bomb threats on the subways here. For all I know, the bodega owners could start swapping out their deli slicers for sub-machine guns. Bedford Avenue would make for nice target practice."

"I'm stuck here. I can't go home. Home makes me wanna change the world too bad. At least in New York I figure I'm only one in ten million. I can rail against the powers that be as much as I want, and nothing will happen. At my mom's, the world collapses in on me. In the suburbs, I'm all alone. It's unbearable."

"That's why I'm going farther away."

"I'd be content with anywhere away from this post-nuclear wasteland." Andrew pauses. With a heavy sigh and a melodramatic glance, he takes in New York's ascending and descending skyline. Although it still travels through the same depths as it did a few months before, it doesn't correspond to anything approximating the symbolism that it contained that night he stood atop the Empire State Building with Michelle. Then, there was mysticism to the ghosts and meaning to the structures. Now, ghosts are no longer possible, and meaning seems even more inane than it did before. "But the problem is that I'd take it with me anywhere I go," Andrew says.

"How do you plan on changing the world?" Michael asks.

"What?"

"How do you plan on changing the world?"

"I'm just going to keep on writing." Andrew goes on in a whisper: "Except that I threw my computer out the window. And if things don't change with my staffing agency, I won't even have anywhere to live soon. Paychecks have become few and far between."

Michael quickly spins his head. It's taken him a moment to digest what Andrew has said. The last couple sentences threw him off, but now the monstrosity of the words, of the whole conversation, has finally registered. He asks very slowly, "If you don't have something to write on, how are you writing a screenplay?"

"In my mind. It all takes place inside my mind."

With a nervous glance, Michael steps away from Andrew. His jaw quivers a little bit. From under his brow, with a needy glint to his eye, Andrew watches him back off the rocks and move closer to the park.

"Yeah, well, I'll be seeing you around then," Michael

says with a timid wave. Shaking his head, he turns around, thrusts his hands into the pockets of his tight jeans, and walks back into the dirty Brooklyn streets.

"See ya," Andrew says. He watches Michael's jean jacket disappear around the corner of a building. All alone on the East River's windy banks, he turns back to face the skyline.

He pulls his cigarettes out of his pocket, sits down on the rocks, and fights with the wind to spark a match. Eventually, the world concedes to his needs, and he begins to inhale ashen sooty smoke. Across the East River, beyond the smoke spiraling off his cigarette, Manhattan's modern splendor resonates with the drab colors of the winter air. Cities appear more ethereal on a gray day, as if they somehow become eternal, but in this instance, eternity was demolished. There is no future. All that's left are infinite memories of the distant past.

Allah is the name of the world's destroyer. He descends in a smoldering ball of fire. The sun reflects brilliantly off of steel buildings. That light, that eternal light, is what we'll see at the end. Michelle wanted to die in a nuclear explosion. Maybe she got her wish. I got mine. I'm being torn apart by wolves. But I'm sick of fighting to stay alive. The wolves can have me.

"I'll check on Charlie tomorrow, Mom," Andrew says over the phone as he sits in his bedroom, staring at the emptiness outside his window.

"It's just that Anne's very worried about him. She hasn't heard from him since before the staffing agency closed, and she knows he wasn't looking for a new job. He was very depressed and drinking a lot she says. She thinks something might have happened to him."

"I'll go by his place tomorrow and check," Andrew says even though he doesn't want to. He hasn't spoken to

Charlie since his last paycheck bounced three weeks ago and his assignment let him go. They told him he'd have better luck getting his money from the unemployment commission. So far, he has. Screw Charlie. "I'm sure he's fine. He probably just doesn't feel like talking to his mother. Speaking of which, I don't have time to talk right now either, Mom. Carey and I have to get the apartment ready for this party tonight."

"All right. Just promise me you'll get over there tomorrow."

"I promise."

"Okay. I love you. I'll call you not tomorrow, but the next day to wish you a happy birthday. I love you."

"All right. I love you too." He presses end on his cell phone. He sits down on his bed and smokes a bowl. Then, he leaves his bedroom and heads through Carey's bedroom into the living room where Carey is hanging decorations.

"Have to see what we can do to make this place a little more presentable," Carey says as he stands on the couch and tapes the end of a red streamer to the wall. So tight, red and white. "Who were you on the phone with?"

"My mom. She wants me to go by Charlie's tomorrow. His mother's worried that something's happened to him."

"He's probably just been in an alcoholic stupor since he lost his job."

"That's what I figure," Andrew says. "But how do you say that to your mom?"

Carey shrugs. "Why didn't you invite him?" he asks.

Andrew narrows his eyes. "Why would I?" he answers coldly.

Carey steps down from the couch. "You should have invited *some*body to your own party, though," Carey says.

"I did. I invited Michael. We're going to get to work on that film. Besides, it's not my party." Andrew squeezes sideways past him into the kitchen. He goes to the broken refrigerator that doesn't really keep anything cold, the reason that there's no milk in the apartment, and grabs a Polish beer. He pops the top and takes a warm sip. "It's the World Trade Center's party."

Carey watches him carefully. They've lived together now for about a year and a half, and Carey knows that he doesn't know Andrew very well, but still, he's worried about him. He glances over at the copy of *The White Album* sitting beside the boombox. He inhales deeply, and he shakes his head.

The guests begin arriving before dark. There aren't too many, people from Carey's theater troupe and a few friends he's made over his years in New York. They're all coming to see the World Trade Center's Tribute in Lights illuminate the night. Nobody knows what it will look like, but it's been built up in the media over the past few weeks as a memorial that will equal the solemnity of the six month anniversary of this event that forever marred the Capital of the World. Andrew's birthday is only pretense. Even he knows that, but he appreciates the rationale of it being the perfect pretense. For him, this whole experience approximates the reality of something purely symbolic.

Mary is the first to arrive. She's wearing a thin wool scarf over a full-length down jacket that dangles down to her ankles. Its synthetic fabric almost brushes the floor. Her outfit is far too warm for the temperature tonight, but it's very stylish for her approach to the door. With her glistening lips, she kisses Carey on the cheek and then grips Andrew's hand in the warmth of her own. Andrew says that she can lay the excess layers of her clothing on the bed in his room. She agrees to do so. He doesn't want to, but he notices the intricacies of her appearance: her high cheeks, her recessed eyes. He smiles at her. She finds his dimples cute, and she smiles back. When she takes her jacket off, he notices the mellow curves of her body, the way that her almost long-sleeved shirt outlines the pointed cones of her breasts and barely reveals her hairless forearms. Her tight jeans add more dimensions, something approximating time, to her attributes. Even though they've never met before, she has a very familiar appearance about her, as if they've already shared some intimate secret. He yearns for what he lost with Ari. She's most intrigued by the dying light beneath the sad surface of his eyes.

Pete and John arrive next. Gabriel shows up after them.

"I don't know why Carey hangs out with him," Mary discretely whispers to Andrew as she takes a sip from the straw of her very first screwdriver of the evening.

It's the first words that she has addressed directly to him since she showed up. He shrugs.

Mary takes another sip from her straw. She smiles, and she steps away to say something to Pete about a casting change that recently occurred in *The Producers* on Broadway. The implication is that it won't be running for much longer. Reality is a million more important conversations away. However, isn't this take ironic for all of the actors who thought they'd sold their souls for a secure gig? Doesn't this teach us all something about life?

Jim, Matt, and Simon show up right after Mary finishes confiding in Pete. They've brought a bottle of cheap champagne with them. Gabriel offers to uncork it. He twists the metal screw. Coupled with a scream of excitement from the guests, the cork flies into the ceiling. The bubbly spills a puddle on the floor. Mary offers to wipe it up, but Carey is way ahead of her. He has the paper towels in his hand before she even finds a place to set her plastic cup down. A few more people straggle in after the first toast.

Andrew wonders where Michael is, when he'll bother showing up. The movie begins filming tonight.

Gabriel sparks up a joint, and it starts making the rounds.

Andrew takes a puff. The paper begins to canoe. He flicks the edge with his finger. The singed barrier disappears beneath the stroke of his thumb. He blows on the spark to make sure it's still bright.

Suddenly, the slight light of the kitchen windows reveal that, outside, it's beginning to get dark. Andrew goes back to his bedroom for a moment. He closes the door. He lights his bowl yet again. Gabriel's joint is done, and Andrew doesn't feel sufficiently lifted in order to deal with people.

Always oozing from the pores of a building, the ghost materializes against his wall. To come through like this hurts. Maybe you see me, maybe you don't. Your eyes are closed. Your forehead rests between your fingertips. I'll move closer to you, breathe across the hairs on the back of your neck. There. As you look up slowly, that's a reaction. Now, do you see me?

For a moment, just one moment, I could have sworn that I saw a face, a woman's jaw line and her hair, outlined against the ceiling. (Andrew blinks, closes his eyes, and rubs his fingers against his temples) this shit's really starting to get to me. Tomorrow, I can't smoke pot, but I say that every night, every day. I'm sure I'll tell myself not to drink either. That'll happen when hell freezes over. Aren't you cold? Don't you realize that even purgatory is frozen?

Andrew sits up on his bed. He shakes his head. Shivering and rubbing his hands down his arms, he gives himself a hug. Somebody's watching me. Quickly, he spins his head to gaze into the corner. Like the smoke off the tip of a cigarette, something gray flitters against the walls. The ghost disappears. There's nobody there.

Leaning his right shoulder against the wall through which, every night, he hears Spanish arguments about money and children even though he doesn't know what the participants are saying, Andrew twitches tumultuously like Joyce's dead. Now personally clearing the scales from his eyes, he wipes his hand down his face. Outside his window, he sees the faint ghost shapes of lights shooting out from Ground Zero into the infinity of space. He stands up. He throws his door open and reenters the conviviality of the party.

"I hope you don't mind, we put The Damned on," Gabriel shouts at him.

As he makes his way through Carey's excuse for a bedroom, Andrew shakes his head, *I don't mind at all.*

Michael still hasn't deigned to attend. A few non-descripts sit around on the couch, the love seat. In the kitchen, Mary is talking to Simon.

Unnoticed, Andrew slips through the living room. He doesn't know any of these people. They don't know that soon it's his birthday. All they know is there's a party. Like a ghost, he disappears, through the fluid flow of conversation, into the miraculous kitchen.

Mary smiles at him. Andrew tries to smile back as he approaches the ledge on which she sits, framed by the windowsill and Brooklyn's buildings behind her petite Asian profile. Simon leans against the wall. He nods his head closer to hers as he speaks. Their foreheads are almost touching.

"I was just wondering where you went," Mary says to Andrew as he approaches. "Do you know Simon?" she asks. She indicates her friend with a nod.

"I…"

"Yeah, we met a long time ago at a different party. You came with Carey," Simon says, smiling. He holds out his hand. "How you doing, man?"

"Fine," Andrew answers. He shakes Simon's hand.

"So where are *your* friends?" Mary asks. "Seems like everybody here I know through Carey."

"My friends are always here," Andrew says.

Mary grins.

Simon says, "I'm gonna go check up on Jim. I'm sure I'll see you guys around." He nods adieu.

"It's hard not to," Mary laughs. In response, Simon laughs, too, but still, he walks away. Andrew slides into his vacated slot against the wall.

"So why do you think Carey never introduced us before?" Mary asks. "You are straight, aren't you?"

Andrew tilts his head to the side. "I don't know why Carey never introduced us before. You look very familiar to me though. Are you certain we've never met?"

"I'm certain." Mary smiles. "Besides, I'm positive I'd remember you."

"How long have you known Carey?"

"We worked together on the September 11th remembrance piece. I guess that's why he thought it would be fitting for me to be here tonight."

"Oh. If it's only been since then… I haven't really been myself lately."

"None of us have."

"It's been hard work just staying alive these past six months."

"Tell me about it," Mary says. She gives an exasperated sigh, and her eyes glaze over with a distant look.

"Where do you live?" Andrew asks.

"Lower East. I'm glad my neighborhood's just a neighborhood again and not a demilitarized zone. I'm sure that when my parents left Korea, they never would have thought that I'd have to live through something like this."

"I used to have a view of them," Andrew says.

Mary nods. "So I hear. It's dark outside, now. Do you want to go upstairs and see the tribute in lights?"

"Why not."

Mary jumps down from her perch. "Do you think I need my jacket?" she asks.

"I doubt it."

"Me too."

Together, they step lithely across the kitchen floor. As Andrew begins to open the door, Gabriel shouts out from behind him, "And where are you two going without inviting the rest of the party?"

Andrew turns around. Holding a beer in his hand, Gabriel is leaning against the stove that works about as well as the refrigerator does. With a grin, he tips his head to the side and takes a sip.

Mary turns around. "We were going up to check out the lights. Do you want to bring anybody else?"

Gabriel narrows his eyes. He juts his head forward like a snake's. His forked tongue slithers between his teeth and laps his upper lip. He tickles the pitted sensors beside his nose. There's even the sensation of a death rattle. "I think we should bring everybody, don't you?" he says.

With his eyes wide, Andrew doesn't answer. Mary feels him shiver beside her.

She says, "Sure. Why not."

Andrew and Mary turn around and step into the hallway together. Behind them, from out the open apartment door, they hear the rustlings of Gabriel gathering the crowd together for the ascent. It's the fluttering of a billion butterfly wings.

"Do you really think they're all going to come?" Andrew leans over and asks as he puts his foot on the bottom rung of the mounted iron stairs that climb to the roof.

Mary shrugs. She looks up and smiles at Andrew. With a look that builds through his cheeks and dies at his eyes, he smiles back, turns, and heads up the stairs. Mary watches his thin legs flex and relax beneath his jeans' clingy fabric. She starts up the steps after him. Andrew flips the trap door open above their heads and hoists himself up to the roof. He reaches his hand back down the hole and helps Mary climb the last few steps.

On top of the building, above the Brooklyn world, they face downtown where the Twin Towers' leopard print used to dominate the nighttime view for miles around. In place of the solid shapes that rose indefinitely but finitely, a physical representation of the mythical Tower of Babel, out of the city's desert skyline, two beams, broad and bright, cut through the darkness, climbing through the smog to the stars and on into eternity. At the base, around the remnants of the skyline, like the fluid for a lighter, as if they've been caused by arson, the beams start out thick and blue. It's only as they are projected up endlessly, as they taper into a needle piercing Olympus's clouds, that they burn into white. They don't stop. For as far as the eye can see, their electric warmth breaks through the emptiness.

"It's like watching all of the people who ever died ascend into heaven."

"What?" Andrew asks.

"It's as if those lights are souls being released from the earth. Not just the ones from 9/11, but ones from all of history, all of time."

Andrew winces. The swaths of light flood the darkness and envelop the stars as if they were the earthbound remnants of God's abandoned Milky Way. At the end of time, the continuum flows backwards. Like the Christian resurrection, the dead rise old and *grow* young again. If life is nothing more than animated electricity, then Mary is right. Our money, our lives are recorded on computers.

The thud of feet and the bark of voices rise out of the hole leading back into the building. Andrew turns around. Gabriel's smiling face pops out of the trap door. "I brought *every*body," he says.

Andrew frowns and turns back around. Mary brushes up next to him. "I liked it when we were alone," she whispers.

The lines of Andrew's frown grow deeper. He nods slowly. Gabriel bursts between them, thrusting them away from one another. "Make room for the party," he says. He spins back around. Like an angel descending from heaven, his silhouette is framed by the bright, distant beams of downtown. He throws his head back, and his staccato laugh bursts through the silent night. All around them, the milling sound of people begins to gather. Ritualistically, it builds slowly like the soft strains at the opening to the fourth movement of Beethoven's Ninth.

Andrew covers his face with his hands. He feels the pressure of somebody's grip on his shoulder. "You okay?" Carey asks.

Shivering, Andrew says, "Yeah." More confidently, he continues, "Yeah. Just stoned."

"Stop smoking so much pot," Carey whispers with his head tilted to the side and a concerned look in his eyes.

Andrew nods. "Maybe. Maybe you're right." He turns and walks over to the side of the building where it meets the next building, and he sits down on a wall raised no higher than a curb. He lights a cigarette. Its cherry burns like the dotted beam of a sharpshooter's laser scope. The target's being zeroed in. Out of the corner of her eye, Mary notices the cigarette burning all alone over there. From the light of the bright street below, she can make out the sharp features of Andrew's profile. She politely disengages herself from another conversation with Simon, and she joins him.

"You mind if I sit down?"

Andrew shakes his head, *No.*

"So what do you think?"

"Of what?"

"The tribute in lights."

Andrew glances back at the streamers searching heaven. "It's weird," he says. "It reminds me of a night I spent with my friend, Michelle."

"Why's that?"

"We were on top of the Empire State Building talking about how amazing the Twin Towers were."

"Oh." Mary glances down. "Where is she tonight?"

"Over there," Andrew says with a nod at the lights.

"In Manhattan?"

"Sort of."

Suddenly, Andrew's cryptic words make sense. Mary whispers, "I'm sorry. Were you good friends?"

Andrew nods. "Pretty good."

Mary stares at her feet. "I remember now that Carey said you lost somebody in the Towers. I really am sorry. I shouldn't have asked so many questions."

"It's okay. You get used to it."

"You're doing better than I am, then." Mary looks up. She smiles. "What sign are you?"

"Pisces."

"I don't know any Pisces. What is that?"

"The fish."

"Hmm… What are they like?"

"I don't know. I never paid any attention to signs. Don't believe in them. Maybe if you talk to me long enough, you could tell me what we're like."

"Maybe. I'm a Virgo, the virgin. No matter what

happens to us, we always stay pure. That's how I've been able to make it through all of this."

"I guess I'm breathing through my gills as I drown. That's how I make it through. I just hope I never wind up on land again. After this, I'd suffocate."

Mary stares at the shadows of the lines accenting Andrew's face. In all seriousness, she says, "You seem like you have something infinite inside of you."

Andrew snorts a short, mocking laugh. "I don't believe in the infinite. Not anymore."

"I believe in the infinite. I feel it inside of me. I see it inside of you."

Andrew glances around the roof. Gatherings of people are leaning into one another, laughing, talking. "Do you want to go downstairs and get a beer?" he asks.

"Sure. I could use another drink." They stand up. Even though they're clean, they brush themselves off and begin their trek across the roof. Mary rubs her shoulders as she walks. "I'm glad we're leaving," she says. "I was starting to get cold."

Andrew nods. He takes one last glance from these heights at the Tribute in Lights. For a second, he witnesses what Mary was talking about. He sees an endless array of spirits flittering through the electric pulse. They wind around one another like a strand of DNA, like Tiamat suckling off Her tail. They're the bright red resurgent trails of the fallen angels to heaven. Lucifer leads the army as the spirit of Ziggy Stardust, the pied piper with his baton. Andrew blinks. Lucifer and his army are gone. All that's left is the brilliant white of the work lights from the past few months exploding due to tension in an upward rush. The noisy silhouette of partying lost souls playing their games on top of the ceiling of Andrew's home invades the blackened foreground.

Back downstairs, on the landing, Mary steps off the last step and onto solid ground, the type of ground that supports your whole foot, not just the ball or arch, again. "I really don't like Gabriel," she says. "He makes me uncomfortable."

"You have to get to know him," Andrew says.

"I don't think I want to."

Inside the apartment, the tail end of The Damned Damned Damned is still playing even though there's nobody there. Like the bass in a symphony, Andrew and Mary hear it as they stroll down the hall. It bounces off the walls.

As they step into the apartment and close the door behind themselves, Andrew asks, "You wanna hear something else?"

"Sure," Mary answers. She heads over to the kitchen counter to fix herself a drink.

"Any preferences?"

"No."

Andrew puts *The White Album* on. A plane begins its descent onto a landing strip in the U.S.S.R. "I'm gonna grab a beer," he says.

"Maybe I'll have a beer, too," Mary says setting her cup aside. "You don't have any Coronas, do you?"

"I don't know. I don't know what people brought."

"I didn't see any in there earlier." Mary walks over to the corner where the refrigerator is. Her shoulder brushes against Andrew's as he opens the door. It's a jolt of electric warmth to both of them. "I'm sure there aren't any..."

"Right here," Andrew says. He reaches into the fridge. Sitting in a six pack of Bass is a single Corona. It seems to have appeared from out of nowhere.

Mary widens her eyes. The tight skin of her cheeks stretches. Trailing her hand along the refrigerator door, she backs away. "Now, that's a miracle," she says. "The first miracle I've ever seen. What's the deal with you anyway?"

Andrew shrugs.

Mary takes the Corona from him. "I believe in synchronicity. Do you?" she says as she tips her bottle forward for a slight *cheers*.

"I don't believe in anything," Andrew says. "To miracles, fish, and crowns, then." Their bottles clink together lightly. "Sounds like a lust for Jesus." He adds, "You wanna smoke some pot?"

"I don't know. Sure. Why not."

"All right. I'll be right back."

Mary plops down on the couch in the tiny living room. She absorbs the atmosphere of the room. The music transports her mind to a place where the balalaikas ring. The run down appearance of the apartment, the sparsely decorated white walls, the crack running across the stained ceiling, has every feature of being the ramshackle dwelling of a Soviet-era worker's communal, comrade-friendly domicile. The image triggers a memory of something approximating Orwell's *1984*. Where are the thought police? Mary leans back, rests her neck on the couch. She takes in the full effect of the room.

Andrew returns. He sits down next to Mary. "I rolled a joint. Figured it would be easier to share than the one-hitter."

"What do you spend your time thinking about?" Mary asks.

"I think about all sorts of things," Andrew answers.

"But I want to know right now. Right now, what are you thinking about?"

"Do you really want to know?"

"Yes."

Andrew turns his head to take a look around the room.

In the corner, at the edge of his vision, right after he passes over the point, he sees the darkened abstract shape that determines his answer. He takes a sip off his beer. Clenching his teeth, he says, "I'm thinking about robbing a bank."

Startled, Mary shakes her head. She coughs. For the second time, with the same emphases as before, she expands her features in an expression of disbelief. "What? You're not serious, are you?"

Andrew checks on the corner for encouragement. Emptiness. He laughs. "Not really. I just need a plot for this screenplay I'm writing. It's supposed to be a film about 'ideas'."

"That's right. Carey said you were a writer."

"Not anymore. I threw my computer out the window."

"Then how are you writing a screenplay?"

"It's all in my head. You'll see. You're in it."

"How can I be in it? You just met me."

"I'm writing your scene right now."

Mary looks at Andrew. The depths and the lines around his eyes lend him the accoutrements of the eternally sad. This must be something like peeking into the faces of the original disciples of Christ. *How long have you looked like this?* Mary wonders. She smiles. "You're odd," she says. "But I like that."

"Right now, we're getting all of the characters together for the robbery. Soon we'll all be rich beyond our wildest dreams. I just don't know how we'll do it yet."

Getting excited, Mary slides one leg onto the couch. She hooks her foot underneath her other leg. "So what's the 'idea' driving this whole thing?" she asks, a desire for comprehension accenting her eyes and lips.

"It's all metaphor."

"You Europeans and your metaphors. When will you

ever grow up?"

"I'm only half-European. Half-Jewish."

"Even worse. Doesn't that make you think you're chosen or something?"

"Or something, but definitely American. I used to like being an American."

"You don't anymore?"

Andrew shakes his head, *No*.

"*I* still do."

"Then you're lucky," he says morosely.

"I didn't have to grow up with wars or anything. This is probably the closest I'll ever get."

"It's only the beginning."

"I don't think so. The world's going to change, Andrew."

"I know."

With that idea, they're both silent.

"Do you really want to know the idea driving the story?" Andrew suddenly asks.

Mary chokes on a sip of beer. She drops the bottle from her lips. "Sure."

Andrew glances around the empty room. He takes a hit off the joint. It's burning nice and slow. He sits up straighter on the couch, and he exhales. The smoke is invisible. The world shifts. He passes the joint back to Mary. "I'm good," she says.

Andrew shrugs and takes another hit. "The screenplay's like an alarm clock, a time bomb, the introduction of the cultural terrorist. It's something that this world's been building up to for years: a recognition of how society stifles the soul, the beginning of the devolution, and I'm going to start the revolution."

"What revolution?"

"The sublation of all dualities: male and female, day and

night, life and death, god and the devil, the devolutionary revelation. It all starts here, on this night. This is the real beginning of the story. I've been writing it for months, ever since the weekend before 9/11, but this is where it really begins. Tonight."

"I don't understand."

"I do. You saw the miracle. You say it's synchronicity. I see it from outside the system. That's why *I* call it a miracle. I finally get it now. I understand the story. It's not mine, and it's not yours. It's relativity. That's the trick. That's the idea driving the whole thing, seeing the world from God's perspective, from the unmoved mover's perspective. That's how you get beyond good and evil."

"I still don't understand."

"Think of the bank robbery I'm talking about as grabbing hold of the Lord's riches. Not the church's money, but God's monopoly on knowledge. If we could get past the duality that came from our invention of the serpent as the devil, then maybe we could finally eat again from the tree of life, and nobody else would ever have to die. Maybe even the dead could come back to life. We could build the New Jerusalem and drink and smoke and fuck in it for all eternity. All it takes is the knowledge of those computerized zeroes and ones that, in a bank, our checks and cash become. Not the knowledge of how to make them, but what they actually are, how they exist. Think of it. You'd be breaking out of the matrix. You could hold electricity in the palm of your hand. Just like those lights shining up, forever outside."

"Are you talking about humans becoming gods?"

"We're summoning the gods."

Mary furrows her eyebrows. "It's an interesting idea, but I don't believe God has a perspective for us to learn. I don't believe that God exists. Certainly not a Judeo-

Christian God, and that blows your whole theory of trees and whatnot."

"Neither do I, but that doesn't negate the reality of the concept. Anything that can be thought of can be done. That's the foundation for Anselm's ontological proof."

Mary nods slowly. She doesn't say anything for a moment. She stares at her hand – the way that the bones of her knuckles wrap her fingers around the bottle of beer. What a fascinating machine. Then, she says, "I don't know anything about Anselm and his proof, but how could you have been writing a screenplay that you didn't understand?"

"Because art is like life. And my art is my life."

Mary shakes her head. "You *are* strange," she says with a smile.

Andrew shrugs. The joint is done, nothing more than a roach. We could step on it, but every death has the right to life.

Something manifests behind them. They can't see it. They feel it. They get colder, move closer together on the couch. The ghost spreads its dark wings over their heads. It leans forward and breathes its cool breath across their faces. Andrew reacts. He's experienced this before. He twists his neck every which way in the hope that he can see it, can catch a fleeting glimpse of what he feels, but he can't. The spirit chooses to remain invisible, especially to them. As her subconscious overtakes her consciousness, Mary drifts off into the world of marijuana dreams. Maybe now all the ghosts can be seen.

"What's wrong?" Mary asks.

"Nothing," Andrew says, and he settles back against the couch, maintaining an edge despite his relaxation. The ghost enfolds them in its wings. It draws them closer together.

"You seem so tense," Mary says. With the trembling

tips of her fingers, she brushes Andrew's arm.

Andrew starts. As if her touch had been fire, he quickly turns his head towards Mary to ask her why she burned him.

She scrunches up her eyebrows. She opens her mouth, and she silently begs, *What did I do? What happened? Did I hurt you?*

Andrew unconvincingly shakes his head, *No.* In the afterlife, amid the afterbirth, every liquid touch burns. *I'd like for you to destroy me.*

Mary leans forward. Eager to meet his fate, Andrew meets her halfway. The grooves in their lips brush against each other's. They open their mouths. Mary gives so willingly. She whimpers in the back of her throat. Her face collapses like rubber. Their tongues twist. There's a barrage of footsteps in the hall. They open their eyes – Mary's so black, Andrew's so blue. Together, they make a bruise.

Leading the troupe that he's not a part of, Gabriel is the first back in the room. "Not yet," he mumbles to nobody as he loosely steps up to the sink to fix himself a drink.

As the rest of the party makes their ramshackle way back into the apartment, Mary whispers to Andrew, "Can we see the lights from your bedroom window?"

Andrew nods.

"Let's go then," she says.

The party's noise envelops them as they stand up and head to the opposite end of the apartment. Nobody bothers them. Nobody shows any interest in them. Only Carey carefully follows their retreat. The edges of his lips tremble, but he doesn't say anything. He vaguely reaches one hand forward not even enough to draw attention from the other guests. Once inside his room, Andrew looks across the apartment into Carey's petrified face. He closes his door, and Carey can't see anymore. Carey frowns and returns to the party. Tension seeps across his movements and features.

"I'm glad we got out of there," Mary says. "I don't feel like dealing with a party anymore."

Andrew nods, but he's not paying any attention to her. He strolls across the room to his window. Like a man contemplating a jump, he presses one hand against the glass and stares into the night. He's looking for ghosts. All he sees is an explosion, September 11th all over again, a nuclear reaction, Ground Zero remains a permanent vacuum, a merger, like the body with the soul, two distinct corporations, of the white work lights into the brilliant buildings that used to dominate Downtown's scene. The lights themselves are a shadow of the once powerful structures, a sort of spirit in their own right, the freed spirit of the hermaphrodite, destroyed by Allah yet brought, by Frankenstein's science, more powerfully back to life. We all have to wrestle with the devil in order to return to this world of light.

"It must be hard to have this view," Mary says. She's followed Andrew. She's standing beside him.

Andrew frowns and shrugs.

"I mean, it's a constant reminder of what we've lost." She ends with a whisper, "Of what you've lost."

"This whole city's a constant reminder. I can't go anywhere without remembering what everything looked like before."

"At least we have those memories."

"I don't want those memories. I don't want any memories."

"Don't say that. We always need to be grateful that we're alive."

Slowly, Andrew turns away from the window. He looks Mary in the eye. Without a smile, without any expression at all, he inhales heavily. She blinks and looks away. He shakes his head and turns back to stare, like a deer, at the mystery of the lights.

"Do you think we could move away from the window?" Mary asks softly as if she's afraid that she might startle Andrew into grabbing her hand, leaping, and pulling her down with him into the alley where glimmers of his laptop, untouched by, useless to the stumbling zombies, still shine. "And just talk?"

Without saying a word, Andrew turns around, walks over to his bed, and sits down. Mary hesitantly joins him on the mattress. They lean back against the wall. She smiles at him. She moves closer to him. She snuggles up against his arm. He runs his hand across her head and smells her hair's fresh scent. Her black hair is smooth to the touch, but it's not as consuming to his senses as the summer smell of Michelle's curls. He closes his eyes and his face contorts. Mary doesn't see it. She's staring at the clothes strewn across his floor. Andrew's room has the appearance and smell of a crypt. She turns and looks at him. His eyes are flooded. His lip is trembling.

"What's wrong?" she asks.

Andrew shakes his head.

She sits up and rubs her hand down his cheek. His flesh has the clamminess of the fevered. Unafraid of his illness, she presses her lips against his. Andrew responds. Slowly, Mary begins to pull off her carefully chosen outfit. With a concerned look on her face, as she stares at the lines around Andrew's mouth and eyes, she throws her shoes, shirt, and pants onto the floor. Like the queen being buried alive with her king, she adds her mess to the one that Andrew has already made. She undoes her bra and slips out of her underpants. Her thighs are thick, Amazon snakes. With his eyes closed, Andrew slowly begins taking off his shirt. Mary helps him to undress.

Naked, they collapse upon the bed, Mary on top of Andrew. As she glides above him, her tongue tonguing his flesh, he smells her musky scent. It's too natural, too feminine for the night, too reminiscent of dreams unrealized. He presses his eyelids tighter together. There's no escape, the thick smell of sex envelops the room.

Like a vampire awakening in his coffin, Andrew comes to life. He pushes Mary onto her back, spreads her legs, and begins to thrust and thrust as hard as he can. He wishes she was a virgin, that this friction could make her bleed. He pulls her hair, forcing her neck straight, the top of her head into the pillow. He's thinking the whole time that maybe with this next action, she'll start to cry, maybe with this much force, she'll feel the pain he feels inside, but nobody can ever make another feel what they feel inside. All she does is close her eyes and breathe and writhe along with every torque of his body. She takes every bit of rage he has and buries it inside her womb.

Weaker than his lover, going limp inside of her, Andrew collapses onto Mary's chest. Breathing soothingly, like a mother with her child, she coos and gently rubs her fingernails down his back.

Andrew sits up. "Get out," he says. "Grab your clothes and get the fuck out of my room."

Startled, Mary doesn't move for a second. Confused, she stares at Andrew. She sees the seriousness, the murder, in his eyes, and she concedes. She wipes off her thighs, stands up, picks her clothes off the ground, gets dressed as quickly as she can, and leaves without a backwards glance at the man she just made love to.

With the tribute in lights burning outside, releasing the dead into the New York night, Andrew and the ghost are alone together, just as they are on every other night, in his bedroom.

When Andrew wakes up on March 12th, the world has the fluid motion to it that every one of his recent mornings contains. It's late, early afternoon. Andrew squints as he sits up in bed. He remembers the promise he made to his mom before the night began. Like a child unhappy with the prospect of cleaning his room, he curls into a fetal position. Playing out his melodramatic role, he grimaces. *I don't want to see Charlie at all.* Can one selfless deed erase the karma of a thousand selfish acts?

The quickest way to Charlie's Midtown apartment is via the G train at Manhattan Avenue. Wearing a scowl, Andrew bounds down his stoop and heads in that direction. His cell phone rings.

"Hello?"

"Is Charlie there?"

"I'm going to see him now."

"What?"

"You've got the wrong number. You know, you've called me a thousand times over the past couple months. Don't you get it yet?"

"I've never called this number before."

"Well, check your digits, brother." He hangs up. Somebody must have duplicated his number. That's the only explanation for all of these calls. *Maybe*, Andrew thinks, *I need to check my phone bill, make sure I'm only paying for my calls. When do I get my next statement?* He drops the phone back in his pocket and nervously runs his hand down his face. He's not sweating, but even in the brisk breeze, he feels like he should be. He blows on his cupped hands.

Waiting on the train, he leans against a tiled post next to the track. He's where he wants to be, three quarters of the way to the end, so that when the doors open at Court

Square, he'll be right next to the stairs that lead up to the Manhattan bound lines. He knows all this from what feels like the distant past, when he worked in Manhattan, when Charlie and he were friends. The dirty station is nearly empty. A sheen of grime coats everything in sight – the walls, the advertisements, the concrete; even the air itself is dirty. Andrew brushes the fuzz away from his eyes. There's an old, Eastern European woman with a shopping bag and a bandana over her stringy, gray hair sitting on the bench. Masticating only with her gums, she chews on nothing. A young man in tight jeans, with long hair and a leather jacket leans against the wall. So eighties for America, he's picking at and biting his fingernails. This part of Brooklyn could easily be Warsaw. On weekends, nobody takes the G. The trains only run every twenty minutes or so. The line, like every line in the city, exists only in order to get people to and from work. When nobody's working, the city doesn't care about transportation. Get out and shop, America. They can't beat us!

A rat scurries in between the track's metal lines. Huge and brown, he's the largest natural predator that the city has to offer. His matted hair sticks up on his back. With his body arched as his little legs scramble, he buries his pink nose in the ground. Like Belial, he scours the scents of Brooklyn's underbelly as he searches for something. He's a virus avoiding white blood cells. Like HIV, he morphs. Unafraid of the tons of steel that pulse through these veins, the king of his little world, he pauses. Something has piqued his interest. With his little rat claws, he paws at the hard ground. It's the most natural, the most serene, that a single creature can ever appear to be in New York.

The sound of the charging subway rumbles in the distance. Suddenly, its lone headlight rounds a corner. At the end of the tunnel, the bright light appears. This is something approximating death. The rat, like a phantom, knew what was coming and has disappeared. The light grows. It expands to fill the emptiness beneath the streets. The sound grows deafening. The hurricane winds blow ever onward. With a squeal and a gust of cool breeze, the train screeches to a halt. Somewhere deep in the earth's guts, the rat's heart beats even faster than usual as he fearfully sniffs the air. He quivers. Andrew and his two compatriots step into the glass and metal monster. The car he enters is bright and empty. He sits down and leans his tired head back against a map that plots the charts for New York's underworld. Beneath plexi-glass, a plethora of colors criss-cross, in jagged shapes, the boroughs from which, once you've entered, there's no escape.

He transfers at Court Square. At Lexington, he switches again and heads down two stops on the 6. He really doesn't feel like getting out and walking. If he's going to make this goodwill trek, then he's going to do it with the least amount of hassle as possible. He's riding on one of the new trains, not one of the ones with grimy, metal hand rails and the perpetual stink of sweat, but one of the ones that are futuristic and clean, with an automated announcer and lights plotting your course. In the midst of his dystopian reality, it's the fantasy of traveling on the perfected transportation of a utopian society. He thinks for a moment about the different colors of green that paint the signs of the two trains, the one that he started on and the one that he's ending on. The G is such a sickly color, reminiscent of fevers and nausea, emptily cutting its course through the ghettoes of Brooklyn and Queens. The 6 is deep and lush, like a forest watered by the pollution in the East River, growing as it barrels below Manhattan. This is the seed that germinated into the theories Ari works with. Andrew closes his eyes, nods forward, and rubs his forehead.

Charlie only lives a handful of blocks from the stop. It's a damn good location for anyone who can barely afford to live in this part of Manhattan, an unbelievable location for a man who just lost his job. There's nothing particularly striking about the building. No reason to include it on an architectural tour of the city, one of a million monoliths crushing the sky. It doesn't have the panache of Madison Avenue's offices, and it doesn't have the character of the Village's homey domiciles. Instead, it's the blank façade of the introductory page to an Ikea catalog.

Andrew buzzes Charlie's apartment. He taps his foot, taps the side of his head, zips his hoody up higher, nearly covers the neck of his thermal shirt, and waits. No answer. He scuffs the toe of his shoe against the step he's standing on. He pulls out his phone and dials Charlie's number. First, his home, then his cell – answering machines on both. He leaves messages for his oldest friend to call him as soon as he can. He's in Midtown, and he was hoping that they could hang out. No reason to try and explain what the hell he's doing in Midtown in the first place. He presses the buzzer again. Still no answer. He decides to wander off and scrounge up a cup of coffee. He's got some change jingling in his pockets. Andrew curses Charlie for fucking up his afternoon. He'll be back soon. He can't have much money. Financial situations aren't quite the same as the days when Andrew first moved to the city and he was staying with Charlie and they'd go out boozing all weekend. How far could he have gone? Maybe they'll even bump into one another at the deli.

Light brown coffee, extra sweet and thin, in the blue paper cups that you get at the delis and bodegas dotting nearly every block of the five boroughs. It's a sweet treat for the afternoon. Andrew sips slowly out of the white plastic top. To cool what he's about to drink, he blows over the mouth hole. Creating an effluence at his lips, the steam mixes with his breath. The cup warms his hand. He tucks his other hand into his pocket. This reminds him of when he had a job, when he and Charlie were friends. He walks down the street back to Charlie's apartment, doesn't bother looking in either direction as he crosses the avenue. Not that he's that cool. He's just that burnt out. Luckily no cars are coming. Andrew keeps walking. It hasn't been more than ten minutes, but even five minutes was enough time for his friend to return from a quick errand.

Back at the door, staring at the wall, at the silver grate covering the box of electronic voice holes, Andrew presses the buzzer again. The sound pounds through the neighborhood's concrete sterility, bounds off of the buildings' emotionless faces. Like a defibrillator, its electronic pulse awakens even the rats. The tiny predator of the subway stops fiddling with the ground. Twitching his nose, he begins to pay attention. All of the demons turn their heads. Everybody on the street is staring. Standing on the steps, buzzing a room that never responds, Andrew feels a fool. He shakes his head, turns, and heads down towards the sidewalk.

A bum, taking a break from his manic strolls throughout the city, is leaning against the bricks of Charlie's building. As Andrew reaches him, from behind his shaggy blond beard, he says, "It's like trying to wake the dead."

"What?"

The bum narrows his wild, blue eyes. "Getting into one of these places is like trying to wake the dead. I've been trying for years." He shakes his head and with a hefty swing of his arms, heaves himself towards the street and begins, at a breakneck speed, to swerve towards Lexington.

Andrew stops in the midst of his retreat. Thoughtful lines crease both his eyes and the corners of his mouth.

With the resounding tune of synchronicity pounding through his brain, the bum's words resonate in his mind. Panicked, he turns around and heads back to Charlie's door. His chest and head feel light. He buzzes his friend's apartment one last time. Still no answer. He remembers, from the days when he stayed here, which buzzer connects to the super's room. He presses it.

Finally, a gruff voice comes through the box, "Who's there?"

"Yeah, you don't know me, but I've been trying to get through to my friend on the seventh floor, Charles Amsterdam, for a while now, and nobody's responding. I was wondering if you could let me in just so I can make sure he's okay."

"Not my problem, buddy. Why don't you try coming back later. Maybe your friend'll be home then."

"Look. His mom asked me to stop by. She says she hasn't heard from him in a few weeks, and she just wants somebody to make sure he's okay."

"I'm not the tenants' babysitter. If they don't feel like talking to their family, maybe somebody should enroll them in counseling. Regardless, it's not something I got time for. Good-bye."

With a shock of anger radiating through his system, as his finger trembles a little from the cold, more so from frustration, Andrew presses the super's buzzer repeatedly.

"Whaaat?"

"I'm not kidding. I think something's seriously wrong. I can't reach him on his phone, and nobody's heard from him in a while. He lost his job, and his mom said he was really depressed. I need to get in there and see him, and yeah, maybe then, I'll enroll him in counseling."

"Listen, buddy, I can't let you in here. I don't know why your friend doesn't feel like talking to you, but nobody's coming in this building unless they're invited. Get it? Now, if you don't leave, I'm gonna call the cops."

"Sounds great, man. Maybe if you call the cops, they'll listen to me and get somebody up there to see him. I'm just gonna sit out here on the stoop until they show up. Don't sweat it, brother. I won't bother anybody. Let the cops know I'm waiting for them."

Hesitantly, the voice comes back over the speaker. "How about if I go up there with you, will you leave after that?"

"Most definitely. I just want to make sure he's okay."

"Okay. I'll be right out to let you in. No way I'm letting you wander in here all alone. Hold on."

Andrew leans against the wall. In his mind, he hears the bum's warning over and over again: *Like trying to wake the dead.* Sometimes, it seems like the dead are already awake.

The door opens. Standing in a pair of sweatpants, tennis shoes, and an untucked white tee shirt, with his gray hair a mess and a beer gut is a man holding a baseball bat. "You the guy been trying to get in here?" he asks.

Andrew glances at the bat. He swallows slowly and nods.

"All right, come on. Let's go check on your friend. You go first. Elevator's over there." With his bat, the man indicates a direction.

"I know where it is," Andrew says. "I've been here a million times."

He zooms past the man and heads over to the elevator. He presses the button, and they wait.

As he picks at the floor with the toe of his shoe, Andrew says, "I hope I'm wrong, but I got a bad feeling about this. And I'm trying to trust my feelings a little more these days. What else can you do when the world's gone insane?"

"Whatever, friend. I just hope your buddy doesn't ream my ass when you show up at his door unannounced."

"Trust me. I'm announced. I've been announcing myself all day. He's just not responding." He mumbles, "I'm sure everything's okay. I'm probably overreacting."

"Well, I don't know what you expect to find. If your friend wanted to talk to you, I'm sure he would have called you back."

"I'm worried that he might have wanted to talk to me a week or two ago."

In the confines of the elevator, the super exudes the sickly stench of a lazy, middle-aged man who spends too much time drinking beer on his couch. It seems he hasn't moved in years, and he stinks of the drunken, stale sweat that has collected in his skin's loose grooves during that time. It doesn't bother Andrew though. His heart is beating too quickly. He stares at the old-fashioned needle as it ticks off their ascent.

The elevator doors open. Andrew steps into the hallway. "Which apartment is your friend's? I don't recall," the super says.

"That one over there," Andrew says, pointing.

"All right. You stand back. I'm gonna ask your friend if he wants to see you?" The super moves over to Charlie's apartment door. "I hear a TV going," he says. He knocks on the door. "Mr. Amsterdam? Mr. Amsterdam you there?" No response. He knocks again. "Mr. Amsterdam?" Still no response. "I don't think he's there, buddy."

"No," Andrew says. His face is stone. His words are automatic. "He's there. I know he is. Don't you have a key or something? Can't we go in?"

The super turns around. "I don't know where you get off. No, we can't go in. Listen. You said that if I brought you up here, you'd leave. Nobody's home. Now I'm gonna walk you back downstairs, and you're gonna get going. You can come back when your friend invites you over."

"I told you. His mom's really worried about him, and now, I am, too. You told me yourself that you heard a TV going. Somebody should be in there. This is my oldest friend in the world. We grew up around the corner from each other. I'm an only child, and so is he. He's a year older than me. We're like brothers. I'm not some sort of psychopath, not yet anyway, and I'm his family's only hope here. If he's not there, we open the door, make sure everything's kosher, you yell at me for wasting your time, and I leave and wait either for him to call me or for me to file a missing person's report. If he is there, well, then, I need to see what the hell's going on with him. Please, I need your help."

The super thinks it over. He purses his lips and looks at the ceiling. He looks at the ground. Playing out as many scenarios as he can imagine, his brain's gears click in clock-like motion. He taps the end of his bat against the ground. It makes a dull thud on the floor – the tick of a grandfather clock. Time flows backwards. His expressions twist with every different ending to the situation. Finally, he looks back at Charlie's door. Beyond it, the television continues its lonely grumbling. Something clicks in the super's desolate eyes. He exhales heavily and says, "Fine. Come downstairs with me, and I'll grab the key out of my apartment."

Back upstairs, in the dingy hall light, the super steps back up to Charlie's door. He knocks. "Mr. Amsterdam? Mr. Amsterdam, this is Dante Beatricio, the building superintendent. I've got a friend of yours here." Dante looks back over his shoulder. He whispers, "What's your name?"

"Andrew Christian."

"Andrew Christian. He and I are going to come in. If you don't want us to, please let us know." Dante waits for a moment. After there's no response, he sticks the key into the lock. Dante twists it. The slight sound of the lock's teeth biting the key's skin clicks through the hall. "Got it," Dante says. "Let's hope he doesn't have the chain on the door." With a small amount of force, he pushes forward. No chain. The door opens.

The muffled TV voices grow louder. They lend the apartment the semblance of retaining an inhabitant. From behind Dante's oversized shoulder, Andrew peeks into the living room. On the couch in the corner, that's where he used to sleep when he first moved to New York, when the world, this city, was a jazzy, beatnik dream. The couch is empty. The apartment is dark. The curtains are drawn. A sliver of sunlight outlines the plastic shades' edges, casts white shadows of tiny dust mites that billow through the stale air.

"Mr. Amsterdam?" Dante asks, a glimmer of concern discernable in his gruff accent.

Andrew peers deeper into the room. In the mild darkness, the television set glows like a worm. On the screen, a man holds a microphone. He's on location in some cold, distant desert. He appears deathly serious, dramatically important, as he reports his fair and balanced view to the news-weary world. In the upper left-hand corner of the screen, it says: FOX. The three letters disappear to be replaced by the word LIVE. Behind the messages, the rectangular shape of a digitized, red, white, and blue American flag flutters. The letters, the flag, the letters, the flag. It's enough to drive anybody mad.

Andrew steps forward. A musty scent, mingled with the smell of excrement, seeps out of the room.

The TV's blue tint casts a pale, triangular light from the

vertex of the screen, out into the living room. Its progression is blocked by the square shape of Charlie's easy chair. Off the side of the chair, cocked at an awkward angle, the shadow of an arm dangles limply. For a moment, Andrew thinks it might be the illusion of the ghost that he always sees out of the corner of his eye. He blinks, but the arm doesn't disappear. It's solid. It's real.

"Charlie?" Andrew cries. He drops his cup of coffee. With a miasma of steam, a tiny model, a science project, reminiscent of the dust and debris that floated over downtown after the towers fell, it spills its dregs across the hallway's floor. In a flash, Andrew bursts past Dante and into the room. He rushes to the front of the chair. He freezes.

The scent of the room is powerful, unbearable, something like the piss covered walls of Paris's sewers, where the rats rule – the overpowering aroma of the flowers of evil.

Charlie is slouched down in his chair. His feet are splayed out in front of him. He's barefoot. His toes seem thick, too fat for his appendages. His neck rests on his chest. His back sits where his ass should. His head is propped up by the chair's stuffing. The bottom of his shirt has risen up, exposing his gut. Dried vomit is crusted to his shirt. It's dripped down his ribs. His eyes are open. So is his mouth. His pale coloring, magnified by the glare of the television, has turned to blue. On the table beside him sits a bottle of whiskey and a bottle of prescription pills. Beneath them is a piece of paper. Scrawled across the page, in Charlie's sloppy, little boy handwriting, are the words: *It's all my fault.*

In the background, the voice of the reporter drones on and on about the positive progress of the United States' war in Afghanistan. Andrew feels numb, more sober even than he experienced life in the days preceding 9/11. A strange noise, like that of the key turning in the lock, clicks in his throat. Deep down in his gut, he wretches. The coffee that he'd poured onto his empty stomach spills across Charlie's hardwood floor, laps at his friend's cold, bare feet.

With tears boiling in his eyes, Andrew looks back at Dante. The super hasn't moved from the doorway. His mouth hangs as wide as Charlie's.

"He's dead," Andrew mumbles. "My best friend's dead."

Andrew didn't wait for the cops to show up at Charlie's door. He told Dante that he needed to get a pack of cigarettes and a fresh cup of coffee, breathe New York's bitter air, and once he hit the streets, he thrust his hands into his pockets, and he started walking, cutting across the island. He stopped at an ATM machine and withdrew some of the money that he was saving for the rent check that hasn't cleared yet. The check will bounce. He doesn't care. It's happened to him before. Now, it can happen to somebody else for a change. He's trembling from the inside out. The wind doesn't freeze him; his emotions do.

He's standing in front of the window at Bellevue, not the lunatic asylum, but the bar. Either way, it's the same thing. Like the breath of angels, both offer the fanatically suffering sheltering wings from life's hurricanes. But sometimes, neither does the user any good. We simply partake of the doctors' dopamine inducing drugs. The angels' violent trumpets lull us to sleep, to dream.

New York's bricks present a more insurmountable wall than ever before. Their drab colors darken the texture of Andrew's soul. Their rough skins harden the cells of his heart. He needs to blow this place apart and set himself free. He opens the door to the bar. He steps inside.

It's early yet. The barroom lights are bright. A thin, blonde girl in a low cut shirt and tight jeans serves drinks to the aged gentlemen lost in their cups. At this point in the late afternoon, only the true drinkers preside over this solemn atmosphere. Andrew sits down at the bar. The blonde girl looks at him and lifts her eyebrows. At any other point in his life, Andrew may have responded to her subliminal advances.

"Give me the cheapest beer you've got," he says distractedly. He doesn't even raise his head to look at her.

She pours him a golden fluid on draft. "Two bucks," she responds coldly as she slides it up to him.

He hands her a twenty. She gives him his change. He leaves her a dollar tip. Some heavy metal song blares from out the jukebox. The tinny sound of its distorted guitars seers beneath the electric slide of operatic vocals.

With the fingers of his right hand holding his pint like a knuckleball, Andrew leans his head over the bar. He still feels sick. His hair has grown longer and wavier over the past couple months. Curling a bit at the ends, it hangs in front of his eyes.

He drinks his beer, fast, gulping it with the thirst of a deserted man. He waves his fingers and orders another one.

He sinks lower, deeper, into his seat. The image of Charlie's grotesquely bloated face flashes across his thoughts. He grimaces and covers his eyes. But you can't hide from what you see on the inside.

Alone at the bar, Andrew's a snake split in two. His brainless tail flops back and forth. His sentient torso slithers on in its horrendous, bloody way. Can we put the hermaphrodite back together again? He runs his hand down his face. He checks himself to make sure he doesn't vomit this time. With his hand at his mouth, he closes his eyes. He doesn't want to see what's happening outside.

A dirty man in a heavy overcoat, smelling of the sickly sweet stench of the homeless, sits down next to Andrew. His presence will leave a stain on his battered barstool's seat. With his grimy fingers, topped by broken, blackened nails, he digs into the pocket of his frayed dress pants, and he pulls out a handful of change. He orders a beer. The bartender brings him the same golden fluid that Andrew's drinking. He meticulously counts out the right amount and adds a quarter for a tip. Beneath his unkempt facial hair, it's neither full enough nor manicured enough to be called a beard, he smiles a decaying grin full of rotten and rotting teeth. The pretty bartender, with her perfectly set lips, doesn't respond. He doesn't care. He's happy enough to get a drink. He slurps it with all the aplomb of a pig at the trough. He scouts around the bar, carefully taking in the appearances of everything. Then, his gaze lights on Andrew. He narrows his eyes and nervously licks his lips. He taps the distraught young man on the shoulder, and he says, "You're not lookin' so good, buddy. Seems like you just saw a ghost."

"I don't want to talk about it," Andrew says. Without looking up from his beer, he waves the dirty man away.

"Doesn't bother me none. I never want to talk about it," the man answers. He goes back to guzzling his beer. He finishes it quickly, and he leans over and whispers in Andrew's ear, "How about buying an old lunatic a drink? It'll be good for your karma. Clean it up a bit. All we got in this world is our karma. Woman taught me that years ago. Women teach you everything."

"Hey," the bartender shouts. She's sitting on a stool, leaning back against the liquor rail, propping her boots on the bar as she smokes a cigarette and sips a shot. "Why don't you get out of here. Quit bothering my customers."

With his hands thrust forward timidly and a petrified look in the depths of his eyes, the man begins to back away. At every half step, he scans the corners of the room for the bouncer who might be on him in any second. "It's all right," Andrew suddenly says, springing to life. "I'm buying him a drink."

"You sure?" the bartender asks. She doesn't move from her place. Her hardened gaze and her set jaw don't soften.

Without looking at her, Andrew nods.

Shaking her head, the bartender slowly stands up. With an air of disdain, she pours the beer out of the tap and sets the pint at the spot next to Andrew's. Andrew forks out the cash.

"You certain about this?" she asks, her hand on the money, unwilling to just take it.

Andrew nods.

The dirty man comes back and sits down. He sighs. "Much obliged," he says. His face breaks into a yellow, broken toothed grin.

"Don't mention it," Andrew responds. "I just did it for my karma."

"Let me tell you a story, then," the man says to Andrew. "Cuz I can see you're a man of intelligence, and I believe you'll understand. This happened to me years ago, back in the eighties, down in New Orleans. That's where I'm from, originally, though I'd just gotten back there from Florida when all this happened, but New York, New Orleans, New Amsterdam... What's the difference? That's what it means to be American. We're all new. None of us have seen the original, only our version of it. But enough about that." With a wave of his hand, he brushes away his ramblings. "Back to the story.

"I'd just gotten back from Florida. I was a contractor in those days, making good money. But who cares about money? All we need it for is to drink, right?" He smiles and nudges Andrew's shoulder. Andrew sways, but he doesn't respond – no grin, no frown, nothing. He's dead. The man stares for a moment, coughs, and continues: "When I showed back up in New Orleans, I got back together with a high school sweetheart of mine." The man's lips turn down. His gaze pierces the infinite, as if instead of New York's cold sadness, he sees New Orleans's dirty, humid streets bustling with the French Quarter's drunks beyond Bellevue's walls. "Her name was Sherry, and she made me drunk. Always had, always will.

"But you see, while I was gone, another guy came into the picture, and he wasn't right in the head. He said he was a writer. That's what seduced her, but when I showed back up, it was coming to an end between them." Andrew bristles at the word "writer". The man notices. "Don't get me wrong. I wasn't jealous. I didn't force it. It just happened. Sherry'd had enough with this guy's rants. She wanted to be with a real man who came home smelling of sweat and work, not an artsy dandy. No offense if you're one of those." Andrew stares blankly at his beer. "But I can tell from the character you possess that you're not. Even if you're an artist, you're not the type I'm talking about."

The man pauses. He looks at his pint, and he buries its dregs. Andrew's down to his last sip or two as well. "You wanna order us another round?" the guy begs. Andrew concedes. He calls the bartender over and points out their empty drinks. She responds accordingly.

After a sip of fresh beer, the man goes on: "This guy, though, wasn't right in the head. He had this theory. What did he call it? *'Liebestod,'* or something like that. I can't remember the name, but it was one of the first things Sherry told me when I saw her again... She looked so good that day in a halter top and a pair of jean shorts, her legs tan from the sunshine, oiled from her sweat. I ran smack into her as I stepped out of a bar I'd been drinking in since that morning. I nearly collapsed in my tracks. We went back to her apartment, smoked some reefer, kissed for the first time in over five years, and she told me all about this guy. He was heavy into her. She wasn't so sure what she thought of him. He was from some small town in Kentucky. She didn't think he was right for New Orleans. His name was Christopher. I've hated that name ever since. She thought the voodoo was taking control of him. His ideas got me to thinking what the hell Sherry'd been up to since I'd been gone." The man sets his elbow on the bar and leans closer to Andrew. "Get this. This guy thought that everybody needed to be ready, at any moment, to die for love. Even if it was murder or suicide." Andrew twists his head towards the sickly sweet smelling man. He's finally beginning to pay attention. "He thought that love transported, that it was the only way a person got into heaven. And if a person didn't die for love, from a broken heart, then they had no chance. Something about how Jesus didn't exist, and somebody needed to intercede for the dead. Like I said, this guy wasn't right in the head. I don't know where he came up with this shit, but the crux of the story is that he'd decided he was in love with the red-headed love of *my* life, and his conclusion, even before she saw me again was that they both needed to die." The man chugs his pint, a necessary step before he finishes his story. "I guess he thought that she was in love with him too. Whatever the fuck that means." With his dirty fingers, the man touches Andrew's arm. "I don't believe in love," he says. "Never have. All I believe in is the way somebody makes your stomach feel. I'm sure you know what I mean, how they put that relaxed feeling in your gut."

Andrew wraps his hand around his pint. He grits his

teeth. "I have no idea what you're talking about," he snarls.

The man cocks his head to the side. He stares briefly at Andrew. He looks away. "You will," he says. "Someday, you will.

"Sherry tried calling it all off with him, but he didn't pay any attention to what she said. I didn't understand how a guy could be like that. Every time I was over at her place, this asshole'd call. Sometimes, he even showed up. That's how he found out about me and what I looked like. He followed me into a bar one night. I saw him out on the street, and I kept my eye on the door as he came in. He didn't walk right up to me. First, he stepped over to the corner and had a few drinks. Guess he was trying to get his courage up. Figuring there was going to be a fight, I started drinking pretty heavy, too. I was in good shape back then. Nothing like I look like now. I had muscles, and my hands were tough from being outside and working all day. After two or three drinks, this guy comes over. He looks me up and down... real scrawny fellow. Built kinda like you, but his face was real pointy. Staring at him, I could have sworn he was a rat, just like the ones that probably live in your apartment here. He says to me, 'I know who you are.' And I answer back, 'I know you, too.' He says, 'Sherry loves me.' I say, 'Man, you don't get it, do you?' He says, 'We'll be married after we're dead.' I say, 'You're one crazy motherfucker.' And he says, 'No, I'm the only sane man here.' And he leaves. Just like that. My blood was up. I had that little tremor in my hands that happens when your adrenalin starts getting pumped up to hit and be hit, but he just left. I never saw him again. Sherry did though.

"The police figured he was waiting outside, waiting for me to leave. All I did was run down to the store to pick up a six pack, some cigarettes, and a couple sandwiches, but it was enough time for him to get in and shoot Sherry and himself. By the time I got back, the cops had already sealed the building off and called the coroner. There was nothing I could do. He killed me on that day, too, but I never found a bride after I died. Maybe Christopher was right. I've been here for going on nine years now. It took me a long time to hobo my way this far north, but I'm done. I'm stopping here." The man glances over at Andrew. He's impenetrable. "Thanks for the drinks," the man says. "Why don't you tell me your story now?"

"I'm not Catholic. I don't believe in the confessional."

The man glances around the bar. "Then make something up," he says. He fiddles nervously with a napkin on the bar. "Somebody else could have told me *that* story. It could all be lies. Christopher might have stolen my woman, and in my mind, I decided they were both dead. For all you know, his story might be mine. You don't know my name. It might be Christopher. I could have killed them both, and I tell people this fabrication because it's what I need to fall asleep at night. I might not even be from New Orleans. I could have been born and bred in New York City, and all I do is pretend like I visit other places just to see what people might say. You don't know anything, and neither do I." Frantically, the man almost screams, "Just tell me a story to keep my mind off my own."

Andrew downs his beer. "Keep your eye on me then," he says. "I'm telling everyone's story." He stands up, kicks his stool back into place, and walks out the door.

For well over three hundred years, the New York streets of New Amsterdam, have seen everything, billions of stories – Hell's Kitchen's, Harlem's, the Village's comedies and tragedies, loves and hates, deaths and lives, lies and truths. They remain silent, emotionless, to those that wander them. There are no answers to learn. Only googles of teeming questions.

Andrew stares at the sidewalk receding beneath his feet. There are so many stains, so much trash – abandoned flyers, discarded newspapers, used wrappers. There's nothing anybody could ever do to make this place clean again. It doesn't matter how many garbage cans the mayor puts out. Humanity has no sense of decency.

The day has been a rush, a blur, and now he's starting to feel a little bit drunk. Life splits him apart from the inside.

Andrew looks up. Ahead of him, rounding the corner, leaving him, he sees (what's this?), not a ghost, not a vision, but a human being, a real person, with her pointed profile, her outfit, her hair, her beautiful curly hair... He starts running. At the corner, he smells her wonderful scent, the same as she smelled when she left him alone that night at Enid's. He wants to stop, to let the sensation filling his nose ooze into his body through every single one of his pores, melt his icy innards from the inside. He turns in the direction Michelle went. She's gone. There's nobody there, only an endless line of stoic buildings and a homeless woman sitting on the ground two blocks up the street.

He stops. He's trembling. His stomach is a pupae filled with a full-grown butterfly trying to escape. He leans back against a brick wall. He touches his fingers to his forehead.

"What's happening to me?" He thrusts himself forward and stumbles along the sidewalk.

He reaches the homeless woman. He leans down. "Did you see which way she went?"

"What?"

"The girl. The girl with curly hair. Did you see where she went?"

"I ain't got no idea what you're talking about," the woman says.

"She was just here. You must have seen her."

"Mister, I ain't seen anybody but you all day."

"Why are you lying to me? What did I do to you?"

"I'm sure you done everything," the woman says. From beneath a kerchief wrapped around her head, she smiles up at him with a mouth that's missing nearly all of its teeth. Andrew turns white. He spins around and wipes his hand down his face.

He begins to frantically retrace his steps. At a quick clip, he rounds the corner and begins heading uptown again. Running his hands through his hair, he zooms past the other few pedestrians on the sidewalk. He reaches Bellevue's black door. He rips it open and steps inside.

The bar looks almost the same as he left it, except that the man is gone. Andrew strides straight up to the bartender. He wakens her from her relaxed stupor: her feet propped up on the bar; her fingers resting on her chin – a feminists answer to the bloodthirsty entrance to a Spaghetti Western. "Where'd he go?" Andrew shouts at her.

The legs of her stool quickly click against the floor. She drops her feet to the ground. Andrew's harried expression puts her on guard. She regains her composure. "Who?" she cautiously asks.

"The man. The man I was just talking to."

"I threw him out as soon as you left. He was bothering my customers."

Andrew slams his palm down, hard, on the wooden bar. The slap thuds above the metal blaring out of the jukebox. The bartender jumps. All of the customers turn their heads. The bartender glances furtively to her right at a big, biker-looking dude sitting on a stool, quietly drinking a beer. He stands up.

"He's the only one who can help me," Andrew pleads. With his lips twisting convulsively, his eyes shuddering in disbelief, he turns around and heads back to the door. The bartender calmly motions the biker-looking dude to sit back down.

"Do you have any idea where he went?" Andrew cries to the bartender.

She shakes her head, *No.*

Andrew leaves. Outside, the day turns to night. Soon, the World Trade's floodlights, filled with an eternity's worth of frozen energy finally set free, will brighten New York's broken skyline. Andrew's cell phone rings. "Hello?"

"Is Charlie there?"

"No." Andrew says. "Charlie's dead." He clicks his phone closed. He touches his free hand to his temple. He stumbles. For a moment, he appears like he might pass out. But then, with as much force as he threw the bottle in the wee morning hours of September 11th, with the same hopeless ambition of somehow striking at the senseless spirits of this world, of toppling the buildings that crush our souls, of vainly flailing against the brick walls of unforeseen events that keep us boxed up inside, Andrew steps and hurls his cell phone across the street. In a black arc, it arches over the pavement and shatters, in a rain of plastic casing and circuitry, something resembling his laptop crashing against the building opposite his window, against a storefront. The shopkeeper, just like the moon, in jeans and a white smock, comes out and glowers at Andrew.

"What are you doing, man?" the shopkeeper yells. He has a Middle Eastern accent. He points a threatening finger in the direction of his potential assailant. He steps quickly in place, a soldier unsure where to march, as he tries to contain his anger. "You want to break my window?"

Trembling, Andrew remains stationary for a moment. He gazes blankly at his accuser. He shuts his eyes, turns to his left, and slowly starts off. A barrage of insults are hurled at his back. Cursed, hexed like a scapegoat, Andrew stumbles beneath his cross. He droops his head, stares at his feet, breathes heavily, wipes dry tears from his eyes, and walks back downtown.

Inside his mind, the killer bees swarm. He moves at a slow, jerky pace, uncertain where to step even though the ground remains firm beneath his feet. He feels his way against the hard, dirty skyscraper walls. The rough surfaces rip his fingers down to the bone. He knows they're bleeding. He looks. They're fine, a little red at the tips, freshly drawn from the oyster's cavernous, satin mouth. With one hand, he pounds on the side of his skull. With the other, he holds the gut wound in his stomach. It's been bleeding profusely now for six months. The bullet's never been removed, and its work's still not done. His heart could drain a reservoir.

Careful now, the Ol' Dirty Bastard might be waiting with Mr. Meth around any corner, sharpening his daggers, his razor edged tongue. Are those fangs I see? Here comes the Ghostface Killah... Andrew pauses to cover his eyes. He doesn't want to know about Lady Stardust. He's certain that she's here somewhere, in leather and lace, with whips and chains, bisexually performing the hermaphrodite's vengeful bidding, seducing men and women like a black widow seduces its lovely mate. But he's not certain if he's ready to meet her, to pay for his sins, for Ari and Mary, Michelle and Charlie. He doesn't know what the Starman has planned for him. What's the penalty for shouting at the moon? He dreamt about September 11th. Does that make this all *his* fault? *I'm still asleep. My alarm clock never went off. How does a human stop a dream?* A whimper escapes his throat. If you can think it, it can be done. It's dark enough now. The tribute in lights releases lost souls into the night. They dance the Lucifugue as the fallen angel waves his beacon baton.

Aliens, demons, zombies, and ghosts drift past Andrew's blindness, brushing his shoulders, laughing and speaking in tongues. Along with pandemonium, Andrew starts up again, visually unaware, but internally certain, of the passers-by who gaze and point their conversations at him as he writhes through New York's city streets. Could this be what it takes to finally move beyond good and evil? Will it ever stop?

Vainly flailing at the empty air, Andrew makes his way to the nearest familiar bar: The Village Idiot. Its entrance reeks of sawdust covered vomit. Andrew steps into it, mashes the gritty texture beneath his shoes. Embracing the stomach-churning scent, he steps up to the bar and orders the cheapest pitcher all for himself. He settles into a seat at the bar and fills his glass. His hand is shaking. Some of the beer spills on the counter.

What's happening to me? What did I see? Where is Michelle? What did the man say? Christopher killed him, too, on that day. What was the woman telling me, the homeless woman with the missing teeth? I'm guilty of everything.

Andrew resettles himself in his chair. Suddenly, his jaw drops. His sudsy eyes turn into flying saucers. He wipes his sweaty palm down his cheek.

The implications are extraordinary. I can't believe what I'm thinking. This can't be true. If I put together two and two, it all means…

"Hey, Andrew, how you doing?"

Startled, Andrew turns around. His eyes narrow back into slits from the wide-eyed zombie stare they had before. Michael is standing behind him, smiling. With his black hair freshly shaped, he's wearing his jean jacket and a pair of bright blue jeans.

"I noticed you from over there, but I guess you didn't see me. Sorry, I didn't make it to the party last night.

Something came up. Things have been in a whirlwind. I'm leaving for L.A. next week, but how are you?"

"What are you doing here?" Andrew snaps.

Michael's expression clouds, "I'm here with a friend. She's taking me out to celebrate. I was going to ask you..."

"Why are you going to L.A.?"

"I'm fed up with New York. Hey, do you want to..."

"Everybody here is dead."

"What? I'm not dead," Michael laughs. He shakes his head. Andrew appears haggard. He hasn't shaved. His hair is a scraggly mess. He's lost weight. Bags hang beneath his eyes. The evening just began, and already, there's a slight slur in his words. He's a ghost of the man that Michael ran into that day, so long ago, in Times Square. He puts his hand on Andrew's shoulder. "Are you doing all right, man? Let me call you a cab. If you don't have any money, I can sport you some for the trip back over the bridge."

"I just bought this pitcher."

"Well, come over and finish it with us, and then, I'll make sure you get a cab and get home."

"I do want to go home," Andrew says. He grabs his pitcher and follows Michael deeper into the Village Idiot, away from the smell of puke, towards the pool table, where a woman sits alone, casually smoking a cigarette, waiting for Michael to return. In the bright lighting, behind the hanging haze of cigarette smoke, she smiles at Michael as he and Andrew walk up. Wearing bright lip gloss and a stylish button down shirt open enough to reveal her lacy bra, she's an attractive blonde with eighties bangs.

"Who did you bring me, Michael?" she asks, licking her lips as he and Andrew approach.

Andrew pauses. A tremor passes across his face. He wraps his hand tight around the handle of his pitcher. The butterflies in his stomach have started flapping their wings again. As Andrew stands there, unsure whether or not to run away, Michael leans down and whispers something into the ear of the blonde woman waiting for them. Her eyebrows furrow. She looks back at Andrew. Something very soft lights the corners of her eyes. She must be an angel.

"You gonna sit down?" Michael asks.

Andrew glances over his shoulder towards the door. Hesitantly, he steps up to the table and grabs a seat.

"You wanna share your beer with me, stranger? Or is it too precious?" the woman asks, a smile tickling the edge of her lips. She pushes her glass forward. Andrew drains part of the pitcher into it. "My name is Noel, like Christmastime. You are?"

"I'm not really sure anymore."

Noel smiles. "This isn't a question of existence. I just need your name."

"It's Andrew," Michael says. Andrew starts at the smooth sound of the letters that spell out his identity.

Noel puts her hand out for Andrew to gingerly shake. He doesn't notice it. With his lips pursed and his eyes crossed, he's staring at his lap. He appears deep in thought, so deep that he's swum to the bottom of the ocean and is now patiently waiting for his oxygen to give out. Whether or not he attempts to make it back to break the surface and breathe again in the sunshine is anyone's guess. "Well," Noel says with a short laugh as she brushes her hands together, wiping away the dust that collected as the one sat alone in the air, "Which one of you boys is going to shoot pool with me while we wait for everybody else?"

"I'm no good," Michael says. He takes a sip off the drink he left behind in order to greet Andrew. "You've beaten me enough times to know that. Maybe Andrew will shoot."

"What?"

"You wanna shoot some pool, hot shot?" Noel asks, smiling.

Andrew thinks for a moment. He tips his head to the side. "Sure," he says. "I'll shoot pool with you."

Noel leads him over to the table. He follows at her heels like a puppy dog with the downcast attitude of the enslaved. The cigarette trailing from Noel's fingertips is Andrew's chain, his leash linked to him by the smoke spiraling off the red tip back into his face, his forehead, his spiritual eye, his brain. He coughs. "Jesus, you sound like you're dying," Noel laughs.

"I am," Andrew answers.

"And the smoke here isn't helping, but I'm not putting it out. You wanna rack or break?"

Andrew shrugs.

"I'll pay. You rack. I break."

Andrew nods. "Do you play backwards?" he suddenly asks, a tinge of fear coloring his voice, a hint of terror evident in the recesses of his eyes.

"Sometimes." Noel smiles flirtatiously. "But you never know until after we start."

The game gets off to an uneventful beginning – Andrew shooting low, Noel taking high. When she leans over the table, the neck of her shirt nearly touches the felt. The white at the milky top of her breasts peeks out from behind the fabric.

"Who are you waiting for?" Andrew asks Noel as she makes a shot down the rail. Her English is impeccable. The cue lands in the middle of the table, lined up perfect for the twelve in the side pocket.

Noel slides down a few steps and leans over again. "Just some friends," she responds disinterestedly.

"Oh," Andrew mumbles. "I was hoping you were

waiting for Michelle."

"Who?"

"A friend of mine."

"Does she know Michael?"

"I don't know. Probably."

"I got lonely sitting over there all by myself," Michael says, smiling as he joins the two.

Andrew starts, jolted out of the thoughts breeding his conversation.

"We were waiting for you," Noel quips. At the edge of her words, implications drip off in liquid perfection.

"Because she's already here as you," Andrew whispers.

"What?" Michael wonders. He turns towards Andrew. Andrew is staring at him, his eyes as wide as the dead's, as wide as the living's witnessing the risen dead.

As perfect as Michelle was, as she is, Michael's beauty, his form, his name, his smile, reflects the ineffable shimmering of her masculine counterpart – the necessary casting reprisal of Shakespearian role-play, of Ziggy Stardust's genderbending game, the motion beyond good and evil, back to the tree, the forbidden fruit, rotting, uneaten, in the garden. Andrew gawks at the coolness in Michael's eyes, the rigidity of his cheekbones, the shock of his black hair, a deeper infusion of the color from his irises, the shape of his body beneath his brilliant blue clothes, the model for turn of the century masculinity as completely as Michelle was, is, that of our understanding of femininity. Andrew smiles.

"What?" Michael asks.

"Nothing," Andrew says, his smile overflowing at the edges with tears building above the ducts in his eyes.

Michael shakes his head and turns back to Noel. Andrew walks away from the game to lean against the wall.

"Your shot, Andrew," Noel says. "Andrew, it's your

shot," she repeats emphatically.

"Oh right," Andrew answers, startled out of his ruminations on the nature of the two that he has confronted in this strange world, at the Village Idiot. *Such a strange, iconographic plane.* Still smiling, he lumbers back over to the table.

Andrew lines up on his shot – cue to the five to the corner. A smile tickles the edge of his lips. He snorts a short laugh, shakes his hair, a magic wand, over his play as he chuckles. With his eyes closed, he watches where the eight will land, eventually. Until that moment, all he has to do is keep on watching the movie and try to follow the script, provided all the other actors will. But the writer can't count on his cast to portray every individual action with his original intention. That's the director's problem. For those who don't believe, it's God's. With all these thoughts, his shot is off.

Noel strolls around the table. Although her build is slight, her frame thin, her body still jiggles and undulates as a woman's. Carrying her stick, her phallic symbol, genteelly between her first and second fingers, she swivels her thin, matronly hips. She purses her glistening lips. This angel looks the same, as androgynously perfect, as all the others.

Noel runs the table as immaculately as the conception. "Well, it's a good thing you weren't betting, Andrew," Michael laughs.

"I thought we were," Andrew whispers.

"What were we playing for then?" Noel wonders, the same flirtatious smile, lit by a starry sparkle in her narrowed eyes, creasing her lips.

"I'm not sure yet," Andrew says. "Gabriel told me all about it once."

"I'd play you again, but I'm out of quarters." Standing on her tip-toes, Noel reaches deep into her tight, hip pockets, searching for signs of silver, Belial's treasure. "Do you have any?"

"I don't want to play again. I lost. It's over."

"What are you talking about?" Michael says. "It's never over. I got quarters. You guys play." With one deft swoop of his elbow, into the outstretched palm of his hand, Michael produces four coins of the blackened at the edges mineral, seemingly quarried, like decomposed dinosaur bones, from the depths of the earth. The clinkety-clank of rusted, moneyed gears is the unmoved mover at the center of our world, the globe's green, apple core.

"Magic," Andrew whispers, his eyes wide. Still, nobody hears him. Michael slips each quarter into its respective slit slot.

As the winner, Noel begins the game. "You ever play last pocket?" she asks Andrew.

Andrew shakes his head.

"It's how the Puerto Ricans play. To win, you have to hit the eight into the pocket your last ball goes into. You wanna play that way? It's more of a challenge."

Don't attempt last pocket with English. It's insufficient. We need a language that better resonates with the hidden features of our abstract, landscape paintings, something more musical like a necromancer's dead, butterfly wings revealing the future's history, an alchemist's potions, the shaman's visions. Andrew shrugs. "Sure."

Some yuppie looking guy in khakis and a button down shirt comes up and places his quarters on the table. "You better win," Noel says. "I don't want to play against that asshole. He doesn't even belong in a bar like this."

"Too well put together," Michael adds with a sly, sidelong look at the mark. "No street cred. A guy who's either really good or really bad, nowhere in between."

"I'll see what I can do," Andrew says. "I know we're in

purgatory already. We've got to get out of this place."

Michael laughs, "Whatever you say, man."

"It's my story, man. I'm the writer." Andrew downs his beer and pours himself another pint. His pitcher's nearly gone.

Nothing falls off the break. The stakes are high. Andrew's nerves flail as he takes his first shot. The tension constricts his already wounded gut. He skims off the side of the six, and with the next play, a straight, sharp shot, Noel takes the three – white to red – for low. *Like Gabriel, one of the lost souls. Michael? Is he your brother? Are you both aliens, angels? I won't let you inside my skull; I don't write with words anymore. Noel is how you see my deeds, my name? I feel groggy. Am I still asleep? You all are my dream. And if this is my dream, then I want to see Michelle again in this time and place, not as a ghost, not rounding a corner a million miles from me, but right here, right now. Do you hear me, God, whoever, whatever the fuck you are?* He screams silently, still shouting, after all these lost months, all this forgotten time, at midnight's morning moon.

The game progresses quickly, with both Andrew's and Noel's shots dead on mark. Suddenly, Noel's trying to put the eight in her last pocket. She carefully moves her shot down the table to leave it resting neatly by the corner. Andrew shoots on the red and white, blood on satin, eleven. It's a cut play to the side. His read is a bit off, and the ball bounces lightly off the rail, leaving the cue in open space. Noel sinks the eight. Using the wrong language, Andrew never makes it to his last pocket.

"It's such a masculine game," Michael says. He's smiling brightly at Andrew. "I always knew Noel was more of a man than either of us." He gives her a hug with one arm around her shoulders, and he rocks her back and forth. As she maintains her balance, her shoes click on the wooden floor.

"Unlike some guys I've known, I always put my balls in the pocket, if that's what you're saying," Noel laughs. "Which kind are you, Andrew?"

Something twists in Andrew's wounded gut. The blood flows a bit stronger. No tampon could ever squelch it. The cotton would grow thick and red, juicy and full with flesh-filled goop.

Behind Noel, a face, a shape, a monster, a werewolf materializes. *Is this the creature that I've been trying to see in the corners of every room in my apartment, in the dark alley underneath my bedroom window?* Drooling grotesquely, it smiles sardonically at Andrew. It growls. It reaches out its claws.

Andrew brings his pool stick back over his shoulder. With an ancient warrior's cry, reminiscent of the battlefields of Ilium, he hurls it, javelin-like, at Noel. She ducks into the enclave of Michael's shoulder, and the wooden cue, striking with and breaking its blue tip, ricochets against the wall and clatters to the ground.

"What the fuck is wrong with you?" Michael shouts, breaking his grip on Noel. He flies at Andrew. His eyes are wild. He shoves him with all of the force that built as he ran from the wall. Andrew stumbles back into a chair. He trips and falls. The people in the back, the people at the bar, all turn and stare at Andrew sitting, dumbfounded, on the ground. Except for the grassy sounds of country music, the Village Idiot has grown silent.

"I was trying to help," Andrew says. Confusion softens his eyes. Noel, in a moment of instinctual motherliness, takes one step towards him.

"I don't know what the fuck you're talking about, but I think it's time for you to go home, Andrew," Michael says.

"I'd love to go home."

"Get up, then. I'm putting you in a cab."

The two of them walk out to Fourteenth Street. To the

south, the World Trade Center's tribute in lights, searching above the low-lying horizon of buildings, releases the dead into the night. Michael hails a cab. He shoves Andrew into the backseat. "Brooklyn," he tells the driver. "Over the Williamsburg Bridge. He'll direct you from there. Whatever you do, don't bring him back here."

Michael closes the door. A disembodied, electronic voice announces to the cab's newest passenger that he's in New York City, the capital of the world. The driver pulls away from the curb. The jangling sounds of Arabic music play. The high-pitched noises of a nomadic, desert language barrages Andrew's ears.

"Where are you from?" Andrew asks the driver.

"Me? I'm from Madagascar," the driver lies. His accent is thickly flavored with sand. He turns off the radio. Silence pervades throughout the cab's leather atmosphere.

"I met my first dead guy tonight," Andrew says.

"New York is a good place for that," the cabbie laughs.

"Yeah," Andrew slurs. "What do you think of the war in the Middle East?"

"Which one?"

"Any of them. Israel and Palestine?"

"There is no Israel. Only Palestine."

Andrew nods. "How about Afghanistan?"

The cabbie sighs. "I think Osama bin Laden is a bad man."

"I don't know if that's what I think anymore."

"Why do you not think that?"

"I think about what he's gone through, and that I'll never be inside his head, and without understanding his experience, how can I ever judge him?"

The cabbie doesn't answer. In the rearview mirror, he glances at Andrew out of the corner of his eye.

"I know I'm scared of people judging me without that

understanding. And now that I'm here, I want everybody to know that's what I believe." Andrew grows silent. After a little while, he says, "Do me a favor. Take me to the corner of A and Ninth. I'm trying to find somebody. Maybe she'll be looking for me there."

"No problem. Anything to stay out of Brooklyn," the cabbie says.

"I know. It's where the aliens landed. Ziggy told me so. It's the Ol' Dirty Bastard's home," Andrew quietly states as he stares at the dark buildings they fly past in the night. "Manhattan's full of ghosts."

The cabbie rubs his hands over the wheel. He swings the car around a corner and down a few blocks where he turns again and cuts quickly across the island. Soon, he lets Andrew off in front of Doc Holliday's. With heavy, drunken breaths, Andrew thumbs through the loose bills in his pocket. He pays the driver, throws the door open, stumbles out onto the curb, and slams the door shut again. In front of him, Doc Holliday's glass front beckons like the portal to another world. There's a face painted onto the window, and Andrew knows whose it is.

"Time for me to go see the witch doctor," he mumbles.

The floor at Doc's is wooden. The walls are country-western. The music is white, rural American. The bar is lit in red. Behind it, a dark haired girl in a cowboy hat, leather vest, and tight, black jeans takes a shot of either tequila or whiskey before she serves a customer his drink. Andrew trips through the collared-shirt crowd and orders a P.B.R. He lights a cigarette and sits down next to an elderly black man in a worn suit with an old guitar. Sipping off a tumbler of whiskey, the man is the full color, iconographic image of the bluesman Robert Johnson if he had survived his trip to the crossroads.

"Nice to see you here," Andrew says to Robert

Johnson.

"I guess so," Robert answers.

"You don't sound the way I expected you to. I figured you'd have a thicker accent."

"My accent's my own."

"The devil can't take everything from you, can he?"

"No. He can't. That's for sure."

"What do you think of hip hop?"

"I don't care much for it."

"Good to know," Andrew says. "I'm petrified of the Wu-Tang Clan."

"Don't believe I know them."

"I heard you'd met the Ol' Dirty Bastard before."

Robert Johnson laughs, "I met lots of them. What's your name, son?"

"I'm not so sure anymore."

"I know where you're at. I'm…"

"You don't have to say it. I already know. Could I hear you play guitar for a little while?"

"You won't be able to hear it here."

"I understand. You gotta be careful in a world like this."

"Ain't that the truth."

"I'm a writer. I used to do temp work for Heavenly Staffing before they went out of business. If you catch my drift."

"I think maybe I do."

"If I can figure things out, I think I might be able to help you."

"Everybody needs help in this world."

"God loves me. I just need to figure out what happened to Him… Or Her, the hermaphrodite. The symbol was destroyed on 9/11, but if you look outside, it's been rebuilt spiritually. Now, we just need to redefine the reality. If we have the power to destroy, we have the power to create. We own the keys. They exist inside our brain. We can let ourselves into Eden. I think, maybe, that's what my job here in purgatory is. I can do it, you know. I see things differently. I read behind language. That's what makes me a writer, and that's why all of this is happening to me."

"God loves everybody."

"It's nice to hear you of all people say that."

"Brother, I'll always say that." Robert Johnson raises his tumbler and takes a sip off his neat whiskey. Andrew drinks his beer. He glances around the bar. So many people… A frown contorts his face. The pool game is over. He lost, twice. It's time to take the hint. He stands up and stumbles over to a group of three guys and two girls sitting in the corner.

"Excuse me," he slurs, interrupting their conversation, leaning close into one of the guys, breathing his drunken breath across his face.

The two girls give him an odd look. The other two guys put up their guard. The guy who Andrew has accosted leans back. He puts on the air of the easily offended. "What?" he asks, narrowing his eyes.

"I need you to kill me," Andrew says.

"You need me to do what?" the guy laughs.

"Kill me. Don't worry, there's no law here. I just want to go home. Michael said he'd send me there, but I wound up here instead. Charlie did it himself. I'm not like that. It's not inside of me, but you're a man. Every man has murder inside of them."

"You look like a man to me," the guy says. "Do it yourself." Trying to return to his friends, he slides a little ways away from Andrew and takes a sip off his beer.

Andrew grabs him hard by the shoulder. He jerks him closer to himself, and he leans in farther. "You don't understand what I've been through, what I've done. I'm not a man. I'm a monster. I've killed my two best friends. I was meant to protect them. I'm supposed to be like my brothers, Gabriel and Michael, a hermaphrodite, but I need you to kill me first. I'm ready to start the final chapter. I'm ready to pay for my sins. I'm ready to be Raphael. Please, goddamnit, kill me."

"I think you just need an operation," one of the girls says. "And maybe some medication."

The guy who Andrew has grabbed a hold of bristles. "You better get your hands off me," he says. With the ultimatum, his two friends stand up.

Andrew lets go of him. He takes a deep breath. The guy is staring at him. His two friends are staring, too, waiting only for Andrew to move away. Andrew swipes a can from off the table and slams it against the side of the guy's head. Between Andrew's fingers, the aluminum crushes through the middle. Beer gushes out of the open top, drenches the guy's shoulder.

The guy leaps out of his chair. With one hand, he grabs Andrew by the throat. Andrew drops the can. It tinkles across the floor. Andrew trips, and with the help of his assailant's momentum, they spill to the ground. Andrew bangs his head on the sawdust covering the wooden floor. The whole world fades to black. The play is over. Let us take our bows.

V.
Hello from the Gutter

Open your eyes. You rematerialize and find yourself supine, perhaps entombed (the velveteen inside of a coffin lid closed to you), on the ground. The back of your head hurts. Your right side throbs as if a spear, kicked in by a boot, has shattered your rib cage. Your throat is on fire. You still feel the pressure of fingers constricting your jugular. Your limbs are cold. You twist your neck. Jagged concrete stones abrasively rub into your scalp. You moan. You thought never to hear yourself again, as if you'd lost your voice. At least the afterlife still contains sensation. This is the entrance to heaven. From out of the clouded sky above you, the golden gates and St. Peter's face should appear. This is the apocalypse, your final judgment. Where's Michelle?

"Andrew, we need to get out of here. Can you stand?"

"Sure. Why wouldn't I be able to?"

A hand grabs you by the shoulder, picks you onto your feet, and shoves you into the street. A yellow cab pulls over to the curb, and you're hustled into the back. Somebody gets in behind you. You look over and see Gabriel Burns settling into the leather seat. This world isn't real, but he's still smiling.

"I'll tell you where in a second," Gabriel says to the driver. "For now, just head towards the Williamsburg Bridge." He hands the driver a bill.

"Whatever you say, my friend," the driver answers.

"Where are we going, Gabriel?" Andrew asks.

"Don't know yet. You feel like going home?"

Andrew drops his head into his hands. "I can't go home."

"Good. I don't want to either. My night just started."

"I'm glad I bumped into you…" Andrew begins.

"It wasn't chance, brother. It was destiny."

"I'm sure it was."

"Those guys were gonna kill you. I'm not big on the term, but call me your guardian angel, brother. The bouncer just called the cops."

"I can't die again, can I?"

"You can always die again. I've died a million times."

"I think I did die again."

"You may have."

"Where are we off to then?"

"Anywhere you want to go."

"I need to pay for my sins."

"Well then, I know just the place for us. Driver, take us to Fourteenth and Hudson."

The cab reaches its destination. It pulls over to the curb and deposits its passengers. Andrew steps onto the sidewalk. A slight, false awning hangs off the building façade. The Village Idiot's large, white lettering graces its top. Andrew begins backing into the street. A horrified look attacks his face. He covers his eyes.

"I can't go back here," he emphatically says to Gabriel. "Michael told me so."

"We're not going there. Who wants to be the village idiot?"

Andrew's asthmatic, staccato breaths settle back into a fluid normalcy. He holds his hand against his heart, presses into the sternness of his sternum, feels his pulse. Even in death, it still beats. "Gabriel, I want them back."

"Follow me." They head out across the street. In the distance, the new World Trade searches for infinity. In front of them, a narrow building, ominous as a vampire's castle, shaped picture-perfectly into the crossroads that it's built upon, slices imaginary spires into the night. Phantasmal gargoyles adorn Andrew's vision of the roof. Gabriel leads Andrew around to the building's side, into its ribs. A metal cage houses a stairway. It's reminiscent of Andrew's childhood memories of Hansel's prison at the witch's candied house. Stepping into the cage, like dogs at the pound, the two of them start down. Gabriel takes a puff off his one-hitter, exhales, and hands it back to Andrew. Andrew hits it, deep, one time, too, and gives it back. Gabriel taps it out and slips it into his pocket. They each light a cigarette.

At the bottom of the steps, they round a corner. In front of them, back up a little ways, Dracula's lights are on. Heat, commingled with the earthy scent of a billion rotting, sweating bodies, emanates from the entrance. The deep thump of heavy techno adds a soundtrack to the scene. It's a lurid sound of unrequited, male lust. One of the demons, a huge black man in the glare of a spotlight, stands with his back to them. He wears leather chaps with nothing underneath, chains strapped across his bare torso, and a thick, spiked collar around his neck. He turns to check out the newcomers, and he smiles a broken grin at them. Andrew quickly spins around. Gabriel grabs him by the arm.

"Where are you going?"

"I can't go in there," Andrew says. His breathing, his

eyes are panicked.

"You said you wanted to pay for your sins. This is the place to do it. Welcome to the Hellfire Club, Andrew. This is where I always go when I'm disgusted with humanity."

The demon enters the club. Andrew and Gabriel stop at a desk housed behind bars. It's modeled after the prison that Chase-Manhattan's tellers, there either for their protection or ours, are locked into. However, if the bank, with its clean scent of laundered money, is heaven, then this – underground, sickly and pregnant with human desires – is the first of the seven gates of hell. Dillinger never tried to rob this establishment. Instead, it robbed him. Some biker-type Charon, with his gut nestled behind the silk-screened eagle of a Harley Davidson tee shirt and his stringy, gray hair tied back into a neat ponytail, hands tickets to the passengers. Gabriel slips him a few bills, something akin to a bribe. There's no computers here, no electronic ones and zeroes to convert cash into; there's only reality. In a gruff voice, Charon mumbles, "Enjoy yourselves, boys." Andrew and Gabriel follow in the demon's footsteps.

The entrance to the Hellfire Club is bedecked in chains hanging the same way that beads hang to separate the rooms in a New Orleans brothel. They clink together, the cold sound of prison rather than the warm tingle of lust. Andrew expected to see Michelle and Charlie waiting there on the other side, smiling at this cruel joke. Instead, he's greeted by a large, dark room with a bar in the center. The stench of humanity is horrendous. The heat of painfully fulfilled desires is unbearable. An overweight, middle-aged woman in a leather bustier hands drinks to the customers – a handful of men and women and those in between in fetish costumes, the dominant and the submissive, in the nude, with their pants unzipped, cocks hanging out, breasts revealed. The bartendress's milky flesh hangs over her belt loops. Andrew cautiously makes his way over to the bar.

"Can I get you something to drink?" she asks him.

"The cheapest beer you got."

"We don't serve beer. Only coffee and water."

"How can you not serve beer?" Andrew shakes his head. He glances around nervously. A naked, elderly man is standing beside him. His bare feet tap up and down on the dirty floor. He's gumming his lips and stroking, with the tips of his fingers, his flaccid, wrinkled penis as he stares at the bartendress's breasts. She pays him no mind. He's a shaman's vision, a ghost in Necropolis, like Robert Johnson, one of the ones who escaped from the Ol' Dirty Bastard's Brooklyn Zoo. *Like me,* Andrew thinks. Andrew looks down and away. "I'll take a water, then," he mumbles.

Gabriel appears beside him. "Give me a coffee," he says. He leans over to Andrew. "Without any liquor, we've got to keep drugs pumping through our systems. They're the only way we know we're still alive. Water's too pure. You should drink coffee, too." Andrew stares at Gabriel. After a second, he nods to Ziggy, his brother, the fallen angel. "Make that two," Gabriel says, holding up his fingers and clapping Andrew on the back. Their coffees are served. Gabriel grabs his off the bar. He says, "Have fun exploring," and he wanders away with the Joker's wicked grin twisting his face.

Andrew sits down on a barstool. Venereal diseases seep through his denim jeans. He's riddled with gonorrhea, herpes, syphilis, HIV. They contort his precious soul. He doesn't want to sip off his coffee. Diseases lurk in that dark concoction as well. Even the walls, covered by a museum of the macabre in ancient torturer's instruments, are possessed with V.D. – a slow death, a permanent scar, a tattoo for your life's short eternity. Like his brother, the elderly vision has vanished, perhaps exploded, vaporized itself even, in an invisible rush of ectoplasmic semen. The bartendress smiles at him. Either cum or saliva drips off of her vampire teeth, sticks at the edges of her mouth. "What's your name?" she asks.

"Raphael," Andrew says. "I'm trying to get to the city of angels. I think it's where I'm from. I had a job to do, but I fucked it all up, and now it's done. I guess Michael's preparing our way."

The bartendress laughs. "Well, this isn't L.A., honey."

"I know. It's New York City, the capital of the world. I haven't been to L.A. yet."

"But you just said…"

"Wait. What's that?"

A fleshy slap echoes above the strangled sound of a man's pained cry. The noise rips through the customers at the bar, piques their piquant interests. All heads turn in the direction breeding the noise. Many of the customers, their heads down, zombies drawn by the oversized magnet of a sensual compass attracted to the rotting cores of their brains – Frankenstein's unholy gift – leave their perches like buzzards homing in on the scent of putrefactive meat. They walk with the awkward gait of the undead, the uncertain shuffle of vultures encumbered by their oversized wings, the last remnants of the heavenly gifts given to Lucifer's host.

"Why don't you go see, Raphael," the bartendress says, a coy smile lifting the corner of her heavily made-up lips.

Panicking, Andrew steps away from the bar to play the role of Raphael and try to rescue Charlie. He's certain that it's his friend's cry. He's certain that Charlie is being punished for the sins he confessed he was guilty of.

Along with a mass of New York's ambling deceased, so similar to crossing the Williamsburg Bridge in the middle of September 11th (the gods visible over his shoulder), Andrew feels his way along a stone wall down a darkened staircase. Here, in the fiery chambers of the Hellfire's depths, so strong that Andrew retches, needs to block his nose, the Club's sweet stench emanates.

Imprisoned by earthen walls, a group of men, seated, like a Catholic, elementary school class, in rows of straight, wooden chairs, stroke themselves, sweating out their impurities, to the nun's lesson. The vague lighting plays unearthly shadows across their frighteningly entranced, unrequited but still lustfully trembling expressions. At the front, the nun has removed her habit. She wears a black tank top and black jeans. She's large and muscular, heavy as the earth's frame. Her face is harsh and chiseled. She holds a wooden paddle, her own Excalibur, between her ringed fingers. Beneath her short, black hair cut like a man's, even in the darkness, her eyes are covered by reflective sunglasses. She appears to be a Southern police officer interrogating a black witness at some point in the mid-fifties.

Her witness, however, is white as an albino bunny, in nothing but a pink tutu with rabbit ears on his head — humiliation for the devil. On all fours, with his naked ass high in the air, his tutu bunched around his flabby, middle-aged waist, he rests atop a raised board. He's trembling. He's an actor on a makeshift vaudeville stage. The dominatrix slowly makes her way around the man, rubbing her fingers along his bottom, his ribs, his chin. She sizes him up as a piece of meat, prodding him here, grabbing him there, tenderizing him like the witch she is. When she reaches his backside, she raises her paddle high in the air, pulls the sword out of its stone, and slams it against his soft skin.

He whimpers. Behind the class, Andrew winces. The dominatrix turns the man to the audience so they can see the red imprint, the raised blood brought about by the paddle. She turns him back to her. She slaps him again, harder. The man cries out. Without a pause, she slaps him yet again, and then again, and then again, and then again. She's possessed, enraptured, fevered as the Bacchae, the Furies. Suddenly, the man crumples.

Buried beneath the stratified applause of a few audience members, the sounds of his sobs trickle down to the floor. The dominatrix stops. She struts around to face him. She squats down to look him square in the eye. As he turns his head up, tears streaming down his cheeks, Andrew realizes that it's not Charlie. The dominatrix takes off her sunglasses. Her eyes shimmer like a sunlit river. She reaches out to the man, grabs him by the shoulders, and hugs him close to her breast. She crushes his rabbit ears against her chest. She caresses his hair as tenderly as a mother would stroke her broken child. Shaken, Andrew turns around and reemerges from out of the deepest of the Hellfire's chambers. He has to find Charlie and Michelle. They can't be left alone in this world.

Making his way in the same direction that he thinks Gabriel disappeared into, Andrew walks straight past the bartendress. She gives him a satisfied glance, similar to that of an older sister on her younger sibling as he struts his way into manhood, but he doesn't pay any attention to it. Oblivious, he strolls past the bar, and heads still deeper into the Hellfire's bowels, where the humans prey upon each other.

He enters a dark catacomb, a Christian crypt lit by dingy bulbs hanging amid their own pale lights. Tombs, cells reminiscent of Michael's bedroom imprisonment, line the walls. In each cell a man or a woman is tortured, flayed alive, sexually punished for his/her sins. Andrew is consumed by the image of an Asian man lost in the sensual crotch, the fragrant scents, of an Asian girl. Andrew remembers Mary. The man shakes his head back and forth, tonguing her clitoris. The girl bends her back overtop the post her man impales her against. The wheel of transmigration spins invisibly. It's here, where Andrew is lost in the thick images and even thicker scents, that he has his first encounter with the mistress of this charade.

Towering over every woman in the place, with legs of black flesh that stretch into heaven from the depths of this hell, she says only three words to him. Flicking her crisp, straightened hair out of the way of her face, leaning close to her prey, the hermaphrodite whispers, "Who are you?"

Andrew drunkenly whispers back, "I'm Raphael."

The hermaphrodite seductively strolls away. In tall, red boots, she wears a white short skirt that deepens the dark hue of her legs, that barely reaches below the feminine bulge of her cheeks, the masculine bulge of her crotch. Her black shirt, revealing her tightened midriff, bubbles out and crushes together her breasts. Lost in the image contained in the four by four cell in front of him, Andrew hasn't noticed her yet.

He moves a few steps to his left and turns around to see the view available in this next cell. Chain linked away from the rest of the Hellfire's party goers, a white couple goes at it while a Spanish man leans against the wall to watch them as he strokes his oversized penis into a veined beast, a shark with a hammerhead.

"It's gorgeous, isn't it," somebody whispers into Andrew's ear.

"What's that?" Andrew asks.

"His cock," the hermaphrodite says. Her voice is deep and melodic. "You know, people used to worship them." With those words, that clue, Andrew turns to take his first good look at her/him. In her heels, she stands a bit taller than Andrew. Her physique is sculpted from marble – hard and taut, a man's body with a porn star's curves, the secret desire of the American pornographic psychology, Venus with arms. She's plastered with makeup – highlights on her African cheekbones, mascara setting off the primal shape of her eyes, and a sheen of gloss coating her thick lips: the glam rocker, the Starman. She shakes her hair as if it's a lion's mane.

"What's your name?" Andrew asks.

"Lola," the two syllables trip off the tip of her tongue.

With a quick glance to his left, Andrew sees Gabriel hiding in the corner of the room, vampirically merging into the shadows. He holds his arms crossed, his lips taut in a thoughtful manner as if delivering a psychic curse.

"Your brother said I should introduce myself to you," Lola says.

"He did?"

"Yes. Gabriel is your brother, isn't he, Raphael?"

"He is."

"I was certain of it. The two of you look very similar. I've known him for quite some time now."

"I'm sure you have."

"Are you from L.A., too?"

"I think so. You're not from L.A., are you?"

"No. I'm from Brooklyn." Lola glances to her right. "Where'd he go?"

"What?" Andrew looks again. Gabriel has disappeared, leaving a puff of purple smoke in his wake. "I don't know. He was just there."

"It doesn't matter. You have me now." In the darkness, Lola moves closer to Andrew. She smells of roses and lilies, red and white, lust and peace wafting off her black skin. With her long fingernails, she touches his shoulder. The feminine sensation of her masculine hands sends a shiver through Andrew's bloodstream. It spurts out his feet into the floor, another psychic memory, another ghost, for the Hellfire Club.

"Are you from Gabriel's neighborhood?" Andrew asks.

"Yes. But I live here, now, in the West Village. Would you like to see my apartment?"

"I would, but I have to find my friends."

"I'm sure they're gone," Lola says.

"You would probably know," Andrew mumbles. He glances down at the floor.

"I do. I know everything about this place. I've lived here my whole life."

"Then, you're the one I need to talk to. Can you teach me the mysteries of being?"

"Raphael, I can teach you everything."

"I'll follow you anywhere. I just can't believe you're real. I never believed in you before."

"Then, it's time you learn how to believe. Let's go."

In Lola's apartment, she turns off the lights, ignites prayer candles and places them advantageously about the room. Beneath the ceremonious lighting so similar to that of the nun's dungeon classroom at the Hellfire Club, with a glass of whiskey in hand, Andrew sits down on the bed. Lola blows out the match, steps away from the candlelight, passes through the darkness, and reemerges in front of Andrew.

Lit from the sides and from behind, framed by bright profiles, she's God transubstantiated into human form emerging from the blinding light of reason. She steps out of her heels, removes her top and skirt. She undoes her bra and slips off her panties.

Her breasts spill forward. Like the Mona Lisa, they're perfect in shape and size. With round nipples, they remain suspended and firm, propped up by her flesh, ready to be nibbled upon by a child. Her penis twitches between her legs. Blood flows through it. It grows immaculate and hard, darker than the rest of her skin, a veined missile ready to create the child to suckle off her teats. A whole world unto herself.

"Are you real?" Andrew asks.

"I'm entirely illusion," Lola answers.

She walks up to Andrew, unzips his sweatshirt and pulls off the thermal underneath. She licks down the sparse hairs dotting his chest, matting them to his flesh. She rolls the tip of her tongue around his nipple. Andrew leans his head back and moans. "You're so thin," she says. "Like a Biafra baby."

"I'm being born again."

"I know." She pulls his pants down. Creating shackles, they bunch up over his shoes. She takes him into her mouth, massaging and exciting him with her lips. Between her cheeks is a cavern, a primitive domicile warmed by the flames of one of our ancestry's first fires, decorated with two-dimensional paintings of the hunt, of animals, of birth and death. A steer is speared in the ribs. One jackal mounts another. Stick figure men make war upon each other, and the goddess, fertile and full, watches over it all.

"Take your pants off," Lola whispers. Andrew obeys. Emancipating himself, he removes his chains. "Now bend over the bed."

Lola probes him with her finger. She opens him up with one, with two. "Are you ready for your lesson, Raphael?"

Andrew nods reticently. Something cold, greasy, and slick is rubbed around his anus. His legs tremble. He can barely support himself with his arms. "I don't want to do this," he whimpers.

"You don't have to."

"Yes, I do." He closes his eyes.

He rips open as Lola slides into him. She grunts and leans in deeper. Is that a trickle of blood? As she slowly, patiently begins to thrust, his sphincter rubs back and forth. He grimaces. She tears him apart from the inside. Going harder now, she pushes around his guts. Andrew can feel her fill his soul into his stomach. He's learning. Losing your virginity can hurt. His eyes brim with tears. Setting one foot up on the bed, settling herself still deeper into his body, Lola grabs him by the hips and pumps away.

Later that night, Andrew collapses into Lola's embrace. He lays his head on Her firm breasts, and he begins to sob. As his tears subside, and he drifts off to sleep, Lola coos, "It's okay, baby. It's okay."

A formless mass ebbs and pulsates with silicone and blood. A catholic sermon spurts through my mind: "Use evil against evil, and like the exorcist, vomit out St. Augustine's confessions — Evil doesn't exist; there's only nothingness." From the woods of the West Village, a howling, black wolf cries to all the gopis, "The devil is a woman, and I've brought you St. Lucifer's derision!" The lamb with the goat's head might never stick his neck between the blade of the guillotine, but I stand and wait, beneath the blinding breath of the sun in a dumbstruck crowd all day, believing in my heart of hearts that I'll catch a glimpse of the face of the executioner responsible for all of this. My hands grow sticky. I feel the wounds, two eyeballs drilled into my palms by the nails of the cross. Like a bullet lodged too deep in my guts for a doctor to retrieve and stick back in the gun to spill another human's blood, they bleed still, to this day. Allah! Why hast Thou forsaken me? I'm a Jew just like your son. In this crowd, this desert wasteland of ten million starving souls, I'm thirsting for madness. I'm dying. Panicking, I force my way through all the monkey-haired, shirtless, sticky bodies struggling like a fire frenzied crowd to reach the tunnel, the exit, but in order to get out of this concentration camp for Abraham's refugees, there's a chain link fence that we have to climb.

Razor wire's strung across the top. I behead myself, hanging by its tortuous rope. With American flags wrapped around their arms, crosses dangling from their necks, the machine gun toting guards pull me down, blow my dead body up in a suicide carjacking on the outskirts of downtown Kabul. But still I am alive. Like a movie played in reverse, I flow backwards through time. Existence is a musical palindrome signed in the bottom stage right, at the entrance to the left-hand path, in God's secret handwriting, with God's secret name. I surrender to my mother, the sky. From the wooden phallus clenched tight inside the muscles between her hips, she buries me deep in the womb of my father, the earth. Henceforward, we bear all of existence. As the only one with the gift of speech (my father has had a tracheotomy), he brings me the world to name, male and female he brings me them to denominate in our own image. I choose a neuter vocabulary to be the secret language of flowers and of all mute things. Like a butterfly's heartbeat, the time signature begins to speed up. I want to spin a new cocoon, crawl back in, and start all over again. A formless mass ebbs and pulsates with silicone and blood. I know the hidden name of God, my love. It's Lola.

"Raphael, you need to wake up. It's time to go."

Andrew opens his eyes. He hears God's voice. He sees God's face. His right ribcage feels like a monster's hand has a hold on it and is squeezing out the marrow. He looks down and sees a black bruise. The back of his head is soft and sore. Recently circumcised, it hurts. His asshole feels so stretched that it just gave birth, so loose that his shit will flow like poetry.

Wearing a silk robe, a member of the Ming Dynasty, Lola gets Andrew dressed in a hurry. She ushers him out of her bedroom and out of the apartment all together. At the door, she kisses him on the cheek. She possesses the odiferous scent of men in the morning. Her eye make-up has run. Her cheeks are smeared. As feminine as she appeared in the night, in the light, she's male. Her cheeks are too rough to be a woman's. She kisses Andrew lightly on the cheek, and she says, "You always know where to find me." The door is subsequently slammed in Andrew's face. No matter. He's got work to do if he's going to save Michelle and Charlie.

He begins the day at a corner bodega along one of the Village's quaint residential streets. He receives a cup of coffee served in the same blue-style cup that spilled across Charlie's floor yesterday, but today the world is completely different. Today, it all makes a bit more sense.

Sipping off his coffee, he strolls down the block. Before noon is the best time of the day. What with his recent vampire nights, it's been a long time since Andrew has seen this face of the world. The pale, Kincaidesque light shining shadows between the stoic buildings conjures images of the angelic glow of a woman's sweat, of Mary, of Sunday morning, of heaven. The scents taste ruddier, more sensual against the tip of the tongue. Andrew is certain that he is most definitely dead.

He finds a small postcard on the ground. **Free Tarot Readings**, it promises. Something resonates in his brain circuitry, an electric message from Michelle, from Lola. Today, he will learn the future of the rest of his life, what it means to be Raphael. He turns around and begins heading towards the address printed at the bottom of the card.

He twines through Greenwich's back streets, stares at the brick facades, the cozy houseplants in the curtained windows, the iron fire escapes of a thousand romanticized dwellings. He approaches the number at the bottom of the card. He presses a buzzer beside the door. "Hello," a woman's voice crackles.

"I'm here for the free tarot reading," Andrew says into the talk box. A memory flits through his brain: being at Charlie's yesterday, arguing with Dante, seeing... His own haywire dopamine shuts his thoughts down. The door buzzes, and Andrew enters the building.

Another door opens at the end of the hall. A middle-aged woman's round face peeks around the corner. She smiles. "Come in," she says. Andrew takes her welcome advice.

The psychic's apartment is small and dark. Muted light filters through a closed window's glass. It streams murkily across a ratty couch upholstered in Asian prints that rests against one wall. A table and a chair, thick with pillows, glittering in the morning sun's dusty stream, are across from it. "Sit down," the psychic says. She nods to the couch.

Andrew sits. He struggles to find a comfortable position. He grimaces. The psychic flutters around her home. Necklaces and bracelets jangle as she moves. Her motion is a tinkling song. She grabs a deck of Tarot cards in a yellow pack and sets them on the table. On the cover, The Magician holds a wand, a candle lit at both ends, aloft. His other hand's pointer finger indicates the ground. This is the number "I". The symbol for eternity halos his head. The psychic pulls a stick of incense from a plastic bag. She lights it, blows out the flame, watches the tip glow red, and sets it in a holder in the corner. Andrew wonders why she doesn't light the other end.

Like from the Trade Towers on September 11th, smoke filters into the air. Its scent envelops the room. With it, it brings spirits and ghosts, memories and dreams. The psychic sits down in her chair.

"What's your name?" she asks.

"Raphael."

"What do you want to know today, Raphael?"

Andrew frowns. "Everything," he says.

The psychic nods. She removes the cards from their

box, flips through them, pulls out a number, and sets the rest aside. "Today we use only the major arcana," she explains. "That's all we need for everything you need to know. Come back some other time, and we may throw in the rest." She stares intently at Andrew, studying every twitch of his features, every emerging line in his skin. Andrew fidgets beneath her gaze. Eventually, she locks eyes with him, smiles, and looks away. She begins thumbing through the cards. "For you, we choose The Hanged Man," she says. "Because you are in the midst of a change, and we need to find out what got you here, what you need to fear, what you need to accept, and what, in the end, you need to do."

The psychic lays the card face up on the table. Upside down, a young man in blue and red hangs from a gnarled tree in the form of a T. His other leg is crossed behind his knee. His hands are tied behind his back. Behind him, the sky is white. This is the self-sacrificed god, crucified by his own decision in order to attain his own forgotten knowledge. He feels no pain. Serenity adorns his lips. His gaze penetrates. Like the sun, a halo surrounds his head. It ends in bursts of energy expanding in every direction. The psychic hands Andrew the remaining cards. "Shuffle them, please," she says, and Andrew begins.

"How long should I do this for?" he asks.

"Until you feel it's right," the psychic answers.

Andrew stops. He hands the cards back to her. She lays them out into three piles. She stares at him the whole time she does this. She takes the middle deck and sets the other two aside. Flipping the cards out of her hands, they appear on the table before Andrew. To The Hanged Man's left: The Hierophant and Wheel of Fortune. To his right: The Fool and The Magician. Below, The Tower and The Chariot. Above, Death and The High Priestess. The psychic has made a cross, a colorful collage of mythical, meaning-filled pictures, the message, the intuition of the Hanged Man's self-sacrifice.

Of all the cards, The Tower commands Andrew's gaze. Of course it's there. Tall and gray, stricken by a bolt of lightning, a crown of flames bursts from its top. A red-caped man and a crowned woman, the dismembered hermaphrodite, leap from its burning windows. It's Andrew's psychic dream of a few months ago, his reality of the subsequent times, the manifestation of all that he's guilty of. He winces. The psychic notices. "A powerful reading," she says. She coughs and repositions herself in her chair, moves a little closer to the cards. Over the incense, Andrew catches a whiff of her patchoulied scent. He rubs his tenderized ribs.

"This is your past," the psychic says. She points to The Hierophant and Wheel of Fortune. "The Hierophant is upside down. I take this to mean that some sort of orthodoxy from your past has been inverted. Perhaps by the Wheel of Fortune." With her ringed fingers, she points to the other card. Andrew stares where she indicates. A disc engraved with nearly Hebrew letters is supported on the back of a flying demon, a feminine, red angel with horns, something akin to what Michelle should look like now. A serpent, the bringer of knowledge, winds down the disc's right side. Sitting atop it, a small, blue sphinx brandishes a sword. In the corners, on clouds, an angel and a griffon, both gold, present open books to the viewer. Below, on another set of clouds, a winged lion and a winged bull, golden again, rich from the Lord's wisdom, study their own tomes. "This is the origin of your questions, why you came here today. The Hierophant has always guided you. That's why he's closer in position to your card. This is order and knowledge, but nobody can avoid the Wheel of Fortune.

Time changes everything. Perhaps you could say that your guardian angel has disappeared, or at the very least, been metamorphosed. In order to understand this process, you must invert your own hierophant. You have the knowledge inside yourself. All you need to do is look at it differently." The psychic raises her eyebrows at Andrew.

"I already did that," he says.

"Good," she responds. She smiles. "To your right is your future." Andrew looks at the cards. The Fool, a young man, walks towards the edge of a cliff. A white dog barks at him. Over his shoulder, he carries a stick attached to his meager belongings. A flower is in his left hand. Above him, the sun burns like a single eye. With a simple look, simply feeling the breeze on his face, he stares at the sky. The card numbers 0.

"The village idiot," Andrew mumbles.

The psychic laughs. "Don't worry about that," she says, waving her hand in order to brush away the negative thoughts. "The Fool is your journey. The important thing is to look at his face. It's this sort of response to the world that will get you off your tree, that will lead you to what you need to be, The Magician. Since this card is inverted again, you still need to maintain the knowledge given to you in your past by the Wheel of Fortune, but your trip with the Fool can teach you how to master the world, only in a way very different from what most people would understand as its mastery. The Magician will replace your Hierophant. He's as powerful of a figure, only with a different type of knowledge. Be careful of the cliff, but you might need to fall off in order to become the messenger of the gods, not literally, but figuratively, whatever that may mean to you. Are you an artist?"

"I'm a writer," Andrew responds.

The psychic nods. "If you can keep the Fool's

innocence in your gaze, you'll be fine. Don't be afraid. The next cards will answer the questions that I see forming in your eyes. Just remember, this is all in your nature. Your parents knew something about your future when they named you, Raphael. Be true to your name." The psychic gives Andrew a serious, penetrating look. He frowns and nods. He has only one parent, the hermaphrodite, Lola.

"Below you are the problems you're going to encounter, The Tower and The Chariot. These are both very strange cards. The Tower tells you to beware of pride. It will bring divine punishment down on you." Andrew shivers. "Not necessarily of Biblical proportion, but you must not use the knowledge obtained in your journey to somehow challenge the existing order of things. For most people, The Hierophant still exists. As The Magician, you have a solitary path. The Chariot is again explaining this. It's inverted which means that you should never assume yourself to be a conquering commander. This would become the origin of your pride, your tower, and like in the card, if you succumb to the chariot, if you try to turn it right side up, your tower will be destroyed."

"How prophetic," Andrew whispers.

"You've already experienced some of this," the psychic says. "Let's move on to the path that you should take, then," she says. "Don't worry about Death. I see you staring at it." Andrew is overwhelmed by the figure in black armor, with a black flag, on a white horse. The skeleton stares at him as it tramples a sickly man underfoot and ignores the bishop's pleas. In the background, beyond a huge chasm in the earth, the sun sets between two towers, a spectacular *mise en scène*.

"In this instance, Death is a piece of your path, a revolution on the Wheel of Fortune. Because it is inverted, it is an event that must be embraced in order for you to transcend your Hierophant. Look at the hierophant himself praying to Death. The High Priestess symbolizes the knowledge you will obtain. Don't turn away from it simply because it's counter to your initial intuition. It's a completely different understanding than you've experienced before. Incorporate it into your writing. The High Priestess will make you The Magician."

Andrew raises his eyes. Satisfied, the psychic leans back in her chair. The air still resonates with incense. To break the spell of her words, she claps her hands. "That's it," she says. "You know where I am. Feel free to come back any day. Next time, though, it won't be free. I can read your palms then if you'd like as well."

Andrew nods. He stands up. Some question nags at the back of his mind, but he can't figure out how to phrase it. All he says is, "They're not my palms." The psychic graces him with an odd look as if she finally saw something for the first time. He stutters, "Goodbye," and he leaves.

Outside, impregnated with his alien knowledge, his aura expands. In a mushroom cloud, it explodes. As he walks, the pope of the Village, he delivers his sermon to the residents with his mind. *I have come to spread the news, to spare the light. I have visited the unmoved mover. Like a nuclear reaction, She resides in Her multi-towered beauty above Olympus among the upper decks of an apartment building not too far from here. Go see Her, if you care. If not, then beware my brother, Gabriel. Man refuses to suffer a rebellious angel. Instead, he chooses for God, himself, to be a child-like man. I choose to make men gods and thus was I born by Zarathustra, the Starman, Ziggy Stardust. My birth canal still aches. Uncut, my umbilical cord throbs. Plugged into the matrix mainline, I'm on the loud speaker. Wake up, New York City! With the simultaneous licks of ten million psychic tongues, you're transubstantiating Raphael! I blow Her trumpet, and right now, She feels like making sweet revelry. Oh, holy Noel, Lola, Michelle, tripartite Christ, triumvirate spirit, the woman, the man, the child, Lilith, Samael, Lucifer, making love to the Virgin Mary taught me that both Ari and my dreams equal Eve. Listen to the music of the spheres! I hear it in the sounds of the city, the squawk of a honking horn, the foul mouthed shout of the pedestrian. In the wasteland, lonely for the tree of life, a bird twitters beside my ear. It sounds like an alien voice nestling its way into my brain. "Chase Manhattan," it says. "Rob that bank." Well, I'm St. John with a Dillinger. This is my revelation. I tucked the pistol up under my robes, strapped it to the inside of my thigh when I passed by Peter at the pearly gates. Since I was on the VIP list, I gave him a high five. Put off by my confident manner, much too nervous and trusting, he didn't bother to frisk me. Like Dracula's reflection, I'm invisible to technology. The cameras never saw me. I put the gun up to Yahweh's head. "Run your pockets," I said. So the bank's been robbed, and I'm going to teach you all how to escape from heavenly staffing. It begins with suffering. Create your destiny. Constantly write your own story. Only then will you be certain of the symbolism at the end. Tell your secret to nobody. Live it for everybody. Maybe, somehow, we can understand one another that way. I'll be the bright star, the shining example, Andrew Christian, D'Angelo Raphael.*

At the basketball courts on West 4th, he pauses. He shuts down his diatribe. Raphael goes offline. He leans back against the chain link fence and lights a cigarette. Zombified, he looks like shit. The shouts and grunts of an early game go on behind his back. The dull thud of a basketball rattles around inside his head. Puffing away on his cigarette, certain that even in death he's still alive, the risen body of Lazarus, of Christ, he gazes across the street. Smoke streams out of his mouth, in front of his sight. The name of a shop catches his eye: *Crazy Fantasy Tattoo.* Manifesting from his dreams, the stigmata in his palms ache. Beneath the surface, there's an itch. Rubbing his hands together, trying to scratch a spot on the inside of his skin, he flicks his cigarette into the traffic and crosses the avenue. He enters the Crazy Fantasy.

A slim, dark haired guy is sitting behind the counter scratching his head. Covered in full sleeves of flames and cryptic designs, he's colorful enough to be an angel. In cursive across his neck, there's one word, *Michael.* Andrew smiles. "I need tattoos," he says.

"I can do that for you," the guy behind the counter answers. He closes a magazine that he's looking at. "What do you want?"

"Can you take my eyes and put them in my palms?"

The guy shakes his head. An uncomfortable grin twists across his face. "What?"

"Can you take my eyes and put them in my palms?" Andrew asks again, more emphatically.

The guy sighs. He doesn't answer immediately. When he does, he chooses his words carefully. "I guess so, but I don't know why you'd want that."

"They've been there forever. I just discovered them today though, and now, I feel them burning to see and be seen."

The guy shakes his head. "Look, a tattoo like that is Xing you out of society, man. You might as well be Manson with a swastika on your forehead."

"It started out as an X. He modified it in prison. Happens to everybody, I guess."

The guy shakes his head. "Is this your first tattoo?" he asks.

"The first one I've ever gotten, but not my first tattoo."

The guy narrows his eyes. He twists his head to the side. "What do you do to make money?"

"I used to work for Heavenly Staffing, but ever since that racket got shut down, I've been doing freelance writing."

"And you're able to make your living like that?"

"I don't need much to stay alive."

"And you don't think you're going to need to work in an office?"

"I know that I won't. I'm done. What I need are these tattoos. How much will they cost me?"

"I guess I could do them both for $100. I just want to make sure that you're certain about this, that you know what it means."

"Believe me. I know precisely what it means."

"All right, then." The guy says. He claps his hands together and stands up. "I just need to see your I.D. I need you to fill out some forms, and I'll take the cash up front."

"You don't take debit cards?"

"No."

"I should have assumed as much. Where's the nearest ATM?"

"Right across the street."

Andrew disappears and returns. He fills out the forms absolving Crazy Fantasy of any responsibility, and he forks over his cash. The guy leads him into the studio in the back.

A mirror stretches across one wall. Andrew is surprised to find that he still has a reflection. He's even more surprised by how worn out he looks, the bags under his eyes, the disheveled shade across his cheeks, the ratty tangle of his hair, the worn creases throughout his clothing. Below the mirror is a counter filled with tools, needles, pigments. Andrew sits down on a chair in the corner. In the long muscle cells of his stomach, for the first time in months, without the use of any substances, he feels good and content. The butterfly is dead. His gut wound has miraculously healed. He smiles. Death isn't a bad place to be. "You want any music while we do this?" the guy asks.

"Sure," Andrew says.

"What do you want to listen to?"

"You got any Clash?"

The guy grins. "Yeah, we got The Clash."

The fuzzy guitar of *Clash City Rockers* resounds between the walls, slices like a circular saw into Andrew's brain. "All right, Andrew," the guy says. "How do you want to do this?"

"My name's Raphael. Your parents lie to you. Someday, I'll use that name across my neck to sew my head back on just like you've done with Michael, Michael, but I'll do it in Hebrew. That way I'm moving in the right direction, backwards, the devolution."

Michael shakes his head. "Jesus, do you always talk like this, in these fucking circles?"

"I talk in ways that everybody can understand because subconsciously, we're all writers, creating our own worlds out of the forms represented with our words. In our dreams, we all see through the punishment of God's languages, languages constructed so that we could never build a tower that ascends into heaven. But it didn't work. Take a look downtown some night. That's the real rebellion, Michael, one that not even you can ever stop."

"Whatever, man. *Raphael*, how do you want to do this?"

"What I want is for my eyes to be face up when I put my hand like this." Andrew raises his palm in a Hitler-type *heil*, similar to the greeting position that a palm reader would look for, so that his fingers point up in the same manner as his spine, as if he's walking, like he does, due to the front loaded pressure of his brain.

"I can do that," the brand-new Michael says as he looks deep into Andrew's eyes. He sees beneath the surface, into the emptiness that his subject's pupils contain.

"I'd expect that from you," Andrew says. "Of all the people left in the remnants of this inoculated city, I'd figure that you, out of all of them, could see what I'm trying to do."

Michael nods.

"You're a true artist," Andrew finishes. "Just like me."

Michael fires up the needle. It rattles like the inside of a madman's brain. Its tip pulses in and out like a nymphomaniac's spleen. He dips it into the ink. "I'm gonna start with black to do the outline with," he says.

Very lightly, he touches the edge of the needle against Andrew's skin. At first, as the simple gyrating pressure licks his epidermis, it tickles. Then, it goes deeper. It begins to slice, to burn. A pool of what looks like blood trails along at the tail end of its path. How Michael can see where it's going to go in the future amid the mild gore is all a miracle to Andrew, but the tattoo itself is a miracle to him to begin with. It's being traced out of a pattern that was cut out of a handbook at the beginning of time, when he came into existence as himself by himself with the simple name of Raphael.

His eyes are tearing, but Andrew manages to say, "I need to get these tattoos done before I see my girlfriend again. She's been gone for a long time, and when she sees me, she's expecting something a little bit different from how I was before."

Michael agrees. At the very least, he nods. With a paper towel held between his fingers, he daubs a tiny slippage of blood. A red, wet spot on the towel grows through the fibers. With grace and a needle, Michael draws his art, his poetry, into eternity on Andrew's perishable skin. The shape's simple outline gives the symbol the effect of a hieroglyph, Michael's very own book of the dead inscribed on the palm of Andrew's Pyramid walls. Michael works in surgically rapt concentration. Beside him, Andrew grimaces. He stares at the fresh wound spilling onto the floor. He wants to close his eyes, but he can't. Like the mob adoring an execution, he needs to bear witness to all the grotesqueries of justice being done.

Against his skin, the ink is cold as water pooling into the hands of a dying of thirst desert man. Lean your head forward. Take a drink. Life is our communion. For a moment, the sensation is akin to vertigo. Andrew's eyes and stomach spin. Michael takes the needle away. Instead of a burning sensation, there's a dull ache. Lola's penicillin attacks the V.D. Michael dips the tip of his needle on his palette, adds some blues. The electric rattle of the needle sings again. Like a virus, its pigment mixes with Andrew's red and white blood cells. It divides the skin of his hand from the black outline. The form begins taking shape.

Unlike the ancient remnants that our outmoded museums possess, the hieroglyph is shaded in with tones as vital as the thing itself. This is a pictograph with the illusion of three-dimensions, the hinting of a fourth, the glimmer of a symbol. Egypt's masons never worked with such mathematical precision. The pupil shines. The iris glares. Spider web vessels twist through the whites. The lashes tremor with a feminine beauty not particularly out of place on the entirely masculine portrait.

Michael looks down on his work. He looks back at Andrew's tangible eye. He makes a satisfied frown, and he nods. Ashen, Andrew nods back. Like his predecessor lying on his back on scaffolding high above the Sistine Chapel's floor while he touches God's finger to man's, Michael bends back over and begins his work again.

He starts from the same point at which he started the last time. However, on this occasion, he dices up Andrew's right palm, tears through his loveline, buries the line for his head, separates his lifeline into two distinct parts. He reverses the tear ducts, continues to paint a watery lens over the all too familiar stare. In the middle of the hand, overtop the stigmata, he drills a black hole for light that leads straight to the hidden workings of the brain. He crucifies Andrew with his subject's very own pupils.

Hands wrapped like a mummy's, Andrew is ready to leave. "Remember to keep the bandages on for a few hours," Michael says. "And when you take them off, put on some A&D. That's an open wound you got there."

Andrew nods. He leaves the Crazy Fantasy. He heads north, then west, then north, then west again. He gets on a train somewhere and takes it to the end of the line.

As he rides, he feels the black people, only the black people (the other races have gone blind), reading his mind. Ashamed of his thoughts, he tries shading them, but there's nothing he can do. A large man in the corner is staring at him with an enraged gaze. Andrew approaches an elderly, black woman clutching a handbag against her chest. Her face is lined with a lifetime of experiences, good and bad, horrific and beautiful, no different but so different from his own. He touches her on the shoulder. She starts and looks deep into his eyes. "I'm sorry," he says.

She stares at the decrepit creature accosting her. Her hard face softens. "For what, child?" she asks. Milk and honey drip off the tone of her voice. A smile radiates across her worn cheeks.

Andrew shrugs. He walks away to lean against the train's windows.

On the platform, as he heads up to street level, he notices eyes staring at him out of the tiles on the walls. They appear to be paint, but Andrew knows they're real. The city's watching him. Large and protruding, colorful as a peacock's tail, runes smooth as the stone surfaces that they're tattooed onto, they gaze at him from everywhere and thus from nowhere. Andrew is reminded of the new scars across his palms.

From out of the tunnel's open mouth, he steps onto the sidewalk. A wooden fence runs along one side. He merges into a crowd and starts on his way. Amid the multitude of the street, as crowded as his personal space is, Andrew feels alone. He stares at the ground. He looks up at the sky.

Without warning, in front of him, to his right, in the midst of the great city, behind a chain link fence, a vast plane, dusty and brown, a 16 acre grave, freshly dug amid the metal tombstones of Manhattan's buildings, expands in seemingly limitless directions. Martian, it glows red beneath the sun. Monstrous pieces of steel, girders and supports, bones snapped so completely that they've broken through the skin, stick out of its flesh. Like dinosaurs petrified beneath an asteroid's sediment, they reach high into the air. Painting the invisible wind currents, clouds of debris circle. This is Ground Zero, the wasteland. Andrew stops. The immensity yawns, consumes his insides. It's the vacuum at a given point in space, the reality of the theory of the Big Bang. A tremor races through Andrew's body, splits apart his face. On the infinite points of Ground Zero's multi-horizons, the city barely begins again.

This is where Michelle was lost. This is the final resting place of the clients who murdered Charlie. Andrew remembers running down the street. He remembers seeing the buildings tumble in, one floor upon the other. Like God's face, it was a giant plume of smoke. As if the devil suddenly came back to life, the other trembled at that moment. Andrew was standing in the middle of Broadway, the defect built into the mosque. Suddenly, the world shook; it had an orgasm. Like everything else, all of existence collapsed.

Overawed by the Saharan monstrosity, Andrew steps slowly. In the pit, miniature people scurry about. Wearing hardhats, they operate cranes, drive trucks – a whole city of the deceased. At the edge of it all, on its own little mound of Calvary, all by itself, an iron cross, large enough to hang a God off of, is thrust into the dirty earth. Beneath it, a tangled mess of metal speaks to the massive destruction, the atomic explosion, by which the cross was created. Andrew gets as close to it as he can.

With walkie-talkies and batons, the police bar his way. There's a National Guardsman. Andrew gazes over the shoulders of tourists snapping pictures. He rips apart on the inside. The wolves devour his sweet meats. This is his Mecca, his Jerusalem, his Bethlehem, his Hiroshima, Auschwitz, and Washington. He wants to kneel in prayer and kiss the earth. He wants a holyman to sanctify those who can appreciate this sight. The tourists are Sharon touching the Holy Dome of the Rock. They're Hitler invading Poland. And suddenly, Andrew feels like bin Laden. His brand new tattoos ache. He stares at the iron cross. It expands to fill his gaze. He notices the rivets nailed through its skin, its joints, the residue of heat burnt into its coloring like a sub-Saharan peoples', the same heat that turned his love to cinders. He feels it all. He carefully massages his wounded palms. He wants to drape the cross in a white cloth and lay it gently to sleep at night.

Nauseous, he turns around and heads back in the direction he came from. He never wanted to see this, the point of impact for the nuclear reaction that destroyed his home. Fighting his way through the gawking crowds of people, following where the dead choose to lead him, reading all of the hermaphrodite's signs, he twists around through a few streets.

In front of a church so insignificant with respect to the economic monstrosities surrounding it, he approaches a blue wall. Flowers, tee shirts, and pictures form a collage of lost loves. It's infinite, a menagerie of colors and emotions. The collage turns a corner and begins again. Its power dwarfs the imposition of the stone church behind it. Certain spots along the wall appear as points of prayer vigils, their flowers watered with tears, grooves dug into the pavement by the knees of a million mourners' from a thousand varied religions. Andrew never believed that death had undone so many.

Here, the tourists find themselves moved in a different way. Some of the more intuitive sniffle and hold back tears. Awed by the violence of reality, children and teenagers grow silent. They realize that most of the smiling people pictured in the pictures they see (in hiking gear, at weddings, proms, and graduations, holding drinks, making toasts, kissing a sweetheart, arms around a friend – so many things that they themselves, if they have not yet done, hope to do someday), like the entire host of the other previously nameless victims, are of the type like Michelle, lost without their parents or friends ever certain of their death or even of their final immolation point other than that it was higher than humanity was ever meant to stand. This may be the only chance they ever have to learn about the people behind the numbers, the programs that ran the computer, the lives that for that one moment in time made up the great beast. It holds them in awe.

Andrew walks up to the wall. He leans his forehead against its immensity. The structure for the icons supports his entire weight. The shock of three thousand dead pounds into his skull. He sees their faces flash in front of his mind: white, black, Spanish, Asian, brunette, blond, curly, nappy haired, gay, straight, hideous, deformed, beautiful. They laugh, smile, cry, fight, argue, love, hate, do everything in the world that he has ever done, feel everything that he has ever felt. The Tribute in Lights burns its floodlights into the space of his mind's eye. The sensation expands. He sees the world's dead: the past's, the present's, the future's. He sees their lives, their births, their adolescences, their marriages, their careers, their deaths. All of existence, all of its regressions and progressions, washes over him. His face twists. He pounds his fists against his skull. There's Charlie. There's Michelle.

Andrew spins around. "Listen to me!" he shouts to the people staring at the memorial. He holds his bandaged hands high above his head as if they're lightning rods directing the currents of God. His ribcage stretches. His wounds ache. A few frightened faces turn in his direction. They take in the haggard apparition accosting them on their vacation streets. With his eyes blazing, Andrew continues: "Where were you when all of this happened? What were you thinking in the moments before the world changed? You were on your way to work. You were sitting in school. You were thinking about your bills, your arguments, your games. A voice came over the radio. It told you that the whole world, all of existence, had just exploded. All of you went crazy. Believe me, I remember everything, every self-centered thought, every worthless action, every trifling moment of the life that I am guilty of, the life that created the pit you'll visit on the other side of those buildings, the life you'll visit on the other side of existence. Why the hell did you come here today? Are you looking for forgiveness, for closure? If you are, then I want to let you know: It *is* your fault you're still alive. What sort of answers do you want? Reason? Science? Politics? God? An answer is an excuse to murder. The only excusable murder is suicide. Tell me, are you willing to die? I am. I concede to that by staying alive. Let me tell you the secret of the universe: Death is the great god, the reality that drives sane people mad. Life is its pawn. Let us worship madness and death.

Sanity is simply a delusion. In this sane world, how is a young woman murdered? Why does a young man take his own life? In this sane world, how are you seeing me, the living, breathing dead? There is no duality, no plurality; there is only one God, devil, us, them, man, woman, master, slave, human, animal, love, hate, life, death. That's how I've been able to escape and come back to you. And I've come back to tell you one thing: Mankind will not survive if our souls remain unchanged. I'm begging you, kill yourselves. Before you maim another innocent life, do like I did, and kill yourselves. Only then will we be certain that this will never happen anywhere in the world ever again." As quickly as he began, he drops his hands back to his sides, and steps back into the drifting crowds. His listeners remain dumbfounded, unsettled, uncertain what to say to one another, and certainly unwilling to believe what the lunatic says. Soon, they all look back at the wall and try to get on with their vacations, but all day something about the strange young man unnerves them. Some of them even tell their friends at home about the odd encounter. What a New York story...

Listening to the voices inside his head, Andrew flits along the streets. The city tells him where to go. There's a red light. Stop. Walk farther along the avenue. Now, go. A car is coming. Don't cross the street. Turn the corner. You need allies. Follow that man on the cell phone. He's got a line straight into the universal mind. He's hung up. Follow the girl in the blue dress. She represents your eyes. Don't trust whitey. They're all devils. There's a black man for you to follow. He's God's chosen people. See that Spanish man. He'll lead the way. He's in tune with the language of this continent. Watch the Asian women glide. They have your best interest in mind. They understand the totality of the yin and the yang. You're in Chinatown now. Bask in its delectable scents of noodles and fish. Stop for a second. Check out the merchandise. Haggle for a pair of sunglasses. Those ones are nice, metal rims with black tints. The jabbering merchant's gone down as low as he'll go. Buy them. Shade your eyes. You're approaching the Williamsburg Bridge. You don't want to go blind. Walk up the sidewalk. When was the last time you did this?

Halfway up the plank leading to the bridge, Andrew stops. The city is silent. If he crosses this bridge, he'll be back in Brooklyn, the Ol' Dirty Bastard's home. Andrew swallows. Saliva slips down his throat. His extremities are numb. For the first time all day, he shivers. He looks over his shoulder at the mad streets of Manhattan. A haze of humanity obscures the city's wandering souls. He taps his finger against the side of his head. From behind the darkness of his new glasses, he looks up at the sun. A bright orb, a blotch on the clear, winter sky, it splinters, at the very edge, into individual streams, angels and demons of blinding light. He can never go home, but this is something that has to be done. He starts walking again.

At the apex of his ascent, recounting a memory from a past-life regression, he glances over his shoulder at downtown's skyline. He frowns.

It's empty now, but not for long. Soon, with the help of all the king's horses and all the king's men, he'll put the hermaphrodite back together again. The male and the female will glitter beneath the strength of the sun. If the beginning is the end, the end the beginning, then soon, Raphael can fly away, and Andrew Christian will reawaken in his bed at 8:46 on the morning of September 11th, 2001. He'll go to work that day. He'll be as bored and frustrated as he is over the course of any other day, but that night, he'll bring Michelle flowers: red *and* white roses. After she smiles, he'll tell her about this crazy fantasy he had where

New York was destroyed in a nuclear explosion. All of their lives ended.

She'll laugh about it. He'll begin to cry. She'll ask him what's wrong, and he'll say, "You'd never believe how scared I was. I missed you all so much, and I was terrified to die."

Andrew stares at the ground. Some graffiti artist has painted a pictograph of stories on the sidewalk: words and images, colors and ideas, a monster here, a siren there, rage in this line, forgiveness in that. It makes no sense. Andrew smiles. That makes all the sense in the world. Approaching the beginning, he follows in the storyline's footsteps.

When he exits the bridge, instead of turning left to head towards Greenpoint, he turns to his right. He wanders through vacant streets of abandoned warehouses. He needs to find allies who will lead him to where he needs to go on the Brooklyn side of the world. In front of him, across the desolate gap of an inner city block, dwarfed by the majesty of decrepit stone buildings, a young woman pushes a stroller. She has two young children tagging along at her heels, a boy and a girl. All three of them are dressed conservatively. The mother and the daughter hide their bodies in long, drab coats, their feet in clunky flats, and their heads in shawls. The little boy wears slacks, patent leather shoes, and a black jacket. They've entered the New Jerusalem from the Old. For them, the commandments of the most powerful, unutterable name of God still have life. They have no hope of heaven, no penalty of hell, but still, they fear the unimaginable strength of the same desert deity as their biblical enemies do.

Andrew follows them. He rounds one corner behind them, and then, he rounds another. The woman glances nervously over her shoulder, tugs at her children's hands, whispers Yiddish into their ears, and moderately picks up her pace. Andrew continues strolling slowly, staring into their brains, trying to read their minds, to see if they recognize him as Raphael, one of the messengers of Lola, their God.

The tap, tap, tap of Andrew's feet rattles closer and closer along the pavement. The woman stiffens. He grabs her by the shoulder. Startled, she gasps and turns to him. She's so meek, a woman who, even though she's lived here most of her life, is out of place on New York's streets. Her features contort with questioning fright. *Please, don't hurt me*, she silently begs of the decrepit stranger in sunglasses with bandages on his hands.

"I need to talk to a rabbi," Andrew says. "Can you direct me to a rabbi? I have a secret to tell him."

The woman doesn't say anything. She shakes her head and starts on her way again. She moves stiffly, as if trying to contain her panic.

Andrew runs up beside her. "You don't understand what I've been through. I'm a Jew. I need to talk to a rabbi."

The woman still doesn't respond. With her jaw trembling, she looks straight ahead and continues to walk purposefully. Andrew stops. He lets her move a small distance ahead of him. Then, sticking to the long shadows at the edge of the buildings, he starts following again. She keeps glancing over her shoulder to make sure he's still there. He's certain that she will lead him to wherever he needs to go.

Brooklyn loses its shady appearance. A homier atmosphere pervades the gray streets. Hassidic children play along the sidewalks. Except for their odd attire, they are like any other children in any other neighborhood in the world. Andrew smiles. Somewhere in the long line of history, these children have something in common with him. Moses told them that they were God's chosen, chosen only to suffer in Egypt, Babylon, Spain, Auschwitz, and Belsen for no reason other than to glorify their faceless God.

He follows his guide and her children into a bustling commercial district that smells of matzo-ball soup. The scent reminds him of his mother's mother, of Passovers where his grandfather recited Hebrew gibberish that he didn't understand. In long, black coats, with huge black hats, long beards and curling sideburns, the Hassidic men rush every which way, intent on perfecting their day. In their conformist uniforms, patiently pushing their neighborhood's gears, they appear to be a human army of embalming ants, gravediggers, coroners. Here and there amongst them, a few silent women stand, carefully watching over the community's children. In the furor, Andrew loses his guide.

He grabs the black coat of a Hassidic man of about his age who hustles past him. "I need to speak with a rabbi," Andrew says. He stares at the bony slates of the Hassid's cheekbones, the thin length of his nose. The face is so Semitically similar to his own that he feels he's looking into a mirror.

The Hassid stares him up and down. He grins at the mad apparition before him. He doesn't understand the clothing that his accuser wears. "Are you a Jew?" he asks.

"Yes, but I was never bar-mitzvahed."

The Hassid's grin stretches. "Then you're not a Jew," he states, and he continues on his way.

Andrew watches him disappear into a million more black coats topped with black hats. He shakes his head. "I was always told I was," he whispers, and he stumbles over to a vacated stoop where he sits down and lights a cigarette. His legs ache from yesterday's and today's manic treks across the city. As he massages his calves, the new scars on his palms throb. His head and ribs still feel tender. Grime, both the city's and his own, has adhered to his scalp and face. It builds up underneath his nails when he scratches through his hair.

The Hassidic neighborhood in front of him, even in the middle of its busy day, is an island of tranquility, a peaceful aviary, amid the Brooklyn Zoo. Pristine and safe, if it weren't for the religious costumes, it could easily be the serene uptown area of his home back in Connecticut. The people on the streets smile and greet one another. The only hint of New York's usual madness is in the angry eyes of the young Latinos sweeping up in front of the shops and taking the kosher trash out to the dumpsters for their Jewish employers.

Reminiscent of the ethnic certainty of the SS, a Hassidic police car drives down the street. Andrew repositions himself on the steps. He crosses his legs and takes a puff off his cigarette. The nicotine opens up his mind, taps him into the thoughts of his Jewish brethren. *I'm the Messiah, Krishna, Jesus Christ.* He begins: *Who told you that you were chosen? Moses? Moses was as delusional as Jesus, as schizophrenic as Mohammed, as murderous as Manson. A book tells you that Israel is your homeland? Well, I'm writing a new Pentateuch. In my Torah, I'm putting forth the argument that it was Christians guilty of centuries of torturing their supposed spiritual brothers, Christians trying to make sure that none of their nations would be responsible for another Holocaust who gave you your new empire of Israel. There is no divine decree that allots a plot of land to any racially charged religion of people – neither Jew nor Muslim, Hebrew nor Arab. In their self-righteous idiocy, Europe has created a brand new holocaust. Zionism is a mentality based on retribution for past persecutions, but there is not a single segment of humanity who has not been, at one time or another, systematically slaughtered and enslaved by their priests, their rulers, their neighbors, their supposed betters, and you don't see any of them as having anything in common with your spiritual heritage. The only slaves I know of on this continent were black. They're the true Hebrews, innocents enslaved under the guise of ethnic superiority, robbed of their homeland, forced to wander for eternity. Yet you go to war with them across arbitrary divides like Crown Heights. Do you believe in miracles? Do you believe that Yahweh gave Moses the ability to send plagues across Egypt? The night before last, I turned one type of beer into another type of beer. If you believe, then you must believe in me. You're wondering who it is that's telling you all of this, who it is that has infiltrated your mind, the most precious of all sanctuaries? It's me, the messenger of God, Raphael D'Angelo, half Jew, half mad, a true American. I was bar-mitzvahed just last night, circumcised through my own anus. I still feel the residual pain of my covenant with the Lord. Now, I'm the prophet, the rabbi. You're not God's chosen people. There is no God. There's only Lola.*

The Hassidic men stare at Andrew glowering at them while he smokes his cigarette on one of their stoops. His brain feels the mild stimulant that the nicotine provides. He's aware of the hatred that he engenders. The Hassidim speed up as they pass him by. The women avert their eyes, tug on their children's hands, try to keep their progeny away from this strange stranger. All of them, the men, the women, the children, bristle at his presence, the physical representation of his rage filled thoughts. He stands up. Twisting his lips, he surveys the scene in front of him. He shakes his head, steps on his cigarette, leaves his perch, and begins walking along Bedford Avenue again.

Tapping his fingers against the side of his skull, letting his neighbors know where their thoughts come from, he weaves in and out of the parting black coats that create his path. They and their subservient spouses know him now. They want his scrambled brains away from the security of their families and their homes.

Without warning, the neighborhood's entire face

changes. There are no more black coats, no more women in drab clothing, no more familial retreats, no more profitable businesses. There's razor wire and an abandoned gas station. There's graffiti and a burnt out building. A black man in tattered rags stumbles across the street, brown bagging a forty, screaming at nothing and nobody. Behind him, like at the currents of Ground Zero, trash swirls around in the breeze. He stops in the middle of the street. He pours his empty bottle onto the pavement. The glass shatters and clinks into the gutters. He raises his arms like he's being crucified. Where the nail hits one palm, he holds an empty paper bag. Where the nail hits the other palm, his hand is empty. Andrew feels that out of deference to Big Baby Jesus he should avert his eyes.

He knows now where he needs to go, where he will find his missing friends. He strolls along Bed-Stuy's abandoned streets, twisting and turning from memory. As he rounds a corner, beneath destructive scaffolding, in front of the fence of an empty work site, a souvenir of the World Trade's grave, he sees, lying on the ground, an abandoned black coat. Dirty and worn, it crumples around itself like a snake. Andrew picks it up and dusts it off. He holds it at a little less than shoulder length. Hanging down to the ground, its width appears to be about his size. He slips it over his shoulders. As it stretches tight, a seam cracks in the back, but other than that, it fits. Andrew admires its cotton length down his arms. It drapes down his legs to his ankles. It's a gift from Lola, a peace offering from the Ol' Dirty Bastard – Raphael's own tattered Hassidic coat. Death can get awfully cold. As Andrew's breath merges with the air, he smiles. Michelle and Charlie will be proud of him when they see him again.

As he starts walking, in front of him, along a brick wall, a familiar picture spreads. Andrew walks up to the portrait.

It's the face of a young, black man. Andrew recognizes it. Like a ghost, it has haunted his fantasies. Above the picture's head, a golden halo rests. This is the servant of the Ol' Dirty Bastard of the Wu-Tang Clan. The blue sky, dotted with clouds, expands behind him. All around him, tiny angels, clothed in white, with white wings and black faces and arms, fly. Beneath the painting's serious, cherubic gaze, a golden banner reads in black: Though your years were short, may you sleep with the angels, Khalid – 1977-1995.

Frenzied, Andrew rips the bandages off of his wounded hands. Their white wrappings pool in the gutters along the edge of the street. His fresh ink glistens beneath the winter sun. He presses one hand against Khalid's forehead. From the ink of the paint to the ink of his blood, through his new tattoos, a familiar sensation shoots in at his palm, up his arm, to his brain. It tingles along his electric sensors. It spreads through his mind like AIDS. He closes his eyes.

In the darkness, a trillion lives appear. Andrew picks one to focus upon. The dead body of a black teenager rises up from the street behind him. Wearing a tee shirt and red Adidas pants with white stripes down the side, Khalid brushes his hands down his chest, checks to make sure that the bullet holes have really disappeared. He smiles. Unsure of the physical world, he starts down the street. He remembers the way. His confidence returns. He begins his familiar strut through his neighborhood. Life is so warm. Along the streets, a hundred girls, hanging out on their stoops, talking with one another, braiding their little brothers' hair, stop whatever they're doing and stare at the apparition amongst them. The boys rapping on the corners, wrestling on the sidewalks, forget themselves. The old ladies' ministers were right. The dead will come back to life. The neighborhood has its own memories of this man, but after the nothingness of death, all Khalid wants is to see his mother and his baby boy again.

Andrew expands his mind. He sees the entire universe. He wills it backwards and forwards in time. He seals off the strange world he lives in. Let nothing ever change. He raises his free hand to the sky. The sensation of a single beacon from the Tribute in Lights shoots out of the pupil tattoo of his palm's eye. It hits the limits of existence, and still it keeps going. The universe has no bounds. He wills it all back to life.

Andrew opens his eyes. On Khalid's thickly painted lips, what used to be a scowl is now a smile. The physical world has changed. Andrew stumbles away from the wall. He drops to his knees in the middle of the street. He stares up at the blinding sun, and he whispers, "I did it." As if his sight were taken, he dangles his head forward. Like the sons of a trillion memories, his white, mummy bandages, the hood that kept his eyes hid, blow through the wind that whips across the street. Tears drip down beneath the tinted glasses shading his eyes. They trickle a path beside his nose, down into the corners of his mouth. He tastes their saltiness. "I know where Michelle is," he says. He stands up. His tears gradually merge into a smile. He turns around and makes his way back towards Greenpoint.

He walks along Bed-Stuy's back to Williamsburg's streets. He passes through the Hassidic community. He stops at a merchant's and buys flowers, red *and* white roses. He remembers the last time he brought Michelle flowers, how he fell to his knees before another's art and cried. With the new bouquet held in one hand, he takes off again. He walks at such a pace that his coat whips behind him in the breeze. It makes him appear a superhero. With his mind, he reminds his Hassidic brethren to heed his directions. We don't want this to ever happen again. He drops his brand-new sunglasses along the way. A Hassidic man crushes them with his heel.

Andrew leaves the old world for the new. The Hassidic costumes are swapped for thrift stored hipsters'. Andrew's outfit is a relic, a merging of the two, the post-postmodern prophet for the new age. He walks in front of The Verb. The chalkboard reminds him again that The Verb loves him. The noun for The Verb is Lola. The verb for The Noun is Lola. He smiles a smile larger than anything that has been on his face since he stood atop the Empire State on the night of September 7th.

Holding his flowers to his chest, he stops in front of the familiar door unseen for so long. He runs his hand through his hair, tries to stick its greasy strands to his scalp. He stares at the eyes in his palm. Are they invisible to everybody else now like a vampire's reflected fangs? Andrew is a teenager ready for the prom. He buttons and smoothes his brand-new coat. He takes a deep breath. Ari's painting will be back hanging on the wall. What did it mean? She told him once during that dream. He buzzes the apartment where so much happened, so many tears, so many bits of fettered joy, murders that he dreamt he was responsible for. It's okay. He willed them all back to life. There's no such thing as ghosts. It's only been four days since their lips first met. Last night sure was a crazy fantasy. What a fucked up dream. Will she remember anything? Andrew was shouting at the moon. He closes his eyes and grimaces at the memory of a six month nightmare. Time does not exist. *Today is Tuesday, September 11th, 2001.* He opens his eyes.

Wearing jeans and a white tee shirt, just like the last time he saw her, her long black hair cascading over her shoulders, Ari opens the door. Like forms to the living, Andrew recalls what the sharp angles of her body felt like.

He remembers her deep, musky scent. He catches a whiff of it again. For him, it was real. For her, it was a... She stares at him in disbelief, as if she can still recollect her dreams. Nobody should ever have to feel. Her eyes light on the roses clutched between his fingers. Uncertain how to express emotions that she's unsure of, her expression twitters between a million different faces, sometimes shock, sometimes rage, sometimes sorrow, and sometimes even love. Her fingers tremble as she touches her throat. She wipes a strand of hair away from her eyes, and her expression settles into a serious, penetrating gaze.

Andrew holds the flowers out to her. "I brought these for Michelle," he says. Wrapped in crinkling cellophane, the red and white roses speak of ashes, blood, and tears. "To apologize for last night."

Ari's face collapses. "You did what?"

"I brought these flowers for Michelle."

Ari draws her eyebrows in. She twists her lips in incomprehension. She says, "Andrew, what are you on? What happened to your hand?"

Eyes aflutter, Andrew looks at where the World Trade's boxes should extend up above the distance beyond Brooklyn's low-lying skyline. This can't be happening. They're not there. "I caught myself on a nail," he says. He trips back from the door. He runs his hand through his hair, spreads it back into a million scraggly directions, and he drops his flowers in the street. Pollinating the dead earth, red and white petals scatter across black concrete. He runs his hands down his face. Utter disbelief transmogrifies his features. He turns around and begins to walk away. Ari stares at him as he rounds the corner. He clutches his stomach, and he disappears. She closes the door, and she walks back up the steps to her lonely apartment. She doesn't know why, but her whole body is shaking. She looks at where her painting used to hang. She immediately picks up her phone and dials Andrew's cell. The signal cannot be found.

The sun begins to set. It casts long, dark shadows out from underneath Andrew's feet as he twists in and out of the Polish immigrants pooling along Manhattan Avenue. Purple edges expand at the edge of the sun's spectrum. They tell tales of insanity, and they force Andrew to squint and shade his eyes. A team of demons brood in his stomach. Trying to dig their ways out into the open air, they scratch their claws down the tender, fleshy walls inside his esophagus. They breathe smoke that condenses as tears behind his retinas. He cries on the inside. Water heats into flames that scorch his brain. Completely numb, his mind shuts down in every which way. Thought itself is painful.

The scent of piss overwhelms him as he pushes open the door leading to the stairs of his own tenement building. He storms up to his apartment, flings the door open, and rushes inside. In the kitchen, he screams, "What did he do with them, Carey?" He stumbles over to the couch in the makeshift living room, crashes into it, and drops his face into his hands.

Carey appears from out his bedroom. He's half asleep. He was just reading. He leans hesitantly against his doorframe. "What are you talking about, Andrew?" he tentatively asks.

Andrew whips his face towards his roommate. Revealing his new eyes, he holds his hand, palm out, towards Carey. Flames shoot out of his pupils. Like a buried fireman struggling to free his crushed legs, Carey trembles from his proximity to the heat. He stumbles from the blast. "Gabriel!" Andrew shouts. "What did he do with Michelle and Charlie?"

An uncertain expression flashes across Carey's face. He

keeps his distance. "I don't understand you," he says. "What the hell is that on your hand?"

"You introduced me to him," Andrew retorts. "That night, he shot pool against me for two souls. He won, and I want to know what he did with them!" Andrew jumps up.

Carey reels back into his bedroom. "I don't know what's going on in your head, Andrew, but don't come any closer to me." He puts his hand on the door, closes it a little ways, looks out of a narrower space.

"Is he in there?" Andrew's eyes grow large. A questionable light shines beneath their soft, blue sheen.

"He's not here. I'm asking you, please, don't come any closer. Andrew, just tell me what you did to your hand."

"Liar! Stop calling me Andrew. I know who I am! My name is Raphael." He takes a step towards Carey's room.

With a cry, Carey slams his door. Its echo vibrates through the tiny apartment's floor and ceiling. Next door, the Spanish arguments stop. "Andrew, if you don't get out of here, I'm gonna call the cops," Carey screams. "Leave your keys next to the boombox. If they're not there when I open this door, I'll call the cops then, too. I'm serious."

A silver exacto knife is sitting beside the boombox. Its razor blade tapers into a thin point perfect for slicing through the fine fabrics, for creating tattoos on the fragile canvases of this world. *With that, I slit my veins...* Andrew licks his lips. He knows what the police will consist of: batons and night sticks from an immigrated Jewish SS seeking to enlist a fallen angel in the role of an immortal suicide bomber to be blown apart and put back together, blown apart and put back together – a Sisyphean punishment devised by Osiris, the penalty for wanting to be torn apart by wolves, for watching the inside of a nuclear reaction, for seeing God's face, learning His/Her secret name. "I believe you," Andrew says cautiously. "He's doing the same thing to you that he did to them. I've been to the Hellfire Club." Andrew picks up the exacto knife. Like a money changer weighing weighted products, he trades his keys with it, slips it into his pocket, and leaves.

After hearing the click of the front door, Carey waits quite a while. He sits on his bed listening to his own breathing. It's comforting. Everything is silent. What the fuck just happened? What did Andrew do to his hands? Who the hell is Raphael?

With his unbuttoned coat constantly flapping behind him in the breeze, Andrew barrels back through Greenpoint. He rounds a corner and stops at a chain link fence. Beyond the asphalt tennis courts, he gazes at the Empire State Building. He wraps his fingers around the fence's links. As the sky turns dark, the needle glows red, white, and blue. It blinks a warning to low-flying planes. Andrew thumbs the razor's edge of the knife in his pocket. With that, he could slice this skyline up, cut his heart out of the center of its Midtown pulse. There's a nuclear reaction. He pictures the skyline with no more buildings, no more memories, no more gods, no more dreams. Everything looks like Times Square's smoky streets. For a moment, it's beautiful. He shakes his head and starts on his way again.

There's another chain link fence topped with razor wire across the avenue from The Turkey's Nest. Andrew stares at it for a moment. He remembers something. He furrows his eyebrows and looks down at the sidewalk. He takes a deep breath and exhales slowly. He opens the door to the bar, and he steps inside.

Inside the Turkey's Nest, there's more heavy metal playing. The jukebox's manic laughter bursts through the vibrant scene. A bass guitar taps out a rhythm before the lead comes squealing in. Although it is just as bright as it ever was, over the course of the six months since Andrew was last here, the clientele has certainly changed. Hipsters patrol the pool games. Young girls sit together at the bar. The regulars are crowded into corners, sitting at full tables, smoking. Perhaps sin has now come to exist even here, in this purest of Brooklyn places. Perhaps the Ol' Dirty Bastard himself is in need of salvation. Andrew heads straight for a drink.

Younger and with tattoos, even the bartender is different. Andrew grabs his old usual, a relaxing remnant from the days when he still knew his name – a Budweiser in a huge Styrofoam cup. He's blinded by the Turkey's Nest's neon signs, its jukebox lights. Enveloped in a haze of cigarette smoke, a familiar figure fills out a chair beside the pool table. Her breasts rest on her stomach, which rests on her lap. In the glare of the pool table's bright, Budweiser spotlight canopy, the goddess notices Andrew and nods. He heads over to her. He smiles, and she smiles back. "I've changed," he says to her.

"You do look a little different." She twists around and looks him square in the face. "Maybe it's your hair."

"I changed my name."

"What is it now?"

"Raphael D'Angelo."

"I like that. It sounds good. Very L.A. Are you a musician?"

"No. I'm a writer."

"Everybody needs a pen name. With your coat, you look like a rock star."

"It's a gift from Lola."

She shrugs. "Regardless, it's nice." She turns back to watch the game. It appears to be fairly even.

"Do you know Christopher," Andrew asks her, "Believes in *The Liebestod*? An old friend of his from New Orleans was telling me about him yesterday."

"You mean Chris?" she says, nodding her head to indicate a blond, shaggy haired hipster holding a pool cue. Andrew can't believe his luck. In awe, just as when he saw Robert Johnson's iconographic legend in the flesh, he stares at the murderer, the suicide. He's wearing a black sweatshirt, blue jeans, and brown boots. Like a mummy unwrapped in the afterlife, his skin has the texture of the eternally young. His brain has been pulled from his nose. Death and New Orleans's humidity have preserved his body. Similar to Gabriel, his eyes are deep and green – replaced with emeralds. Andrew fingers the blade in his pocket. He wants Christopher's sight.

"Yeah, him. I need to shoot against him," Andrew says with a snarl. "Something like a duel. He has to explain something to me." He sets two quarters, one for each dead eye, on the table.

The goddess laughs. "Well, I'll see what I can do." She closes her eyes and nods her head.

Andrew nods along with the rhythm she feels. "By the way, have you seen a girl in here who's a little shorter than me with long, curly hair? She might be dressed like she was going to work. Her skin is soft and smooth. Her face is long and thin. She's something like an angel. I've been looking for her everywhere."

The goddess winks a heavy eyelid at him. She shakes her head. "Not yet," she says.

Everything about the goddess, her misshapen body, her grotesque face, her easy smile, relaxes Andrew. The panic that he'd felt overwhelming him ever since Ari apparently remembered their nightmare together begins to dissipate. He sits down in a chair against the wall and begins the ritualistic process of getting drunk.

With his hands in his pockets, his fingers on the shaft of his knife, he suddenly leans forward. "Today's my birthday," he blurts out.

"Congratulations," the goddess answers. "How old are you?"

"I thought you might be able to tell me."

"I don't play games."

"Neither do I." Andrew leans back into his seat. "I've been thinking a lot about what you were trying to teach me the last time I was here, about playing pool backwards," he says.

"It's the only way I ever win."

"I think I know how to do it now. Last night, I lost, but a lot's changed since then."

Christopher drops two balls. He misses the third. His opponent droops down and draws a bead for a shot. He strikes, squeezes the trigger. The bullet is released; the cue takes flight. It strikes the six and sinks it in the corner pocket. A gut wound.

"The last time I saw you was on September 10th, right?" the goddess asks.

Andrew twists his neck. A frown trembles across his face. He nods.

"I remember everything about that night," she says.

"So do I," Andrew responds frighteningly.

"You remember how it was raining?"

Frowning painfully, Andrew nods. From the window of Enid's, he watches Michelle disappear beneath an umbrella around the corner.

"And you told me about a dream. By the way, whatever happened with your girlfriend? Is she the girl you're looking for?"

Andrew wraps his hand around his stolen knife. "I brought her flowers just like you said."

"Like The Stones said." She smiles. "And what happened?"

"It worked." Andrew smiles back. Tears gather in the corners of his eyes. "It really worked. We've spent every night together for the past six months."

"I can tell you love her," the goddess says. With her pudgy fingers, she squeezes Andrew's arm. "Did you make sense out of your dream yet? Did it come true?"

"Yes. To both."

"Good." She lets him go. The white imprint of her grip is left on Andrew's flesh.

At the end of his pool stick, Christopher skewers his man. Twisting the knife in his pocket, scraping the blue veins of his leg through the fabric of his jeans, Andrew steps up to the table. He leans over and swipes his quarters off the wooden runner, drops them into their slots, and slides the contraption in. "Hey, Christopher. I'm Raphael," he says. Christopher glances his adversary up and down. He smirks at the modern costume hidden beneath Raphael's Hassidic coat. From across the table's green felt divide, unaware of what his opponent's other hand holds, like a model, like a dog, he grabs Andrew's outstretched hand and shakes.

"Those are some crazy tattoos you got," Christopher says. "I've never seen anything like them before."

"Not crazy. Just true, past wounds," Andrew responds. He racks the balls in what is known as a J.C. rack – placing the golden one up front and the black eight in the heart. The corpus is composed of a few solids, a few stripes together, and the eleven and three at either side. "Do you mind playing last pocket?" he asks.

"Not at all," Christopher responds. He wears a Cheshire grin.

Andrew's expression turns extremely sincere. "It means a lot to me."

"Sure, man. Whatever you want."

Christopher bends his legs to break. Nearly on his knees, licking a whole alphabet across his lips, he slides his stick in and out between his downward V'd fingers.

"For Sherry," Andrew says.

Christopher agrees. He thrusts forward as hard as he can. He winds up standing, his arm outstretched, his stick hanging in the air. From out the tip of the cue, a white egg spews forward, flies into Andrew's colored cells. With speed tails trailing out of their sides, the three and the eleven break in opposite directions. The energy of forward motion is transferred to the seven. It slips through and finds a home in the corner pocket. The other balls break apart and spill their contents all over the pool table's grassy felt field.

Christopher sinks the six deep. Inflicting his desires, the balls slice every which way. Like a mental rape, their tell-tale trails rip across the green bed. Christopher slips the stick in his thumb and forefinger's slick O. He runs the rail down the three. Skimming off the side, he spills away early. "Your shot," he says.

"Don't forget how you play, Raphael," the goddess interjects.

In his own pocket, gouging a hole through the pocketed air, Andrew twirls his knife. His eyes grow wide. His brain turns off. His wounds bleed. "Guess I'm high," he says. He gulps his Budweiser, leans forward, and aims for the gutter. His first stab is for the eleven to stick in Christopher's side. His slice is perfect – thirteen down the rail. He lines up for the eleven again. "Nine to the corner," he says. Like the Sultan of Swing, he points to the fence where the ball will fly home. The tip of his stick punctures the air, pounds the cue. With a yellow stripe, the nine, like a copperhead, slides right into its hole. Always keeping his eye on the eleven, for the first time since September 10th,

Andrew runs the table. Michael and Noel would be proud.

Andrew carefully chooses where the eleven will fall. There are certain things in this world that we can control. He looks for his shot on the eight. Leaning against the wall, he twists the knife deeper into his pocket. He wants his last pocket to be the corner. A rail shot will do the trick. Without revealing his intentions to anyone, he lets go of his crutch, the knife, and focuses on his weapon, his spear, the stick in his hand.

Stepping beside him into the Budweiser shade's spotlight, behind what he hopes will be his last pocket, he sees, to his right, the grisly creature, the werewolf, that he tried to kill over Noel's shoulder the night before. It grins mockingly at him. With its claw, it covers the hole. It shakes its head and growls. Andrew's features harden. His heart beats so fast. A bead of sweat drips down the side of his face. He gets control of himself, stops looking aghast at the monster. He tries not to see it at all but instead to focus on the end of the game.

He strikes. Like a rocket, the cue ball is ejected from the stick's chamber. In an Apollonian arc, the eleven bounds off the rail. With a cry, the werewolf whips its hand away from the pocket, but the eleven's mathematically vicious path severs its lazy finger. With a parabolic trajectory, the eleven slips into the table's guts. Andrew's been waiting for that for six months. Bleeding profusely, the werewolf's single digit flops around, a skewered snake, on the table. In a howling puff of smoke, the monster disappears. Andrew begins to laugh. His skin stretches tight around his manic eyes. His lips lift into a Jokerish grin. He doubles over and holds his stomach. For the first time ever, it feels good to be dying. That thought only makes him laugh even harder. He holds onto the knife in his pocket. As suddenly as he started, he stops laughing.

With his eyes, he slices Christopher apart, dissects him on the pool table, runs his hands through his entrails, reads the necromantic future from his guts. It looks like the energy of the world is shifting. In homage to his bicameral god, Andrew bathes himself in Christopher's warm semenic blood. With the claw of the werewolf's severed finger, he carves out Christopher's green eyes, exchanges their emerald beauty with two rusty quarters from his pocket. He sews Christopher back up, ignites him with Frankenstein's electricity, and sends him out to wander New York for all eternity.

"Those quarters are yours," Andrew says. He stares Christopher down, dares him to question his authority, to come closer to the knife in his pocket. "I'm not playing anymore."

Christopher backs away and looks strangely – his head to the side, one eyebrow arched over his eye – at his adversary. Pursing his lips, he glances around for the bar's other customers to explain something to him. The goddess sits up higher in her chair.

With heavenly eyes, Andrew watches himself walk out the door, button his coat, and strut down the street to Enid's. He sees his breath in the night air. Without thinking, he scoots around the table and sinks the eight in his last pocket. From her harpy's perch in the corner, the goddess begins to clap. Like an approach to orgasm, her rhythm builds with her enthusiasm. Andrew can finally go home.

He walks over to the bar and orders a shot of whiskey. He downs it in a single gulp. Its nectar scorches his throat. He orders another one, tips his head back, and pours it down his gullet. He orders one more. He twirls the glass, watches the golden fluid lick the rim. The image of its sweetness causes him to lick his lips. Thoughtlessly, he tips the contents into his mouth. With his head swimming, he returns to the business of drinking his beer.

For a change, the goddess sashays over to him. She leans her elbow against the corner of the bar, flips her long, wavy hair over her shoulder, and asks, "So when will I meet your girlfriend?"

"Soon," Andrew answers. "She just got back in town."

"Where was she?"

"She went home for a little bit."

"And you're not with her?" the goddess wonders incredulously.

"We've had some difficulties meeting up, but I'll see her tonight. I'm certain of it."

"Is she coming here?"

"I don't think so. This place is too bright for her. Ever since September 11th, she prefers darker atmospheres."

"Well, I can't wait to meet her. You learn well. A teachable man is the best man in the world."

"I've been trying with all my might to learn. I've been trying so hard it hurts."

The goddess's fat face glows with an unearthly, sexually pleasurable light. Her aged eyes shine like an underage girl's. "I'm jealous of her," she says. "I've wanted to find a man like you for forever."

Andrew nods. He mumbles, "The angels, not half so happy in heaven, went envying her and me." With a push against the bar, he slips off his stool and weaves to the door.

"Take it easy, Raphael."

In the street's cold air, Andrew buttons his Hassidic coat around himself. It encapsulates him like a serpent's shed skin reclaimed. He's moving backwards through time. It's not raining tonight. The world has been flushed clean. His breath, reminding him, like cigarette smoke, that he's still alive, appears in front of his lips. He walks up the block, past McCarren Park – opening wide and verdant, an empty, baseball field covered block in an asphalt wasteland – and turns right.

Passing Enid's large open windows, he gazes through his reflection at the frivolous scene inside. A packed, swirling crowd of twenty-somethings laugh and drink and smoke and talk. It could be any bar on any night in any city in the world. It could be this bar in this city at a different time in a different world.

As he steps up to the large, double doors, he stumbles and trips back down to the sidewalk. An icy rain of tear drenched memories drowns him. Tasting the rising sea of their salty deluge, his lips contort. His eyes roll back into his head. His hands tremble epileptically. He opens his mouth to scream, but like an insect pinned to a piece of foam, its wings spread for observation, no sound escapes.

The door opens. A giggling girl, waving goodbye to somebody still inside, steps out onto the sidewalk. Framing her round face, her blonde hair is cut short. Her bangs are very cute. She's dressed in striped pants and a thrift store tee shirt, some silk screened print peeling off its design. With woolen fringe around its collars and cuffs, a long, pink coat flows down to her ankles. Shaking her head, she gives Andrew a sidelong glance as she walks uncaringly past him. He braces himself against the sidewalk, retches emptily, wipes his dry mouth, stands back up, and steps into Enid's. As if he were suffering from the acrid remnants of a flu, his fit still causes him to shake.

With his eyes tearing, he slips through the crowd and up to the bar. In his stomach, the living heart of his alien progeny beats – the brooding brood of spiders from Mars. Still suffering from the torrent outside, his skin is clammy. He recognizes the slim, pretty bartendress from an eternity ago. He orders a gin and tonic from her. "Have you seen Michelle?" he asks her.

"Who?" she responds. She leans in closer to him to try and shield the din. Her expression is painfully serious and attentive. The bar lights brighten a halo around the fading wisps of her blonde hair.

"Michelle."

"I know lots of Michelles. Which one?"

"I don't know. She must be somebody different."

The bartendress shakes her head and rushes around to the other side of the bar to take some mod hipster's order. Andrew tries finding a lonely spot in the happy crowd where he can sit down.

He squeezes in at a table with two girls and a guy. The guy glances menacingly at him, frustrated over the invasion of his territory (he seems to feel like he already pissed on Andrew's seat, and he doesn't understand why the stranger can't smell it), while the girls grin salaciously at Andrew's haggard appearance. In the darkness, he cuts out an odd apparition.

Andrew smiles – a supercilious lilt to his lips. He sticks his hand in his pocket and fiddles with his knife. He plays the stringed music of the spheres. He lolls his head back on his neck, swings it around in rhythm to the symphony that only he hears. Like the rush of a conch song, the rest of the world is silent.

Tapping him on the arm, one of the girls says, "I like your tattoos."

Andrew opens his eyes. All the way across Enid's warehouse, standing at the end of the trendy bar, not too far from a group of laughing hipsters huddled around and thrusting their hips at the frustratingly difficult pinball machine, Andrew sees her.

Glancing in disarray at the mass of people surrounding

her, she appears lost. The dim lights behind the bar highlight half of her soft profile. A single strand of short, dark hair dangles out of her beret-like cap. At the end, at her chin, it curls up just a little bit. She turns her head. The lone strand of hair swings to the back of her neck. Her face comes straight again. The strand of hair licks the side of her lips. Adding a sense of sensual misgiving to her features, her eyebrows furrow. The adolescent puffiness of her cheeks' skin appears translucent, like something that you could push straight through in order to feel her pointed, muscled tongue. Beneath her striped, button down shirt, her slight, round breasts tug at the cotton fabric. Her waist tapers in, expands at her hips, fills out into her legs. Although her accoutrements are different, she looks exactly like she did when she was fifteen.

Andrew holds on tight to his exacto knife. With his other hand, he grabs his gin and tonic. He stands up and takes one step towards the lost, little girl. He pauses. In his wrist, in his neck, his pulse pulses frenetically. The guy at the table sighs and pretends like nothing's happened. Under the dim lighting, the girls watch Andrew step away. He walks cautiously with his head cocked to the side, his eyes tight, and his lips questioning. He carefully places one foot in front of the other, makes sure that he doesn't step out of line. Meticulously, he picks his way through the crowd. With one hand still in his pocket, he stands dumbstruck in front of her.

Between her perfectly spaced lashes, her flitting eyes come to rest on the disheveled specter before her. She blinks. Her heavy mascara gradually pulls apart to reveal the most innocent, the most questioning of emerald green irises. Against her ghostly skin, they shine. Her caught breath lifts her breasts with a silent hiccup.

"I just saw you," Andrew says. "How long have you

been here?"

"Way too long," Michelle answers. "The guys I came here with abandoned me. I'm just starting to realize that." She slips the white end of a straw between her deep red lips, and she sips off of her oddly colored mixed drink. A smile toys with the fresh edge of her mouth.

Andrew smiles back at her. He leans against the bar's edge. Michelle's smile extends all the way across her lips to her mouth's other side. For a moment, just in his face, Andrew looks precisely like he did six months and two and a half days ago. He takes his hand out of his pocket, lets go of his murderous crutch.

Michelle's gaze glitters. "You've been watching me, haven't you?" she says.

"You've been watching me."

"Maybe." Michelle pauses. In a moment, she perks up. "This is Belle and Sebastian," she says.

"What?"

"The DJ. It's Belle and Sebastian. I was listening to this CD earlier." Her smile slips inside of her. It lights her whole body. Her wide, drunken eyes glow.

"We used to like Belle and Sebastian a lot," Andrew says. He looks down and frowns. "You remember that," he mumbles.

Michelle's face softens and opens up. On an inner level, her expression draws an inquisitive sentence. "What's your name?" she asks. An innocuous turn shapes her features into a renaissance portrait of immaculacy. "You seem familiar."

"Raphael. And you?"

"You can call me Belle."

"That rhymes," Andrew states.

Michelle laughs simply. Her staccato breaths puncture the crisp barroom air. "You're strange," she says.

Andrew shrugs.

"How about if I call you Sebastian?" she asks with a girlish giggle.

"That's okay," Andrew answers. He's still looking down. "Names don't mean that much." Hesitantly, he adds, "I just can't believe I'm talking to you."

"I can't believe I'm talking to you," Michelle responds. "When those guys left me, I didn't know…" She blinks, looks away, and returns her sheepish gaze to him. "You look like a rock star."

"Do you like it?"

"I like the coat," she says. Moving a step closer, she runs her hands down the coat's rough cotton texture. Her proximity ignites Andrew. She smells of flowers and youth. The scents waft off her neck with every subtle shift of her body. To be this close to her again, illuminated beneath the bar's lone light, is to step into and snuggle amid the long, flowing grass of Rome's Elysian Fields. The meaningless sky expands endlessly above your innocent gaze. With nothing to die for, there's no such thing as God. She crumples the coat's black fabric between the tips of her fingers. Electricity passes through the vegetable material. She starts from the shock. For a moment, her fleshy lips flash a pained expression. In a second, she returns to her awkward happiness. "What's that on your palms?" she asks.

Andrew opens his hands. As if trying to remember something, he stares at them. His lips contort. Eventually, he says, "An open wound."

Michelle giggles. Her teeth sparkle beneath Enid's mood-lit darkness. Her laughter cuts through its constantly chattering din. "Do you have any other tattoos?" she asks.

"I'm covered in them."

Entranced with liquor, Michelle gives him a knowledgeable glance. "Maybe I'll see them someday."

"Maybe."

"What do you do?" she asks, a chaste expression, the most enticing of sexual meanings, flashing over her lurid features.

Andrew's eyes widen like a holy fool's. "I'm a writer," he says.

"Are you writing anything now?"

Andrew pauses. In a moment of reflection, he looks up at the high ceiling. He exhales heavily and tilts his head to the side. He answers slowly and thoughtfully, "I'm finishing a screenplay."

With a tinge of excitement evident in her voice and her eyes, Michelle says, "Really? Where are you now?"

"The climax."

"What's it about?"

"A bank robbery, but it's really our love story."

"I love love stories," Michelle says. Her entire demeanor relaxes. "I think writers are fascinating."

"I know," Andrew answers. He glances away and frowns. "I've always known that."

"You're so perspicacious," Michelle responds in an attempt to try and regain his attention.

Her device works. Andrew turns back to her with a child's wide stare. "Do you really think so?" he asks.

"I think you've already got me figured out." Their eyes meet. Michelle smiles at him. Her eyes sparkle with the same starlight that shined in them that night atop the Empire State Building. She reaches out with her fingers and touches his arm. "I'm gonna go to the bathroom," she says. Slowly, she draws her seductive gaze away from him. Even slower, she removes her fingers' tingling pressure from his coat.

She slips away a few steps to the unisex bathroom's door. In the darkness, Andrew watches her leave. She's shorter than he remembers her being, but their connection, the same connection that enflamed his soul the Halloween of his sophomore year, when she was a vampire who mischievously taught him to unfasten her garter belt, remains as binding and powerful as it did when their lips and tongues finally met to impregnate one another with the other's loving seed.

With a quick peak over her shoulder, a sweet grin shot at Andrew, Michelle opens the bathroom door and steps inside. Her look contains too many memories, too many dreams. It tears Andrew apart. Uncertain but trying to have faith that, this time, she will reemerge from the bathroom's lonely cell, he frowns as she disappears, and he returns, to quell his fluttering stomach, to his gin and tonic. He reaches into his pocket, feels the knife's cold razor blade. With a forlorn glance at the ceiling and the nothing that lies beyond it, he exhales and relaxes.

Drunken thoughts float through his brain. From out of a whiskey whirlpool, they cling to the spinning, saturated remnants of his shipwrecked mind. Trying to hold himself together, Andrew rests his forehead between his fingertips. He closes his eyes.

"Sebastian!"

Andrew spins around. At the bathroom door, Michelle has reemerged. In a shaft of light, through a narrow crevice between the door and the frame, she's grinning and biting her lip. Her beret is cocked to the side. Her hand appears out of the same crevice through which her face is visible. With a simple wave of her finger, she draws Andrew towards her.

He succumbs like a puppy on a leash, shuffles through the stylishly dressed bodies clumped across Enid's hardwood floor. Brushing against somebody, he almost spills his drink. He lets go of his knife and steadies himself against another party-goer's arm, his own Simon Magus. In a seemingly drunken daze, the same as on many of their high school nights, Michelle slides half way down the door. She throws her head back and guffaws at his fall. Andrew licks the liquor off his fingertips. He continues onward to the bathroom as if there were a sacrifice to make.

At the door, Michelle grabs Andrew by the arm and ushers him inside. A plain white cell with a simple mirror above a single washbasin flashes across his vision before Michelle slams the door closed, locks it, shoves him against the wall, and flips out the lights. Through the closed door, Enid's party noises muffle as if he were being suffocated by a pillow in his own bed. The acrid scent of disinfectants overwhelms him. He spills his drink. Ice tinkles across the tile floor. Panicking, he grabs hold of his knife.

In the clean darkness, Michelle presses her eromanic lips to his. He quickly responds by opening his mouth. She opens hers. Their tongues, their saliva, their diseases, their loves merge. The magical world of Eden and humanity without sin opens inside of Andrew's mind. He sees himself as Adam, Michelle as Eve, as they recline nude underneath a tree. Whether it's life or knowledge, Andrew will never know. Michelle flips the lights back on.

The alien bursts out, chews its way through Andrew's stomach. With spider-like dexterity, it latches onto Michelle and claws and bites its way inside. The world flashes red. Andrew squints.

"I wanted the first one to be in the dark," Michelle says. As reality comes back into focus, her eyes glow with youthful intensity. She's the same teenage girl who Andrew remembers – the embodiment of the spirit of the dream he told to the goddess. Only then, he never got to feel the contours of the pout of her lips as he writhed against the wall in a unisex bathroom.

Trembling from his soul to his hands, he sets his empty glass on top of the toilet. He closes the seat and sits down. He rests his face in his hands. Michelle walks over and caresses the back of his head. He looks up. A rush of compassion washes over him out of her eyes. "You're so sad," she says. "What makes you so sad?"

"You'd never believe what I've been through."

"Since September 11th?"

Andrew nods.

"It's been hard on me, too. I lost a good friend that day. Somebody I'd known my entire life."

Andrew mumbles, "I lost my best friend."

Michelle tips her head to the side. A distant look invades her eyes. A frown, permanently etched into her features, needing only the right light to throw it into relief, comes into focus. She quickly masks it with a smile. "I knew I loved you," she says.

Andrew wraps his arms around her waist. "I know," he answers, and he presses his cheek to her stomach.

"I haven't really been myself since then."

"Neither have I."

"That's what you're going to turn me into tonight, Sebastian, my real self."

"I'd love to," Andrew says. He looks up at her again. She unwraps his arms from her waist, takes his palms to her face, and kisses each of his fresh tattoos. Her pecks tingle into the holes in his skin. They heal him all the way through. They force the last, lingering remnants of his bloodstream out of his stomach wound. They kill the alien, his parasite, and in turn, they kill him. "Michelle, my Belle."

"How did you know my name?" Michelle giggles and swoons.

Andrew undoes the bottom two buttons of her striped cotton shirt. As gently as he touched her lips the last time he ever saw her, as he begged, in the only way he knew how, to please not let that be the end of his dreams, he kisses her smooth stomach. Goose pimples quickly constrict her flesh into a rigid texture of dots. Andrew runs his scarred hands across her seemingly pock marked skin. Although they come from pleasure, the goose bumps feel like the sadistic work of a torturer's device. Andrew puts his cheek up to her waist, feels her hairless torso expand and constrict beneath his unshaven face. He listens to her breath, her life, fill her diaphragm and her lungs.

"This is better than drugs," Michelle whispers as she runs her hands through his hair. She's trembling. "Sometimes you just need drugs to get here."

"I want to stay here forever."

"Me too." She leans over. In the bathroom's bright, blinding glare reflected off of mirrors, white tiles, white paint, and white porcelain, she lifts his chin so that their lips can meet. They close their eyes. For that moment, that one moment, the extremities of their bodies commingling as subtly as a tire touches the road, with each of them lost in his or her own personal darkness, they are one being, the hermaphrodite, unity.

Their kiss parts. Andrew presses his lips to her stomach again. Lost in the soft contours of her skin, his whole world is white. With the tips of his fingers, he feels the endless hole of her belly button's implosion. That was where her life began. Never taking his lips from her flesh, he unbuckles her belt. Michelle closes her eyes. Bliss transforms her face. Her cheeks glow. She takes off her hat and sets it on the toilet next to Andrew's drink. She shakes her head. Her short hair, with its two extra long strands in the front, something akin to horns, seems to stand on end. Light shines through its capillaries. Andrew takes off his Hassidic coat and tosses it into a ramshackle heap on the floor.

Tugging at her belt loops, he slides her pants down her hips. The waist catches on her curves. Andrew kisses her above her underwear line. The rough, metal teeth of her open zipper bite his cheeks. The satin sensation of her underpants tickles his bottom lip. At this proximity, the oceanic, life-giving scent of her insides fills both his mind and the bathroom's entire cramped space.

Andrew spins off the toilet. Like when he brought Khalid back to life, like when he brought this same girl flowers months ago on a sad, sad night, he drops to his knees. Michelle backs up a few steps. Andrew pulls her close to him with one hand on each of her cheeks. "Hold on a second," she says.

She takes two steps back. Through his jeans, Andrew feels his knife bulging in his pocket. Michelle steps out of her shoes. She slips off her pants. Beneath the glaring bathroom light, her bare legs are as blinding as the sun off of snow. In stockinged feet, she walks on tiptoes back up to him.

Starting at her knees' bony caps, Andrew rubs his hands up her roundly muscled thighs. Her skin tingles beneath the touch, the vision, of his eye tattoos. She shivers. Andrew grabs hold of the tops of her underpants. He pulls them down to her ankles.

Her vagina is carefully manicured. A line of spiky pubic hair, a punk rock mohawk rises overtop her full lips. Andrew sticks his hand between her legs. With two fingers, he spreads her velveteen lips and enters her coffin. A warm, sticky wetness dribbles across his fingertips. He catches it in his palms, lets its ointment spill across his tattoo. He probes deeper into her, feels the flesh packed walls inside her sepulchral cave. She's so warm, so tight, red *and* white. Suddenly, he's overcome by the blues.

Michelle sighs softly. She stumbles back a step. Nearly banging her head against the sink, she falls to the floor. Her ass flattens against cold, white tiles. A melting ice cube from Andrew's spilled drink slips out from underneath her leg. It leaves a glistening trail on her skin. Her partially unbuttoned shirt opens over her flat stomach. Her breasts push against the closed portion of its fabric. Drying quickly, Andrew's middle finger crinkles from her dampness. He crawls across the wet floor and drags her underpants over her socks, off her feet.

He clings like a poet to Michelle's thighs, inverts the world, and draws himself up to the island of purgatory. Reminding him of his covenant with Lola, even in his drunken state (as if the pain were somehow deeper inside him), his entire anal cavity throbs with the hermaphrodite's ghostly memory.

Michelle leans back, rests her head amid dribbles of piss across the floor. Her pale stomach is visible over her mound of Venus. Admiring the winged diamond of her lips, a jeweled bat given as an engagement present, Andrew tilts his head to the side. He leans forward with a kiss.

She tastes as pure as a mermaid drawn fresh from the crystal Aegean. She is the foam delivering Aphrodite in an oyster shell. He parts her with two fingers and sticks his tongue inside. He tastes her burgeoning pearls. He feels her smooth inner surfaces. His tongue is wrapped, enraptured with unlocking the doors of her body. Through a tiny hole, he enters a cell that every human being can fit inside. The walls are warm and moist. Coated in candy, they're a child's dream of prison. He senses the essence of existence, of the earth, of blood.

Like a zombie awakening from its empty slumber, Michelle moans mildly. She twists her hips a bit, lifts them off the bathroom floor. Her slick drippings slide across

Andrew's chin. He opens her up with one of his fingers, spreads her apart, caresses her caverns. He loses himself in the sensations of feminine lust. He returns to her everything he learned from Lola. Her stomach throbs from the intensity of her breaths. Reminiscent of his own epileptic fit on Enid's steps, her hands begin convulsing.

The same as when Dante tried in vain to reach Charlie, there's a frenetic pounding on the door. Michelle shifts her leg. She almost knocks Andrew in the face. He stops. Michelle grabs him by the back of his head. In a second, with the moment broken, she changes her mind and pushes him away. She leaps up, grabs her underpants and jeans, and jumps back into them. She rebuttons her shirt and steps back into her shoes. Her cheeks are flushed, but her eyes are flitting and nervous.

Andrew stands up. The powerful depth of her scent has melded itself to his skin. He grabs his Hassidic coat off the floor. It's a little damp. It doesn't matter. He puts it back on. "Where are you going?" he asks

"Back to Manhattan," she says.

"Will I ever see you again?"

Michelle shakes her head in frustration. "There's a lot of bars in New York City," she says, and she grabs the door handle.

"Wait!" Andrew screams.

Michelle pauses. She turns back around slowly and looks at him with her eyebrows furrowed.

His eyes are mad. His lips are trembling. He reaches into his pocket. This isn't the same person she invited to share the bathroom's unisex cell with her. As insane as the Joker revealing a stacked deck of playing cards, he pulls out his knife. Michelle freezes. She refuses to believe what she sees. Her Sebastian's face is frightening. Tormented by the repressed memory of the true, past death of a true, past life, recognizing the significance of the recurring feeling of dejá-vu that has disturbed her through all of this life, her gaze grows wide. Her mouth opens, but nothing comes out. Pointing the knife ahead of himself, training it on the mystical life-giving properties of her belly, Andrew steps towards her. The metal blade sparkles beneath the bright bathroom light. Like the pointed dome of the Chrysler Building's pleated skirt, it glitters. Like a paragraph, it tapers into a razor's edge.

"Don't hurt me," Michelle whispers. "Please..." Her eyes pray for some sort of escape.

Andrew doesn't hear. "In case you ever want to see me again," he says as he offers her the knife.

Michelle's breath slows in her chest. In the glare of the bathroom light, framed like a fallen angel in God's angry glare by God's angry white walls, white porcelain, and white tiles, Andrew stands as still as stone, as stoic as a monument. Michelle can't believe she's alive. The knife is so close to her guts. As if it had already happened in another dimension, in another time, she can sense the sensation of its cold point pressing into her warm womb. She puts her hand to her chest, stills her fluttering heartbeat. The knife quivers between Andrew's fingers. His lips twitch as he begs her to take it away. Shaking, unsure of herself, she reaches out and grabs the knife from his hand. Their fingers slip across one another's. Her nails click against his. The sensation is kinetic. At the same instant, for perhaps the last time ever, their eyes meet – his blue, hers green. Andrew stammers, "I thought I'd never see you again."

Michelle feigns a nervous smile. Andrew trembles. In a flash, she's taken his knife, and she's gone, buried beneath the rubble of lower Manhattan, entombed once more in the delicate corners of his mind.

All alone again, just like on September 10th, Andrew stumbles backwards to the toilet. He crashes down on top of the seat. His face falls into his hands, and he dry heaves a sob. Michelle's scent, a scent that he waited a lifetime to experience, dries into, becomes a permanent stain on his hands, his tongue, his lips. A piece of him now, he can't escape it. The bathroom walls close in on him. The bathroom's light blinds him. Constricting his breath, the tight space presses against his chest. He can't breathe. He can't think. He needs an umbilical cord, an IV drip, to feed through. He claws at the walls of his tomb, his womb. There's no light at the end of the tunnel. It's here, in this cramped, painful space, that light both emanates and dissolves. Buried alive, Andrew knows he's going to die.

The door opens. Enid's volume bursts in on his solicitous solitude. With his lips twitching, he turns towards the dark, gaping hole in the wall. A red-headed girl, as perfectly vengeful as Saint Michael, is standing there. Apparently disappointed, she frowns at him. "Sorry," she says, and she closes the door, re-inters Andrew in his bright white emptiness.

"Sherry?" he whispers, and he shakes his head. His head lolls on his neck. It's hard to visit the dead. He runs his hands down his face. Forgetting himself for a moment, he reaches into his pocket for his knife. He feels nothing but nothingness.

In a frenzy, he jumps off the toilet seat and bursts out of the bathroom. The scene in Enid's is some sort of post-civilization madness. Andrew runs smack into Sherry waiting to come into the unisex cell. She trips to the ground. Her drink pours onto her stomach. In his possession, Andrew doesn't bother to help her up. He tears around people moving their liquored concoctions out of his way. He finds himself in the middle of the bar, his head spinning beneath dark lights, his eyes blind from the fluorescent bathroom. Hanging on the wall, the only thing still bright enough for him to see, an artistically golden tangle of coins in some postmodern rendition of a relic from the Roman Empire shimmers like leaves beneath Enid's ensnared breeze. "Michelle!" Andrew screams.

The way too cool for you crowd breaks in the middle of a pointless phrase of conversation. They stifle their ironically forced laughter and glance nervously at Andrew out of the corners of their eyes. As soon as they realize that any response might impress upon their interlocutors that they care, might imply that something in New York has actually disturbed them, they lean back into the glare of their tables' candle flames and return to their social schemes. There isn't even a pause in Enid's hip rhythm.

She isn't there, anywhere.

Andrew rushes out Enid's door. It slams shut behind him. Like for one forever banished beyond his castle's gates, for one forever told he can never return to the promised land of his mother or father, like for Adam, for Moses, for Lucifer, for Cain, Enid's frivolity immediately disappears. No siege engine will ever break down those walls. Awakening on the lake of the abyss, Andrew stands on the corner at one of Brooklyn's many crossroads. Dead and ready to go to war with God, he's cold. Beneath the streetlights, rubbing his arms through his jacket, he rushes back and forth on the sidewalk. He glares in the direction Michelle disappeared into beneath September 10th's rains. He strains to scour north, south, east, and west. He's trying to see through dimensions, through time, back to a vacuum at a given point in space. Light years away, there still exists the memory of the lightshow from the Big Bang.

Brooklyn's alien streets are empty. Andrew knows now where he needs to go. Michelle told him so. He needs to travel backwards to the land of ghosts. Twisting and turning, writhing with every jerky motion of his walk as if he were the living dead newly loosed from his coffin, as if he were the living newly dead pissing and spasming with his neck tight in a noose, he begins retracing his steps. The rope around his neck physically dangles out of a spiritual heaven. It's a marionette string in the devil's grip picking him up and moving him forward, forward, always forward. He can't resist.

He passes McCarren Park. When his name was Andrew, some time over six months ago, when he could still stand to be sober and alone, he'd often sit on the park's wooden benches and contemplate God and life and death. The infinite blue sky expanded above both the city and him, proved forever that the infinite existed. In the distance, over the corner of the park, high above huge, tiny trees, the World Trade Center embodied New York. He'd watch the squirrels gather nuts, the elderly stroll, the immigrant kids play soccer. None of them were really so different from each other. None of them were really so different from him. He'd read books, and he'd dream a famous future for Michelle and himself.

But tonight, as he walks through the cold, he doesn't pause to sit and contemplate. He shakes his head. Like a strangled rat, a snake's meal, his lungs, stomach, and throat constrict. Andrew Christian never existed. His life was Raphael's dream, a means for escaping an eternity in hell, an angel's attempt at art. *What was I imprisoned for? I think maybe we lost the war. I remember twisting in barbed wire as the demons licked my blood off the cold, steaming floor. They sodomized me with razors, plucked the feathers from my wings and replaced them with broken glass. They laughed with forked tongues and mangled teeth. They spit urine on me and told me I would never be free. They pumped fire up my urethra, slit my veins, and watched me bleed steam.*

They tied wires around my throat, used ice picks to cut through my gums, to slice through the roots of my teeth. Flies buzzed in my stomach; spiders crawled through my intestines; bees stung the inside of my brain. They sewed up my lips so I couldn't scream. They peeled off my eyelids so I would always see. This is what it means to never be able to die. All this for all eternity. These demons are my past, my future's dreams.

Somewhere along Bedford Avenue, Andrew doubles over. He closes his eyes and holds his stomach. He pounds his fists against the sides of his head, attempts to crush his memories, bury them in the gelatinous mass of his scrambled brains. Out of his wide open mouth, a cry so intense that it curdles the blood, so high that it bursts the eardrums, so painful that it cuts the listener to the quick, screeches from his throat. It echoes back and forth between the brick buildings up and down and across the street. It goes on and on forever. In their lonely apartments, Williamsburg's residents – the young and the old, the hipsters and the immigrants – turn their searching faces towards closed windows. They glance nervously at their roommates, their children, their lovers. Both appear worried, but in the city, what can anyone ever do. Outside, in the world beyond their rooms, an androgynous somebody is being raped or killed, beaten or stabbed. In hell, Raphael's lips are no longer sewn together. His scream is the pure emotion behind Christ's doubting words on the cross. It's the grief of the gods at the doom of their Ragnarok, the trumpet of the seraphim meant to bring about the revelation, the rage of Kali completing her fearful age for mankind, the sad song of the tortured Israfel, whose heart strings snap beneath the playful strain of humanity's suffering.

Andrew continues stumbling forward until he reaches the Williamsburg Bridge. He gazes up the ramp to the concrete monstrosity. Like the entrance to the Hellfire Club, it's a cage. He takes one step underneath the chain link overhang. "Follow me," he snarls. "All you ghosts, angels, demons, aliens, all you souls released by the Tribute in Lights, follow me back into Manhattan. As pure energy, we'll stake our claim, seize the town, possess their bodies, their minds, and raise our flag of red, white, and black atop the Empire State's spire. We'll begin our revolution, humanity's devolution. God has kept this world's riches to himself for far too long. Until it's swallowed by the earth, this island will be our capital – Necropolis, the New Jerusalem. Chase Manhattan. Nobody will ever have to die again."

Leading his invisible army, rewinding the exodus of September 11th, Andrew treks over the East River towards Manhattan's glittering, skyscraping windows. Behind him, a billion banshees scream. Three thousand angels, fired by vengeance, fly above. They hold spears in their hands, trumpets to their lips. A counterpart of demons slithers up the sidewalk. They snarl and seethe, rabidly foam at the mouth. The only way to win is for each side to surrender to the other. The ghosts stumble along *en masse*. Even in the darkness, they're blinded by the living's starlit world. They reach forward, praying for the day when they can feel again to come soon. Aliens follow in carefully trained lines. They are the future, the myth of evolution, the truth of creationism. They all hate us – unevolved beings raping one another, killing the world, perfecting more and more insidious means of self-destructive blues.

The sidewalk's random graffiti recedes beneath Andrew's feet. The story that he followed to Brooklyn's streets is being played in reverse. Sometimes, that's how the world works. But even on the second trip through, from an entirely new angle, it doesn't make any more sense than it did before.

Michelle's sweet taste burns his lips. Her lighter fluid ignites his fingers, his palms, his tattoos, his soul. From in between Downtown's spires, cutting through the black sky high above the city's glowering haze, the Tribute in Lights heats up the freezing night. It's the last remnants, the peaceful death rattle, of an entire world age. Did America think its reign would never end? The cruel defeater of Communism, the world's financial and political Athenian savior... The final gasp of the World Trade Center projects a beacon, a bat signal, to heaven. It's the landing lights for the alien starships that will either kill us or save us. Either option would be better than what we've got. Humanity needs to be put in its place – 5 billion insects with the hive mentality of bees, the caste system of ants searching for their misplaced queen, crackers, slave drivers, betas in the monetary guise of the alpha whipping one another forward, chewing through each other's abdomens when the selfsame workers refuse to starve for the glory of the state of their worthless colony. Bring on the flying saucers! There has to be somebody there. There has to be.

I want this whole goddamn country to see this, feel this. I don't want to be here anymore. I want this world destroyed, consumed in a mushroom cloud, a bright ball of indivisible, invisible flames.

From Chinatown and Bleeker, Andrew trips through Manhattan's phosphorescent darkness. He stumbles into the East Village, bumps into the twenty and thirty-somethings in their catalog attire out for yet another night of partying and forgetting. They're laughing, shouting, in love with themselves and their single, solitary lives, trying to pretend like nobody wants them and their desired middleclass lifestyle dead. He passes NYU's dorms and bars and restaurants – the meager beginnings of a million meager American dreams. What did those kids think, babies at the age of eighteen, when they showed up in the big, bad city only to have reality vomit ash and soot over their primrose fantasies? This is a world that nobody makes art out of. The wolves revealed their teeth, devoured the Sugarplum Fairy, took their first chunk out of every suburban child's shanks. It becomes more difficult to walk, to run, to escape. Death is closing in. They were only a handful of blocks away. The university certainly paid for their counseling. Andrew slips down Fourteenth, gazes into the late night traffic headlights going past him in the opposite direction, so many people, so many conflicting desires, so many fights and misunderstandings. As long as we all, madmen and psychotics, schizophrenics in everybody's own individual way, live together on this planet with multiple personalities, there is no way we will ever be safe. He arrives at the corner of Hudson Street in the Meatpacking District.

Waiting for the devil to pick them up, cross-dressing prostitutes stand around on the corner. In short skirts and knee-high boots, they're laughing and talking, smoking cigarettes and spending their down time with their working sisters/brothers. They've traveled to this neighborhood from every ghetto in the city. None of them are as perfectly feminine, as quintessentially masculine as Lola, the Starman. They have an air of oppression and need, a hint of addiction, an angel's existence in this world of human demons preying upon the Lord's freak show. Stark and defined, dwarfing them and their psychological suffering in the way that all human creations dwarf the individual, the same vampire's castle from the night before rises behind them above them. Andrew stumbles around to the side of the building. He slips into Hansel's cage and walks down the steps where Gabriel had passed him the one-hitter. He goes to open the Hellfire Club's heavy, black door, but it's locked from the inside. What secret games are being taught in the underworld tonight? What private punishments are the nuns handing out?

Andrew leans back against the wall. He closes his wild eyes. He'd hoped that Lola had something more to show him, that She could explain to him how to keep Michelle alive forever, that She would reveal more than just the mystery of Her being, that She would give him the golden keys to God's bank vaults. He couldn't have learned those secrets already. Could he? If he did, if they're in his possession, then they're as worthless as a made-up paper currency, Monopoly money. They don't make any sense to the human mind, but like the mural of the Williamsburg Bridge, that makes all the sense in the world. *There's a lot of bars in New York City.* Andrew trudges back up the Hellfire's steps.

With nowhere else to go, the prostitutes still spread across the sidewalk. A few random gangster looking guys, smaller but broader than most of the prostitutes, with hardened expressions of horror and malice, mostly either drug dealers or pimps carrying side arms somewhere underneath their baggy sweatshirts, twine in and out between them. Andrew crosses the street. There's a bright, white diner next door to the Village Idiot. Like a single floor from the World Trade Center, it's encased in glass. Somehow, it was stolen, lifted out of the towering inferno like Dorothy's Kansas house and dropped down safely near the spiraling beginning of the yellow brick road. Ding-dong the witch is dead. Maybe it was the same whiskey tornado that whipped Andrew's mind through the city's destruction on the night that he threw his computer out the window. That diner is where his Belle, Michelle, wants him to wait. He's certain of it. He just doesn't know how long he has to be there. Then again, he doesn't know how long he has to be anywhere.

Inside the diner, the strung out *maître d* in his half-assed white jacket leads Andrew over to a Formica covered table where he has a view of the entire well-lit room. As he sits down, Andrew flips his long coat out from underneath himself and over his crossed legs. A young, blonde waitress comes over. Extraordinarily thin, almost anorexic, she gives Andrew a strange look. Who is she? What does she know? She must have starved to death somewhere in time. "Coffee," Andrew orders. With interest, he watches her leave. He pulls out a cigarette and taps it against the table to pack it. He lights it. It tastes pungent and fresh.

The diner is full of drunken couples and drunker youths chowing down on after midnight meals of hamburgers and eggs that will hopefully help their poisoned stomachs better deal with tomorrow's hangovers. Vibrant and alive, they're laughing and arguing, shouting and swearing, so certain, even after whatever they've been through, that they'll wake up and everything will be the same as today. The world never ended. They've never seen a nuclear explosion. Ghosts aren't flittering along the streets outside, trying to find bodies with possessable minds. The archangel Raphael is not sitting at a table not too far from them condemning them in the eyes of Lola, the one, true God. The only real question worth their asking is whether or not their buddies put in enough money to cover the tip. I'm not going to be left footing this goddamn bill.

With wide eyes and a terrifying gaze, Andrew sips off his weak coffee. The bitter water mixes with Michelle's saliva. It washes her down his throat. Caffeine enlivens his taste buds' memories. It redirects his synapses. His stomach twists and turns from swallowed acids. It follows his schizoid paths through the city. To burn the butterfly, he takes a drag off his cigarette. Smoke spirals in front of his eyes. The ashy taste is the dust of September 11th, the powder of the grave. Andrew wipes his eyes. This world is madness.

When he looks again, the diner is flooded with the World Trade Center's dead refugees. They've come to this place to recount their memories, to ennoble their friends with the stories of their deaths. They've returned younger than they were, with self-murdered ghosts of the lovers who they want to spend eternity with. They're every face off every missing poster that's been plastered across the city's drab walls. They laugh in ways that they're trying to remember after six months of being buried in effigy. That guy in the baseball cap had to jump out the window. He had no other place to go. His tie flapped against his face in the breeze. The black woman over there, the one in the hip hugger jeans, burned to death on the stairs. Behind her, her coworkers were pushing and kicking. She couldn't back away from the fire. Smoke choked that girl with the dimples and the pony-tail who's talking to that guy who still has acne. She knew she was going to die, but even on her knees, clawing at her neck, she couldn't gulp enough breath to scream. Andrew hears their stories, three thousand of them. He shakes his head and holds back his tears. Only he still sits alone. Michelle remains his dream, but he knows she's somewhere in the city. He felt her body. She's inside of him now. Raphael's a hermaphrodite. Is there anybody to make love to when you die? All of existence isn't quite what it seems. Andrew gets a refill on his coffee.

The caffeine makes his drunken digits tremble. Its stimulant expands his mind. His aura explodes in a mushroom cloud emanating from his brain. He is the vacuum at a given point in space. At moments like this, this mismatched world suddenly makes sense.

It's not that you ever have to know the future. You only have to know the next moment… perfectly. Forget about time. Evolve beyond it. Most animals don't even know it exists. Time is only real for us because we have words to describe its passing, futures and pasts coming to be simultaneously. The present is the only thing that matters. Right now, I'm sipping my coffee. Next, I'll swallow it and set the mug on the saucer on the table. In my mind, I see myself doing these things. That's how I know they're true. Existence only occurs inside the mind. What we experience with our senses is nothing more than the visible, auditory, olfactory, and tactile manifestations of the universal mind, the truth of mythology, the heaven and hell where we all do our time. Being in touch with this thought continues to animate my being, embalms me with zombifying fluids. In each second of my life, my death, I'm devouring God's body and blood. I'm sacrificing myself upon the tree of life. I'm going to take a drag off my cigarette. During those moments, I will determine what my next course of action will be. If I keep myself open at that time, I'll see what the immediate future intends for me. To flow is the best that a human animal can ever hope for. We have to flow. This world is in flux. We have no control. This is the universe. This is how it works. It's the calculus come to life, moments compounded into motion on an infinite line. Motion manifests itself out of the fourth dimension of time. Let us move without thought. Right now, I'm sipping my coffee.

In the wee hours of the morning, when the sun shines its shattered spectrum onto the broken pavement outside, dark visions move across Andrew's sight. The diner has emptied out. The living dead have gone home to make love, to smell and taste and feel the sheets and sweating bodies above. Remembering nothing, they cling to their lovers tighter than they ever have before. They relish every twist, every vibration that makes them sense again. Across the street, the hermaphrodites have all retired for their morning's evening. Like vampires ready to die for the day, they've taken subways and taxis back to their rented, coffin-sized rooms where nobody necessarily knows the treasures they hide inside of themselves. They take off their make-up and take their places amid schizophrenic lives.

Ever civilized, Andrew raises his finger and asks the waitress for the check. She's a different waitress from the one who was there when he sat down, the one who, all through the night, filled his coffee every time he asked, but who, well beyond the midnight hour, never even bothered to smile at his requests. This new waitress looks like a deranged version of the psychic. In her middle age, she has pits in her face. Her stomach billows over her apron, and she regards him in no less strange a manner than his previous server. They're all dead. She gawks at his clothing, blinks at his gaze. She pours steaming coffee into his cup, but she doesn't smile when he says, "Thank you." A lazy wind – like dry ice, it burns straight through you – kisses her shivers through the syllables of his voice. It bites her coldly from the depths of the pupils in his hands, his eyes. *It's time to go*, Michelle says.

Andrew pays and leaves. The entire establishment breathes a subliminal sigh of relief. On the corner, Dracula's castle lights are off. The city smells of the residual grime, the many varied sins from the night before. The invisible sun is engulfed by a polluted haze. Andrew slips past the Village Idiot closed for the morning. Its vomitous smell seeps through his memories. He wanders down Fourteenth to the L. As he stumbles down the stairway, holding onto the rail, bags gouged beneath his eyes, he realizes that it sure would be nice to be deep in the pressurized heat of New Orleans. Coffee and cigarettes can only do so much for the manic mind.

With his legs crossed, swinging his foot in time to his own silent rhythm, he waits patiently at the end of the line. This is what it means to be an angel stuck in time – you do nothing but wait for the world to end. Rats scurry along the tracks. With their twitching noses, they search the scents for some sort of meaning. The train comes in for its final stop of this trip. Less than a handful of people get off. Andrew steps inside and sits again. With a shudder, the subway's rumbling heart dies. The car goes dark. Buried and unable to move beneath his city, Andrew sits quietly. A dirty man in a smock, straight from a night and a morning at some unforgiving kitchen-type work, still holding his smeared apron, comes into the car, sits down, leans his head back against the window, and immediately goes to sleep. His heavy, somnambulant breathing rolls through the silent subway. Through Andrew, Raphael tries reaching into the man's dreams. Without warning, the subway comes back to life. The lights spring on. The world's so bright. This train could take Andrew back to his once upon a time Brooklyn home.

The train starts up slowly, groaning along the tracks, going back the way it came. Its swift music builds. Top speed is reached for a brief moment, a single underground block. The dark underworld outside passes quickly. The mole people, compatriots of the rats, pasty, silent inhabitants of this indiscriminate arena, build their cardboard homes somewhere in the distant depths of this hovel. They shoot up with used needles, warm canned bean meals on portable stoves. The train slows to stop at 6th Avenue. A minor exchange is made, barter and trade. With a few new passengers, a few less old passengers, the spiritual balance slightly tweaked, the train rumbles along again. Raphael shows Andrew the world inside another man's mind. His dreams are light and bright, dark and sinister, both at the same time, the same dreams as yours and mine. Andrew closes his eyes. As the train pulls into Union Square, alive inside of him, transplanted by her own vaginal secretions, Michelle says, *Get up, Sebastian, it's time to go. We're never going back to Brooklyn. There are plenty of bars in Manhattan.* Andrew opens his eyes, leaves the cook's fevered, work-infused dreams, unplugs himself from the other's mind, stands at the glass doors, and waits for them to automatically slide open.

Buried under earth, unable to escape, the air in the station is stale. Andrew breathes deeply. It reminds Raphael of hell. A tremor twists Andrew's body. He heads up the platform steps. The virtual station is virtually empty. Closer to the Lord's world, Andrew pauses. Ahead of him, trickling down another set of steps, just like in death, he can see the light. Up there is the square where six months ago a million people gathered to express their grief in candles and words and pictures with which they decorated the insignificant statues from America's momentous history – so innocent, so pained and worthless. To his right, another set of steps descend down to the subway again. The numbers determine Andrew's decision. He makes his choice and heads to the 6.

The deep green number, watered by a thousand years of the city's tears – gang violence, HIV, rapes, and wars – that he took through the tunnels two days ago flies into the Uptown side of the tracks. Andrew waits for the doors to open, and he steps inside. Unlike the other day when everything was so fresh and so clean, this is one of the old cars, grimy and feeble, faded and dejected like its holy trinity of passengers, Raphael, Sebastian, Andrew. Winged beneath the city, the three of them fly uptown on the 6. At Grand Central Station (*is that still there? It doesn't seem like it is*), Michelle tells Sebastian to switch trains again. He steps into the bright light of the city's nuclear explosion. Its vast halls are void, devoid of life and breathing. So frightening. New York City, empty. He walks past a blue partition of poster board. On this wall remains one of the last places to hang postcards of those lost in the World Trade. They're here again. Andrew switches to the 7.

In a purple limousine coming out from above ground out of Queens, he makes his way underneath the drowsy early morning city on the eve of its billionth night of insomniac insanity. Through the air above him, Times Square's bright heart – defaced and devalued, pimped out and tormented like every American – pulses. Andrew feels its dying energy pulling on him. Right before the door closes, he squeezes off the train. Lost in the mazes beneath the city, twisting through the eternal corridors of his endless mind, he eventually finds himself waiting on the blue A. This is Robert Johnson's note, played into a closeted microphone through his slack guitar. The music sings through Andrew's bones. Like wolves' teeth, it vibrates along his nylon marrow. At 14th Street, he switches back to the L and begins his closed, eclectic, electric circuit all over again.

Through the morning hours, the number of subway passengers gradually but steadily increases. At Michelle's behest, Andrew switches from Gray to Green to Purple to Blue – a symbolic rainbow outlining right corners at the blurred edges of the yin and the yang. He waits on the trains, stares disbelievingly at the increasing numbers of the dead, so many of them still dressed for their funerals, so many of them in tired shock at the living world. This is the army he conducted over the bridge last night, a zombie battalion of fallen saints, the stillborn future of humanity. Holding onto the metal strap above his head, locked in place by jiggling bodies on every side of him, a mass Kosovar grave, an Auschwitzian shower, Andrew grins knowingly and shakes his head. He chuckles. One of his allies raises her eyebrows at him. She gives him the same odd look that he got used to from the waitresses at the fallen World Trade's single diner floor. With a shiver, he stops smiling. It's not safe yet for the angels to be who they are. The living never dead must still pollute the New Jerusalem's pure waters. They must be dispersed. They must be destroyed. Necropolis must be purged for it is our home.

After hours of Andrew's going in circles, the 7 pulls into a bustling station of a billion rats in self-imposed cages. Like some strange experiment, they're suffocating and dying in suits and skirts. They stare like mine-working slaves at the concrete ceiling imprisoning them. Frozen at Pompey – it happened like this when they gassed the entire city, when the sun exploded a blinding flash across the island. This isn't Paris. There are no sewers to hide in – only the polluted ghosts of the East River's dead fish. Andrew crushes towards the train door. Some guy's briefcase spears him in the back. He hasn't felt this sensation in a while. It's been so long since he was awake at rush hour. The tiles on the wall that replaced the World Trade's eyes read Times Square. Andrew rubs the eyes in his palms. This is Michelle's stop. *It's time to go, Sebastian. I'll meet you at the crossroads.*

The train door swooshes open. Pitchforks prod Andrew into hell. He descends to the platform. A woman exhales into his face. Her breath is a waft of laudanum from a suddenly unstoppered vial. Volcanic statues melt back into life. Shadows jump off the walls. Sin creeps in. The city of Lazarus rises.

Immediately, a frenzied crowd hustling towards the exits sweeps Andrew into its midst. There has to be some way out of this madness, the lab rats say. With noses twitching for freedom's scent, they shove him along the platforms, hurry him up the stairs, breeze past him in stony, twisting walkways. Writhing in his own mind, Andrew flows along with the traffic. He stares at the ground, stumbles into the cave paintings on the walls when the mole people brush forcefully past his shoulders. As if he were Osiris exploring the dank catacombs interring the pharaoh and his suicidal living court deep beneath their pyramidal tombs, searching for mummified survivors versed in the Book of the Dead, asking those able to answer the riddles that permeate death, the underworld's mazes enthrall him.

Trying to find Michelle because he can hear her voice even if it is only in his head, following a different route than the one he followed the previous hundred times that he twined through the station this morning, he stumbles into a wide space open under the earth. Given the confines that the past hours have restricted him to, it's like standing in the middle of Ground Zero's vast emptiness in the middle of the monstrous city. This is the Great Pyramid's great hall, the descending point of the gods, the entry point for the afterlife. After accustoming himself to the closed space of the grave, the walls ascend to infinity. They support flying buttresses. The ceiling rises for miles. It's limitless. Even below ground, there must be clouds at that height. Like Jacob's ladder, an escalator climbs to heaven. This is a vision. Angels make their way back and forth between the sky and the earth. Ready to claim his prize, to stick the gun to Yahweh's head, to stop chasing Manhattan, to steal those electronic ones and zeroes once and for all and never have to collect unemployment from Heavenly Staffing ever again, Andrew smoothes and buttons his coat, flattens his tangled hair, and begins walking across the hall towards the ladder. Halfway there, finally almost free, he stops.

To his right, near the decaying wall of this fallen world, a group of young, black angels – the physical manifestation of the mural behind Khalid, a living scene that, like all great art, came to be from inanimate spray paint on bricks – are clearing a circular stage for themselves. The travelers, the tourists, the demons who feed off of New York City and who aren't in too much of a hurry to escape are forming a barricade around them, waiting to see what happens next. Since they woke up today, deep inside, they refuse to believe anything other than that they're alive. Still never dead, they must succumb in order for our pandemonic Necropolis to become the Jerusalem of pure gold, like unto clear glass. Spiritually, they're frothing and foaming, ready with their checkbooks to devour the children of God. But Lola only takes cash.

The four black angels are wearing red Adidas pants with white stripes and sleeveless black shirts. Their arms are toned – defined shoulders and triceps, long biceps that bunch at every motion. With faces young and smooth, they probably don't even have to shave. They're the age that America wishes – in gyms, at the beach – to be eternally. The tallest and obviously oldest, still a teenager, has a white du-rag tied around his head. Reflecting the ghastly, fluorescent lights, it makes his face even darker, richer with color. Leaning over a large boombox that he's setting up on an overturned bucket that will eventually collect their money, he's the general. His soldiers are stretching. Despite their proximity to the enemy, they don't seem scared. Preparing throughout all of eternity for this one single moment, they're serious, contemplative, reigning in their thoughts. From the four corners of the earth, they hold invisible trumpets to their lips. This is how the battle for heaven begins. Andrew pauses and leans against the wall. He needs to watch them work, to learn how angels go to war. He hopes that in the ensuing melee he doesn't get hurt.

He makes eye contact with the general in red, white,

and black – the colors for our new American flag. Symbolic of the daylight sky, blue is meaningless. Black is the tone for our earth, our world, our transmogrifying cave, the nighttime, African field that, as the birthplace of humanity, represents the ancient domain of the goddess and her consort, the hermaphrodite, the most primitive and therefore truest of our relationships with the divine. Upon this color, our stars will shine. Andrew nods. Recognizing Raphael from repressed memories of their previous lives, the general nods back. In a Hitler style salute, the same as he showed Michael when he told him how his stigmata should set, Andrew flashes him the eyes in his palms. The general smiles (he has a gold capped tooth – a symbol of wealth stolen from the Lord), presses play on the stereo, and quickly steps away. "Ladies and gentlemen," the general announces to the crowd. He has an accent developed somewhere deep in Brooklyn, in one of the neighborhoods yet to be gentrified, the Ol' Dirty Bastard's home. "You are about to witness a wonder of nature."

Music thumps out of the speakers. It resounds through the pyramid's sonic halls. The pumping bass is an old skool break beat, but the drumming rhythm beneath the scratching tones is older than even history itself. It resonates deep within the hidden prehistory of humanity, forces everybody, the good and the bad, the rich and the poor, to clap their hands and tap their feet, to move their hips and try to reach into their former lives to feel the gospel beat. Andrew's subconscious latches onto a universal memory of tribal fires and the celebration of the hunt. He remembers sharpening wooden spears and speaking guttural sounds, scarring himself to prove his masculinity and learning the divine mysteries of taking a mate.

In regimental order, the soldiers stand still at attention –

their feet together, their hands at their sides. Suddenly, with a universal shout, they come to life. Motion's energy flows down their line. Transferred from the music to become combustible fuel for their bodies, it animates one after the other in time to the beat.

From the middle, the youngest of them all, barely yet a pre-teen if even that, steps forward. The others take one step back. The baby soloist shoots his knees together, kicks his feet to the side, and drops to the ground. On his knees, hobbling like a rhythmic penguin, the arctic Jonathan Livingston Seagull begging for his flock's understanding of the sounds his body's tune can fly with, he dances towards his audience. The demon tourists clap and guffaw. Impressed but frowning still, Andrew claps, too. The baby soloist isolates his ribs and wobbles back upright. He jumps back in line, and the other two soldiers, the middling aged, come forward.

Playing off of each other, blindly mirroring one another at a distance, connected somehow spiritually as if in the same manner that Andrew once upon a dream believed (a kiss birthed that kind of connection) he shared with Michelle, they work in tandem. They pop and lock. They worm and robot. They dance together, clapping feet, always keeping the beat, and they slide back into place.

The general steps forward. His movements flow like jazz. Arhythmical, they're in perfect harmony. He slides around the downbeat, hits the upbeat, then switches it all around. His pace increases. He falls to his hands, flips onto his back, and becomes a blur. His legs twirl. His arms whirl. He traces the atom's spinning path. Without a pause, he's on his head, as perfectly erect as most men on their feet. He slides back down to his back. His ring of electrons expands. Like watching a Cheetah run, it's impossible to follow his speed. And then, as quickly as it began, the atom splits, all motion stops. Supporting himself upside down, he's a nuclear freeze. One arm's muscles are contracted, the other's extended. His face presses against the concrete. His neck twists at an odd angle. His legs splay in the air. In order to know an electron's place, we cannot know its speed. In order to know an electron's speed, we cannot know its place. Testing Heisenberg's uncertainty principle, the general plays with his audience. With tiny twists, he pretends his madness will begin again, but instead, letting us all know where he is at this one moment in time, he remains motionless – only a slight trembling where his frail fingers meet the ground. He makes eye contact with Raphael. He winks and smiles a golden grin. And then, like the world reborn after the death of the gods, he explodes in an atomic reaction, the Big Bang all over again.

Shock waves resonate seismically beneath New York City. From out of the pyramid's great hall, the subway tunnels rumble. Their walls crack. They crumble. The fears of six months all come true. The fault line beneath Manhattan yawns. Fire and brimstone shoot into the air – a divine punishment coming from below. As if struck by airplanes, by lightning, skyscrapers break apart in the middle. Uptown, Midtown, and Downtown collapse together in a miasma that magnifies the minor destruction of September 11th, 2001 to a million degrees Fahrenheit. Drowning the city's panicking inhabitants, the East River and the Harlem River meet at the hips. They swap spit. Buried alive, suffering from insomnia eternally, the capital of the world is swallowed into the earth's crusted womb.

Andrew blinks. Thirty million souls escape their bodies for a tribute in lights. No matter what happens, nothing will ever change. Andrew feels his own body to make sure that he's still real, that, unlike the music, he hasn't turned into pure energy. His head hurts. His ribs are sore. His asshole, after more than a day, still feels stretched. Like the smoke from a cigarette, the pain makes him realize that, even at the end of time, he's still alive. In complete control, he steps away from the wall. He gazes over the audience's heads at the angels' makeshift stage. It's a concrete, fluorescent emptiness. The battle line has broken apart. In a billion simultaneous poses, evolving into their many-armed forms, the angels are dancing war. With nothing more to do, Andrew waves goodbye to Khalid and heads for Jacob's ladder.

Sloughing off living skin, ascending to heaven, dead souls come to life again. Before blind eyes, a lifetime of memories flash in less than a millisecond. Birth – the traumatic fight to be free from the womb. Crying and screaming at unknown doctor's faces. Who are these creatures? They must be aliens. The bright light of the hospital fields growing confused newborns, brains in a vat. Latching onto your mother and father, a connection deeper than thought, your blood and genes, learning by osmosis to speak and walk. A happy childhood ruined by divorces, remarriages, adolescent assimilation. Fighting for years to establish oneself in relation to one's peers. All of it, meaningless, a lifelong psychosis. The afterlife nothing more than a dream before the brain in the vat dies. Andrew reaches the end of his trip. His scrambled brains leak out over a wooden barroom floor. Somebody must be arrested for this. Somebody has to pay the consequences.

Times Square. The crossroads of the world. From the sky, where the tip-tops of glass towers overreach Babylon, to the ground, where the pedestrians are imprisoned on sidewalks, hurrying past one another, protected from bumping shoulders by invisible shields, a grayness hides in the light. The excess of New York City's smoke, fumes, and exhaust sticks to the humans' skin, collects in their breathing lungs, merges with the scents of hot nuts, hot dogs, tobacco, and trash to create a cacophony of flavors circling through every square inch of the atmosphere. In the space that isn't occupied by a body, sounds resonate – laughter, horns, voices. Maddening. Exhilarating. Tempting.

Across Broadway, a little ways from Chase-Manhattan, on a projection screen that takes up the entire wall of a building, a gigantic, pixeled eye watches over the scene. Its iris fades from brown to blue to green. When it slid down New York's brick veins from the walls of the subway at Ground Zero, somehow, it grew. It's the world's lens, the god, the goddess, the hermaphrodite, Michael, Gabriel, Lucifer, the Starman, Ziggy, Lady Stardust, the Ol' Dirty Bastard, Khalid, Ari, Mary, Christopher, Sherry, Carey, Charlie, Noel, Lola, Michelle. The eye darts back and forth, scanning the zombies in their suits on their varied ways to work. Simply watching life unfold, it passes no judgment. It gazes directly across the crossroads. It sees Andrew. Its pupil bores into his brain, reads his thoughts, his dreams, his past, his future, his sins. Andrew smoothes his coat and stands up straighter. The serious look of a soldier under review passes across his face. The eye blinks, and it disappears.

Andrew turns left. The sun's so bright. The world's so alive. He shuffles along Broadway. He notices a homeless man a few feet from him sitting on the sidewalk, asking the pedestrians to spare some change. The few who do acknowledge him, in their suits or with their tourists' maps, say that they have nothing to give. They can afford their apartments, they can afford their hotels, but they can't spare a penny. "Fuckin' devils," Andrew mutters. He approaches the homeless man. The man's stench is so sweet it's vomitous, like the Village Idiot's entrance. Andrew pulls his wallet from his back pocket. He pulls out his Chase-Manhattan ATM card. Leaning down to the homeless man, he says, "Whatever I have is yours. The key is 0313."

The homeless man takes the card. His fingers are trembling. His features are uncertain. He glances sidelong at Andrew. "Do you want it back?" he asks.

Andrew shakes his head, *No*. "Go ahead," he says, and he nods across the street to Chase-Manhattan's ATMs. The homeless man stands up. Like a gentleman, he brushes off his hands and tattered pants. He nods at Andrew, smiles, and rushes across Broadway. Andrew starts walking again.

He stares at the dirty sky. He stares at his worn feet. On the street, all the people that he meets stare at this haggard stranger with the eyes in his palms more vibrant than the eyes in his head and the Hassidic coat rustling against his soiled jeans. It's a shock, a jolt that they forget about pretty soon. Only in New York, as the tourists often say. Ahead of him, a crowd has gathered outside the darkened windows of one of the morning television talk shows. Inside, pretty people smile for the camera. After hours spent in hair and make-up with stylists whose only job is to make sure that they don't look anything like everyday life (the public doesn't want reality. There's no market for that), they posture and pose, interview happy people promoting themselves with nothing to say. On the chilly smog encrusted streets outside, their subjects smile at one another and wave to nobody, to friends and families who aren't even watching, to cameras not trained on them. This is their vacation, their chance to be a face on TV, even if it is only a face in the background, a face nobody ever cares to see. You can understand why all their kids want to be on MTV. Childhood dreams. New York fucking City. Andrew shakes his head and keeps walking. There are so many more deserving faces. It would be nice someday to know them all.

On a postcard rack outside a tourist shop, a gray picture catches his gaze. Andrew stops. Tears gather in the corner of his eyes as he looks downtown. What should be there isn't. He stares at the ground. Somewhere beneath him, the angels are dancing. Their vibrations gyrate him onward. In his mind, he sees the general's golden grin. He sees the general, like the eye on the wall, wink. Running his hand along the rack, he pulls the postcard from its place. Underneath his palms gaze, he holds the thick paper against his chest. Its pigments bore into his heart. In the city's hustle and bustle, nobody notices.

Paying no attention to the cars swirling around him, Andrew crosses the street. A taxi cab honks. Deaf from September 11th's conch shell, Andrew doesn't hear it. On a tranquil island in the middle of the crossroads, he sits down on a concrete slab. Across from him, a naked cowboy plays guitar. Young women smile and have their pictures taken with his buff body. None of them notice the hipster Hassid sitting on concrete, his legs dangling towards the street while he stares at the picture he holds in his hands.

Above Andrew, the eye comes on the screen again. Its chameleon pupil changes again. It stares down on its subjects, and it seems exceedingly interested in the one with the disheveled hair and the long, black coat.

Andrew holds the stolen postcard on his knees. All around him, the crossroads of the world barters madly with ten million souls worth of currency. The giant business card enticing everybody to chase Manhattan twirls. The homeless man waits in line for his money. Lucifer licks his lips and waits. Andrew inhales deeply. The picture on his lap is of two buildings, two twins, a hermaphrodite, a male and a female. Like a butterfly escaping its cocoon, smoke billows out of their Siamese ribs, hangs like a gray angel in the blue sky. *Wish you were here.* Andrew sniffles. He heaves. He grabs his own kicked in ribs. He wipes his eyes, but tears already drip down his unshaven cheeks. He throws the picture away. Like the trash at Ground Zero, like his bandages in Bed-Stuy, it's caught by the breeze. It falls to the concrete a few inches from his feet. Andrew stares down at his empty hands staring back at him. His pupils' gaze is vacant: Saint Christopher's carved out, stolen eyes. He looks up at the sky. The eye on the screen blinks at him again. "It doesn't matter, Michelle," he says. "It made us how we are... dead." Maybe on the third day, he'll rise again.

Portrait by PJ Adams

About the Author

Michael Anthony Adams, Jr. is originally from Whittier, CA. He holds a master's degree in Philosophy from the New School for Social Research in New York City. As a teenager, he was the lead vocalist and lyricist for Richmond, VA-based hardcore band Broken Chains of Segregation. In 2012, he began publishing his collected works under the pen name Israfel Sivad. He's the founder of Ursprung Collective, a spoken word/music project referred to as "fantastic brain food" on ReverbNation. He was the primary lyricist on indie rock group One & the Many's first two albums, *Forms* and *Hours*. His writing has appeared in the *Santa Fe Literary Review*, *The Stray Branch*, *Badlands Literary Journal*, and more. He currently lives with his partner and collaborator, artist PJ Adams, and their children in Baltimore, MD.

www.MichaelAnthonyAdamsJr.com